MW00479997

FAYCALIBUR
A LESS VALUED
KNIGHTS
NOVEL
II
LIAM PERRIN

For Kelly & Abby
my love and my joy
always

With special thanks to:
Bethan the Conscionable
and Richard the Congruent

ISBN-13: 978-1-7904-3658-3

Ordering and contact: liamperrin.com
Cover illustration by J. Caleb Clark

One of the last paragraphs in one of the last volumes of *The Merlin Continuation of the Old French Arthurian Post Vulgate* by Lacy & Asher reads:

Know that there were three kinds of tables there. The first was the Round Table. King Arthur was companion and lord of this one. The second table was called the Table of Errant Companions, those who went seeking adventure and waited to become companions of the Round Table. Those of the third table were those who never left court and did not go on quests or in search of adventures, either because of illness or because they had not enough courage. These knights were called the less valued knights.

I shall now (continue to) set the record straight.

Liam Perrin
Somnia Salvebis

OUR TALE THUS FAR

A Refreshment of Select Memories

In a village not far from Camelot, the people languish under drought, famine, and the machinations of a greedy baron who hoards anything that seeds, sprouts, or shines. Thomas, a farm boy from the village with no talents or possessions to speak of, dreams of righting injustices by becoming a knight.

When a herald arrives proclaiming King Arthur will bestow gifts and knighthoods to celebrate his upcoming wedding to Guinevere, Thomas asks his father if he can go to Camelot and become a knight. His father can't think of anything more ridiculous.

Meanwhile, Thomas' charming and beloved older brother marches to the evil baron's keep and demands the baron open his storehouses. The baron throws him in prison for treason. When Thomas' family discovers their predicament, sending Thomas to Camelot becomes a wonderful idea. They rush Thomas out the door to reach the King and petition him to pardon Thomas' brother.

Thomas passes through a strange forest where he helps a cursed knight escape torment, repairs an enchanted bridge, rescues a shrinking giantess, and completes a quest for an allegedly reformed evil wizard. The allegedly reformed evil wizard awards Thomas with a blessed sword. 'Blessed' is in the eye of the beholder. These things take practice, and the wizard's experience lies on the other end of the spectrum.

Thomas arrives in Camelot, makes fast friends with an exceptionally unlucky aspiring knight, and catches the interest of a young lady-in-waiting. When Thomas finally meets Arthur, Thomas is unwilling to sacrifice his dream and rationalizes that if he is knighted, he'll be able to help his family and do so much more. He leverages his magic sword to achieve his dream.

Arthur knights him, but Thomas discovers the Round Table is reserved for the notable and privileged. Thomas is assigned with the rest of the nobodies to a seat in the back at the Table of Less Valued Knights which, notably, lacks an actual table. The honor is in the Order not in the furniture, say the people with the furniture.

To Thomas' consternation, the baron's son, Bane, is also assigned to the Table of Less Valued Knights. Bane bullies Thomas. Thomas stands up for himself, but he is no match for Bane's athleticism. Nevertheless, Thomas impresses his friends with his wit and his commitment to do right.

Thomas grows increasingly convinced that Bane and the baron are up to something even more nefarious than oppressing their village. The allegedly reformed evil wizard lends Thomas an enchanted, not-exactly-moral compass which Thomas uses to uncover details of the baron's plot. Thomas also learns that Bane has been sorely mistreated by the baron. Taking pity, Thomas confronts Bane and exhorts him to do the right thing: help Thomas free his brother, expose the plot, and redeem himself.

Bane concedes, gives Thomas sealed orders to free Thomas' brother, and instructs Thomas to deliver the orders to the village warden. Thomas rides alone through the night, delivers the letter, and discovers he has been betrayed. The orders instruct the warden to imprison Thomas along with his brother and execute them both the following day.

Back in Camelot, a series of accidents place Thomas' unlucky best friend in a position to discover Thomas' predicament. He gathers Thomas' friends, and they all head to Thomas' village where they break Thomas out of prison. Thomas makes a final stand against the baron. Inspired by his goodness and bravery, the townspeople rally to Thomas and drive away Bane and the baron.

The townspeople head to the village keep where they discover knights of the Round Table have arrested the baron and Bane. The knights reveal that the baron has poisoned the grain as part of a plot to deliver the grain to Camelot in order to sow unrest in the kingdom and distrust of Arthur. The Round Table knights privately congratulate Thomas for playing an instrumental part in foiling the plot. The townspeople want to make Thomas the new baron, but Thomas gives the crown to his brother who, unlike himself Thomas says, had the town's interest at heart the whole time.

Having learned that true heroism requires sacrifice, Thomas finally embraces the role that initially seemed like such an insult to his dream. When a messenger arrives with a summons from Arthur regarding a quest for a magic cup that's gone missing, Sir Thomas the Hesitant of the Table of Less Valued Knights answers the call.

Meanwhile, as the tale is recounted by Sir Thomas Malory, King Arthur has entrusted Excalibur to his sister, Morgan le Fay, for safekeeping. You see, before they were enemies, they were family…

Said Arthur, "Here may ye see what adventures
befall oft time of errant knights..."

Sir Thomas Malory, Le Morte d'Arthur, *Book IV, Chapter XII*

CHAPTER I

THE SENDING

"Watch," said Merlin.

They watched.

Nothing happened.

This is not entirely accurate. Lots of things happened. For example, a candle flame danced and sputtered as it reveled in the cave's cool draft. A drop of water clung desperately to the tip of a stalactite, terrified, listening to the rhythmic demise of its brothers echo through the chamber. Mushrooms luminesced because, well frankly, they could. And the forces that hold the universe together delighted in the orderly molecular structure of the crystal at the center of the room.

Merlin hit it hard with his staff.

That's a wizard's job – perturbing the forces that hold the universe together. Merlin was good at it. He'd been good at it for a long time. He was tired now and looking forward to retirement.

He'd trained his replacement, Nimue. He'd introduced her during Arthur's wedding in a manner of her choosing. It had been a bit flamboyant for his own taste with the mad hart and the braying hounds and the ruined desserts, but it was important she make it her own. He was ready to hand over the reins of this grand enterprise. Not the royal, governing, public reins. Those weren't his to give. No, the secret reins. The reins that steered not the coach, as it were, but the coachman.

But now this. He sighed. It was important they see this. There were things Nimue and her apprentice needed to learn – especially the apprentice. And that unlikely knight. Merlin frowned.

He hit the crystal again. A satisfying resonance accompanied the strike this time.

Images formed in the crystal. Fuzzy.

He hit it again.

The image focused:

Arthur in a battle for his life with a dark champion. Arthur driven back, near death, wielding a sword.

Nimue leaned in squinting. "What weapon is that?"

"Not Excalibur," said Merlin. "An impostor. Watch."

The impostor-sword shatters. Arthur falls. The dark champion raises his sword.

The crystal went dark.

They watched.

Nothing else happened.

The candle flame was steady. The water drop swelled.

"There is a plot afoot," said Merlin, gesturing at the empty crystal. "As you have seen."

"But," stammered Nimue, "How? Where is Excalibur?"

"He gave it to her," said Merlin.

"Morgan?"

Merlin nodded.

"But why?"

Merlin shrugged. "'Safekeeping,' he said."

Nimue's apprentice rolled her eyes.

Merlin draped a cloth over the crystal. "He'll soon learn she isn't to be trusted," he said. "I only hope he survives the lesson."

"We should put a stop to this," said Nimue.

Behind the beard and beneath the eyebrows Merlin could be quite expressive when he chose to be. But at times like this he was simply too lost in thought to bother operating his face for the benefit of others. Hotter heads often mistook his preoccupation for indifference, but if you wanted to know what was going on in Merlin's head it was best to ask, not guess.

Nimue's apprentice guessed. "You're not seriously going to let this happen. This isn't some life lesson or laboratory experiment where the student will learn best by being allowed to fail. This is Arthur being murdered. Surely it's Morgan behind this. We have to stop her!"

Merlin straightened.

"We," he said, "don't have to do anything."

He stared at her. She stared back.

Nimue's apprentice looked away. Her hands were balled in white-knuckled fists.

"Nimue," said Merlin. "Go to Morgan's court. Find what you can find. Unravel this plot."

"Yes," her apprentice hissed with excitement.

"Elisante," said Merlin.

The apprentice clenched her jaw. "I'm going too," she said.

Merlin nodded. "Find the one who bears the impostor-sword, and do what you do best."

"And what is that exactly?" Elisante asked warily.

"Get in the way."

Merlin chuckled.

Nimue frowned.

Elisante glared.

Merlin cleared his throat. "Find Sir Thomas the Hesitant," he said. "And stop him."

CHAPTER II

THE SELF-APPOINTED SQUIRE

Sir Thomas hesitated at the outer gate of Fogbottom Keep. "Summoned to Camelot," the herald had said. "Something about a missing cup." *Typical job for a Less Valued Knight*, Thomas thought. A royal summons seemed like overkill, but you muck the stall you're standing in.

It was time for him to find his family and say goodbye. He was told he'd find them in here, the new Farmer residence. Or was it now Farmer Keep? Or – the thought curdled his blood – were they now Fogbottoms? He tried the name on. Thomas Fogbottom. It felt wrong. Thomas *of* Fogbottom was difficult enough.

His attention turned to the two thoughts all siblings consider when new information presents itself. One, how could his brother William use it to badger him and two, how could he use it first. His brother, the new baron, William Farmer. William Farmer Fogbottom. Good, kind, and wise were three words Thomas wouldn't use in public to describe William. Privately though, he believed one or two of them.

Someone jostled him.

"Standin' in the road, son. Make like a heifer and mooo– Oh. Hi Thomas." Wendsley Cheston Hunter still wore his guard's uniform, such as it was. He carried a loose assortment of nondescript items Thomas recognized as the Farmer's meager and unremarkable belongings. The only thing the Farmer belongings really had going for them was that they belonged to someone. Belonging was important, Thomas had come to understand. Especially for the nondescript.

Wendsley had acquired a helmet from somewhere. That was new. He tried to shift it now with his shoulder and nearly dropped the belonging things. Thomas reached out and helped him.

"Thanks. They're all inside," said Wendsley. "Movin' in day!" And he lumbered into the keep, helmet askew again already.

Places that hold powerful histories – places like Fogbottom Keep – tend to cling to those histories long after the people who perpetrated them have departed. The old baron was gone, but he was still present. Thomas felt him brooding in the heaviness of the dark stone and leering from the sharp angles of the cloistered arches. His banners drooped like wet socks in the stagnant, humid air.

Thomas shook himself and breathed.

The Parson would say the place had a spirit. Thomas' father would say the place had men, and men were bad enough. Thomas figured either way the place had something it hadn't had in a long while. Hope.

He stepped through the gate, made his way into the keep proper, and stopped short again. Few things jolt a person out of their own thoughts quite like hearing their own name.

"You've got it all wrong!" A girl's voice. Angry. "*Thomas* is the hero. I *saw* it. I was *there.*"

Thomas peered around the corner. Not a girl. A young boy. Heavy. And squeaky. Thomas jerked back.

"We were *all* there." An older, taller voice. "Kay, Gawain and Bedivere bound the baron and Bane and dragged them off with the poisoned food. End of story."

"End of—issnot—isn't," sputtered the boy.

"Spit it out Augustus." The other boys laughed. "If you can."

"That's *not* the story." said the squeaky boy. "Mmmph," he grunted in frustration.

Thomas put his palm to his forehead. "Don't," he said under his breath.

He heard the boy stamp his foot.

"He did," said Thomas.

The laughter faded as the group broke up. Thomas frowned and listened. He could hear the squeaky boy breathing. He seemed not to be moving.

"The truth will out!" blurted the squeaky boy. "I have been and espied the Court of King Arthur." He sounded like he was reciting something. "And there is such fellowship." He breathed easier. "And well-nigh all the world holdeth with Arthur." He was calm now. "*Thomas* stood up to the baron. *Thomas* inspired the town to stand up for itself. *Thomas* made the others care."

Thomas straightened up. He didn't know what to make of the squeaky boy. He seemed to have acquired a fanatic and was surprised how much this tickled him. The boy's courage was to be applauded. Thomas was also inclined to find another route to his destination.

Augustus was still mumbling. "It was Thomas—" he said, and smacked right into the man himself as he rounded the corner.

They stared at each other. One more wide-eyed than the other.

"Um," said Thomas. "Hello."

The boy's mouth opened and closed and opened again.

Thomas cleared his throat. "I was just on my way... That is, I'm off to see–" In the manner of departing,

Thomas decided *gracefully* was out and went for *quickly* instead. He took a step.

"You're Thomas," said the boy and inhaled.

"Er," said Thomas. "Yes," he admitted. Embarrassment gave way to concern. "You should breathe, I think."

The boy somehow managed to inhale again with no intervening exhale.

"You're Sir Thomas the Hesitant!" said the boy. There was another breathless pause, and then the rest came pouring out in one uninterrupted stream. "Formerly and not un-presently I suppose that is to say one doesn't stop being who one was when he starts being a knight after all except in the case of a knight who specifically sets out to distance himself from a previous identity for instance perhaps in the case of someone like Accolon of Gaul though everyone still knows who *he* is," snort, "or the Green Knight for example but in any case that's not the kind of thing Sir Thomas the Hesitant would go in for so it's safe to say: Sir Thomas the Hesitant formerly *and*," wink, "presently Thomas Farmer of Fogbottom, brother William, sister Elizabeth, natural parents and one grandmother surviving, knighted by King Arthur on the occasion of his wedding – that is, Arthur's, not Thomas'," snort again, "to Lady Guinevere and assigned in proper haste to the Table of Less Valued Knights subsequently distinguishing himself by foiling the poisoned pastries plot and ousting the recreant Baron Fogbottom – the falsest baron who ever took breath – wielding an enchanted sword, Ambrosia, now lost under the collapsed Fogbottom dungeon, sacrificed to free the eponymous town and her people and don't you worry, Sir, the truth will out!"

"The truth will–" said Thomas. "How did you know the name of–" said Thomas. There were too many competing concerns and not enough words for all of them. "How do you know all this?" said Thomas.

The boy inhaled.

Thomas panicked.

"Wait," he said. He pinched the bridge of his nose. "That was something," said Thomas. "The thing is–"

The boy grinned at him.

Thomas sighed. "What's your name?"

"Augustus Ditcher of the Fogbottom Ditchers at your service, sir."

"The thing is, Augustus–" said Thomas.

"Gus," said Gus.

"Pardon?"

"Call me Gus, sir."

"Right," said Thomas. "The thing is, Gus..." What was the thing? "The thing is," said Thomas. "The truth is complicated." He shrugged.

"My pa always says, 'Truth is easy, it's lyin' that's comp-located.' He means 'complicated.' That's just how he talks."

Thomas nodded. "Uh huh, but see, that's a little simplistic is all."

Gus snorted. "Aye," he said. "That's the point, sir. The truth is simple. You're Sir Thomas the Hesitant, and I," he pulled himself up to his full height which primarily involved stretching the neck and jutting out the chin. "I'm your new squire," said Gus.

He bowed dramatically. One thick leg thrust forward. One heavy arm went back. Front hand circled wrist circled forearm circled elbow until Gus stood head bowed with one palm up behind him and the other before him as if he would summon the world if Thomas asked and place it at his feet. The whole affair involved far more grace than Thomas expected from a boy with an uncanny resemblance to a half-sack of potatoes.

Thomas grinned. He couldn't help it. And then, with Gus bowed before him, Thomas quietly removed a familiar "Kick Thee" note from his back. Gus seemed the type who would attempt to explain to the hooligans that their joke didn't make sense. "It means, 'Kick You,'" he'd say. "You meant 'Kick Me,'" he'd tell them. "You heard 'im lads!" the hooligans would say. And then there'd be kicking. Experience was a cruel but effective teacher.

Thomas tucked the note away, pulled Gus upright and saluted him. Gus returned the salute. Thomas, at a loss for words, hoped Gus felt his gratitude. Thomas dropped his salute, gave Gus a manly nod, and failed to tell Gus not to follow him into the keep.

If there were vestiges of the previous baron lingering in the quiet spaces of the keep, his influence was thoroughly banished from the throne room. William stood dazed in the center of the hubbub. Thomas' father, Mr. Farmer, stalked from one corner to the next with a slate under his arm and a chalk pencil dirtying his ear. From her threadbare chair plonked down right next to the throne, Grandma Farmer was receiving and dispatching servants with an ease that Thomas recognized – she'd been treating her children and grandchildren in the same manner all their lives. Unlike the other Farmers, treating the whole town as her realm was merely a quantitative not a qualitative adjustment of disposition. Only young Elizabeth enjoyed Grandma Farmer's unconditional favor as she climbed on the Fogbottom throne itself talking to, and for, her tired stuffed bunny.

But all of this was lost on Thomas because on the edge of it all was his Mum talking to Marie. He panicked. He spotted Philip standing by a low table working on a leg of indeterminate meat. Thomas sidled to him crab-wise, nodding and smiling at a variety of servants.

"Philip!" Thomas exclaimed through his teeth.

Philip choked and recovered himself.

"Thomas! Been wondering where you'd gotten off to."

Thomas tilted his head toward the other side of the room. "You were supposed to keep them separated."

"Aye," said Philip. "'Twas a doomed enterprise that. Those two drew together like, er, like two things you can't keep easily apart."

"Like peas in a pod," said Gus.

Philip looked down. "Who's this?"

Eyeing Marie and his mum, Thomas ignored the question.

Gus snapped to attention. "Augustus Ditcher, sir!"

Marie caught Thomas' eye and smiled. Mrs. Farmer followed her gaze and spotted Thomas. Her face lit up and she beckoned Thomas over.

Thomas groaned.

"Philip," said Thomas, "best mate, comrade, brother-in-arms..." Thomas put his hand on Philip's shoulder and squeezed hard.

"Ow," Philip winced. "Yes?"

"You'll get yours," promised Thomas. He stood tall and strode purposefully and directly to his doom. Half way there, Mrs. Farmer leaned in and said something to Marie that made her giggle. She patted her on the shoulder, and Marie excused herself. Thomas wanted to follow Marie, but courage demanded a straight line and that bore him to his mother.

"Thomas," she said with an unsettling grin. "She," she said, "is lovely."

"Um," said Thomas. Mrs. Farmer was considering the retreating Marie. She seemed to be inviting Thomas to consider her as well. There were whole areas of Thomas' brain where his mother and Marie shouldn't be together. Thomas glared at Philip instead.

"Oh, hello Augustus," said Mrs. Farmer.

"Greetings, your ladyship. How dost the day fare ye? Well, I hope!"

Gus bowed.

"You know Gus?" said Thomas.

"Of course I know Gus," said Mrs. Farmer. "You may stand up Augustus."

Thomas supposed he shouldn't be surprised. There were children born every day that Thomas never heard about, but if his mum and Grandma Farmer didn't know about it, it hadn't happened.

Gus laughed. "If a hen has a chick your mum don't know about, there'll be no eggs for dinner!" Gus winked at Mrs. Farmer and snorted.

Thomas squinted. "I don't… Right... Can I talk to you, Mum?" Thomas eyed Gus. "Privately?"

Gus bowed and dismissed himself.

Thomas tried to look professional.

"What's the matter? You look upset," said his mum.

"We've been summoned back to Camelot," said Thomas. He felt the futility of trying to behave like an adult in the presence of his own mother, but he wasn't giving up just yet.

"We who? Summoned! By whom? You have duties here young man."

"Philip–"

"Philip's right over there, dear."

"No I mean Philip and me. Have been summoned."

"And I."

"Pardon?" His mother couldn't possibly have been summoned to Camelot, could she? There were too many worlds colliding already.

"Philip and *I* have been summoned."

"Oh," said Thomas relieved. "Right," said Thomas.

His mother seemed to be expecting more. There'd been another question. Thomas was as certain of that as he was uncertain of what he'd been saying.

"Surely whatever tasks your superiors have for you can wait, Thomas. I'm sure your brother wants you here to help organize the town."

Mrs. Farmer took an idealistic view of her children's relationships.

"Talk to William and your father. I'm sure they'll appreciate having the extra hands, and then you can return to your responsibilities in Camelot. We're all very proud of you, Thomas."

He was dismissed with a pat on the arm. This wasn't going well. He meandered over to his father.

Mr. Farmer was craning his neck staring up at a high window in the southern wall. Thomas took a spot next to him and stared. After some time, Thomas decided it was definitely a window. High up there. In the wall.

"Whatcha lookin' at Dad?"

"Masonry needs pointing." He made a mark on his slate.

Mr. Farmer liked his sentences like he liked his stonework. Pointed. Thomas laughed at the thought.

"Something funny?"

The answer to that was always no, regardless.

"Nope." Thomas shook his head for emphasis.

Mr. Farmer stared at Thomas a moment longer, then turned his focus back to the wall. He stuck his pencil in a joint and wiggled it, dislodging bits of damp mortar. "Seepage," he said, and made another mark.

"Dad, we–" started Thomas.

Mr. Farmer frowned at his slate.

"I've been summoned back to Camelot. Important duties to attend to. I've come to say goodbye."

Mr. Farmer shook his head. "That's neglect. Plain and simple."

"Dad! I–"

"Don't know why I expected that baron to take any better care of his home than he did his town."

"Oh," said Thomas, both relieved and deflated.

Mr. Farmer glanced at Thomas. "Right. Camelot. Important duties. Bonnie voyage then, as the French say. Lots to do. Better get a move on." He tucked his pencil back behind his ear and strolled away squinting at the molding.

"Right. Good luck," said Thomas, "with the stone and... things." He circled his hand in the kind of useless wave a person gives when the intended recipient isn't looking, turned on his heel, and headed toward the one person he was certain would give him a proper goodbye.

"Kneel!" said Elizabeth.

"Elizabeth I–"

"*Lady* Elizabeth," she said. "You will kneel before the Cottontail King and address his court properly, pheasant!"

"Peasant," corrected Thomas.

Elizabeth gasped and posed the Cottontail King with his paws in the air aghast. "WHOM are you calling peasant, pheasant?"

Thomas took in the scene. He hadn't noticed several hastily but lovingly constructed courtesans arranged before the throne. Elizabeth spotted him looking, dropped the King and introduced him to the court.

There was half an egg shell painted green with eyes drawn on. She picked it up and held it close so Thomas could appreciate the craftsmanship. "Sir Turtle," she said. She put him down gently, then pointed in turn to four nearly-identical dustballs. "Lady Lion, Lady Kitten, Rat, and Wolf. I haven't named them all yet," she explained.

"And that one?"

Elizabeth looked where Thomas was pointing. She rolled her eyes. "That's just a string Thomas."

"Could be a snake," he said.

She considered this, then hopped onto the throne with King Cottontail. "Now why have you come to our court, Pheasant?"

"Your feathers, sir!" said Gus.

"Where did you–" started Thomas.

"You will address the King when he speaks to you," said the King.

"Um," said Thomas holding the feathers uncertainly. "I've come to report a... snake?"

The King gasped. The courtesans glanced at each other, alarmed.

"Yes," said Thomas. "A snake in the court!" It felt good to redirect the King's attention away from himself.

"Well, I never! Where?" demanded the King.

Thomas stood tall, stretched his arm full length, and pointed directly at the bit of string. "There, Your Majesty."

"Seize him!" said the King.

"Wait!" said the string.

The courtesans held their breath.

"It is I," said the snake. "Merlin!"

The courtesans cheered.

"He does that you know," said Thomas in his Thomas voice.

"Does what?" said Elizabeth.

"Disguises himself," said Thomas. "Quite effectively. Not, you know, like a snake, but–"

"I know that Thomas," said Elizabeth. "Everyone knows that."

Gus shrugged and nodded.

"Listen, Elizabeth–" started Thomas.

"How do you know who's who?" said Elizabeth.

"What do you mean?"

"If a bad person can make himself look like a good person. How do you know who's who? How do you know who to help? You know. If you're a good person?"

"Well," said Thomas. "With knights it's easy. They wear their colors. On their shields or on a tabard or something, or they just tell you who they are and where they're from."

"But they could dress up in other people's colors," said Elizabeth. "Or lie. Since they're bad."

Thomas nodded. "Well then, I suppose you have to decide if they're a good person or a bad person by how they behave."

Elizabeth considered this.

"You watch what they do," said Thomas. "And see if it matches what they say. Especially when it's going to cost them something."

She seemed satisfied.

"I came to tell you I have to return to Camelot now," said Thomas.

Elizabeth dropped Merlin, threw herself at Thomas, and gave him a tight hug. Thomas was certain there wasn't anything else quite like it in all the world. Eventually he put her down.

"Thomas," she said.

"Mmm-hmm?" said Thomas.

"I'm glad the baron is gone, but you should have been the hero."

"Wait. I was–" he said and then saw what she'd seen over his shoulder – William, in the middle of the room, at the center of everything. As usual.

"Oh," he said and turned to explain, but she was engrossed in her court.

Thomas sighed. "Here," he said to Gus and handed him the feathers. "Do something with these."

"Right you are, sir!" said Gus. He stuck them behind his ears and presented himself to the Court of King Cottontail.

Thomas turned and stepped into the path of one of his Grandmother's newly commandeered servants. They collided. The servant apologized and bowed himself away. Thomas, more accustomed to apologizing than being apologized to, replied with awkward silence.

"And watch where you're going!" bellowed Grandma Farmer at the flustered servant. Then to Thomas: "Close your mouth or you'll let the flies in."

Thomas hadn't been aware his mouth was open. He closed it, realized he was going to need it to speak, and opened it again. It was a risky move. Grandma Farmer had held a schoolroom for most of the lives of most of the living citizens of Fogbottom. She knew how to shut a person's mouth.

A smile broke across her face, and she stretched her arms wide. "Thomas," she said. It was all she needed to say. Thomas folded himself in for a Grandma Farmer hug.

"I'm going back to Camelot, Grandma."

"Of course you are dear. You've got better things to do than hang around here. We'll get things all sorted. AMANDA APPLEBUTTER THAT IS NOT FUCHSIA AND YOU KNOW IT TRY AGAIN! You've got bigger stalls to muck."

A frightened girl on the other side of the room gathered up a roll of cloth and backed quickly out of the throne room.

"Thanks Grandma," said Thomas. *I think*, he thought.

Her gaze turned conspiratorial. "And Thomas, when you get there..."

"Yes?"

"And you've settled back in Guarding the Realm and Seeing to the Order and Doling Out the King's Justice..."

Finally someone understood.

"Don't forget your Grandma."

"Never."

"Hop on over to Chamber's. They've got the sturdiest pots and kettles. Iron. Solid. And Decorative. Not these plain old things the baron–" she coughed. "*Previous* baron kept."

"Pots," said Thomas.

"And kettles. Send some back. There's a good boy."

She promptly dozed off.

A servant who'd been sneaking across the room behind her chair visibly relaxed. It was a mistake people under Grandma Farmer's rule rarely made twice. The servant took one incautious step toward his destination.

Grandma jolted. "BUXTON YARLBERRY YOU KNOW VERY WELL THAT IS *NOT* THE WAY TO THE KITCHEN."

Eyes wide and ears back, Buxton turned on his heel and made quickly for the proper exit.

"I'll see you again soon, Grandma," said Thomas. But she was asleep again.

Thomas surveyed the room. That was all of them. There was no one left to forestall it. He inhaled, pressed his palm to his forehead, pulled his tunic straight, exhaled, and made his way toward William in the center of the room.

William Immanuel Farmer. If you took Thomas, fed him better, exercised him more often and more rigorously, bathed him, taught him to move gracefully, and lowered his voice an octave, you'd have an impressive Thomas, but you wouldn't have William. Everything beautiful loved William. It's just the way it goes with some people. But William had recently been nearly starved to death in the old baron's dungeon and wasn't quite himself yet. It was a perfect opportunity.

"Baron von Frogbutt," said Thomas.

William turned.

"That your best?" asked William.

Thomas shrugged.

"Von Sogbottom?"

"Am I German now?"

Thomas shrugged. "Wouldn't want to insult the Germans."

William laughed. It wasn't like him. His declining to return fire meant there must be something more important going on. He was taking his barony seriously. And he'd one-upped Thomas by doing so. He'd beaten Thomas by not playing. Thomas punched himself mentally.

William put his arm around Thomas. Thomas tried to figure out what to do with his hands.

"I heard you're heading out," said William.

Thomas nodded and hooked his thumbs in his trousers.

"I have to say, I'm jealous," William continued.

Thomas crossed his arms. But his brother's one-arm embrace was already throwing him off-balance, and this just made it worse.

"Jealous?" said Thomas. "You're a baron. *The* baron. All of this..." Thomas' arm swept the room taking in the crumbling water-damaged walls, the newly appointed keep personnel tiptoeing around a snoring Grandma Farmer, and the Cottontail Court conspicuously minus one Augustus Ditcher, Court Pheasant. "…is yours," finished Thomas.

William dropped the awkward embrace. "And thank *you* for that. I should've liked to decline. But crowning me publicly, in the heat of things... That was a masterful stroke. And now you get to ride off on adventures like a real knight–"

Thomas' grin slipped. "What do you mean 'like?'"

William looked genuinely surprised at Thomas taking affront. Thomas wished he didn't. It meant it wasn't a dig. It meant William really didn't think of Thomas as a real knight.

"What's a *real* knight then?" said Thomas.

"I didn't mean anything by it. It's just, you know. There are knights, and there are *knights.*"

"I'm sure I don't know," Thomas frowned. "What's a real knight got that I haven't?"

"Well, let's see," said William. "Proper armor?"

"It's being fashioned."

"Fashioned. Right. Okay. A sword?"

"You know mine was buried in the rubble when I *saved* you."

"Buried. Right. So, no sword. How about colors?"

Thomas fumbled, then an idea struck. "I could wear Fogbottom's colors," he declared triumphantly.

"Could you?"

Thomas frowned. This was a bad move. It put him directly at the mercy of William's good pleasure. But there was no way out now. "May I?" he said.

William scratched his chin. "Your recent manner of address to the Baron of Fogbottom – that'd be me – doesn't demonstrate what I would call 'respect for the office' so-to-speak."

"William," Thomas groaned.

"He has a horse!" said Gus.

Thomas' head snapped. "Gus. What–"

Gus bowed. "Pardon, your lordship. Knights have horses. Thomas has a horse."

William guffawed. "Booker, right? You're talking about Booker?"

Booker had been called many things. Most of those things were things other than 'horse.'

"So," said William, counting on his fingers, enjoying this. "No armor. No sword. No colors. One animal that was, once upon a time perhaps, a horse. That hardly makes–"

"And the blessing of King Arthur," said Gus. "Your Lordship," he added, bowing as they both stared at him.

"And the fellowship of his peers," said Sir Philip the Exceptionally Disadvantaged at Thomas' elbow. He'd lost the leg of meat. Lost wasn't quite the right word. Everyone knew exactly where it'd gone. And given the quality of victuals in Fogbottom recently, most suspected it'd turn up again of its own accord in the not too distant future.

"And the adulation of woman," said Marie at his other elbow.

Thomas smiled.

"Women," said Thomas, correcting Marie.

Marie squinted at him. "What women?" she said.

"Woman," said Thomas, correcting himself.

William laughed. "Right you are," he said. "And you'd be wise to remember what it is you have and what it is you don't when you're bearing this. Wendsley!"

Wendsley Cheston Hunter was Fogbottom's most recently reappointed, less recently demoted, and not long before that, newly appointed Guard of Town and Keep and Sundry. He was large enough to hide a shield behind his back. This was, in fact, what he was doing. He stepped forward, grinning, and brought the shield around in full view.

The collective reaction was underwhelming.

Wendsley looked down confused. "Oh," he said, and flipped it around.

The collective gasp was more like it.

"It's beautiful," said Marie.

"Aye, that's right nice," said Philip.

"Allow me, sir!" said Gus. Gus received the shield from Wendsley, who was generally inclined to go with the flow of things for the simple expedient that it was easier than paying attention.

A passing cloud passed just in time to allow a ray of sunlight to beam through the window high atop the water damaged outer wall, and the shield caught it as Gus knelt and presented it to Thomas, face up.

"Your shield, sir."

The shield's face bore, in all its refurbished glory, the red and white Fogbottom colors, but the white moon had been replaced with a cross, and the Less Valued Knights motto had been inscribed around the border in careful letters. *Somnia Salvebis.*

Thomas took the shield from Gus and slotted his arm through the leather straps. He felt its heft. He gave it a swish or two.

"New crest?" said Thomas.

"New crest," said William.

"Thank you William."

"You're welcome Thomas."

"Yes!" said Gus. "Woo!" He clapped.

Marie laughed. "Who's your friend Thomas?"

"That's Gus," said Thomas. "He's my new squire."

Philip snorted. "You're getting a squire?"

"Already got one," said Thomas, nodding to Gus. "Someone's got to carry this shield around."

Philip frowned. "He's what, eleven? We can barely keep ourselves safe if you recall. He won't last a week."

"Nonsense," said Thomas. "He'll be fine."

Thomas handed the shield to Gus.

Gus beamed. "*Somnia Salvebis*," he said, blinking madly to dry his eyes.

CHAPTER III

SECRET MISSIONS

It felt good. Gus was grinning. William was grinning. Wendsley Cheston Hunter was grinning. Marie was smiling. Philip was not. Philip was squinting at Thomas.

"What?" said Thomas.

Philip pulled him aside.

"Are you mad?"

"What?" repeated Thomas.

"A squire?"

"Look at him!" said Thomas, grinning.

"You look," said Philip. "What do you need a squire for? Hmm?" He held up a finger. "You don't have a horse to take care of."

"We've been through this. Quite recently in fact," said Thomas matter-of-factly.

"Go through it again."

"I have Booker."

Philip rolled his eyes.

"Booker. Okay." Philip pointed at Gus. "He's not tall enough to saddle even Booker."

Thomas opened his mouth. Philip held up a second finger.

"It's not like you've got a dozen weapons to truck around and hone and oil and sharpen and... hone."

Thomas felt the emptiness at his hip where Ambrosia once rested.

"That's a low blow Philip."

Philip held up finger number three.

"You don't need help with armor–"

Thomas nodded toward the shield and raised his eyebrows.

"You can carry your own shield."

"But look how much he likes it. Besides, it's not about how much I *can* do *without* him. It's about how much I *could* do *with* him." Thomas grinned and tried to look wise.

Philip frowned. "Like what?"

"Um," said Thomas. His grin faded. "Well, for instance..."

"Yes?" said Philip.

"He can..." said Thomas. "He can gather kindling. You know, while we, um... While we hunt. He can cook! I bet he's an excellent cook. Gus!"

"Yes sir!"

"Can you cook?"

"Cook what, sir?"

Thomas shrugged. "Anything?"

Gus laughed. "Well it'd be quite the cook who could cook anything wouldn't it? I'm flattered you think I might be one, sir. But I'm afraid I have to admit I can't cook anything."

"Can't cook anything," repeated Philip.

"Nothing at all?" said Thomas hopefully.

"Well," laughed Gus, "that's a right trick there too isn't it? Cooking nothing at all. I heard a tale once of a fairy market where you can buy anything, but what would cost a person the most was to try to come away from there with nothing at all."

Thomas blinked. "Thank you, Gus, that will be all for now."

"Right you are, sir."

Gus produced a handkerchief from somewhere and began carefully wiping down the edge of the spotless shield.

"Look," said Philip. "I get it. He's eager. He makes you feel like a real knight."

"There it is again," said Thomas. "Philip, we *are* real knights."

"You know what I mean. If you go walking into Camelot with a squire... What do you think Tuttle will say?"

"Mmm," said Thomas doubtfully.

"And how are you going to pay him?"

Thomas scratched his chin. "Hadn't thought of that. Don't we pay squires with, you know, learning experiences?"

Philip shook his head. "We *don't* pay squires because *we* don't *have* squires. And," he said, softening his voice. "It's dangerous. You're not the sort of Less Valued Knight that is really taking the stay-in-Camelot-and-keep-your-head-down directive seriously."

"That's exactly why I need someone like Gus," said Thomas.

Philip just stared at him.

"Really?" said Thomas. "That's a directive?"

"Implied," said Philip. "Don't you think?"

"'Suggested' is more what I thought."

But Thomas had to admit his own justifications were beginning to feel pretty selfish and impulsive, and the idea of managing and training Gus was beginning to look like work now that he really considered it.

Marie sauntered over. "What are we talking about?" she asked.

"Philip doesn't think I should bring Gus along."

"Oh," said Marie.

She was being 'quiet and thoughtful' Marie. Thomas found it unnerving.

"What do you think?" said Thomas. He cringed inside. Whatever she said when she was like this was normally shrewd, sensible and smart. It was infuriating. And he liked her for it. Liked her a lot. There was another L-word he wasn't using yet. Wasn't even thinking it. Nope.

"I think..." said Marie.

Philip glared.

"I think it'd be good for you to have someone to look after," she said. "To train up in chivalry. To mold into manhood. To lead by example."

Thomas grinned at Philip. Philip frowned.

"You can teach him how to ride a horse," said Marie. "How to sit right in the saddle to joust. How to care properly for leather and iron and steel. How to field dress your quarry. How to salute and march and about-face. How to properly furl, unfurl, fold and carry colors..."

Thomas' grin was fading. Philip's frown was transforming.

"How to choose one's battles. How to fight. How to fence and grapple. How to handle oneself in court. How to address one's superiors. *When* to address one's superiors. When not to address one's superiors. How to recognize rank, title and office. How to speak to the ladies of the court. Oh!" she said. Her face lit up. "You can teach him how to dance."

Thomas was flattered that Marie appeared to think Thomas was not only capable of all of this, but capable enough to teach it as well. He wasn't about to admit that he hadn't known that there were proper ways of doing half of it.

"Yes," she said, considering her own thoughts, "yes, I think the responsibility would be good for you Thomas."

"Um, right," said Thomas. "You've both made some excellent points. I'm off to talk to Gus," he said, and ducked away.

Philip grinned at Marie. Marie smiled innocently.

Away from Marie and Philip was the right direction, but beyond that Thomas was at a loss.

"Where did he—"

"Sir?" said Gus.

"Gus!" said Thomas, startled.

"Yes sir!" said Gus and saluted.

"You don't need to salute indoors Gus."

"Right. Sorry sir!" He saluted. "Sorry."

"Gus, I've been re-thinking some things."

"Important not to overthink, sir. At least that's what I always thought 'til I heard of Sir Thomas the Hesitant and I said, 'Gus, what does that mean? Hesitant?' And I said, 'Well, it means one is careful and thoughtful and thinks about things ahead of time.' Look before you leap, that's what hesitating is all about, am I right? My pa always says follow your ink-stinks." Gus laughed. "Ink stinks. It does, you know?" He shook his head and sighed. "He means instincts. And my ink-stinks say think it out and when you've got it sorted think about it some more and after that consider the other's prerogative."

Gus had stopped talking. It took a moment for Thomas to realize it.

"Perspective," said Thomas.

Gus nodded. "Yes sir, that too."

"Right. As you say, I've been doing some re-considering," said Thomas.

"I'd expect nothing less, sir."

"And I've come to the conclusion–"

"Bound to happen eventually, sir. Even to the best of us."

"–that I've been thinking selfishly," said Thomas.

Gus absent-mindedly buffed the pristine shield.

"About what, sir?"

"About how it wouldn't be right to put you in danger, Gus. You've got your whole life ahead of you."

Gus paused. "What do you mean, sir?"

"I can't employ you at the moment, Gus."

"But you're employing me right now. See?" he said, buffing more consciously.

"I mean I can't bring you along with me to Camelot."

"Oh," said Gus. His buffing slowed and he stared at the shield.

He was quiet for a moment, then his eyes brightened conspiratorially and his buffing resumed. "Oooh," he said. He whispered theatrically, "I completely understand, sir."

He winked and then raised his voice, "I am besot with woe that I canst not travel with thee, Sir Thomas, at this time. T'were my dream, but alas I see now it must abide and I with it here." Then quieter to Thomas: "What's my mission, sir?"

"Pardon?"

"The secret mission. I will not fail you sir."

"Gus, there's no–" Thomas faltered. He'd looked into the eyes of the crazed before. He'd seen the eyes of the deceiver before. Gus' eyes were neither of these. Gus' eyes were alight with reckless optimism and unconditional trust, and the optimism and trust were shining directly at him. At Thomas.

Perhaps it was his emotionally off-balance subconscious seeking some reassurance of stability: Thomas' left hand tried to come to rest on the pommel of his sword. It failed. There was no pommel to come to rest upon. His muscle memory sent an alarm to his brain that cut through the current crisis.

The alarm said, *Your sword is missing.*

Thomas' conscious mind responded, *It's not missing. It's buried under the collapsed prison.*

Gus, keen-eyed, alert and watching for top secret orders assumed Thomas was being purposefully indirect.

"Consider it done sir."

Thomas faltered. "Consider what done?"

Gus looked significantly at Thomas' hip where Ambrosia should be, touched his nose, winked, pressed the shield into Thomas' hands, and with a surprisingly well-executed about-face, deployed himself on his first mission for Sir Thomas the Hesitant of the Table of Less Valued Knights.

"Wait!" said Thomas. But it was too late. Gus was making his way out of the room, looking rather conspicuously inconspicuous. Thomas glared at his left hand. The betrayer.

Philip and Marie moved up beside him.

"How did he take it?" asked Philip.

They watched Gus leave the room.

"Why would that even be a secret mission?" said Thomas.

"What secret mission?" said Marie.

"He's gone to try to dig out Ambrosia." Thomas shrugged. "Secretly."

"Ha!" said Philip. "Good one. That'll keep him busy for a few years." He slapped Thomas on the back.

Marie frowned.

"I didn't. That wasn't–"

"Come on boys," she said, with what Thomas felt was undue emphasis on the word 'boys'. "We have responsibilities to get back to at home."

Home, thought Thomas. She meant Camelot of course. He took in the scene before him one last time: his family, making the Fogbottom keep their own. The whole town was their home now. Somehow, Thomas had never felt more displaced.

Thomas watched his family occupy themselves. Then after a moment, he followed Philip and Marie out of the keep and headed toward – for lack of a better word – home.

৵

There was Britain, and there was Gaul. It wasn't difficult to tell the two places apart. For one thing, there was a wide body of water between them. Crossing the Channel by boat was the preferred method – as opposed to, for example, the front crawl – though crossing by any means was memorable. Navigating the currents was a bit like trying to traverse a series of conveyor belts operating at differing speeds and laid haphazardly in opposing directions. A voyage in such waters tends to be a humbling experience. The average person loses their cheek, their brass, and their lunch in roughly that order.

Not everyone who crosses is the average person.

Elisante appeared average. She appeared average because that's how she wanted to appear at the moment. Elisante appeared however she liked to appear – within certain limits. The primary limit was what the observer expected to see. She wasn't a shape-shifter. She was an illusionist. She didn't actually become what she was trying to be. She simply seemed to be what others thought they would see. Her mistress, Nimue, could do it. She rarely chose to. Merlin could do it. He used the ability, as far as Elisante could tell, to play practical jokes. In fact, most people could do it. The difference between the practicing illusionist and the average person is whether or not one does it on purpose.

Elisante was doing it on purpose.

"Merci, maman," she said to the kind woman who was doling out breakfast to her brood beside the busy market stall. The woman ran out of sweet rolls before she ran of children. Puzzled, she began counting, but Elisante had slipped away.

In a nearby alley, Elisante sat, picked at her roll, listened to the woman argue with the stall owner and mused on her mission.

She'd seen several knights since her arrival in the French port, but all of them had been, not surprisingly, French. An English knight would be easy to spot. In contrast to the French, there would be a certain proud absence of flair. She wasn't certain what a 'Less Valued Knight' would look like. She supposed he would look like someone trying to be something he wasn't. She had experience in these matters. She knew what to look for, and it was easier to wait and let him come to her than to traipse around the countryside searching. She just needed to find a way to pass the time.

She scanned the market. She tossed a crumb to a fat pigeon. She listened to ships' bells tolling in the nearby docks. She fiddled with a pendant hanging at her throat. She scanned the market. She scraped a pattern in the dirt with her toe. She chewed. She rubbed her neck. She scanned the market. She groaned.

Elisante stood up, brushed herself off, and placed the remains of the half-eaten sweet roll on a derelict barrel deeper in the alleyway. She shooed the fat pigeon away and concentrated. Time passed. The sun climbed. The shadows in the alley grew short and began to disappear. Beads of sweat formed on Elisante's forehead until finally she exhaled. She examined the half-eaten sweet roll. It looked very much like a half-eaten sweet roll. But that's what *she* expected to see.

She pocketed the roll and waited at the mouth of the alley. When the stall keeper turned his back she slipped the half-eaten roll in amongst the others and retreated. Pressed against the alley wall, she held her breath and watched.

The man wheeled a cart around to the front of the stall and began unloading the morning's contents to make room for the afternoon's. He seemed to take no notice of the half-eaten sweet roll. One after another he moved unpurchased pastries from the stall to the cart, and with each transfer Elisante's heart pounded harder. Had she really done it? Surely, he would have noticed it by now.

Now he turned. Now he put his hand on the half-eaten roll. Now he placed it in the cart. Now he stood. Now he–

Elisante bit her lip.

Now he stared. Now he frowned.

Elisante gritted her teeth.

Now he spouted curses and scanned the crowd. He retrieved the half-eaten roll from the cart and tossed it in a waste barrel beside the stall. Muttering, he returned to his task.

Elisante slumped against the alley wall.

To make oneself appear to be what others expected – that was basic illusion. Anyone could do it. To make something else appear to be what others expected – that was the advanced stuff. Nimue could do it. She was famous for it. Merlin could do it, certainly, though she didn't think she'd seen him do it; which meant, probably, he was just that good at it. Apparently, Morgan le Fay could do it, hence the impostor-sword, hence the mission, hence Elisante standing in an alley trying to make half a roll look like a whole.

But the stall keeper had spotted it.

Elisante couldn't do it.

Not yet.

CHAPTER IV

THE DOWNCAST SHEEP

It was morning in many places. One of those places was roughly halfway between Fogbottom and Camelot, down an overgrown path which led from a small bridge with quite a story to tell – for those who are interested in that sort of thing – to a hermit's old ramshackle shack.

The hermit had retired from hermiting after previously retiring from evil-wizardry, and was now seeking new ventures in the big city. The allegedly-rehabilitated, no-longer-evil hermit-wizard, Pyralis, had nursed Thomas back to health after a brave but ill-advised confrontation with a ne'er-do-well on Thomas' first trip to Camelot. Pyralis had given Thomas a poultice and a sword, which had both really stunk, and set him on his way to knighthood.

To Thomas, it felt like a lifetime ago.

Raindrops splashed in muddy depressions, pattered on drooping colorless wildflowers, and lost themselves in the cloudy stream that loitered despondently beside the hunched and abandoned shack. Inside, water dripped rhythmically through gaps in something that might have once been thatch and streamed into the shack through wide gaps in the decaying wattle and daub.

The site had been abandoned for quite some time now. It hadn't changed a bit.

Thomas rolled over and nuzzled his head in a scratchy pile of musty hay. He kept his eyes closed, breathed through his mouth and tried to drift back to sleep. The morning air was cool. The rain patter was soothing. He was vaguely aware of Philip's presence elsewhere in the room. He was strongly aware of the precise location of Marie's presence not far away.

He sighed and smiled. He'd felt let down by his family yesterday, but a long walk and a good rest in a place with fond memories had done the job. The floor was a little hard, but if this moment stretched Thomas wouldn't complain. He let himself sink into it like a bather easing into a bath. Content. That was the word. He felt good. All was well. Things felt right.

And then the bleating began.

Thomas Farmer was a country-boy, but you didn't have to be a country-boy to know the sound was an animal in distress. Thomas did what an experienced country-boy does at times like this. He stuffed his fingers in his ears and tried to go back to sleep.

Philip was sitting up and hollering. Marie was up and searching, concerned that the unfortunate animal was in the room with them. Thomas groaned.

"What is it?" snapped Philip.

"It's a sheep," said Thomas.

"Why is it crying?" shouted Marie. "Is it in trouble?"

"It's going to be," said Thomas.

The bleating continued.

"We have to help it," said Marie.

"Yep," Thomas conceded. It's hard to count sheep when the first one won't shut up.

Thomas pulled on his boots, shook the hay from his hair, hiked up his britches, and stepped out of the shack. There was a squelching sound, and his right boot sunk half a foot into the mud.

"Yep," said Thomas, as he examined his stuck foot. He was dampening quickly in the rain. "That's about right."

Philip stepped around him, scanning the tree-line, trying to locate the source of the incessant alarm. Marie stepped carefully beside Thomas and tried to help him pull his foot up.

She was partially successful. Thomas' foot came up. His boot didn't. Trying to catch his own balance without toppling Marie, Thomas executed the expedient, time-honored maneuver familiar to anyone who has found themselves in a similar predicament. He put his socked foot right back down in the welcoming mud.

"There we go," he said. "Even better."

He pulled his boot out of the mud with a slurp. With the deftness of someone who's done a thing more than a few times, he held on to the top of his sock so it would come with his foot as he lifted it, gave the muddy foot a useless soggy shake, and stuffed it firmly in the boot.

"Come on, ya dew-beaters!" yelled Philip from somewhere up ahead.

Marie grimaced sheepishly at Thomas. "Sorry," she said.

"Not your fault," said Thomas with a forced cheerfulness. "Let's go rescue a baby lamb," he said, hoping by means of the obvious redundancy to convey his true feelings on the matter. He hobbled after Philip who was meandering his way into the wood.

"You think it's a baby?" cried Marie and rushed ahead.

Thomas stepped through a curtain of dripping water and into a clearing where the rain assaulted the ground unobstructed by the forest canopy. Someone familiar with masonry and the construction of basic water pumps might have graciously called the well in the middle of the soppy clearing 'rustic'. Thomas had only recently become aware of rustic as a category. It seemed to mean everything outside of Camelot. To Thomas it was your basic well: hole in the ground, low stone wall, frayed rope, leaky weathered bucket.

An old man knelt at the well moaning and crying out. Out of the hole came incessant bleating and occasional splashing. Philip and Marie stood on either side of the old man and stared over the wall. Thomas stepped up and peered into the deep, dark void. It was roughly three feet deep. Standing in an inch of water, the ugliest sheep Thomas had ever seen stared back at him.

Bleat, it said, and stomped its hoof. Splash. *Bleat.*

"What is that?" said Philip.

"Please help," the shepherd pleaded. "She's trapped," he said. "She's going to drown," he moaned. He looked up blinking against the rain. "She's all I–" He abruptly let go of Thomas' leg. "Who are you?" he said. He glanced quickly at Marie and Philip, suspicious. He pulled himself up onto his feet and backed away pointing a weathered finger at them. "Stay away from my sheep," he said.

"That's a sheep?" said Philip.

"She's in distress," said Marie matter-of-factly. "And she needs our help."

"The well's only three feet deep," said Philip.

"That's not a well," said Thomas.

"Is too," said the shepherd.

"That's a walled puddle is what that is," said Thomas.

"Is too a well," said the shepherd. "My one and only prize sheep is stuck in a well and don't you touch her."

"It's like a... whatcha call. There's a French word," said Philip.

"Faux," said Thomas. "It's a faux well."

"It's a foul predicament indeed," moaned the shepherd. "A veritable plight! Who will help me? Not you three. Move along now."

"Not foul," said Thomas. "Faux well. Fake. False."

"It's decorative," said the shepherd.

"It doesn't matter," said Marie. "She can't get out."

"Stay away from my sheep," repeated the shepherd.

"There's a ladder," said Thomas.

"I'm no shepherdess," Marie said, "but I'm reasonably certain sheep can't climb ladders."

"That's not a sheep," said Philip. "Can't be. Sheep have, you know, better um, dispositions and such. Don't they?"

Bleat. Splash.

Thomas examined the well. The wall looked solid. The ladder was undamaged. There were grooves in the mud leading up to the well. There was a chaotic array of foot and hoof prints at the edge. Mud was tracked up and over the wall.

Thomas turned to the shepherd. "How exactly did she get in there?"

The shepherd squinted at him. "Fell," he said.

"I see," said Thomas. "Before or after you tossed her in?"

Bleat.

"I resent what you're implying," said the shepherd. "Now, get away from there."

"Yes sir," said Thomas. He turned and started hobbling back to the trees.

"Thomas!" said Marie.

"He put her in there." Thomas kept walking. "He can get her out."

"But he can't get her out." She looked sadly at the sheep. "And she can't get out herself."

Thomas stopped and slouched.

"Fine," he said, and hobbled back to the well.

Snap. Philip pulled his hand back just in time.

"It tried to bite me!" he said.

The shepherd chuckled.

"We're going to help you," said Thomas to the shepherd, "and then–"

"What? No! Get back. I won't allow it."

"Why not?"

"It's not for you. What'll it look like if I go back and say I lost my sheep–"

"Your prize sheep," corrected Philip.

"What? Oh. Yes. My prize sheep–"

"One and only prize sheep," said Philip.

The shepherd glared. "What will it look like if I go back and say I lost my one and only prize sheep down a well, but oh some nice young people came along and helped her out. Who wants to hear a boring story like that? I didn't go to all this effort for some lousy, run o' the mill Samaritan to pop out of the woods and do a good deed that doesn't belong to him. GET AWAY FROM THERE!"

Marie stopped petting the sheep.

Bleat?

Thomas moved toward the well.

"No wait," said the shepherd. "Please, it's got to be a knight that helps us, see?"

"He *is* a knight," said Marie. "And so is he," she said pointing at Philip. "Sir Thomas the Hesitant and Sir Philip the Disadvantaged."

"Exceptionally Disadvantaged," Philip corrected.

The shepherd snorted. "Right," he said. "And the young lady's one too I bet. Look, I know knights when I sees 'em. And you three are not knights."

"And that," said Philip, "is not a sheep."

"Fair enough," said the shepherd. "But you're still not touching her."

Philip hadn't expected the shepherd to agree. He took a step away from the sheep-like animal.

It started to lay down in the muddy water then changed its mind. It gave a forlorn half-bleat.

The shepherd took up a position between Thomas and the animal, arms crossed.

An idea struck Thomas. "You've heard of Gawain?"

"Aye," said the shepherd, eyes narrowing.

"He saved my life," said Thomas.

The shepherd shrugged. "Says you."

"It's true," said Marie, a little too enthusiastically. Thomas shot her a look.

Philip nodded. "There's even a song about it." He hummed the bridge. "*Who is the subject of my refrain...*"

The shepherd began to nod in time.

"*The glorious the noble* the something *Gawain*," sang Philip.

"Yeah, I know that one," said the shepherd.

They sang together, "*Gawain! Gawain! Gawain! Gawain!*"

"You've got to be kidding me," said Thomas.

The shepherd was grinning. "Ah that's a good one. I wish he'd shown up instead of you lot. That'd be a tale to tell."

"Right," said Thomas. "Well, he's not here, but we are. And like I was saying, Gawain saved my life."

"And like *I* was saying," said the shepherd, grin gone, "so what?"

"So," said Thomas, "if I save your... animal, I'd only be able to do so because Gawain saved me and so it'd be like Gawain saved your shhh– her. It."

The shepherd considered this. He chewed his cheek. He peered at Thomas. He squinted at the rain clouds. He came to a decision.

"No," he said.

Thomas sighed.

"Oh come on," snapped Philip.

"Be reasonable sir," said Marie.

"No knight, no good deed, no negotiations. I know my rights."

"What'll it take to convince you he's a knight?" asked Marie.

"That's easy," said the shepherd. "A knight's gotta have a crest–"

Thomas brightened. "I'll get my shield."

"A steed of war–" continued the shepherd.

Thomas paused. He could fetch Booker. He wondered how Booker would react if someone called him a steed. He didn't think it had ever happened before.

"And most of all," said the shepherd, "a magic sword."

"That's a king," said Philip.

The shepherd frowned. "Don't think so."

Philip rolled his eyes. "Look, almost no one's got a magic sword."

"Gawain does," countered the shepherd.

"He does not," argued Philip.

Someone stepped out of the trees then and shook himself. He made his way to the group assembled at the well, squelching heavily with each mud-sucking step.

"Galatine," said Gus, trying to catch his breath.

"Gus?" said Thomas.

"Gawain does have a magic sword," said Gus. "It's called Galatine."

He turned to the shepherd. "I am Augustus Ditcher, sir. Squire to the renowned Sir Thomas the Hesitant, Table, Less Valued. And I'm here to confirm that he also—" Gus dropped to one knee with an uncomfortable squish. "Has a magic sword," he said.

Gus swung a bundle from behind his back, laid it on his knee, rolled it out of its protective cloth with a dramatic flair, and presented it to Thomas.

"Your sword, sir."

Even in the rain, you could smell it.

"Mission accomplished sir," Gus whispered. "More or less." He winked.

*

Thomas grunted, aimed the front of the animal at the ladder, and shoved. The stone wall was no taller than the well was deep, but added together they formed a formidable barrier to the would-be rescuer. He was putting a great deal of hope in the animal's ability to adapt to the concept of a ladder. There was a moment of stability. Hope bloomed. The sheep bleated and scrabbled at the rungs. Thomas pressed harder. Philip reached. The sheep recoiled. The mud squelched and released Thomas' feet.

Thomas hit the mud face first. Philip held the sheep by its armpits. The sheep flailed wide-eyed at Philip.

BLEAT!

It tried to bite Philip's hands. Philip twisted and turned trying to hold onto the crazed animal.

"Don't you hurt her!" cried the shepherd.

Thomas pushed himself up on all fours.

"Hrnnghaaaw! My nose! It's got my nose!"

Marie grabbed Philip and pulled. Philip let go. The sheep came down on Thomas and flattened him again into the muddy well bottom.

That was the first attempt.

Philip nursed his nose. Thomas and the sheep sat in the mud eyeing each other warily for quite some time.

Bleat, said the sheep.

"Likewise," said Thomas.

In the end, it took all five of them working with the rope to get both the sheep and Thomas out of the well. Marie suggested using the ladder as a make-shift stretcher.

"What's she need a stretcher for? *She's* not hurt," complained Philip.

"And let's keep her that way, mm?" said Marie.

"It would certainly make her more… manageable," said Thomas.

Philip volunteered Gus to wrestle the animal onto it. But the shepherd insisted it should be people who at least claimed to be knights to do the heavy-lifting in his quest, so Philip and Thomas had the honor.

Now Thomas slumped against the well. He was water-logged and heavy with mud. The rain had ceased at some point, the clouds broke, and the afternoon sun began to bake a thick crust on Thomas.

"Give my thanks to Sir Gawain," said the shepherd, and he started trundling off making slashes and stabs in the air with a wet stick, soggy animal in tow. They could hear him talking to an imaginary audience as he departed.

"And then Gawain showed up," the shepherd said. "With his mighty sword Guillotine–"

Gus winced.

"–and he held it up–" The shepherd demonstrated with the stick. "And the clouds parted. And the sun came out." He giggled. "That'll do. Come on, Esther," he said. He disappeared into the trees on the other side of the clearing humming. "*Ooooh* something something *my refrain, Gawain, Gawain, Gawain, Gawain!*"

"Gawain was here?" said Gus, suddenly standing taller.

"No." Thomas shook his head. "No, Gawain was not here."

Thomas tried to unfold and stand up, but the dried mud resisted. He grunted and heaved himself up. A small avalanche of moist detritus crumbled from him.

"If Gawain was here," said Thomas rather mad-eyed and too loud, "you'd know it, because Gawain is great! How great is Gawain? I'll tell you how great Gawain is. Gawain is so great that he doesn't even have to show up to get credit for someone else's good deed. That's how great Gawain is."

Thomas was steaming. Literally. It wafted up from him as the sun baked him.

Gus looked frightened.

Marie frowned.

Philip said, "Um, Thomas?"

"What?"

"Two things," said Philip. "One, that's the job, remember? Less Valued Knights, right? It's right there in the code. Article Nine." Philip took a breath, "It's–"

"Not about you," Gus chimed in, standing at attention. "It's never about you. Except, of course, when it would be better for your superiors that whatever it is be not about them." Gus relaxed and grinned.

Marie looked impressed.

"Right," said Philip, more than a little suspicious. "And two–"

Thomas glared at Philip.

"You stink," said Philip.

Thomas hesitated. He sniffed. He smelled wet sheep and well-bottom, but – oh, there it was.

He sniffed again. "That's not me," he said.

"Oh I think it's you mate."

Thomas shook his head and shambled over to a stump where his sword leaned, glinting in the sun.

"It's the sword," said Thomas.

Gus fidgeted.

It was Philip's turn to look impressed with Gus. "How did you get her out from under all that rubble?"

"Er," said Gus. "Sorry, sir. That's a lost cause. A sailed ship. A shorn sheep, if you will. Ha ha."

Thomas glared.

"Right. Too soon for the sheep jokes. Sorry sir. I took one look at the ruin where Ambrosia is buried and said to myself, 'Augustus, no one's getting in there and no one's getting anything out again, either.'"

"It looks like Ambrosia," said Thomas. He turned it over, careful to breathe through his mouth. "Smells about right too."

Gus beamed. "Been working hard on that," he said. "Ever since I heard of Sir Thomas the Hesitant and his magic sword."

Philip squinted. "You didn't. You couldn't have. You? Augustus Ditcher, are you saying you enchanted that sword?"

Gus twisted his fingers. "Marinated is more like, sir. Enchanting? No way, no how sir. That's second tier witchcraft and wizardry stuff, enchanting is. Practically sorcery. Heck, I can't even do your basic illusionism. I'm ashamed to admit I tried to hustle a free pie from Old Lady Applebutter once. She saw through me right away. Enchantments? No sir. Can't even do the first level stuff. I'm too me to not be me I reckon." He shrugged.

Marie smiled at Gus' genuineness and tried to share a delighted glanced with Thomas and Philip. Neither reciprocated. She frowned.

"Where's the cloth you brought this in?" asked Thomas.

"Right here sir."

Thomas wrapped up the sword.

"Okay then," he said. "I'm going back to the cabin. I'm going to wash this mud out. My new squire is going to feed Booker. And then we'd best get on to Camelot."

"Your new what?" exclaimed Philip. He shot a look at Marie for support.

Marie crossed her arms. "I think he might just do you both some good."

"You heard me," said Thomas, ignoring the barb. "I've got a crest, a war steed, a magic sword–"

"A facsimile," said Philip.

"–a loyal companion-knight," said Thomas pointedly, glaring at Philip.

Philip's nostrils flared. His lips went tight. Then, "Aye," he said, and saluted.

"A lady..."

Marie considered him for a moment.

"A lady?"

"As she chooses," said Marie, and curtsied.

Thomas grinned, emboldened. "And I'm headed to Camelot," he said, "with my squire, Augustus Ditcher of the Fogbottom Ditchers. Come along, Gus."

Thomas aimed himself toward the ramshackle shack and hobbled into the trees. Gus followed, so excited he might have been walking on springs. Marie laughed and joined them. Philip frowned, looked at the well, looked at the sky, looked where the shepherd had exited the clearing, then sighed and followed.

CHAPTER V

ANOTHER FINE PICKLE

Thomas, Marie, Philip and Gus made their way along the wooded road to Camelot. Birds sang. Lush green grass waved in the summer breeze. Bumblebees bumbled about rather purposefully, actually, and butterflies labored frantically to get their minds around the concept of wings. Gus marched pleasantly leading Booker, who now carried Thomas' shield strapped to his saddle. Marie picked a yellow wildflower and stuck it behind her ear. Thomas tried not to stare.

Thomas had insisted, but Marie had declined to ride Booker out of concern for the volunteered. Booker was the kind of horse who was happy to help. You just feared for his well-being all the while. Probably due to the wheezing.

As they climbed the final hill before the city, Gus grew more bouncy and Philip more stiff.

"Breathe, Gus," said Thomas.

Gus let slip an excited squeak.

"And you too, Philip."

"I'm telling you," said Philip through clenched teeth, "it's a bad idea bringing him along."

"You know what I think?" said Thomas.

"What?"

"I think you're jealous."

Philip looked shocked. "What? Look. Fine. You know what? It's not my problem." He pointed his chin up the road and outpaced the rest of them as they crested the hill.

At the top of the hill, Gus halted.

Blue pennants flapped gracefully atop high towers. White stone arches arched artfully. A river circled part way round the outer wall, under an iron gate and into the city. The setting sun turned the river into bronze fire. Words like buttress, bulwark, bastion, and battlement drifted into the usual onlooker's mind and failed to stick because the usual onlooker didn't know what those things were; only that if they were anywhere, they were certainly here. Gus wasn't the usual onlooker.

He made a choking sound. There were tears in his eyes.

"Oh come on," said Philip.

"Sorry sir," said Gus. "It's just so... It's everything I'd hoped it would be."

Thomas considered the view before him.

"Me too," he said. "Let's go," he added kindly.

Thomas grinned and followed Philip and Marie down the hill. Gus swallowed and allowed his feet to carry him into Camelot.

❧

"I need to check in at the Palace," said Marie. "I'm sure the Queen hasn't missed me, but the ladies covering for me will have."

"Meet you at the Pickle?" he asked. "Eight o'clock?"

Marie smiled. "I'll see what I can do."

She winked, spun, and was off down the street taking Thomas' attention with her.

"The Pickle!" said Gus. "The Fine Pickle! They've got all the famous battles on tapestries on the walls, right? King Ban versus the Eleven–"

Philip snickered. "It wasn't just Ban," he said.

Gus didn't seem to hear.

"And Pellinore killing Lot!" Gus sobered briefly. "Phew that's got to irk Gawain eh? Pellinore immortalized killing Gawain's dad right there on the wall for everyone to gawk at."

"Lot rebelled against King Arthur," said Philip in the tone of someone for whom the case was simple and closed.

"Oh!" Gus brightened. "Balin fighting Garlonde! Garlonde could go invisible you know. How'd they embroider that anyway? For the tapestry I mean. It must look like Balin's not fighting anyone." Gus paused. His brow knit. "Or looks like he's fighting nobody. Looks like he's *not* fighting nobody?"

"We get the idea," said Philip.

"He looks like he's fighting someone, but the other person isn't there." Gus trailed off. "Balin the Savage. The Knight with Two Swords. '*Whether life or death, whichsoever adventure befalleth me...*'" Gus straightened and peered so hard into the distance that Thomas had to look where he was looking. There was nothing there.

"'*I will take it*,'" said Gus finishing the quote.

"Death mostly," said Philip.

Thomas shot him a questioning look.

"Death 'befelleth' Balin. And nobody talks like that."

Gus continued. "They say Merlin put Balin's sword in a stone and floated it down a river and it will arrive in Camelot on the day it's needed and the knight who can wield it will."

"Will what?" said Philip.

"Wield it," said Gus.

Philip rolled his eyes. "There's only one sword in a stone. Arthur's. And if Merlin were going to do something like that he'd be a little more... I dunno... inventive. Don't you think?"

"Sounds impressive to me," said Thomas.

"It's a sword in a stone," he said. He crossed his arms. "It's derivative."

"But Merlin's stone floats," said Thomas.

"Yes sir," said Gus. "Right down the river." He made a motion with his hand to demonstrate.

Philip frowned.

They stared at each other until Gus remembered another crucial fact. In the hushed and startled voice of a person who doesn't want to frighten off a skittish fairy creature: "They've got iced creams," he said, "at the Pickle."

"Only in the right season," said Thomas.

"And this is definitely not," said Philip, wiping his sweaty brow with his sleeve, "the right season."

But Gus was already on to the next thought. He stared at his feet.

"These are the very stones," he said.

"Pardon?" said Thomas.

"These are the very stones King Arthur treads upon. Well," Gus snorted, "rides on, right? I mean, he's the King. He doesn't walk anywhere anymore, right?" Gus' brow knit. "Does he?"

"Of course he walks places," snapped Philip. "You know, Gus, speaking of stones... We've got the stone Arthur pulled Excalibur from over at Saint Stephen's. You should check it out."

Gus smiled and wagged a finger at Philip. "You're pulling my leg sir. King Arthur didn't pull *Excalibur* from the stone. That sword was broken when he fought Pellinore. Excalibur came from the lake." Gus laughed chummily.

"Right you are," said Philip with a forced smile. "Just testing you. But we do have the stone. And it's a sight to see. What do you say? See you later?" He waved his hand invitingly in a direction other than his own.

"Oh, Sir Philip, you're tricky, but everyone knows the stone's in London. Unless King Arthur had it dug up and hauled here." His smile faded. "He didn't. Did he?"

"No, he didn't," said Thomas glaring at Philip. "To the barracks, Gus. I'll show you where to stable Booker, and I'll introduce you to the men."

Thomas headed toward the palace grounds. Gus followed, leading Booker and interrupting himself with observations. One after another, ordinary landmarks were rendered extraordinary by their association with people Gus admired.

Philip clenched his fists and stewed. Aping Gus he mumbled, "Garlonde could go invisible you know." He sneered. "Floating rocks. I'll float him a rock, arrant little windbag." A passerby gave Philip a nervous look and a wide berth. Philip cleared his throat. "Pardon," he said. "Off to the barracks, ma'am. Knight's duties. Have an evening." He backed away bowing and hurried after Thomas.

෴

Thomas threw the barracks door open. The door stopped short with a muffled grunt. Mendhel the Misfortunately Placed stepped out from behind it, eyes watering, holding his nose. "Ow," he said. He blinked. "Oh! Thomaf! Hey everyone, it'f Thomaf and Filip."

Choruses of "Thomas!" and "Philip!" rang out. Shoulders were manhandled. Backs were slapped. Ox the Monosyllabic gave bear hugs. Remi the Imperturbable, snoring on his bunk, looked for a moment like he might stir, but he didn't.

"It's good to be back," said Thomas.

"Who do I hug?" rumbled Ox, squeezing Gus.

"Sir Ox, this is Augustus Ditcher. Gus. My squire."

Ox's eyes went wide.

Gus grunted.

"Maybe enough hugging for now," said Thomas.

"Right," said Ox. He set Gus down gently.

Gus inhaled, wobbled, then knelt. "At your services sirs!"

"You can stand up Gus," said Thomas.

"Yessir."

Thomas made the introductions. "Sir Ox the Monosyllabic, who you now know."

"Intimately, sir," said Gus.

Thomas pointed around the room. "Anyone in Camelot is bound to bump into Mendhel eventually. Remi over there gets along with everyone. This is Dedric."

A lanky man stepped forward, smiled, and saluted the space to Gus' left.

"He's a–"

"Diplopian," said Gus. "Faces unflinching twice as many enemies as other men. Slays two with a single stroke."

Dedric beamed. "Sometimes I flinch," he admitted.

"And that's Edgar the Erstwhile," said Gus saluting. "Nice to have met you, sir though I must say I feel as though I've always known you."

"Likewise," said Edgar.

Thomas was impressed. "You've done your homework."

Gus laughed. "Everyone knows the Less Valued Knights, sir."

Philip frowned.

Thomas caught everyone up on the events in Fogbottom, right up to the summons calling all knights of every order back to Camelot.

"You are just in time," said Ox. "We meet in the morn."

Dedric nodded.

Edgar interpreted, "An assembly has been scheduled for tomorrow."

"The summons was... succinct. Any idea what it's all about?" said Thomas.

"Don't know. But the spell man is gone," said Ox.

"Merlin," explained Dedric. "No one's seen Merlin."

Gus snorted. "How would you know if you had?"

"Gus!" said Thomas.

Gus' face went red. "I mean– I didn't mean Dedric specifically. I meant, it's *Merlin.* He can look like whoever he wants to look like."

"Mmm," said Thomas. "That's a good point."

"Except," said Philip, "he prophesied his doom before he disappeared."

Thomas frowned. "How do you know that? You were in Fogbottom with me."

"You mean after I came to rescue you," said Philip. "Before I came to rescue you, I was here with everyone else. And then I came to rescue you."

"Thank you," said Thomas, who could see Philip was put out about something, "for rescuing me from the Fogbottom dungeon, Philip."

"You're welcome," said Philip. He crossed his arms and sat back.

"'*I warn you Arthur I shall not endure long,*'" said Gus. His eyes were closed and he was affecting the voice of an old man. "'*Alas! I shall be shut in the earth alive despite all my crafts. Keep well your sword and scabbard, my King, for they shall be stolen by a woman you most trust. And also, I will miss you.*'"

Gus opened his eyes. They were all staring at him.

"It's what Merlin said to King Arthur by way of portent," said Gus.

"Aye," said Ox, clearly impressed. "What he said."

Gus beamed.

Philip rolled his eyes and grumbled in the lengthening shadows. Edgar lit some lamps.

"Merlin missing," mused Thomas. "You think it's got something to do with the missing cup?"

"Cup!?" blurted Gus. He caught himself and clamped a hand over his mouth. "Sorry, sir."

"You know something about the cup, Gus?"

"You mean the Sangreal, sir." It was a correction, not a question. "The Royal Blood. The Holy Grail. The Cup of Redemption."

"May...be?" said Thomas, wanting to know what Gus knew and reluctant to admit in front of the others that he didn't already.

"Held our Lord's blood. Carries his promise. Redeems anything it touches. Undoes any curse."

Ox made a noise. Thomas glanced at him. Ox coughed once, cleared his throat, and held up a hand to indicate he was okay. No one else seemed to notice.

"And it can't have gone missing sir," said Gus.

"Why is that?"

"Well," Gus chuckled. "We never had it in the first place, did we? The Fisher King had it. And then Balin wounded him with the sword Merlin went and stuck in the floating stone after..." Gus glanced at Philip. He faltered.

"And then the Grail went missing?" asked Philip.

"Aye," said Gus. "Right. I suppose so. But if you could find it," he rallied, "you could heal the Fisher King and restore the land! That's probably what everyone's on about."

Philip was unamused.

"Gus," said Thomas, "Why don't you take a break. I think Booker could use some care and attention."

"Right you are, sir." Gus excused himself. "It really is a pleasure to meet you all," he said at the door.

"Gus," said Thomas. "Booker."

"Yes sir." He shut the door behind himself.

Thomas leaned forward. "You think Tuttle wants us to look for the Grail?" He sighed and rubbed his face. "Can't be," he said. "I mean, we can't even rescue a sheep, right?"

"We did rescue the sheep," said Philip. "We can rescue sheep. We can do things, Thomas. We just, you know... We can't hog the glory."

Thomas leaned back. "That shepherd. He's going to tell everyone Gawain rescued his sheep and it grates on me, but this? Finding the Grail? That would change everything for everyone. Who cares who gets the credit?"

He frowned. "Why do you suppose the little things hurt more than the big ones? Why is it harder to be selfless with the little things?"

Philip shrugged. "Maybe you're not doing the little things for someone else. Maybe you're doing them for you."

Mendhel dabbed at his bruised nose.

Remi snored.

Thomas raised a dubious eyebrow. "You're saying that I'm not being selfless. And the reason I'm not being selfless is that in those matters where I'm not being selfless, I'm failing to approach them, for example, selflessly."

"Now you're getting it," said Philip, grinning.

"As usual Philip, your logic is inescapable."

"It's a fine pickle, isn't it?" said Philip.

It sunk in slowly. "Oh!" said Thomas. "Son of a sea cook what time is it?"

❧

The late spring evening air was just right. The Fine Pickle's shutters and doors were propped open. Laughter and light spilled into the street and danced among the cobbles. Inside, couples cavorted and groups guffawed. Marie sat beneath a tapestry depicting two kings who seemed to be in a heated discussion over the veracity of one another's pedigree, or perhaps the quality of the other's upbringing, or the relative worth of each other's land holdings. The argument appeared to be about to come to blows. A slice of White Chocolate Heaven sat untouched before her, slowly collapsing under its own weight.

She eavesdropped until she grew bored. She picked up a fork. She set it back down. She sighed.

There was movement in the crowd near the door. "Pardon me," said a voice. "Pardon." And there was Thomas, excusing himself through the patrons. He spotted her and made his way to the empty seat across the table. He was out of breath.

"Sorry," he said. He smiled. He noticed the melting confection. His smile drooped a bit, then rallied. "You needn't have waited. I'm so sorry. Got caught up catching up."

Marie shrugged. "The ladies wanted to hear everything, too," she said. She smiled.

But I made it here, she didn't say. She didn't have to. Thomas' conscience said it for her.

"I'm sorry," he repeated.

This was the Pickle. This was the girl. This was the same slice of cheesecake. *Well, not exactly the same*, he thought. It felt chillier.

He handed her a fork. "Cheesecake?" he said.

She accepted, and they tucked in.

"It's a nice night," Thomas said.

"Mhmm," said Marie.

She chewed. She had beautiful eyelashes. She was hiding beneath them.

Thomas laughed at a memory, "Philip tried to get Gus to go crawling around under Saint Stephen's."

She smiled.

"He's too sharp though. Ox almost broke him in half with a hug. I think he's going to get on well."

She took another bite.

Thomas swallowed. He cleared his throat. "That tapestry there. That's Pellinore, you know? Pellinore fighting Lot."

She chewed.

"Kings both," he said. "They fought to the death. It was a terrible battle. True story."

She looked at him.

"Pellinore killed Lot," she said. "Gawain's father. And now Pellinore is in line for the Round Table. It maddens Gawain to no end. Guinevere doesn't know what Arthur is thinking. It's no wonder Gawain won't come in here."

She took another bite.

Thomas swallowed.

He searched frantically for anything to change the mood. He found it. "I think they're going to send us to find the Sangreal," said Thomas. "The Holy Grail." *Isn't that great?* said his face.

Marie's face didn't seem to think it was great. She frowned.

"The Grail quest has been side-tabled," she said.

"Side-tabled?" said Thomas. "Like, given entirely to us? The Less Valued?" he said. He couldn't believe his luck. "I mean, if anyone's the Side Table..."

She shook her head. "Postponed. Suspended. Delayed inevitably. It's had a pin stuck in it." She impaled the dilapidated cheesecake with her fork and let go. It stood upright for a moment then gradually began to list. She ignored it.

Thomas' forehead compressed slowly and thoroughly. "But why?" he said.

"Because of the armies attacking from the Uplands."

Thomas froze. "Because of the what now?" he managed.

Cheers erupted from the front of the Pickle. The crowd shifted and parted with cries of "'Awain!"

Thomas dropped his fork. "Gawain is here?"

A tall knight came through the crowd, or more accurately, with the crowd. He held his gleaming helm in one arm and shook hands with the other. He embraced the men. He winked at the ladies. He had the kind of smile that made the ladies feel safe and the kind of hair that made men reach for their hats.

Thomas turned to watch. From where she sat facing the entrance, Marie could see more clearly. "Not Gawain. Owain, his cousin. Morgan le Fay's son."

Thomas thought he heard something in her voice. He turned back to her. She was smiling. He had heard the smile. And it wasn't for him.

"The Crown Prince of Gore," she said.

That was for me once, thought Thomas. *I want that smile back.*

The crowd flowed toward them. Owain's glance fell on their booth and stuck.

"Marie," said Owain. He took her hand and kissed it. Thomas didn't have a great deal of experience in these matters, but through diligent observation he'd developed a strong sense of how long certain kinds of kisses should be given and this one was most definitely taking far too long.

Marie gave a small delighted laugh that she would have insisted wasn't a giggle.

"Sir Owain," she said and managed to curtsy. Sitting. In a booth.

Thomas fumed.

"It's a pleasure to see you outside the palace. I see the Queen gives her ladies their…" he glanced at Thomas, "freedom."

"It's my honor to serve– Ow!" She jerked, rubbed her shin, and glared at Thomas. Thomas tried to look innocent.

"Who's your friend?" said Owain in a tone that could crack a rock.

"Sir Owain, this is Sir Thomas. Sir Thomas, Sir Owain," said Marie.

Their corner of the Pickle had chilled several degrees.

"An honor to meet you–"

"A knight," said Owain. "Which order?"

Thomas coughed. There was no way around it. "The Less Valued."

"Ah," said Owain. "I see. Well, well met." He nodded at Thomas and turned his attention back to Marie who was all too happy to return her attention to him. He was still holding her hand. He leaned a little closer and dropped his voice a few decibels. "We're having a little get-to in Mum's suites later. You should come. Your radiant countenance might just be sufficient to brighten that dark space."

Marie stared. What was it about his eyes? The color? It occurred to Marie that it was her turn to speak. "You're too gracious. I'd love to attend," she recovered.

"Delightful," said Owain. He let go of her hand, straightened, and returned to his tavern-voice. "Bring Timothy if you like." And then he turned and moved away with his entourage.

Marie sat back. She straightened her dress and sighed. She reached for her fork. It had drooped to almost parallel the plate. "Ha! Look at that," she said. "Sad little fork." She noticed Thomas. She froze.

"What?" she said.

"Timothy?!"

"Pardon?"

"Timothy!" said Thomas "He called me *Timothy*."

"Oh," she said and laughed again. "Did he? I'm sure he just misheard."

"Inviting you to his suites! The blasted rotter. I ought to–"

"You ought to what exactly?"

"I ought to..." Thomas wasn't sure what he ought. "He's a miserable cox-comb and someone ought to put him in his place."

"Is that what you're going to do? Put Morgan le Fay's son in his place?"

Thomas frowned.

"And where exactly is his place that you would so like to put him in?" she said.

"His mum's suites, apparently," said Thomas sullenly. "And they're resplendent I'll have you know." He realized who he was talking to. "Which you know. Which everyone knows. 'Sufficient to brighten that dark space,' says he."

"He was being gracious to me."

"He was being dismissive," Thomas shot back, "to me."

Marie sat back. Thomas fiddled with the cutlery.

"Are you going?" asked Thomas.

"Hmm?"

"To his 'get-to'. You told him you'd go."

"I didn't say I would go. I said I'd love to go."

"You lied?"

"I didn't lie."

"So you'd love to go."

"That's what people *say*."

"That's what *you* said."

"Well maybe I *would* love to go."

"Well maybe you should."

"Maybe I will."

"Fine," said Thomas.

"Fine," said Marie.

It was too much. He could do trifling good works all day and all someone like Owain had to do was walk in the room and kiss a hand.

"Have fun," said Thomas. He stood, dropped some coins on the table, and left without a backward glance.

"Thomas!" Marie called to his back.

Marie sat alone again beneath the tapestry of two men squaring off. She stared at the decimated slice of heaven. She was certain the world would be a better place with less of the one and more of the other.

CHAPTER VI

THE RASH VOW

Sir Tuttle the Authorized was a bit of a mystery. Though Tuttle was tasked with overseeing the Less Valued Knights, it wasn't clear to Thomas whether the man was one himself. Despite Tuttle's ambiguous relationship to any specific order, there was no man who embodied the general notion of order more thoroughly. Diminutive and quiet, he formed the backdrop to the background that propelled a particular subsection of Camelot's overall operations. In addition to overseeing the Less Valued, he functioned as liaison for all new minstrels, knights, courtiers and ladies-in-waiting.

Tuttle was good at waiting. He was practicing it now.

Meticulously polished, combed, scraped, brushed, buffed, oiled, straightened, aligned, tucked, creased, buttoned and buckled, he stood outside the doors to the Great Hall unmoving. Mostly. If one looked very closely, one might notice his nostrils move. They were flaring.

There was hubbub beyond the closed doors behind him – the sounds of milling could be heard: vocalizations of camaraderie punctuated here by convivial laughter and there by a mocking wit enjoying itself at the expense of another. Tuttle despised milling. But his attention was in front of him, not behind. He was listening for the footsteps of his missing charge. Sir Thomas the Hesitant was late.

The footsteps came shuffling but steady. The word 'brooding' came to Tuttle's mind. It was dismissed as irrelevant. Tuttle inhaled.

Thomas rounded the corner.

"Farmer. You're late."

"Yes sir. No excuse sir."

It was the correct excuse.

"This isn't going to be a pattern with you, is it Farmer?"

Tuttle had a way of making one's own name sound like a demotion. Thomas steeled himself against it.

"Difficult to say, sir."

It was a truthful response. It was also very incorrect.

Tuttle glared.

"No sir."

Tuttle glared a moment longer. Thomas held steady.

Tuttle made a doubtful sound with his throat and produced a clipboard.

"Anything to report before we make our grand be*late*d entrance?" The word 'be*late*d' was over-articulated and came with its own italics.

"Mm," said Thomas. "Saved the people of Fogbottom from their sorning scobberlotcher of a baron and his malcontent son."

Tuttle checked his list. "Confirmed," he said. "We'll have to replace Bane. Anything else?"

Thomas reeled at Tuttle's efficient dismissal of his accomplishment.

"Anything else?" repeated Thomas, confused.

Tuttle raised an eyebrow.

"Anything *else*," said Thomas. The hallway outside the Great Hall was getting smaller and hotter.

Tuttle stared.

Thomas clenched his jaw and forced himself to breathe. "Rescued some kind of sheep-like animal for some saddle-goose shepherd on the way here."

"No need for that kind of language," said Tuttle, scanning the clipboard. He made a note, then turned his attention back to Thomas.

They looked at each other.

"Something on your mind, Sir Thomas?"

The restoration of his title did not escape Thomas' notice.

"Yes sir," he said.

"And," said Tuttle, "what would it be? This thing on your mind."

Thomas had never been very good at being direct. He'd tried it a few times. It generally hadn't gone well for him in the short-term, so he liked to avoid the strategy when possible. But it was difficult to avoid with Tuttle. He was the kind of man who peered brazenly straight up your nose. Thomas decided it was time to chin up and stick his neck out. He did both and snapped to attention.

"Permission to pursue the Holy Grail, sir."

"Denied," said Tuttle.

"But–"

"Anything else?"

"Permission to aid the war effort in the Uplands."

"Denied." Tuttle's brow furrowed. "What do you know about the war?"

"Aha! So there *is* a war."

Tuttle frowned.

"Denied!" said Tuttle. "And if that's all–"

"Permission to search for Merl–"

A trumpet sounded. It meant Arthur was entering the Great Hall, and the assembly was being called to order.

Tuttle spun toward the doors and pulled one open.

"Get inside," he said. "Now."

"But sir–"

"Sir Thomas the Hesitant, if you hesitate one more instant I shall inflict on you an amount of paperwork the likes of which you have never seen." Tuttle wasn't known for his colorful metaphors. He was known for his paperwork. "And that paperwork will be followed by more paperwork. And when you're done with *that* paperwork you will have only *begun* to understand the reports, bulletins, memos, summary statements, land-bills, write-ups, rundowns, records, communiqués, details and dispatches that will be involved in relation to aforesaid and previous paperwork do I MAKE myself CLEAR?"

"Yes sir!"

"NOW MOVE."

Thomas moved.

Philip waved. Thomas excused his way through the Less Valued to an open spot on the bench next to him. The Great Hall was just as he remembered. Like most organizations, one generally found the nicest people in the back of the room and the nicest furniture at the front. Three wooden tables for three chivalric orders dominated the front of the hall.

On one side was the table for the Table of Errant Companions. The table's seats were empty of course due to errant knights being, by definition, errant, i.e. not present. The empty seats were there primarily, Thomas and Philip had decided, to remind those present that they weren't allowed to sit in them.

On the other side was the table for the Knights of the Watch. At fifty percent occupancy, it was currently the most occupied table. Thomas clenched his jaw and watched Owain lounge in his seat at the polished table and laugh at his own jests. Gawain, next to him, seemed oddly tense. Thomas looked away and caught the eye of the Watch's leader. Marrok's eyes were sad, but he smiled at

Thomas. Thomas' face grew hot. He returned the smile and tried to shift his attention inconspicuously. Marrok had adopted Thomas as a sort of informal mentee-at-a-distance after Thomas inadvertently discovered Marrok's secret and subsequently didn't come unglued about it. Marrok was an exceptional knight, wise and measured. He exuded an ever-present air of self-control. Thomas was in no mood for wisdom, measured response, or self-control, and was certain Marrok would disapprove.

Between the table for the Knight's Watch and the table for the Table of Errant Companions was something else entirely. One might describe the wooden appointment there as a table. Similarly, one might describe the legendary kraken as a sort of fish.

The Round Table's table was in fact round and also a table. But, for example, it didn't have place-cards – it had magically-etched prophetic appellations engraved in heavenly, golden calligraphy. And it didn't have 'seats'; it had 'sieges' – which are like seats in the way that an office is like an Office. Amongst the thirteen sieges was one Merlin had dubbed the Siege Perilous. Only someone of the greatest virtue and the noblest heart could occupy it and live. It was currently empty. But so were most of the others. Arthur had been dragging his heels in the promotion department.

Kay and Bedivere arose from their sieges as Arthur entered the hall and Guinevere processed into the balcony with her ladies-in-waiting. Marie wasn't looking at anything in particular. Thomas noted that one of the things she particularly wasn't looking at was him.

Beneath the noise of a hundred knights standing, Philip whispered, "Where were you?"

"Killing dragons and rescuing princesses," said Thomas with a fierceness Philip mistook for veracity.

"Really?" he said.

Thomas looked away. "Maybe. I might have been." He shrugged. "Of course not. But who cares?"

A head appeared by Thomas' shoulder from the row behind. "I would care, sir," said Gus.

Thomas turned. "Thank you, Gus. I know you would."

Philip gave Gus a look that made him slowly and carefully ease back into his own row.

"That's not fair you know. Bedivere and Kay and Gawain up there were very appreciative of your help in Fogbottom–"

"My *help*?"

"Just as I know *you* are appreciative of Marrok's help," Philip said pointedly. "And mine."

Thomas brooded. But Philip had a point. Thomas knew he did. He sighed, deflated a little and shook his head. "You're right."

Philip sat back. Here was the Thomas he knew.

"It didn't look like Tuttle was too keen on your dragon killing and princess rescuing."

Thomas said nothing.

"I mean, punctuality and promptness – that's Tuttle's whole bailiwick, for sure, but I don't think I've seen him that upset over someone just being late."

"It wasn't just that," said Thomas.

"What was it then?"

"I asked him for permission to go look for the Grail."

Gus gasped excitedly. "What did he say?"

"Denied."

Philip sighed, relieved.

"What?!" said Gus. "That's preposterous. Who's to say who can and can't or who should or shouldn't ought to want to search for the Holy Grail?"

"Sir Tuttle the Authorized," said Thomas stressing the sobriquet. "That's who. Whom? That's whom."

Philip said, "Well that's that then. Oh well. But it doesn't answer my original question."

Thomas gave him a tired look that said, *I have no idea what your original question was.*

"Where were you all night?" said Philip. "There was some big hoo-hah in the palace. We thought you might be there, but Mendhel got stuck in the dumbwaiter and overheard most of everything. He came back in the middle of the night and said Marie was there but there was no sign of you."

"I took a walk."

Philip raised an eyebrow. "A walk."

"Yes, a walk."

"And what did you do on this walk?"

"I was thinking."

"You were thinking."

"Yes, Philip. I've been thinking. And you know what I think? I think things stink, and I'm going to do something about it."

Arthur sat. So did everyone else. Arthur cleared his throat.

"Sir Gawain, please rise," he said.

"Here we go," muttered Thomas. "'Congratulations on your glorious victory at Fleabottom!' 'Pardon me my King it's not *Flea*bottom.' 'Oh my mistake Sir Gawain.' 'It's *Frog*bottom.' 'Right you are. Well, wherever it was, the kingdom owes you its thanks. Known for its frogs is it, Frogbottom?' 'Didn't see a single frog the whole time now that you mention.' 'Toads?' 'No sir–'"

Philip elbowed Thomas hard.

"Ow," said Thomas.

Arthur took a breath and spoke in an unmistakably kingly voice. "Let the trial begin," he said.

"Wait, what?" said Thomas.

~

"Bailiff, please present the charges," said Arthur.

No one moved.

"Who's acting bailiff today?" whispered Arthur.

Kay frowned. "Doesn't Merlin normally take care of this sort of thing?"

Bedivere did some hasty mental calculations and determined that a) he was one of only two knights seated close enough to the King for him to reach out and grab hold of, and b) he was one of the furthest knights from the King relationally. He cleared his throat and preemptively volunteered his table-mate. "Wouldn't the honor fall to Sir Kay, sire?"

Kay sputtered. "I'm Seneschal."

They both looked at him.

"Remind us again?" said Arthur.

Kay, seeming very put out, said, "The Seneschal of England – which is what I am, by your decree – is responsible for the King's estate and the royal household."

Arthur nodded.

"Like a steward," said Bedivere.

"Seneschal," said Kay, sitting tall.

"Bedivere," said Arthur.

Bedivere's stomach sank.

"Yes sire?"

"Are we presently occupying the King's estate, would you say?"

Bedivere brightened. "Oh, yes." He made a show of considering the hall's appointments and ordinances. "Definitely your estates, sire. And I daresay we do appear to be presently occupying it."

Kay glared at Bedivere.

"Right then," said Arthur. He took a breath and engaged his Great Hall voice: "Sir Kay, Seneschal of England, shall now present the charges against Sir Gawain of Orkney."

It was rumored that Kay, Arthur's foster brother, could turn himself into a tree. It was rumored he could light a fire just by rubbing his hands together. It was rumored he once went nine days without breathing. There were, however, no rumors of his fear of public speaking. The most successful knights carefully managed their public affairs.

Kay arose from his siege and stood as tall and stiff as an ancient oak. He held his breath. His palms began to sweat.

A portly knight burst through the hall doors, jogged down the center aisle, and knelt before Arthur. He held a scroll partly crumpled in one meaty fist and did his best to present it to Arthur through puffs and wheezes. He smelled of herbs.

"Sorry... late... sire."

"Constable Baudwin!" proclaimed Arthur. Arthur turned to Bedivere. "It's the Constable that reads the charges," said Arthur. *Puzzle solved!* said Arthur's grin.

"Indeed," said Kay, in the delighted tone of someone who has been relieved of unwanted responsibility.

Constable Baudwin was not an ambitious man. He liked plants, he had a bit of a talent for herbal remedies, and he asked simple questions like "Why not try doing it another way?" and "Are you certain that's the best place to be spending limited resources?" Those kinds of questions can land a person in a great deal of trouble, so Baudwin had aspired to be a hermit. But he'd been a friend of Arthur's father and Arthur's father hadn't minded the questions – though in truth Uther had never heard Baudwin's questions, because Uther had a habit of talking over people especially when they seemed the type to ask questions. In the end Baudwin the aspiring hermit had wound up in the wrong place at the right time and been appointed Constable.

"Constable Baudwin," said Arthur, "please rise and relieve Sir Kay."

Baudwin pushed himself up. Kay sat and exhaled with visible relief.

Baudwin unfurled the scroll. "Sir Gawain of Orkney," he read, "it is asserted by your own confession that on or about the final weeks of May this year, you willfully withheld mercy and failed to provide succor while in pursuit of a white hart alleged to have caused substantial property damage–

"And emotional!" interjected Guinevere.

"–and emotional damage at the wedding of King Arthur and Queen Guinevere. You are to submit on a day of the King's appointing – that would be today – to a trial by inquest of ladies for judgment and sentencing in aforesaid matter. Fine print and so on. Signed, Arthur, Lord and King of Britain, Wielder of Excalibur, Puller of the Sword from the Stone, etcetera. What say you?"

Gawain cracked his neck.

"What did he do?" whispered Thomas.

"Cut a lady's head right off," said Gus.

Thomas grimaced.

Gus mirrored Thomas' grimace. "Says it was an accident."

At the front of the room, Gawain spoke.

"'Twas an accident," he said.

Thomas didn't know what to think. On the one hand, some form of justice was long overdue as far as Thomas was concerned. On the other hand, Sir Gawain was *Sir Gawain*, possibly the most celebrated knight in the room. What reflected poorly on Gawain reflected poorly on all of them. And, frustrating as the whole event had been, Gawain had in fact saved Thomas.

"This really happened?" whispered Thomas.

Gus frowned and nodded. "Says he was aiming for a knight that was fighting him over the white hart, and the knight's lady threw herself in the way."

"That's..." said Thomas, "That's terrible! But surely an accident?"

"Problem is," said Gus, "the knight had surrendered."

"Oh," said Thomas.

"How do you plead?" demanded Baudwin.

Gawain had been looking at his feet. He stood now, stared straight ahead, and held his chin high.

"Guilty," he said.

The crowd gasped.

Arthur stood slowly.

"My Queen," he said. "Ladies of the inquest, please rise."

In the balcony, Guinevere and her ladies-in-waiting stood. A hush fell upon the chamber. Kay held his breath.

"We judge Sir Gawain of Orkney," she announced, "guilty."

Gawain's jaw muscles bunched, but he didn't blink.

Arthur inhaled. "And your sentence?"

"But it was an accident!" whispered Thomas.

"We commend Gawain," she proclaimed, "that forever as he lives to be on the side of all ladies and to fight for their quarrels. And that he should be courteous and never refuse mercy to one that cries mercy. And to swear upon the Four Evangelists that he will never stand against ladies or gentlewomen."

"Do you so swear?" said Arthur.

"Ah dae sae swear," said Gawain in his thick Scottish accent.

A copy of the gospels was produced for Gawain to swear upon.

"Huh," said Thomas. "That's it? I mean, he cut a lady's *head* off."

Gawain paused. "One question, if ah kin," he said.

"Yes?" said Arthur.

"Well, as ah ken, A'm suppose tae rammy fur all lassies, aye?"

"Ladies. And gentlewomen," corrected Guinevere.

"Rrrigh' – an' A'm just supposin' – bu' suppose thare ur two lassies, 'n' thae lassies, see, thare oan opposin' sides o' th' rammy?"

"Mmm," said Arthur.

"Ye see mah kinch?" said Gawain, eyes wide.

Everyone carefully failed to react.

"His problem," said Owain, helpfully.

"Ah," said Arthur, relieved. "Aye. My Queen?"

Guinevere huddled with her ladies. "Right," she said. "We've agreed to amend the sentence as follows: Forever as he lives and so on to fight for quarrels etcetera and to swear upon the Four that he will never stand against ladies or gentlewomen *excepting* the case where Sir Gawain of Orkney fights for a lady and/or gentlewoman and his adversary fights for another."

Arthur turned to Gawain.

Gawain said, "Um, righ'. It's jus' tha' – nae tryin' tae be pernicketie – bu' 'tis important tae be precise, you'd 'gree? Whit if, say, thare wur *thrrree* lassies? Or four?"

Guinevere stared at him.

"'N/or gentleladies," he added. "Ilk oan their ain side?"

Guinevere reconvened her ladies.

She turned back. "Please amend the sentence to indicate any number of ladies on any side," she said.

Marie leaned in quickly and whispered something in her ear.

Guinevere nodded. "And," she said, "we require Gawain eat only fruit from this day forward to soothe his temper and foul humors."

"Wha'?" Gawain was mortified.

The crowd was mortified.

Arthur reeled.

Guinevere stood firm.

Baudwin frowned and nodded in approval. He held the book out to Gawain.

"Ah suppose th'alternative...?"

Arthur mimed a hangman's noose.

"'Tis jess' tha'–" Gawain shook his head. "Froot?"

Arthur shrugged.

Gawain crossed himself, placed one hand on his heart, placed the other on the gospels, and vowed.

Arthur invited the crowd to sit.

"He kills a lady," whispered Thomas, "and all he has to do is promise to do better."

"And eat fruit," added Philip.

"And eat fruit," said Thomas, baffled.

"Said to calm rash tempers," said Gus.

"It's true?" said Thomas.

"I guess we'll find out," said Philip.

At the Watch's table, Owain tried to console Gawain whose face had gone pale. "'Tis jess' pure nasty," Gawain said.

"Right. That's done. Announcements," Arthur said, visibly relieved to be moving on. "Good news everyone!" Arthur was wise to follow trauma with something cheerful – something that would bring everyone back together and provide a renewed sense of meaning and purpose.

The crowd waited.

He grinned.

The crowd waited some more.

Kay bit first. "What's the good news sire?"

"We're going to war!" said Arthur.

His grin was not returned. There wasn't a hoot or a holler in the whole hall. Perhaps he hadn't spoken clearly enough. He cleared his throat and broadened his smile.

"To war!" he bellowed. He brought his fist down with a disappointing thud. The Round Table was very, very solid. It was nearly impossible to make cutlery bounce by punching it. It was even more difficult when there was no cutlery upon it. Arthur's hammering was vigorous however, and if there had been cutlery upon it, it would have bounced in sympathetic enthusiasm at the very least. The men in the room were a different matter. They very carefully failed to react in any way whatsoever.

"What's wrong with you lot?" Arthur demanded. He turned to Kay. "What's wrong with them?"

Kay raised his eyebrows. "Well..." he said.

"It might have something do with the matter you just mentioned, sire," said Bedivere.

"Which matter?"

"The bit about the war," he said. "And – forgive me if

I'm putting words in your mouth, Your Majesty – but some listening may have interpreted your statements regarding it in a way that suggests you rather think we might be going to it."

"That's precisely what I'm suggesting–" said Arthur. "Stating," he corrected himself. "Commanding," he amended. "Look," said Arthur. "Five armies are assembling in the north and it's going to be a great adventure. Even Guinevere is coming."

"I am?" she said. She coughed. "I mean of course I am. Wouldn't miss it." Guinevere had only been on the job for a couple of weeks, but she was learning quickly: Support the King in public; question his sanity in private.

Kay rallied. "Nor would I," he said.

Arthur sat tall. This was more like it.

"Except," said Kay.

Arthur raised an eyebrow.

"It's just that I've got a prior engagement," he said.

"What engagement?"

"The Grail, Your Majesty. I'm off to find the Holy Grail and save the land."

Arthur shook his head. "The five armies are more pressing I'm afraid. All Grail quests are hereby postponed."

Baudwin inhaled and drew himself up to his full, abbreviated height. It was the thought that counted. "ALL GRAIL QUESTS ARE HEREBY POSTPONED BY ORDER OF THE KING," he declared.

"Thank you," said Arthur.

Kay slumped.

"Time is of the essence," said Arthur. "We'll catch them off guard. We'll end this before it begins. Every knight is to make ready – we march tomorrow."

Thomas caught Marie shoot a worried glance in his direction. Her concern despite his recent behavior cheered him. Briefly.

"Did he say *every* knight?" Thomas whispered.

"Kay," said Arthur, "assemble the Round Table."

Kay looked at Bedivere. Bedivere shrugged.

"The Round Table is ready, Your Majesty," Kay confessed. "Both of us."

"ROUND TABLE READY!" bellowed Baudwin.

"Excellent. Marrok, assemble the Knights of the Watch."

Marrok saluted. "It will be done, Your Majesty."

"KNIGHTS OF THE WATCH MAKING READY!" thundered Baudwin.

"Outstanding. And Tuttle?" said Arthur.

Tuttle snapped to attention. "The Less Valued Knights are assembled and prepared to lend our entirely competent and ready assistance at each and every juncture in support of a smooth and polished battle-ready operation, sire."

Arthur glanced over the men in the back of the hall. Words like prepared, competent, and polished were decidedly front-of-the-room words. He came to a quick conclusion.

"The Less Valued Knights will remain in Camelot to effect the, er, smooth and ready operation of the kingdom's day to day operations and what-have-you here. At home."

"LESS VALUED KNIGHTS STAYING PUT!"

Tuttle saluted and sat.

"He smiled," said Thomas.

"Who?" said Philip.

"Tuttle. He did that on purpose."

"Did he?" Philip was impressed. And relieved.

"Day to day operations," said Kay. "Very important. As Seneschal I must say I approve. And I'm willing to sacrifice any glory I might obtain in battle to lend my assistance to Sir Tuttle here in Camelot."

"Denied," said Arthur.

Kay slumped and drummed his fingers on the arms of his siege.

Bedivere traced the etching of his name on the Round

Table. "I miss Merlin," he said to no one in particular.

"Merlin," mused Kay.

His fingers stopped drumming.

"Merlin!" he repeated, excited.

"What about him?" said Arthur.

"He should be found!" said Kay. "I take upon myself this quest, My King, to find and rescue our beloved court wizard from whatever fell fate ensnares him."

"Denied," said Arthur. "Merlin will have to take care of himself for the time being. Every Knight of the Round Table, every Knight of the Watch, and every Queen's Knight will march on the Five. There's no time to spare."

"Now what's next on the agenda?" he asked.

"The recognition of heretofore unrecognized deeds of valor," said Tuttle. He unfurled a scroll. "One hundred and eight of them, Your Majesty."

"Commence," said Arthur.

❧

These were the early days of Arthur's kingdom. Recreant knights were just beginning to contrive their foul deeds, and the economy simply wasn't strong enough to support any noteworthy growth in the evil enchantress population. Yet. These changes would come with time as Arthur's kingdom prospered. Meanwhile, in the relative vacuum of widespread villainy, the countryside found itself replete with "rare" white harts, one honest-to-goodness questing beast, and the occasional monstrous boar which could be goaded into a foul temper with a little persistence on the part of an ambitious knight. It was these sorts of adventures that dominated the accolades this day.

Despite his recent chastisement, Gawain received the most distinctions. His long list of credits included demonstrating exemplary initiative and significant contribution to the quality of life of Camelot's citizens by effecting the dissolution of the Sloppy Pants Gang–

Gawain bowed.

"That was me," hissed Thomas.

"Not... exactly," said Philip.

–noble spirit and keen insight in the ousting, with Kay and Bedivere, of a tyrannical sub-ruler in the village of Fogbottom–

Gawain winked at Thomas from across the hall.

Thomas smiled sardonically. "Also me," he said without moving his teeth.

"Not... entirely," said Philip.

–godly persistence despite setbacks in the retrieval of the white hart which ran amok in, around, through, and throughout the wedding of King Arthur and Queen Guinevere–

"I helped with that," said Ox.

"Good on you, Ox!" said Philip.

Ox beamed.

–and a humble and selfless spirit in the rescuing of a sheep-like animal for a destitute shepherd–

Gawain grinned, shrugged, and frowned as he tried to recollect that one.

"That takes the biscuit," said Thomas. The points of contact between Thomas and his seat were rapidly decreasing.

"Leave it be," said Philip, firmly. "All of the accolades, do you know where it gets them?"

"Seats up front?"

"War," said Philip. "War is what it gets them. If you want that kind of honor, go for it. But things seem alright by me."

"That's the problem," said Thomas. "If you want a seat at the Table – a *real* Table – you've got to have deeds. And to get deeds, you've got to have a seat at the Table."

"We *are* a real Table," said Philip. "And there are lots of deeds you could do."

"Like what? We can't go to war. We can't seek the Grail. We're supposed to just sit here and do all the things that need doing and odds are when they get back they'll get the credit for those things too. So you tell me Philip, what can we do?"

"You could find Merlin," said Gus.

Thomas and Philip continued to stare at each other.

"What did you say?" said Thomas.

"You could find Merlin," repeated Gus.

But Thomas had heard him the first time. Philip could see clearly that Thomas had heard him the first time. Thomas had grown frighteningly calm.

"We can't," said Philip. "Arthur said we couldn't."

"King Arthur said you couldn't go after the Grail," corrected Gus, matter-of-factly.

Philip's voice came fast and high. "Arthur said we were to lend our effort to the smooth operation of the day-to-day operatings of the kingdom."

Thomas' voice came easy, like an oiled blade pulled from a clean sheath, "What's more essential to the smooth operation of the kingdom, than the restored presence of a capable and beloved court wizard?"

Desperation gripped Philip. "Tuttle denied you."

Thomas slowly shook his head.

"But you asked him," pleaded Philip.

"I started to," said Thomas. "But we were interrupted."

Thomas grinned, wide.

Philip frowned. "You wouldn't."

Thomas raised his eyebrows, still grinning.

Gus sat back. "Phew that would be something wouldn't it? Us. Rescuing Merlin. Merlin! Ha!"

Tuttle had reached the end of his scroll.

Philip shook his head rapidly. "Don't do it."

"Oh, I'm doing it," said Thomas.

Arthur stood. "If there is no other business–"

"Please don't."

Thomas stood sharply, stretched himself to his full height, and took a deep breath. He'd never felt more sure of a thing. But he wouldn't do it for himself. He'd do it for all of the Less Valued. It was time to set things right. If he had to prove it, he'd prove it. He'd show them. Once and for all.

Tuttle squinted at him. Marrok raised his eyebrows. Philip buried his head in his hands. Marie closed her eyes and slowly shook her head.

Thomas' voice rang across the Great Hall of Camelot. "I pledge on my honor and that of the Less Valued... My King, I will find our beloved court wizard. I will find Merlin. Or I will die trying."

There was only one person in the room who didn't seem surprised.

Arthur pursed his lips. "Baudwin," he said.

"Yes Your Majesty?"

"Reserve a seat at the Table of Errant Companions for Sir Thomas the Hesitant."

Baudwin glanced at the empty-seated table. "Yes... sir," he said. His brow furrowed.

"Godspeed, Thomas," said Arthur. "Let not even the King himself deter you from finding our friend."

Arthur's gaze lingered, then, "The rest of you make ready! We ride tomorrow. To war!"

Gus whooped and applauded.

Philip groaned.

Tuttle fumed.

Marie exited the hall with Guinevere and the other ladies-in-waiting. She didn't look back.

Thomas' grin began to fade. The sounds of the crowd dispersing took on a tinny edge. Gus slapped him on the back, and it almost knocked him over. The floor leered at an odd angle, and his stomach seemed to be trying to hide behind his spine.

"Well, now you've done it," said Philip.

"Nonsense," said Thomas. "I'll be–"

He wanted to finish the phrase, but he decided to close his mouth and keep his breakfast to himself instead.

CHAPTER VII

A TIGHT SPOT

It was the second lonely night in a row for Thomas. Tuttle had pulled him aside as the Table Hall emptied. He explained to Thomas, calmly and matter-of-factly, that Thomas' temporary – he stressed the word temporary – appointment to the Table of Errant Companions didn't mean Thomas could shirk his commitments as a Less Valued Knight. It was a dual citizenship sort of thing. Tuttle's calm demeanor was extremely off-putting. Thomas was being left to his own fate. He felt sick.

Tuttle departed, and Thomas sent Gus off to find some squire-ly things to do. Gus obeyed reluctantly. "You should at least try having a sit-down at it," he said nodding at the Errant Companions' table and backing out of the hall. Gus was still watching Thomas as the great door swung shut leaving Thomas alone in the hall. Thomas was fairly certain if he pulled the door open again Gus would still be standing there. Thomas didn't care.

He stood where everyone had left him and stared at the Table of Errant Companions. He couldn't seem to get his stomach out of his throat. He forced himself to breathe.

Muffled laughter filtered in from the palace grounds. He could hear the rhythmic banging of a hammer against metal in the distance. The emptiness of the hall wasn't oppressive. It was just... empty.

He moved toward the Table twice. After a third failed attempt, he resolved not to sit at it until he'd earned it. He spun around and exited the hall without looking back. There was no Gus on the other side of the door. Thomas made his way to the barracks alone.

Philip wouldn't talk to him. The others' reactions were mixed. Mendhel the Misfortunately Placed was concerned about what would happen to the Less Valued if Thomas failed, but he was even more worried about what would happen to them if he succeeded. Remi the Imperturbable was certain everything would work out for the best. Edgar the Erstwhile wondered why anyone hadn't already been looking for Merlin. Dedric the Diplopian was of two minds on the matter. Ox was disappointed they weren't going to war.

In the morning Thomas' stomach was still knotted. The Less Valued stood in parade formation at the palace gates to send off the others. Trumpets blared from the direction of the palace. They heard the horses clopping first. Then Arthur and his knights appeared, blue and gold pennants streaming from raised lances. The sun sparkled, shone, danced and bounced off a thousand polished surfaces. The crowd behind the Less Valued cheered, clapped, stomped, hollered and gesticulated, for the most part, appropriately. The horses pounded the cobbles so close to Thomas that he could feel it in his teeth.

Beside Thomas, Philip saluted each passing knight with misdirected fury.

"Talk to me," said Thomas.

Philip's gloved hand sliced the air. His whole body was as stiff as his jaw.

"No talking in formation," Philip growled.

"He speaks!"

Philip shot him a look. "Reprimanding you is not the same as talking to you."

"It's a start."

Knights passed. Philip swatted his forehead.

"You don't have to do that," said Thomas. "You can hold the salute until they all pass." He nodded toward the others.

Philip's arm stopped. Now there was nowhere for the energy to go. It only took a moment before it burst out of his mouth.

"What I want to know," said Philip, "is what you don't understand about the word 'hesitant?'"

Thomas looked at his feet and shook his head. "I don't know. I haven't been sleeping well. The way the whole Fogbottom thing ended. The thing with the sheep. Marie..."

"And the solution is to publicly declare in front of everyone. *And* Arthur. And *everyone. Publicly.* That you Thomas. On behalf of the Less Valued. All of us. That you're going to go find a missing wizard. A *wizard!* Who's missing. You're going to find him."

Thomas shrugged.

"*Merlin* of all people. The greatest wizard who ever lived. Have you thought about what kind of forces would have to be involved to make *Merlin* disappear?"

Thomas shook his head. "I–"

"Thomas the Hesitant," Philip snorted. "They should call you Thomas the Ridiculous. Or Thomas the Stupid Face. Or Thomas the–"

"Easy now," said Thomas gently.

"You're going to get yourself killed. *Again!* Or you're going to wander around the country and just disappear yourself and that empty Errant Companions seat will be a reminder to everyone of just how less valued the Less Valued should remain."

"So you *are* worried about what people think about the Less Valued."

"Of course I am."

They stood silently.

Thomas considered pointing out that he couldn't technically get himself killed *again* since he hadn't, in fact, been killed at all yet. Only nearly killed.

"So," he said instead, "help me."

"Thomas the Missing," said Philip. "Thomas the Foolhardy. Thomas the Big Headed. There'll be tiny dolls made of you with really giant heads."

Thomas laughed despite himself. Philip was calming down. More knights passed.

"How do you even know he's alive?" asked Philip.

Thomas frowned. "I hadn't honestly considered the alternative. Until now."

"Even wizards don't live forever," said Philip. "Especially ones that predict their own doom and then disappear."

Thomas blinked. Philip saluted.

"You could check the tapers," said a voice.

"Gus?" said Thomas.

The squat squire shoved the bystanders aside and stood at attention. "At your service sirs." He saluted, which lead to a confusing round of return salutes and return-return salutes while trying to maintain salutary synchronicity with the passing knights.

"Just," said Thomas, "hold." Thomas stopped return-saluting and held his salute facing the procession. Gus snapped a final salute and held it. Philip glared at Thomas and returned to his serial saluting.

Thomas sighed. "You were saying?"

"Tiny dolls with great big heads," said Philip.

"Not you. Gus."

"Oh," said Gus. "I was just saying sir, that if you wanted to know if Merlin was alive or, pardon, I should say still is alive and presently living, well then, you could check the tapers."

"What tapers?"

Gus swallowed. "Carefully guarded secret sir. Probably best I don't say too much."

"But you brought it up."

Gus' face was blank. "That does appear to be the case sir."

"Out with it," said Philip.

"Merlin's tapers sir. In the tombs under St. Stephen's. As long as they're burning, Merlin's alive. Or so it's said."

"So it's said?" said Philip. "Said by who?"

"Whom," said Gus.

"That's what I'm asking you," said Philip through clenched teeth. He was holding his salute now.

Gus bit his lip. "The squire network?"

"The squire network," repeated Philip.

"There's a squire network?" asked Thomas.

"He's been a squire for," Philip shook his head, "what? Two days?"

"Three days," Gus corrected. "Officially." He raised his chin perceptibly. "Longer in my heart sir."

"This is a big deal. Why don't we know about this?" asked Thomas.

"Carefully guarded squire secret?" said Gus, in the manner of someone who doesn't expect to be believed.

Thomas could tell Gus was stalling, but he didn't know why. And the idea of a secret squire network was a bit unnerving. A group of under-appreciated people who are supposed to be quietly serving and maintaining and keeping things running smoothly but whom, it turns out, actually have their own lives and hopes and motivations and are watching and talking and making plans…

Thomas found himself battling a feeling of vertigo.

"There's no squire network," Philip scoffed. "I've lived in this city all my life and this is all news to me. I mean, I've been to the memorial, but I've never heard of this Merlin life-taper business. Hang on–"

Philip cracked a mischievous grin. "You went to St. Stephen's."

Gus looked cornered. "That's where the tapers are sir."

"You went to St. Stephen's but you weren't looking for the memorial," said Philip. "You were looking for something else."

Gus drooped. "Yes sir. You got me."

"I don't follow," said Thomas.

"He went looking for the sword in the stone!" Philip laughed.

Thomas sighed.

"Just the stone," said Gus without much enthusiasm. "Everyone knows the sword–"

"It's not important Gus. Sir Philip the Exceptionally Disadvantaged has had his fun," said Thomas.

Philip, ignoring Thomas' reprimand, giggled.

"Is there a squire network?" said Thomas.

"Whether there is or isn't," Gus confessed, "that's not how I found out about the tapers, sir."

It didn't escape Thomas that Gus didn't answer the question, but he was happy to put the subject out of his mind and focus on the mission.

"Out with it," said Thomas, not unkindly.

Gus swallowed. "The stone's not there," he said. "Under St. Stephen's. But I had to be certain." He gave Philip an aggrieved look. "These things are important. Locations of legendary artifacts."

"Very important," agreed Thomas encouragingly.

"So I was down there making sure the stone wasn't, and while I was, I was looking around and I found the memorial to all the kings that fought King Arthur and did you know Gawain's dad is the biggest? I was thinking, *Who makes a memorial to honor your enemies?* but then I spotted

King Arthur – not King Arthur *per se,"* snort, "his statue of course. And he's standing over them suchlike with a sword and all the kings are honoring him by holding up these candles to him. And I thought, *Okay that makes sense.* And I thought, *That's really clever to honor your enemies giving them this rich memorial tomb but at the same time sort of you know eternally submitting to you,*" wink, "I bet Merlin had a hand in *that* arrangement."

Gus laughed, chuckled, sighed, and continued.

"So I was looking for a closet or something maybe for storage for things like stones-that-used-to-have-a-sword-in because I hadn't found it yet," shrug, "and Sir Philip who's a knight *said* the stone is there, and knights are honorable see, and so maybe he *wasn't* pulling my leg and maybe the stone really *is* there."

Gus took a breath.

"But if it is I didn't find it."

He stopped.

"The tapers?"

"Oh," said Gus. "Right. I got up and back around behind the statues see. Looking for the storage. And back behind there is where I saw it."

"Saw what?"

"The inscription that explains about the tapers."

Philip shook his head. "Everyone would know about something like this. He's trying to prank us back."

"Prank *you* back," corrected Thomas.

"It's no prank. It's the truth sir."

"So why hasn't anyone heard of this?" said Philip.

Gus rubbed his elbow. "Well," he said. "It's kind of hard to get to. I was stuck there for quite a while." Gus looked suddenly pale. "You were probably wondering why I was missing."

Philip hadn't been wondering.

Thomas wondered about the difference between 'not present' and 'missing' and how to spot the difference. It seemed to depend on whether you expected a person to be there or not. Or whether you *wanted* them there or not.

"I'm sorry Gus. This kind of thing won't happen again," said Thomas. "Will it?" he added looking at Philip.

Philip pursed his lips. It probably would. A future bright with shiny moments of innocently tormenting squires unfurled before him. It would be character-building. For them.

Philip grinned. "Sorry Gus." *Need to get myself a squire*, he thought

"There," said Thomas. "The team's back together."

"Hang on," said Philip. "What team?"

"You know you want to come and help me find Merlin," said Thomas.

Gus brightened considerably.

Philip stared at Thomas for several long moments.

"If the tapers are burning—" said Philip.

Thomas raised his eyebrows.

"—and if *he*," said Philip, pointing at Gus, "can show us this inscription—"

"Of course sir," said Gus.

"—*and* if it says what he says it says," said Philip.

"Yes?" said Thomas.

"If all of those things, then fine I'll help you find our beloved all-powerful court wizard who, despite his all-powerfulness was bested by whatever has bested him, having recently predicted his own doom. What could go wrong?"

Thomas clapped him on the back.

"Gus, take us to the tombs," said Thomas.

"Yes sir!"

The war procession continued. They held their salutes. Nobody moved.

"As soon as we're done here," said Thomas.

"Right you are sir."

ං

Underneath St. Stephen's, in the hands of twelve penitent brass and copper kings, Merlin's tapers burned. The statue of Arthur stood encircled by the others, larger, sword pointed heavenward, gleaming in the candlelight. Philip clung to Lot's shoulder, perched on his metal arm. He stretched toward Lot's candle, inhaled deeply, and blew. The flame wobbled.

"You've got to stop him sir," Gus pleaded.

Thomas was certain what Philip was doing was a bad idea, but he'd been unsuccessful in dissuading him. And deep down, he wanted to know what Philip wanted to know.

"He'll kill Merlin!" cried Gus.

"You said that the inscription says that if the tapers are burning, Merlin's alive," said Philip.

Gus gave a panicked nod.

"What does it say it means if the tapers aren't burning?"

Gus looked dumbfounded. He shot a frantic look at Thomas.

"Look," said Philip. "Let's say, if it's raining then the duck is wet."

"O…kay…" said Gus. He was clearly dealing with a madman.

"But it's not raining."

"No, sir." Gus shook his head, bewildered.

"Is the duck wet?"

"No?" said Gus in a small voice.

"Incorrect. What's the correct answer? Anyone? Thomas?"

Thomas had no idea where Philip was going. "I have no idea—"

"Correct!" said Philip. "We don't know. All we know is that if it's raining, then the duck is wet. But if it's not raining, then the duck *might* be wet. It might not. Who's to say?"

Gus turned to Thomas. "Sir Philip's gone mad sir. He's trying to kill Merlin and going on about ducks. Permission to take matters in hand."

Thomas managed to turn the laugh into a cough as it left his throat. He didn't know what Gus taking matters in hand would look like, but it seemed like something he should prevent if possible. For all their sakes.

"Philip, maybe this isn't such a good idea."

Philip continued, "We need to establish if these candles are enchanted or not, and unless you've got a better idea–" He inhaled.

"Sir!" said Gus.

"Philip, maybe we should rethink—"

Philip blew hard. The flame sputtered and went out. Philip straightened up with a satisfied grin.

Gus stopped breathing.

Thomas grimaced. Wanting to be prepared but wanting not to instigate, he took a step and eased himself between Gus and Philip.

In a voice he'd used to calm angry cows, Thomas said, "Now, as Philip was *trying* to say, if the candles are out, we don't know—"

There was a tiny scraping noise, a series of clicks, and a *phoof*. The candle re-lit itself.

Philip leaned back against Lot's torso. "Huh," he said.

Gus exhaled in relief.

"Well, look at that." Thomas grinned and patted Gus on the back.

It took a moment for the relief Thomas felt for Gus to make way for the excitement of the implication it had for Thomas' quest.

"The candles burn!" he shouted.

Thomas high-fived Gus, who was looking both happy and traumatized. "Merlin's alive!"

Philip dropped from his perch. "Not so fast," he said. "Let's see this inscription."

Gus' hands were shaking, but he managed to produce some parchment, a charcoal stick, and a small tin from his backpack.

"What's this stuff for?" said Philip.

"To make a rubbing sir. I was going to squeeze back in there and make a rubbing of the inscription."

They looked at the gap Gus indicated.

"How did you get in there Gus?" said Thomas.

"It wasn't easy sir. Getting out was even harder." He took a breath. "But fear not for me, sir. Our quest demands—"

Philip grabbed his shoulder. "Oh no you don't," he said. "If you got in there, so can I. I want to see this with my own eyes."

❧

Philip wouldn't admit it, but he was stuck.

"Push," he said.

Thomas and Gus grunted and pushed.

"Ow ow ow stop," said Philip. He was finding it hard to breathe, compressed as he was. He adjusted himself. "Okay, one more time."

Philip let all the air out of his lungs and tried to make himself small. Thomas and Gus pushed. Philip twisted. He angled his head. He moved his shoulder just so. He tried to think small thoughts. He gave one long sustained grunt during which nothing noteworthy seemed to be happening, but suddenly he was through.

"Ha ha!" he said. He inhaled through his teeth. "Okay that hurt."

"What do you see?" said Thomas.

"Nothing," said Philip.

Thomas frowned at Gus. "No inscription?"

"Can't see anything," said Philip. "It's dark as peat in here."

"Try moving away from the gap, sir."

Philip moved. "Ah," he said. "That works."

"Do you see the inscription?"

"Aye," said Philip.

"Does it say what Gus says it says?"

"I really couldn't say," said Philip.

"What do you mean you couldn't say? Does it say the thing about the candles or not?"

"It's some sort of nonsense limerick. It says..." said Philip. His voice reverberated a bit in the tiny chamber.

"Yes?"

"It says 'Some are dumb see some vee vum," said Philip slowly and carefully.

"Some are dumb..." repeated Thomas.

"See some vee vum," finished Philip.

Thomas tried it again and applied some rhythm. "What's a vee vum?" he said.

"*Vivam,*" said Gus. "It's Latin."

"Oh," said Philip.

"Do you know Latin, sir?"

There was a silent pause. "Do you?" said Philip.

Gus shrugged. "Just a little. It's not the construction I'm used to. That's why I was worried about how precise you were being with my translation."

Thomas squinted at him.

Gus' face flushed.

"Alright," said Philip. "Hand me the stuff. I'll make a copy and we can take it to the abbot. He's sure to be able to translate it."

A few moments later Philip passed the parchment back through the gap.

Thomas read it, "*Sum ardeam si sum vivam.*" He shrugged and handed the parchment to Gus, who stowed it in his pack.

"I have to be honest," said Philip eyeing the gap. "I'm not looking forward to squeezing back through here."

"I've got something for it, sir," said Gus. He handed Philip the tin.

"What's this?"

"Grease," said Gus.

Philip frowned and shot him a look. "Why didn't you tell me about this the first time?"

"You seemed determined, sir."

Philip glared.

"And–" started Gus.

Philip cracked open the tin and smelled it. "Pellinore's beast this stinks!"

"–and it stinks," repeated Gus.

"What is it? Pork fat?"

"Good nose, sir."

Thomas snickered. Long days with his older brother had honed Thomas' nose to smell feigned innocence a mile away. All he could smell right now was justice. It smelled like pork fat.

Philip glared at Thomas, but he wasn't about to act squeamish in front of the squire.

"Fine," Philip said, and started stripping.

It wasn't easy to stand still on a stone floor with greased feet. Philip did his best. Putting his clothes back on was proving a hopeless task. He finally gave up and allowed Gus to help him.

"You brought everything else," said Philip. "I suppose a towel was too much to ask."

"To be honest sir, I thought I'd be the one going through and..."

"And what?"

"And, well..." Gus twisted his fingers. "I would have greased the gap sir."

Gus considered it part of his job to avoid embarrassing his superiors. Some superiors made his job very difficult.

"No need to go through in your altogethers, if you pardon my French, sir."

Philip glared.

"Schloop," said Gus. "Right through." He demonstrated a schlooping motion with his hand.

"You could have said something."

"You seemed determined, sir."

"Yes, you've said that."

Thomas tried not to laugh, but he didn't try hard.

ૐ

"The abbot is out," Brother Loquacious would have said. He didn't. He was six hours into his latest attempt at a vow of silence, and he was determined to make seven. Instead he pointed to the empty pallet, then the empty desk, then the empty hall, and shrugged.

"Confound it," said Philip. "I don't suppose you can translate Latin?"

The monk waggled his eyebrows. It might have meant yes. Philip went with it. He took the parchment from Gus and handed it to the monk.

"CAN YOU READ THIS?" Philip said, slowly and loudly.

The monk rolled his eyes, frowned and tapped his ear with one finger. "I'm not deaf," he didn't say. "I'm voluntarily mute."

"Sorry," said Philip. "Right." He pushed the parchment at the monk. "Can you read this?"

The monk took the parchment. His face screwed up. He started to make a grunting noise and caught himself. He held the parchment at arm's length, pinched his nose, and gave a pleading look. His eyes were watering.

"Oh," said Philip. "No." He backed up. "It's not the parchment. It's me."

The monk took a grateful breath as Philip moved away. He squinted at the parchment in the dark hall, then motioned for them to step inside the abbot's cell. Thomas and Gus moved inside and Loquacious raised a firm hand toward Philip.

"You stay here," he firmly didn't say.

Gus lit a taper and handed it to the monk.

"Thank you," Loquacious communicated with a bob of his head. He smoothed the parchment out on the desk, set the taper down next to it, rubbed his chin and stared.

His gaze grew suspicious. He pointed a questioning look at Thomas and held both hands palm-up.

"Oh," said Thomas. "Of course." He patted himself down searching for coins.

The monk shook his head vigorously. He grabbed a piece of charcoal and wrote a word on the parchment.

"Where?" it said.

Thomas opened his mouth. "Can't say," said Philip from the hall. "Matter of national security."

Thomas closed his mouth.

The monk frowned. "You're full of duck feathers," he didn't say. "I have a mind to expel you from the premises," he didn't continue, "but this puzzle is admittedly intriguing." He turned back to the parchment and scratched his head.

He picked up the charcoal again, underlined '*Sum vivam*' and wrote '*I am alive.*'

"Aha!" said Thomas.

"Hold on," said Loquacious' hand. He underlined '*ardeam*' twice, paused, and wrote '*burning*' underneath. He made a few more notations, rendered his final translation, circled it, then set down the charcoal and handed the parchment to Thomas.

"*I am living fire*," read Thomas.

A thought struck the monk and he snatched the parchment back. After more energetic scratching he held the parchment aloft examining his work. Satisfied, he handed it to Thomas again.

"*I am burning alive*," read Thomas. "Oh dear. Are you certain?"

The monk shrugged. He held up a finger, took the parchment, underlined '*burning*' and wrote '*possibly figurative.*'

"We don't understand," the others didn't say.

Loquacious snatched the charcoal again and wrote '*not literal.*' He underlined it. He underlined it again.

"Oooh," said Thomas.

"Like," said Philip, "burning with anger. '*I am living rage.*' That sort of thing?"

The monk's face scrunched to one side and seemed to say, "Mmm, probably not." He made to write a word on the parchment and stopped. His face turned red.

Philip laughed. "Not anger," he said. "Passion. '*I am passion brought to life.*'"

The monk looked horrified. "No no no," he struggled not to say.

He paused. Then he thrust his hip sideways, fanned his heart, and batted his eyelashes at them.

Thomas took a step back.

The monk stopped to reassure him. He pointed at '*ardeam*' and reenacted the pantomime.

"Love?" said Thomas. "'*I am loving life.*'"

Gus interjected, "But what about the '*si*'? And '*vivam*' is subjunctive. I'm sure of it."

They all looked at him.

Gus cleared his throat. "Um," he said. "Is that the only way to translate this part here?" he asked innocently.

The monk reexamined the phrase. His mouth went down and his eyebrows went up. Underneath '*si*' he wrote '*if*' and underneath '*vivam*' he wrote '*perhaps.*'

Thomas was the first to put it together. "*If I am perhaps alive, I am in love.*"

"For the love of Uther," said Gus. "What does love have to do with it? Every student of languages knows context is king, and this was written on the back of a statue holding a ruddy candle. Look." He shouldered the monk aside, took up the charcoal, scratched out the word '*not,*' circled the word '*literal*' and wrote, '*I am burning if perhaps I am alive.*'

He held the parchment up to show them.

"If the candles are burning, Merlin is alive," he said.

"Sirs," he added.

"Ooooh," said Loquacious and clamped a hand over his mouth too late.

ꟹ

The trio had left. Brother Loquacious turned the brass and copper valve that cut off the gas to the memorial candles and lit some incense to try to mask the lingering odor of matters relating to national security.

A larger, more serious looking brother strolled in.

"We had some visitors," he said. Brother Compendium liked to mix up the proper uses of "we" and "you." When he said the one he almost always meant the other.

"They're worried Merlin is dead," said Loquacious.

"Can't be," said Brother Compendium.

Loquacious raised his eyebrows. "Why's that?"

"I investigated his quarters with the abbot," he said. "And his hat was there. Plain as day."

"Ah," said Loquacious. "Of course. No practicing wizard would be caught dead without his hat."

Brother Compendium touched his nose. "We've broken our vow of silence again I see."

Loquacious tightened his lips and made a motion over them with his fingers as if he was locking them with a key. He placed the imaginary key in an invisible box, then locked the invisible box with another imaginary key. He swallowed the second key and the box and then stood stoically before Brother Compendium.

Brother Compendium regarded Brother Loquacious for several moments. "See we don't break them again Loquacious." He turned and left the room.

At evensong, Loquacious came down with a terrible case of indigestion. He took it as a sign that God wanted him to start working harder at who He'd made him to be rather than who He hadn't. Loquacious became famous in the order as an exceptional orator on the one hand and not a terribly good monk on the other.

CHAPTER VIII

THE ENCHANTED LOOKING GLASS

The sun on his face felt comforting to Thomas after the cold stone halls and candlelit catacombs beneath St. Stephen's. Camelot was active doing the things a healthy city does, but things felt different now that Arthur and Guinevere had departed with the war party. The city felt less safe yet more at ease. Less busy but more productive. Less exciting but more good-natured.

"Oi, what's that smell," said a passer-by.

"Okay," said Philip ignoring the disgusted glares. "Fine. Merlin's alive. I'm with you. What's the plan?"

"I propose a two-pronged approach." said Thomas. "Prong one, you go take a bath."

"Har har," said Philip. He sniffed himself and immediately regretted it. "And prong two?" he asked.

"While you go take a bath," said Thomas, who felt that this part of the plan bore repeating, "Gus and I will consult Pyralis."

Philip didn't object.

"Because who would be better at finding a wizard than another wizard?" asked Thomas in defense.

"I'm not objecting," said Philip. "Sounds like a good plan."

"Good," said Thomas.

"Good," said Philip.

"Alright then. We're off," said Thomas.

"See you soon," Philip said, and headed off toward the barracks.

"He makes me nervous when he's like that," said Thomas.

"Agreeable?" suggested Gus.

"Yes, that. Agreeable."

Gus nodded. "Pyralis," said Gus. "He used to be evil?"

"Mmm-hmm," said Thomas, watching Philip retreat. "Former evil wizard. Rehabilitated. Good fellow."

"Who did the rehabilitating? Is there an evil-wizard-rehabilitation programme?"

Thomas looked at Gus. He hadn't really thought about it before. "It was kind of a self-taught, go-at-your-own-pace sort of thing. I think."

Gus nodded. "And we're off to ask his advice? The former evil wizard. On a matter of national security, as it were."

"Mmm-hmm," said Thomas.

Gus nodded and seemed to come to an internal agreement with himself. "Right then," he said. He stood tall. "Ready when you are sir."

"How should I know where Merlin is?" Pyralis snapped. "A wizard's business is a wizard's business." He pointed to a needlework sampler on the wall that said so.

They sat in rocking chairs inside Pyralis' cluttered room overlooking the cemetery. Gus held his teacup and saucer with both hands and struggled to keep things from jittering, splashing, spilling, or upsetting in any way. His eyes hadn't left Pyralis since he and Thomas had entered.

"If Merlin doesn't want to be found he won't be," Pyralis said. "And if he ever does want to be he won't be until he does. How's the family?"

Thomas was well aware of Pyralis' conversational tactics and was ready for the abrupt change of subject. Two could play at that game.

"The family is grand. Moving into the new abode. But what if someone *made* Merlin disappear? Gus drink your tea."

Gus' cup rattled against the saucer.

Pyralis snorted. "Make a wizard disappear. Ha! Although..."

As Gus raised the cup to his lips he spotted the shelves lining the back wall. They had jars on them, and the jars had things in them. Gus whimpered and examined his tea. It looked normal. That didn't prove anything. He lowered the cup and returned to his rigid stare.

Thomas paused with a biscuit halfway to his mouth. "Although?"

"Well, I never did trust her."

"Her who?" said Thomas.

"Nimue. The Lake-Lady."

"Lake-Lady?" said Thomas.

"There's always a lady," said Pyralis. He waved an impatient hand. "Cherchez la femme."

"Find the woman," interpreted Gus despite himself.

Pyralis shot him a look. His old watery eyes twinkled, and he grinned. "A man of letters," he said.

Gus waited for Pyralis to turn into a giant toad and swallow him up, or to be turned into a toad himself and *then* swallowed up. Or to be turned into a swallow and shut away in a jar and added to the shelf. Nothing of the sort happened. Gus focused on breathing.

"She's a sorceress?" said Thomas.

"Of course she's a sorceress," said Pyralis dismissively. He frowned and studied the ceiling from underneath a pair of great, bushy gray eyebrows. "It's not the *what* but the *what sort* that causes the trouble."

"Powerful?" said Thomas.

"Allegedly," said Pyralis.

"Nefarious?" he asked.

"Suspected," replied Pyralis.

"Mysterious," said Thomas.

"Most assuredly," agreed Pyralis.

Pyralis drummed his fingers on the chair arms and peered at Thomas.

"Merlin should be more careful who he gets friendly with. Was friendly with a sorceress myself once," Pyralis said.

Thomas raised his eyebrows.

"She was a sight to see," he said, "as long as she knew you were lookin'." He cackled.

Thomas lowered his eyebrows. He sipped his tea. "How's Gorgella?" he asked.

Pyralis squinted at him and pointed at the needlework.

Thomas held up a hand. "Message received." There was no doubt that Gorgella could take care of herself. But the giantess' world was an inherently lonely one, and Thomas worried about her. Nevertheless, it didn't seem like a good idea to press a wizard where he didn't want to be pressed, allegedly formerly evil or otherwise.

Pyralis cleared his throat. "Back to the subject. Sorcery starts with illusion," he said. He levered himself up out of the rocking chair. Gus shrank when Pyralis teetered toward him, but the old wizard found his balance and shuffled away from them.

He shoved some clutter off of a trunk. He spoke louder now that his back was turned to them. "When they start to get good," he said, "they can imbue objects with the illusion. Make the illusion stick so it still works when they're not there to make it work."

He opened the lid and rummaged in the trunk. He dropped his voice as if he was talking to himself. "Then they stop carin' that you're lookin'."

The pause felt sorrowful and heavy.

Pyralis harrumphed and reached into the trunk. There was a clatter, some grunting, a cascade of sparks, and an explosion of dark feathers as Pyralis strained to pull a small object wrapped in velvet from the depths of the trunk. Something pushed its way up after it. Pyralis shoved it back and slammed the lid shut. He leaned against the trunk cradling the object with one hand and holding down the lid with the other.

He held the object toward Thomas. "Take this would you?" he said. He examined Gus. "You look just the right size."

"For what?" blurted Gus. As soon as he asked the question he knew he didn't want to know the answer.

"To keep this closed. Come sit."

Gus obeyed. Pyralis' will was compelling. Gus reflected that he didn't actually *feel* compelled. It was probably an indication of just how powerful Pyralis was – he could make you feel you ought without making you feel you must. Fascinated and terrified, Gus sat.

"That's a good little wizard," said Pyralis.

"A what?!" is what Gus might have said. Instead he smiled, pleased to have pleased the Evil Wizard, Former. *Diabolical*, thought Gus. *He's making me help him by making me want to help him so that he doesn't have to make me help him.* Gus shook his head in horrified admiration.

"This," said Pyralis, taking the object again from Thomas, "I made this to help me, um..." He glanced at the young wizard. "…to combat, yes… combat other illusionists and sorcerers."

"...and sorceresses?" asked Thomas.

"Hmm? Of course. Yes. And sorceresses. Cherchez la femme." He turned the object over in his hands and pulled the velvet cloth away.

"It's a mirror," said Thomas.

Pyralis nodded. "A looking glass, you might call it," he said, "if you wanted to be more poetic." Pyralis drifted off.

"An enchanted looking glass?" Thomas prodded.

"Mmmm," said Pyralis. "What? Oh. In a manner of speaking. It's not like your normal looking glass. A normal looking glass just shows you want you to see. That's not going to help with an illusionist."

"Hang on," said Thomas. "Mirrors have always shown me what's there." He gave a sardonic chuckle. "Whether I want to see it or not."

Pyralis shook his head. "They show you what you expect. And despite protestations to the contrary, people want what they expect. Makes them feel clever when they get it. But when you're dealing with someone who wants to show you what you want to see, what you need is something that will show you what you don't want to see." He offered the looking glass to Thomas. "That's what this does. Take it from me."

Thomas stared, trying to work it through.

"No, I mean literally," said Pyralis. "Take it from me."

"Oh," said Thomas. He accepted the glass and turned it to look at himself.

Pyralis' hand shot out and stopped him. "Whoa!" he said. "Careful where you point it. You've got to be certain you want to see what you don't want to see before you go looking for it."

Thomas pulled the cloth back over the glass. "So," he said, "this will show me the truth instead of the illusion."

Pyralis shook his head. "This will just give you another frame of reference. A disillusioned frame of reference if you will." Pyralis seemed quite amused with himself for a moment, then he sighed. "But I'm afraid sussing out the *truth* is left as an exercise for the viewer. So to speak. It could be that what you want to see is what is there to see. In that case, what's there is probably there."

Thomas considered this. He felt he should ask some questions. He wondered what those questions might be.

"But none of it will do you any good," said Pyralis, "if you can't find her."

Pyralis stared at Thomas. Thomas stared at the cloth bag. Gus stared at Pyralis.

"Don't you have a girlfriend in the court?" asked Pyralis abruptly.

Thomas' brain seized at the word 'girlfriend'.

"He does," said Gus. "I met her. She's lovely." The trunk thumped underneath him. He remembered to be terrified.

Thomas cleared his throat and tried to act nonchalant. "Why do you ask?" he said.

"I'm sure she'd have access to some pertinent information not readily available to the average citizen," said Pyralis.

"We're, um," said Thomas. "We're not on the best speaking terms at the moment," said Thomas. It felt more manly to confess they weren't getting along than it would've been to confess they were in a relationship.

"Then you have the first noble challenge on your quest," said Pyralis.

Thomas gave him a quizzical look.

"Be a man, and apologize to your lady," said Pyralis.

Thomas was neither the first nor the last to experience the friction between feeling like a man and being one.

CHAPTER IX

A DARING JOURNEY IN A STRANGE LAND

Thomas slouched along the palace corridors. He kept himself moving forward by telling himself he could always turn back. As he neared the quarters of Guinevere's Ladies-in-Waiting, things began to transform.

On the farm and in the barracks everything had a purpose and every purpose a place. The pitchfork goes with the hay. The hay goes in the hayloft. The polish goes with the boots. The boots go in the footlocker – for those with the good fortune to have acquired a pair of boots, and except for Ox who'd requisitioned but not yet received a larger footlocker. But the point was—

What was the point?

The point was that things that go together go together. Thomas was entering a different sort of territory.

The objects that occupied these spaces wanted him to suppose they were purposeless. He had the sneaking suspicion this wasn't at all the case. He suspected they had in fact mysterious purposes he wouldn't understand until it was too late. There had to be a reason to put a flower in a jar and put the jar on a shelf.

He had to admit, it smelled nice.

Amidst this land of strange things placed in strange places for no apparent reason, there sat a hand bell. A card near the bell read in an elaborate script: "*Gentlemen Callers muste please ringe the belle.*" It had little flowers expertly drawn upon it and a diagram of a man daintily ringing.

Thomas swallowed. He cleared his throat and tried to relax his neck and shoulders. He reached for the belle.

"Thomas Farmer," sang an operatic voice.

Thomas recognized the voice instantly. It was a voice associated with a particular sort of trauma Thomas had hoped never again to suffer. It was the voice of Madame Rhapsody, sole proprietor of Madame Rhapsody's Dance Emporium, Self-Appointed Liaison to Inexperienced Young Gentlemen, and evidently the Palace-Appointed Ladies-in-Waiting House Matron. Her presence and her voice seemed always to be accompanied by wafts of perfume which might have been not unpleasant in smaller quantities, distracting source-less tinkling noises, and a sinking hopeless dread in most men.

She embraced Thomas and began to squeeze the life out of him.

"It's wonderful to see you dear," she crooned.

Thomas grunted noncommittally.

She deposited him back on his feet, smiled and surveyed him head to foot and back again.

"Stand up," she said. She adjusted his hip, his shoulder and his chin. "There."

All pleasantness left her face. "Do you have an appointment?"

Thomas opened his mouth.

"Of course you don't. If you had an appointment, we would have been aware of your visit, wouldn't we have?"

There was just enough of a pause for Thomas to fail to respond.

"And if we had been aware of your visit, we would have known what it was regarding and with whom it was with–" The sternness fled her face for a moment and her eye twinkled. "–though I suspect I know whom you're here to visit, no?

"So *if* you would be so kind as to kindly state with whom you are here to visit and for what purpose and to what end, I shall endeavor to see if the young lady is disposed."

"Dis..." said Thomas, confused. "Disposed?"

"Agreeable," said Madame Rhapsody. She waited, unblinking.

Thomas blinked. "Um," he said.

Madame R's teaching posture returned. "No *um*'s dear. State your statements. Punctuate your proposals. You're doing it again with your chin."

Thomas straightened. He swallowed.

"I'm here to see–"

Madame R frowned.

"–visit," corrected Thomas.

Madame R stopped frowning.

"Lady Marie?" he said.

Madame R stared at Thomas. Thomas stared at Madame R.

He'd missed something. He mentally surveyed his hips, his shoulders, his chin. He'd stated whom he was present to visit, and to what purpose–

"Oh!" he said. "In order to apologize for my recent churlish behavior."

Madame R's posture melted. Her countenance lifted like a balloon. She blinked rapidly and fanned herself.

"What did you say?" she asked.

"I'm here to visit Marie, Madame Rhapsody."

She held her breath.

Thomas said, "To apologize."

Madame R produced a handkerchief from somewhere Thomas didn't want to think about. She dabbed at the corners of her eyes. "I'm so proud of you," she whispered. She grinned. She winked. "I knew you were special," she said. "I'll just go fetch her."

Madame R bustled out of the room. Thomas sat in a flowery chair with an overstuffed cushion.

This is going much better than anticipated, he thought.

He was awakened some time later by Marie clearing her throat.

"Sorry to disturb your rest, Sir Thomas," she said. A thawed out woolly mammoth upon hearing her tone would have asked if it could return to the cozy warmth of its iceberg tomb.

❧

"I'm sorry," Thomas stammered. He sat up and rubbed at the chair's imprint on his cheek. "I haven't been sleeping well."

Had he drooled? He hoped he hadn't drooled. He tried to inconspicuously inspect the corner of his mouth.

Marie stood tall and proper, hands clasped behind her. "Mother Rhapsody said you'd come to apologize. Was that it? Your apology?"

Thomas stood. Apologies were good things. Why couldn't she be more like Madame R? Belay that thought.

"Look," he started.

She raised an eyebrow.

"I mean," he veered. He dropped his hands. "I'm sorry," he said.

Marie waited.

Thomas hadn't actually mentally reviewed what he should be sorry about. *I'm sorry that you're mad at me* was where it started, but he wisely decided to keep that one to himself.

"I'm sorry that," he began, hoping the words would come to him before he got to them. In fact, they did. The thoughts started spilling one over the other now that he really gave the matter some consideration.

"I'm sorry that I acted the way I did at the Pickle. I'm sorry I didn't trust you. I'm sorry I let Owain get under my skin. I'm sorry that–" his voice caught at the realization. He continued in a smaller tone, rather horrified at himself. "I'm sorry that I... left you there."

He couldn't believe what he'd done. He looked in her eyes.

She looked away quickly.

"Marie, I–" he said. But now there were no words.

He turned. "I'll just go," he said. He paused staring at the floor. "I'm sorry I'm an idiot," he said. He headed for the door.

"You don't have to be sorry," said Marie.

Thomas stopped.

"For being an idiot," she said. "You don't have to be sorry for being an idiot. Being an idiot is something a person is born to. It can't be helped."

"Right," he said. He thought about laughing, but her expression was unreadable and her tone wasn't amused.

He took a few more steps toward the hall.

"But I accept," she said.

He froze again.

"Pardon?" he said meekly.

"I accept your apology for your behavior," she said. "I forgive you."

"I..." said Thomas. "I don't know what to say."

"It's what friends do," she said. She drew herself up. "Sometimes they hurt each other. And then they apologize. And they forgive each other."

Thomas' elation deflated. "Right," he said. "That's what friends do," he said. *Friends*, he repeated in his head.

"So," she said. She adopted a more convivial pose. "How are things with you?" She gestured toward a seat.

Thomas moved toward it hesitantly. He sat.

Marie sat opposite him.

The woolly mammoth backed deeper into its iceberg.

Thomas swallowed.

"Well," he said. He looked at her. "As you know," in the calm and careful manner of someone who's just heard a cracking noise while making his way across the frozen lake, "I'm off to find Merlin."

"Yes," said Marie. "I was there when you undertook the quest. That will be a grand adventure for you."

"Yes," said Thomas. "I quite think it will be."

"He ought to be searched for," said Marie.

Thomas gave a sick smile and a nod.

"And found," she added encouragingly. "And why shouldn't it be Thomas the Hesitant to do so?"

"No better reason than *why not* I always say, ha ha." He'd never actually said it before.

Marie smoothed her dress where it had bunched on her lap.

"Of course the reason why a person does a thing like that is as important as the thing itself, I should think," she said.

She glanced at him meaningfully.

Thomas nodded. "Quite," he said. "That's the thing really. The reason." His mind was blank.

"And what is your reason?"

Don't move a muscle, said Thomas' brain. *Don't even breathe.* But Thomas' eyes didn't listen; they looked everywhere for an escape.

"I, um," he said.

"You must have your reason," said Marie. "Thomas the Hesitant isn't known for his brash acts and thoughtless commitments."

That stung. And Thomas was suddenly quite tired of feeling trapped and toyed with.

"That I do," he said. And shut his mouth.

She stared at him. He stared back. He sat up. He put a metaphorical hand on the steering wheel of the conversation.

"Lady Marie, in your position on the court, perhaps you might have been privy to information that might aid in our investigation. Merlin's last movements, notable acquaintances, significant conversations, anything odd or out of place leading up to his disappearance."

She raised her eyebrows. "Anything odd? About Merlin?" She laughed and rolled her eyes.

Thomas remained stoic.

"Oh all right," she said. "Sir Thomas the Royal Investigator. Rumor has it amongst the court that Merlin was more than a little besot with one Lady Nimue. She's pretty, and she's mysterious, and she's more than a little creepy about it if you ask me. Which makes her just Merlin's type."

"We're aware of the relationship, ma'am," said Thomas. He wasn't sure where *ma'am* had come from.

Marie squinted at him.

He cleared his throat and shifted in his seat. "Did they mention any plans, destinations, what-have-yous? Any..." Thomas waved his hand lazily. "Any... zhunsaykwas?"

Marie looked sideways at him. "Zhunsay... Oh." She laughed. "*Je ne sais quoi.* No," she giggled some more. She stopped. "Wait. Yes." She sat up. "There was talk of France. And a knight! King Ban's son. They were going to France! To Ban's realm. To Benwick!"

Marie fidgeted with excitement and laughed at herself. "You're a good investigator Thomas. How odd that I'd forgotten all about that. It seemed so… unimportant, at the time."

Thomas watched her eyes and found only genuine admiration.

"Thank you," he said.

They were quiet for a moment.

"I'm a little worried–" started Thomas. There were a lot of things he was worried about. He didn't know where to begin.

"Nonsense," said Marie. She held his gaze. She smiled. "You'll be fine."

He laughed and blinked at the sudden stinging in his eyes.

"I'm glad you came to see me," she said.

"Yes, well, I can't take all the credit there," he said.

"Oh?"

"We went to see Pyralis thinking he'd know where Merlin might've gone – maybe a wizard could find a wizard sort of thing – but he didn't – or couldn't – or wouldn't – and he said don't you have a girlfriend on the court?"

Marie's face brightened.

Thomas replayed the last few words that had just come out of his mouth. *Oops*, said his brain and then sat back to watch.

"He said 'girlfriend?'" she asked.

"Um," said Thomas. "Yep, yes, that's what he said alright ha ha."

"And," she said, "what did you say?"

"Well," he swallowed. "I said, um, well, yes, I said..." He shook himself. When in doubt stick to the facts. "I explained how I'd been an idiot and..."

Sticking to the facts was a good idea. He'd just recount everything up to now and that seemed like sure-footing except talking was proving rather difficult now that she was kissing him.

She was kissing him.

Thomas' mind slipped out quietly and gently closed the door.

CHAPTER X

THE SEA FAIRY AND THE SAILING RATS

It was that time of day when the setting sun lances people right in the eye. Too much light makes it hard to see. But Thomas wasn't walking by sight. He trod sure-footed over broken cobbles. He passed unharried through jostling crowds of citizens who seemed to him to be in need of a good cheering up. He felt courageous. He felt confident. He felt like he could face a thousand nefarious sorceresses, rescue a thousand kidnapped wizards, love a thousand ladies-in-waiting. He paused. He felt like he could love a single lady-in-waiting a thousand-fold. He resumed. He trod on cobbles, gave cheery smiles to citizens, hummed a tuneless melody, and finally threw open the barracks door.

"We head for Benwick on the morn!" he declared.

"Where is Benwick on the Morn?" said Mendhel.

"In the same place it was the evening before I should think," said Edgar.

"Could someone shut the door? That light is blinding."

Ox obliged and they all squinted at Thomas.

"Why's he like that?" said Remi.

"Like what?" said Thomas.

Ox smelled him. "You smell like fruit," he said. He stepped back and looked at him. "Why do you smell like fruit?"

"He's been to see Marie," said Philip grinning.

"And ate fruit?" said Ox confused.

"Sounds about right," said Philip. "From the looks of it."

"Is it hot in here?" said Thomas.

"Not as hot as elsewhere I'm guessing," said Philip.

"Pardon?" said Thomas.

"You know," said Philip. He made a snapping sound with his cheek, pointed a finger at Thomas, and winked. "Hot."

"I'm sure I do *not* know, Sir Philip–" said Thomas.

"Must have been *very* hot to forget his friends," snickered Edgar.

Philip chortled.

"Got more fruit?" said Ox, genuinely wondering.

"No I do not have more fruit," said Thomas. "I do not have any fruit in fact. Nor *did* I have any fruit." He grinned and shrugged. "Well, okay maybe, you know, one fruit."

"I knew it!" said Philip.

"But that's not the important thing here."

"Does she know?" said Philip.

"Of course she knows," said Thomas. "Know what?"

"That she's not the important thing here."

"That you think she's a fruit."

It went on like that for some time.

~

To a man, the Less Valued had bowed out of accompanying Thomas across the Channel due to former commitments. Thomas suspected Tuttle had worked overtime to secure said former commitments. The only knight to join him was the one whose former commitment had been, in fact, to join him.

Now, a day later, Thomas, Philip, Gus and Booker stood before a large block of nondescript stone in London.

"There it is!" said Thomas cheerfully.

Gus stared quietly. It wasn't at all like him.

Even Philip was worried. "She sure is a beauty, isn't she?" He shook his head encouragingly. "A sight to see. A real marvel."

"You can see the slot right there where the sword was," said Thomas. "See that, Philip?"

"Aye. Sure do. A sight to behold," he said.

Thomas and Philip exchanged worried glances.

Philip gave Thomas a subtle conspiratorial nod, "That's the very spot Excalibur lodged for all those months."

"Years," said Thomas.

"Aye, years," said Philip.

Gus mumbled something.

Thomas brightened. "What's that Gus?"

"Not Excalibur," said Gus.

And that was all they could get out of him that day.

"I'm worried about him," said Thomas.

"He'll cheer up when we get to the sea," Philip replied. "Who doesn't like to see the sea?"

The sun climbed over Dover. The sea gently lapped the beach. Gulls cried. Gus was still not himself, and the air smelled of dying fish.

Thomas' only goal was to secure passage across the Channel. He'd been thinking about how to go about this for a few days now. Every reasonable method that came to mind would have been improved substantially by the transfer of coin in a direction that was unfortunately dependent on him having some. He worked up the best persuasive strategy he could think of and memorized it. He told himself no honorable captain loyal to the kingdom could possibly refuse them. He hadn't anticipated the difficulty of finding an honorable captain loyal to the kingdom.

Three captains so far had proven unpersuadable. The fourth was Captain Ulmir 'One-Ear' Soames of the *Winged Sea Fairy*.

"*Wing-ed*," corrected Soames. "Two syllables."

"But I'm an Errant Companion of the Table of Errant Companions of His Royal Majesty King Arthur," said Thomas.

"Aye," said Captain One-Ear. "Ye said that. Yer an erring company of a whole table of erring accompanies who ain't got no coin. An' if ye ain't got any coin, then I ain't got any ship."

Philip stopped counting Soames' ears. "Sure ye– sure you have. She's right there."

"Ye know what I mean," said Soames.

"What I don't understand," said Philip, "is why you've got two ears."

"How many should a person have?" said Soames.

"Well," said Philip, "two I suppose."

"Smart lad. Now let me ask *ye* a question since yer so good at countin'. How many coins should a person have who wants to take a ship across the sea?"

"Well," said Philip, "presumably more than none I'd say."

"And have ye got the right number?"

"No sir."

"Exactly precisely right on the nose," said Soames. "So supposin' if I was someone who didn't have the right number of things, would I say I should or shouldn't go askin' another fellow about why he has or hasn't a certain expected number of things?"

"No sir."

"Right again. I'd say, 'Well met,' to ye, but then one of us would be a liar, wouldn't he? Can't stand around socializin' all day," said Soames. He turned away.

"What about honor?" said Thomas.

"What about it?" said Soames.

"It'd be the honorable thing to do – to transport Arthur's men across the Channel," said Thomas. "And back," he added hastily.

"Would it now?"

Thomas nodded. "And loyal. Why, if– *when* Arthur hears of it, I'm sure his good will would extend to whomsoever it was that did such a kindness to his men. For–" he corrected. "For his men."

"No no no," said Soames. "Not today. No more good deeds. Not after that last lady."

Thomas and Philip exchanged glances.

"Mysterious lady? Kind of unsettling? With an older man? Twinkling bits of astronomy on his robe? Gnarled white staff?"

"You mean Merlin? Nay, that was weeks ago. This was a little slip of a gel." Soames shivered. "Merlin always pays well. But this girl–" he tapped his temple with a finger. "Does things to yer head that one. Things you don't want done." He widened his eyes meaningfully. "Not a chance," he said. "No more good deeds."

The sun was climbing. Thomas didn't want to waste time waiting for another ship to come in. "How about a trade in kind?" he asked.

Soames looked sideways at him. "What, you mean like a do-fer?"

Thomas nodded. "A what?"

"A do-fer. You do fer me, I do fer you."

"Yes," said Thomas. "That. I'm an errant knight–"

"So ye keep sayin'."

"–surely there's something I can... do-fer you."

Soames twisted his beard, looked Thomas up and down, and said, "Alright. Aye. There's somethin' ye can do."

ঌ

Gus was finally speaking. In fact, he'd gone from talking less and less to not talking at all and then straight through to not shutting up. He also seemed to be staring at things that weren't, strictly speaking, present.

"Not Excalibur sir. Excalibur came from the Lady in the Lake and that sword there, or rather, *not* there, that is to say the sword that *was* there, that's the sword that established Arthur as King, the one I'm talking about. The sword that was in the stone. *That* sword. That one was broken, everyone knows, in the battle with–"

"So why's Arthur still king?" interrupted Philip, annoyed.

"What?" Gus focused on him. It seemed to take great effort.

"If having that sword is the sign that made him King, then now that the sword is gone, why is he still King?"

If you ask a person to describe a tree, one person will talk about bark, and color, and branches, and leaves, how they flutter and fall. Another will point at a tree and wonder what kind of fool he's dealing with that needs to have a tree described to him. Gus had the look of the latter.

"The sign is for the King sir, not the other way around."

Philip frowned. Gus went quiet, but it wasn't the wide-eyed quiet of before. This was a quiet quiet.

Thomas reached gently into the quiet. "What's going on Gus? Are you okay?"

Gus pushed his toe at nothing in particular on the ground. "It's the water, sir."

"Can't swim?" said Thomas.

Gus shook his head.

"That's alright. The whole goal with ships is to stay out of the water."

"It's just I don't like anything you can't face head-on like, sir."

Thomas nodded.

Gus twisted his sleeve. "You have to just sit there. Bobbing up and down. And wait. And you can't do anything about it. You can't make it go faster. You can't make it go away. You have to just let it happen to you until it decides it's done." He started to breathe in gasps.

"It's a short trip. It'll be over before you know it," said Thomas.

"Couldn't we wait for Merlin here?" said Gus.

"He may have already come back," said Thomas. "Or he may not be able to come back. We won't know unless we go inquire. It's our quest Gus. This is what being a knight is all about."

Gus looked morbidly depressed. He tried to paste a smile on. It hunched and slunk on his face like a cat caught in a downpour.

"At least you were able to find us passage," said Gus.

"Looking on the bright side of things!" said Thomas. "That's the Gus I know."

Gus swallowed. "Did Captain Soames say what he wants us to do? At least it'll be something we can face head on."

"Aye," said Thomas. "He mentioned 'bilge rats'."

"Oh," said Gus. "Bilges. That would be a whatchcallit. A tight space?"

"Aye," said Thomas. "Usually is."

Gus started breathing with his shoulders again.

"You managed the tight space under St. Stephen's just fine," Thomas said, encouragingly.

Gus considered this. "You're right," he said. He brightened a bit. "I must have been distracted by the mission, sir."

"There you go. We'll just do that again. Focus on the mission."

"The mission," Gus agreed.

"The mission," he said again, less confidently.

"The mission being… rats, sir? Of the disease-carrying vermin-ish sort?"

"Maybe we should focus on the bigger mission," said Thomas.

"The bigger mission," repeated Gus, nodding rapidly. "We're going to tackle our problems head-on, for the bigger mission."

He exhaled. He could do this.

"There you go," said Thomas.

Gus made the kind of chuckle people make when they don't have a chuckle in them. "Problems like for instance the plague…" he said.

"…in a bilge…" There was the chuckle again.

"…on the water." He looked ill.

Thomas put a hand on him. "I think you should sit this one out Gus."

"Nope. No sir. Augustus Ditcher doesn't sit things out. Where Sir Thomas the Hesitant goes, his squire goes." Gus stood up, gave a determined nod, and passed out.

❧

Soames' beard flapped as he pressed his leathery face into the wind. The waters roiled beneath the *Wing-ed Sea Fairy*, but the skies were clear and the currents familiar. It was a good day to be a sailor. But the crew had taken note of his white knuckles on the wheel and the set of his jaw, and they were keeping their distance. Sailors learn to sense the temper of their captain and the temper of the sea in that order.

The crew suspected their captain's bad humor had something to do with the passenger he was now lashing to a barrel.

"It's fer yer own safety see?" said Soames. "If anything happens, ye'll float."

Gus tried to find the comfort in this.

"Can I ask, sir, how many voyages the *Sea Fairy* has made and how many with you as her captain and how many voyages you've made prior to the *Sea Fairy* and how many ships were lost in those prior voyages and what role you played in those ventures? Maybe you have some logs or records I could take a look at? Is your license posted?"

Soames examined Gus. If he wanted to maintain the *Sea Fairy's* ferry license, he was only supposed to do things to his passengers that were in their own best interest. He was trying to figure out how to explain to Gus that a gag was in Gus' own best interest. It would save Gus' life, Soames was sure of it. An idea struck.

"Got any stories?" asked Soames.

Gus paused. "Why, yes," said Gus. No one had actually asked Gus to tell a story before. He'd usually had to take the initiative and tell the stories he knew people needed to hear.

"Good," said Soames. He maneuvered the barrel to one side, gripped the ship's wheel, pressed his leathery face into the wind again and told Gus, "Tell us a story."

Beside the Captain, Gus shifted against his ropes and searched his mind for the right story.

Thomas knew about rats. Once a year, the farmers in Fogbottom would collect all the pitchforks, shovels, big sticks, and mangy dogs they could find. Then they'd go from farm to farm, surround anything that could be hoisted – feeding troughs, storage bins, poorly constructed tool sheds – and they'd hoist them. The rats would scurry, the weapons would swing, and the dogs would pretty much do all the work. Dealing with rats on a ship couldn't be much different.

"This 'ere is yer bucket," said the gaunt and toothy sailor. He handed a bucket to Thomas and another to Philip.

Thomas pursed his lips and looked at his bucket.

"This 'ere is yer disinfectant," he winked and poured a chemical into two mugs with hinged lids. Like a priest handling sacred elements, he picked one up with both hands and handed it to Thomas. He waited until he was sure Thomas had a good grip before he let go. He repeated the operation with Philip.

"Buckets?" said Thomas. He shared a puzzled look with Philip. Philip shrugged.

"Could use a few dogs if we could round some up," said Thomas.

The sailor guffawed. "Ha! Ye got a long way to go if yer lookin' fer sea dog. Nope, it's the bucket and the 'fectant fer bilge rats, and yer lucky we've got the magic pipe. In my day–"

"Magic pipe?" said Philip.

"Aye," said the sailor. "Ye'll see it down below." His haphazard teeth made an untidy grin. "Fashioned her meself. Now git." He made to slap Philip on the back but glanced at the mug and pulled short. Then he weaved away cackling at some private joke. Thomas and Philip made their way below decks and located the hatch leading to the bilge.

Philip examined his bucket. "Maybe we're supposed to trap the rats?"

"Could be," said Thomas. "It's got to be an initiation sort of thing." He sniffed his mug and snapped his head back, blinking.

Philip tipped his lid up and approached the contents more carefully.

"Hey now, that's not disinfectant," Philip said. "That's rum."

Thomas propped the hatch open. Dark foamy sludge sloshed beneath them. There were misshapen bundles of slimy things floating in the muck. Thomas gagged. Philip swallowed the contents of his mug.

"Down the hatch," he said.

⸙

"Arthur had just been crowned King," said Gus, "when the Eleven Kings assembled against him. King Lot was one – that was Gawain's father. And Uriens another. Lot and Uriens are King Arthur's own sisters' husbands. Half-sisters of course. I don't think Morgan le Fay–" Gus shivered. "She's his *sister* if you can believe it. I don't think she'll ever forgive King Arthur for the death of her father even though King Arthur had nothing do with it." Gus' chin went up, but there was no argument from Soames. "Her father's death was Uther's business. And Merlin's, if you ask me. But King Arthur was the product of all that, and that's bad enough in le Fay's eyes, I suppose. And then they sent her off to a convent." Gus' voice dropped. "But it turns out it was a secret coven. And it doesn't matter that they didn't know where they were really sending her. It wasn't right. And she wasn't right after, if you take my meaning."

Gus paused to admire his own turn of phrase.

"Arthur keeps trying to make them all into a family, but some relationships – some people – maybe they're just broken."

He was quiet again for a moment. "The parson says God can mend anyone who wants to be mended. I guess that's the problem with someone like Morgan. She's so twisted she doesn't even know she's bent. It'd take a miracle for someone like that to admit she's broken." He trailed off. He shifted uncomfortably and glanced at the ropes.

"In any case," he said, "the Eleven go to war against young King Arthur. He's still got the sword from the stone – *not* Excalibur, not yet –" He shot a firm glance at Soames again. Soames did not disagree. "And they say when he held it up in battle it shone like thirty suns. I don't know how they decided thirty and not twenty-nine or thirty-one. I should think one sun close up like that would be plenty, but that's what they say." The ropes binding Gus to the barrel prevented a full shrug. It frustrated Gus that he couldn't accurately convey his disapproval of unnecessary and suspect embellishment. He wiggled briefly, then gave up.

"But one magic sword wasn't enough to deter the Eleven, so Merlin tells King Arthur to go fetch two brothers from France – King Ban and King Bors. Merlin says they're good with their hands, by which he meant they know how to use a sword, and probably some other weapons," Gus snickered, "and he proposes King Arthur send for them and say he'll help them against *their* enemy, King Claudas, if they come help him against his.

"'What say you of my counsel?' says Merlin. And King Arthur and all the barons say they think that's a good idea. So Arthur sends two of his knights – Sir Ulfius and Sir Brastias – with letters explaining the deal. And the Sirs sail to France. Just like we're doing!" Gus swallowed. "Just like we're doing…" he repeated, in a smaller voice.

He closed his eyes. "Well, the Sirs meet a party of eight other knights on the road and the Sirs say, 'Hail!' And the eight knights say 'Hail!' And the eight knights say 'Who are ye?' And the Sirs say, 'We're messengers from King Arthur to King Ban and King Bors.' And the eight knights say, 'Therefore you will die!' because they were from Claudas see? And they all fight on horseback but Sir Ulfius and Sir Brastias smote them all, every last one."

Gus threw a sideways glance at Soames again, looking for protestations, but Soames was turning out to be the perfect audience. "Now when they finally get to Ban and Bors everyone in France is *very* impressed. So the Sirs give Ban and Bors the letters, but it takes some time for them to get the message because they have to have the letters translated see? Because the letters were in English, but at that time everyone in France was French."

Gus paused again. He looked at the sky. "I don't know how they were able to explain about the battle with the eight whereas meanwhile they couldn't explain about the letters." Gus couldn't reach his chin to rub it thoughtfully. "Maybe they pantomimed the battle. It'd be more difficult to mime a war negotiation. That could explain it. Mimes are a French invention, aren't they?"

He shook himself. "Anyway that's how the story goes. So Ban and Bors agree of course, and they show up to help King Arthur in the war with the Eleven. King Arthur at this time is at Castle Bedegraine, by the way, in Sherwood. On the border there between Logres and Cameliard where Queen Guinevere is from. Merlin said once that there's a great treasure buried there, at Bedegraine, but they all thought he was just playing a prank. But you know, it's Merlin, so who knows? *I* think there probably *is* a great treasure under Bedegraine, and he just let them all *think* it was a prank so they won't go looking for it. I mean who's going to look now? Everyone would think you'd gone soft in the head."

Gus chuckled. Soames did not reciprocate. It dawned on Gus that for someone who may or may not be a pirate, buried treasure was likely not a joking matter. He quickly continued.

"So Ban and Bors arrive and they find out the Eleven have fifty thousand mounted men and another ten thousand on foot. It's clear King Arthur is vastly outnumbered, so Merlin devises a surprise midnight attack – King Arthur's got the sword of thirty suns so that'd help in the dark I'm sure. *And* he's got his pair of able fellows now, Ban and Bors. Well here's why I'm telling you this see, because we're on our way to visit King Ban, and here now is what he is like in his manner of person as the story goes."

Gus cleared his throat. "Bors says to Ban, 'Let's see how these Britons fight, eh?' Except he would have said it in French. And King Lot, when he sees Bors charge in driving his spear straight through armor and man, Lot says 'What *is* he?'" Gus laughed. "'What *is* he?' he says. Ha! And then Ban rides in wearing his green and gold, and they say you could hear the sound of his mighty strokes rebounding off wood and water, and when King Lot sees him he says to the Hundred-Knights-King – That was his name, that King. Because you can probably guess how many knights he had."

Soames didn't guess. Gus was used to people not guessing.

"Anyway, Lot says, 'We must flee, I should think!' But the Hundred-Knights-King spurs his horse and rides straight at Ban. And for a while no one can see exactly what's happening except that both horses get killed and both men go down.

"So King Arthur," Gus paused to shake his head in wonder, "King Arthur, who is horseless himself at this point and covered in blood so no one can tell who he is, fights his way into the fray. And there he finds Ban surrounded by dead men and dead horses, fighting on foot like a mad lion, and anyone that gets within reach of his sword dies." There was no way to satisfactorily demonstrate the fighting techniques in question while strapped to a barrel. Gus' hands and feet squirmed. Gus seemed unaware. "King Arthur manages to convince Ban he's a friend, and he tells Ban he should find a horse and get on it. Ban says, 'I trust God.'

"Well, King Arthur does too, and he figures maybe God wants him to get this man a horse. So King Arthur smites another knight on the head and takes his horse and leads it to Ban and they ride out and meet Bors in the woods. Then Bors says to his brother, 'I have answered my question.' And you can imagine by now everyone's forgotten the question, so Ban says, 'What question, my brother?' and Bors replies, 'The Britons. They fight pretty well.' And they all have a good laugh and from then on they're all fast friends."

Gus leaned his head back and rested it on the barrel. "Of course it helped too that shortly after all that, before the brothers sailed home, they helped King Arthur help Leodegrance in Cameliard, and that's how King Arthur met Leo's daughter Guinevere."

Gus slowed down. He wasn't quite certain how to approach the end of a story. He rarely made it this far. "So, there you have it. We're going to see King Ban because Merlin went to see King Ban before he disappeared with some important information about King Ban's son."

There was some commotion on the deck. Gus lifted his head and saw Thomas and Philip approaching. They were covered in muck. Thomas was carrying two buckets and supporting Philip, who seemed to be focusing all of his concentration on his feet.

"Wooo," said Philip rolling his eyes. "I feel like I'm on a ship."

Thomas spotted Gus tied to the barrel.

"Everything alright Gus?"

"Yes sir. Was just telling the Cap'n a story," he said proudly.

Thomas nodded the kind of nod meant to convey support more than understanding.

"What happened to the Sir, sir?" said Gus indicating Philip.

Philip steadied himself and stood at a wobbly but passable attention. "Deporting for ruty!" He saluted and fell over. He tried to lift his face off the deck but his head was too heavy. The last thing Philip saw was Booker whose mane would have been blowing in the wind if he were that kind of horse. Philip's eyes widened, then softened, then closed.

"He um," said Thomas. "He drank the rum."

"What – all of it?" said the gaunt and toothy sailor.

Thomas grimaced.

"The whole ration?" said the sailor. He seemed impressed.

Philip snored.

"Let me see that." He took the mugs, popped the lids, and peered inside. Thomas' was full. Philip's was empty as reported.

"Ye mix it, ye fool boy. It's grog! The rum kills the water so the water don't kill you. Ye didn't drink the water without the rum did ye?"

"Nothing on this ship is going in my mouth. You can be sure of that," said Thomas.

The sailor snickered. "Fair enough. What's in the bucket?"

One of Thomas' buckets was clearly heavier than the other.

"Ah," said Thomas, smiling through the drying mud. "We just got the one, but she's a corker," he said.

The sailor looked confused. He peered into the bucket and reeled back gasping. "Ye didn't. What've ye done, boy?"

"We got the bilge rat," said Thomas.

"Oh, laddy," the sailor reeled. "Ye weren't supposed to *get* the bilge rat. Ye *are* the bilge rats. The rats what clean the bilge." He pressed a hand to his forehead and stared at the dead rat.

"Ye'll have to tell the Captain," said the sailor.

Thomas opened his mouth.

"C'mon," he said and pulled Thomas to the other side of Soames. "He's deaf in that ear."

Gus frowned. "He's deaf in this ear?"

Philip giggled in his sleep.

"Land ho!" cried another sailor from the crow's nest.

"Could someone cut me loose?" said Gus.

"Go on," said the sailor. "Tell the Captain what ye've done."

Soames kept his eyes on the sea as they neared the port.

Thomas opened his mouth to speak, but the sailor pointed a finger with too many knuckles at the rat and interrupted. "They've killed Bella!" he blurted.

Soames glanced at the bucket. His shoulders drooped a little. "It'll be alright Fred. We can get another."

"Won't be the same," said the toothy sailor shaking his head.

"Nay, it won't," admitted Soames. He glanced at Thomas. "Rats flee a sinkin' ship," Soames explained. "Fred likes to think of Bella as a lucky charm and an early warnin' system all rolled into one."

"She were a full member of the crew," Fred pleaded.

"An *honorary* member of the crew," said Soames. Fred clammed up. Thomas got the impression this discussion had been had before.

"But the bilge is cleaned, aye?" said Soames.

"Cleaned," said Thomas. *Of rats anyway*, he thought.

Soames threw another glance at Thomas. "Tell me, Sir Thomas of the Table of Less Valued Knights, how did you manage to kill Bella?"

"We used the magic pipe, Captain."

Soames repeated the words slowly and carefully. "You used the magic pipe."

"Aye," said Thomas. "I'm afraid, well, we might've broken it."

"*Might've* broken?"

"Definitely broken."

Fred wailed and pulled at his hair.

"They broke the pipe?"

"Fred?" said Soames.

Fred was wheezing.

"Fred!" said Soames.

"Yes cap'n."

"Dismissed. Make ready for port."

"Yes cap'n."

Fred shouldered his way through Thomas.

"What did you do before you were a knight, lad?" said Soames.

"The Farmers are farmers, sir. Captain."

"I see," said Soames. "And your friend there?"

"His father makes cheese."

Soames nodded and chewed his lip. The land grew closer. Thomas could see people moving about.

Soames sighed. "I fear I might've put too much responsibility on Fred. I don't mind about the rat. But the bilge – the magic pipe is magic see, because it makes the waste water disappear. Pipes it overboard before we get to port. Otherwise you have to pay the port authority to dispose of it."

"I see," said Thomas. "That's a different sort of magic than I'm used to Captain."

"I can see that," said Soames. He shrugged. "We can get another magic pipe. And paying the fees once in a while abates suspicion. But do me a favor will ye?"

"Aye Captain?"

"Dispose of the pipe for us?"

"Yes sir. Captain."

Soames eyed Thomas but kept his hands on the wheel. There was a fatherly air about him. "Ye'll want to keep yer eyes open here in France, lad. I suspect yer goin' t'encounter more magics yer not used t'before yer adventure is over, Sir Thomas the Hesitant."

CHAPTER XI

OUT OF THE BILGE AND INTO THE BARROW

"I'm tellin' you," said Philip. He was too close to Thomas' ear. "There's something wrong with your 'horse.'" He started to make air quotes but got distracted by his own fingers. His eyes widened. "I saw it," he said. He squinted at Thomas' forehead. He reached out to touch it. Thomas slapped his hand away. "There was something..." Philip leaned in conspiratorially. "On its head."

"There's nothing wrong with Booker," said Thomas. "The one there's something wrong with is you." Thomas shifted the broken magic pipe to his other hand and tried to get a better grip on Philip. Someone had to keep Philip upright, and Philip himself didn't seem up to the task.

They stumbled down the gangplank and set their feet uncertainly upon the foreign shore.

Elisante counted the trees. Three. No change. She counted the barrels. Five. No change. She started to count the bricks. She gave up and did the math. Four hundred and fifty bricks. Same as always. She yawned. She counted the guards. Five.

She sat up and squinted. There should have been three. She counted again. By the east entrance to the market, one. To the north toward the docks, two. At the west entrance, three. And now four and five. There were two new guards confronting a disheveled sailor with a broken pipe on one shoulder and an even more disheveled sailor on the other.

She sighed and leaned back. Her opinion of sailors had been sinking like... well, like a sinking ship. Soon it would submerge and drag anything sailing-related with it into the oceanic depths of her gall. "Sea gall," she said to herself. She sneered and threw a crust at a pigeon.

She'd had enough. Even her own cleverness was boring her. She was tired of waiting. She had set the trap. Everything was prepared. But she could sit still no longer. She was no spider spinning a web and waiting. And waiting. And waiting. She was a... she was a... she wasn't happy with any animals she could think of at the moment, but she was definitely *not* a spider.

She stood up and brushed herself off. She sneered at the three trees. She sneered at the barrels five. She wouldn't even spare the bricks a sideways glance. She sneered at the vapid guards and the doltish sailors. The wobbly sailor was pleading his case. She made some mental predictions. The charge being leveled against them would be tedious. The sailor's excuse would be dull, unoriginal, and ineffectual. If her predictions were correct, it would be all the evidence she needed in the case against staying put. She eavesdropped and sneered again in anticipation.

⁂

"Allow me," said Philip to Thomas. "I speak…" He gave an explanatory wave. "...the language."

"You speak French," said Thomas doubtfully.

Philip reeled back in exaggerated astonishment. Thomas had to catch him from falling over.

"Gussn't the only one who is a person who knows about langwiches." He poked Thomas in the chest with his finger. He nearly missed. He poked him again for emphasis and for practice.

"Go right ahead then," said Thomas.

"I will," said Philip. He turned to the guards. He focused on one. He adopted a theatrical stance with one arm raised, one arm back, one foot forward. When he was satisfied, he inhaled. He bowed.

He didn't come up.

Thomas touched his shoulder.

Philip reared up and focused. "Oh, hello."

"Hello," said Thomas.

Philip smiled.

"Are you going to talk to these fine gentlemen, or shall I?" said Thomas.

Philip swung his attention to the guards. "I'd be happy to. There's just one problem," he said swinging back to Thomas.

"And that is?"

Philip grinned amiably at Thomas. "I don't know French."

"You just said you did."

"Prepsosterous!" He pursed his lips. "Presosperous? Nope." He shook his head.

"Preposterous," said Thomas.

"Well I am sorry," said Philip with great affront. "We can't all go around being polyglots like your squire Wossname can we?"

Philip took a breath. "I mean half of us don't even know what a polyglot is. And the only French I know is the sort that one begs to pardon if you catch my meaning.

And these fine gentlemen…" He waved a finger at the guards. "…don't look like the sort that pardon." He smiled and nodded at the guards.

"Let's start with your names," said one of the guards slowly, clearly, and in perfect English.

Philip gasped. He grabbed Thomas' shirt. "I *can* speak French," he said.

"This," said Thomas putting his arm around Philip's shoulders to steady him, "is Sir Philip the Exceptionally Disadvantaged. And I am Sir Thomas the Hesitant."

Philip eyed Thomas in astonishment. "You speak French too," he said.

৵

They propped Philip up in a chair in the Port Authority building, where he promptly dozed off.

"Grog," explained Thomas when the Guard Captain raised an eyebrow at him.

The Guard Captain frowned. "Doesn't usually have such a profound effect on sailors. Unless they're new," he posited.

"That," said Thomas. "And we're not sailors. And he didn't quite get the rum to water ratio correct."

"How much rum?" said the Guard Captain.

"All of it," said Thomas.

"I see. How much water?"

"None, sir."

A small old woman shuffling papers behind the counter snickered.

The Guard Captain ignored her. "And this is how Arthur's men comport themselves abroad?"

"I wouldn't know sir. It's our first time. I'd like to think not."

The Guard Captain examined Thomas.

"Are we being arrested?" asked Thomas.

The Guard Captain shook his head. "Just questions.

For now. You understand we like to keep track of who and what go in and out here."

"Anything to declare?" the old woman screeched.

"We'll be done shortly ma'am," said the Guard Captain.

"Short or tall, comin' or goin', they've got t'declare! What's that device he's carryin' there?"

The Guard Captain turned his attention to the pipe. He held out his hand.

"Kindly answer the woman," said the Guard Captain.

The old woman's face spread into a toothless grin.

"It's a..." Thomas' face grew hot, and he handed the Guard Captain the pipe. "It's how we were told we could pay for our passage sir. We were…" He slumped. "We were the bilge rats, sir."

The Guard Captain turned the pipe over in his hands.

"Did the operators of the *Wing-ed Sea Fairy* make any claims in your presence about the nature and or function of this pipe, sailor?"

"We're not sailors, sir. Like I said."

The Guard Captain raised an eyebrow.

"Aye, they did."

"And what sort of claims did they make?"

"They said..."

Thomas didn't *want* to shop Soames in. But a bald-faced lie to the Guard Captain was out of the question.

"They said it was a magic pipe, sir."

Great. Now I really am *a rat,* he thought.

The Guard Captain pursed his lips. He looked at Thomas from underneath his eyebrows.

"This…" said the Guard Captain.

Thomas braced himself.

"This is good work."

"You two–" The Guard Captain indicated the guards that had escorted Thomas and Philip. "With me. Madame, pay these men." He glanced at Philip lolling on the chair then tilted his head toward Thomas. "Correction. Pay *this* man the whistle-blower fee. And get *that* one some tea."

"And you–" said the Guard Captain to Thomas. He waved a hand at Philip: "Intoxicating beverages." He held up the pipe: "Dubious claims."

"Welcome to France," he said. "Careful what you swallow." Then, "Vite, vite!" he said to the guards, and they exited.

"Everyone's full of advice after the fact," Thomas muttered.

He turned. The old woman wasn't at the counter. Puzzled, he turned some more.

And there she was, leaning over a snoring Philip, with a bucket tilting precariously at the end of her wiry, outstretched arms.

"Tea time!" she cackled, and dumped the bucket of water on Philip.

Philip sputtered and shook his head.

Thomas didn't know if he should laugh or run, so he did neither.

The old woman tossed the bucket aside and pressed a sack of coins into Thomas' hand. "Whistle-blower's fee," she explained.

"Didn't blow no whistle," said Philip, slicking his hair back and wiping his eyes.

"That's right," she said. "You didn't. But I got you two hooligans out of that mess and got you paid too and now you owe me."

Her tone was fierce, but her eyes were wet. The old woman's lower lip trembled, and she fidgeted with a cameo necklace at her throat.

Thomas softened. "What's going on?"

"It's my little sister," said the old woman. "She's been taken."

"Taken? Where? By who?"

"Whom," corrected the old woman.

"Pardon?"

"By whom," she said. She shook her head and closed her eyes. "That's not important right now. Focus."

The old woman opened her eyes. There was fire there. "Rescue my sister" she said. The knuckles on the hand gripping her necklace went white. "Please?"

Now here was a proper good deed. For the moment, all else was forgotten.

"Where is she?" asked Thomas.

❧

A soft drizzle pattered amongst upturned leaves and dampened the forest floor. Thomas and Philip stood on the slope of a shallow, wooded ravine. There was a hole here amidst a jumble of large stones. It was large enough for a person but not by much. The old woman carefully picked her way around the rocks and trees and joined them.

"In there?" said Philip.

The old woman wrung her hands. "Yes sirs," she said.

They peered into the dark.

"You're certain?" said Philip.

She nodded.

"How did she get in there?"

The old woman swallowed and glanced around. The hand-wringing continued. "We were houby hunting and she…" The old woman shrugged. "She just slipped." She glanced at the hole and made a downward motion with her hand.

Philip looked around the forest. "Husband hunting? What? Out here?"

The old woman dropped her hands and tilted her head at Philip. "*Houby* hunting ye dull boy. Houby."

"Mushrooms," said Thomas.

She nodded. "Don't need a husband. Don't want a husband. Not lookin'." She glared at Philip. "Now are you two going to get in there and find my sister or not?"

"Have you tried calling to her?" asked Philip.

Thomas' expression indicated that he considered this a most welcome and reasonable question.

"Called to her?" repeated the old woman. "'*Did I call to her?*' he asks. Well let me think. Hum." Her face screwed up in disapproval. "Of course I called to her. What do you take me for?"

"Did she answer?"

"No."

"Could be knocked out," said Thomas.

"Or worse," said Philip.

"I can think of one way to find out," said the old woman. She shooed them toward the hole.

Thomas felt his pockets. He was looking for a rope. But he had suddenly realized how many things besides a rope were missing, and his hands were performing an unconscious inventory. They confirmed his suspicions.

"We're lacking all our gear," he said.

Philip frowned.

"And Gus," said Thomas. "And Booker."

"What do you need all that for? You're knights, aren't you? Sure, sailors need paraphernalia. Ropes. Boats. Oceans. But *you're* not sailors. You're *knights!*" Her eyes flashed impishly. "Or aren't you?"

Philip was too distracted to notice the challenge. "What's this?" he said. He was staring at something on the ground near the hole.

Thomas and the old woman leaned in.

"Looks like a–" started Thomas.

"Chicken print," interrupted the old woman confidently.

Thomas and Philip looked at her.

Philip compared his hand to the size of the print.

"That's a big chicken," he said.

"Got little chickens where you're from?"

Thomas picked up something that looked an awful lot like a bone.

"You're not afraid of a *chicken* are you?" said the old woman eyeing the bone.

"Depends what ate it," said Thomas.

"Look here," said Philip. "Does this look charred to you?"

The old woman threw her hands up.

"You two are exasperating. Really. I'm exhausted just watching you come up with excuses to not get in there and–" She punctuated each word with a finger to Thomas' chest. "Find my sister."

"Is there a dragon in that hole?" said Philip.

The old woman's face went blank. She stared at Philip. Then she burst out laughing. She held her sides and bent double and breathed deep and cackled some more. After a while she wound down, wiping a tear from her eye with one finger.

"Dragons," she said. She sighed. "Haven't been dragons in these parts for years. Lizards, sure. Maybe there's a lizard down there. You're not afraid of a lizard are you?"

"Depends what ate the lizard," mumbled Philip.

The old woman adopted her pleading pose again. "Look, let's say there's a lizard. And I'm not saying there is, but saying there's a lizard, and a big one. You could cut off its head and take it back to your land of tiny animals and tell your mates it's a dragon and what an adventure you had in Gaul, Land of Dragons."

Thomas raised his eyebrows.

"We've got real-sized animals," said Philip.

"Whatever you need to tell yourself, love," said the old woman. She fiddled with her cameo. "Now how about it? Will you brave the dark and find my sister?"

ୡ

Gus shook the ropes off, peeled himself from the barrel, stretched, and rubbed life back into the places that had been bent and pinched for too long. He thanked the Port Authority guard who set him free and rescued another guard from Booker. Booker was braying outlandishly. He would have reared up if he had been built for it. Instead he was executing a series of unsettling, nervous hops.

Gus held Booker's reins, put a hand on his shoulder and spoke soothing nonsense. Booker stopped the hopping and hollering, but he was still breathing hard. His eyes rolled.

"Shh, shh, shh," said Gus, petting him.

But Booker refused to settle down. He headed toward the gangplank. Booker wasn't hard to keep up with, but he proved impossible to stop.

❧

Thomas slipped into the hole and landed hard.

"Ow," he said.

Safely sheltered from the wind and drizzle, he tore a piece of his shirt, soaked as it was in bilge-oil, and wrapped it around a damp tree branch. A few sparks from a piece of flint set the makeshift torch ablaze.

'Ablaze' was overselling it. The flame guttered and struggled, angry but fragile. Thomas moved the torch around carefully, watching it more than what it revealed.

"It's working," he called. "Come on down."

Philip slid down and completely failed to land on his feet.

Thomas helped him up.

"Thanks," said Philip. His tone was genuinely devoid of gratitude.

They squinted at the chamber revealed in the torchlight and peered into the darkness beyond.

Something was happening to the light.

The torchlight grew slowly brighter.

Nope, that's not right, thought Thomas. *The darkness is getting... darker.*

He looked back up at the hole. It was shrinking. The sky was disappearing.

There was a heavy clunk above him.

The sky was gone.

The torch sputtered. Shadows stretched and jittered. The stalagmites on the cavern floor were too big. Anything could hide behind them. The stalactites on the ceiling were too sharp. The charred bones on the chamber floor were too many. And too charred.

Philip took a breath and tried to speak as calmly as possible. "Hrnng," was all his mouth was able to contribute. He inhaled again and wheezed.

Thomas put a hand on him.

Some situations are so preposterous, so unlikely, so unreal that the mind fails to panic. Some measure of comprehension is required in order to feel fear. If there is no comprehension, there is no fear.

Thomas comprehended his situation.

"Focus on the mission," he told himself.

The words sounded feeble and small.

Philip was gasping for air now. Frozen, he managed to lift a hand and point at something on the edge of the light.

A shadow grew and separated from a concealing boulder. It danced maniacally in the frenetic torchlight.

Thomas jumped and dropped the torch. The flame faltered and flared. The torch rolled across the floor. The shadow grew larger and larger until it consumed all other shadows.

The torch died.

The darkness was complete.

"Hello," said a voice.

CHAPTER XII

THE DRAGON, THE PRINCE, AND THE PERFUMED ARMADA

The voice was deep. It was the kind of voice that came from under a mountain, from a time before. It slithered and clawed its way into the mind. The words came slowly and carefully, each a morsel savored.

"You are not from here," it said.

"I can tell…" it hissed, "the acsssent..."

Honest confusion, it should be noted, is an effective antidote to paralyzing dread.

"We…" said Philip, honestly confused. "We haven't said anything."

"Have you not?" it said. The tone was considerate. "I recall '*hrnng*.'" The voice did its best to imitate what it had heard. "Wuzzz that not you?"

Thomas pointed at Philip. In the pressing darkness, the gesture should have gone unnoticed.

"Ah," said the voice. It was on the move.

"You can tell where we're from by that? By… '*hrnng*?'" said Philip.

"I have some exsssperienssse exsssstracting

exsssclamationsss of disssmay. I am... What izzz the word...?"

The voice stopped moving.

"An admirer?" said Philip hopefully.

"Hmm," said the voice. "Yesss and no."

"A devotee?"

"Clossser."

Thomas took a step back.

"A..." said Philip. He swallowed. "A connoisseur?"

"True but incorrect. No," said the voice. "Ah." It moved again. "A *collector.*"

Thomas put his hand on his sword. If the creature could see in the dark then there was no point trying to be sneaky about it. He drew his sword in one swift motion. It sang in the still air and utterly failed to shine in the dark.

"Ah. One duzzz not need to ssspeak to sssay what izzz on the mind yesss?"

"We're here to rescue, erm..." Thomas made a note to himself to gather more details in the future.

"There izzz no one here by that name I am afraid." It chuckled. "'*I am afraid.*' A figure of ssspeech. What have *I* to fear? You, on the other hand..."

"You sir!" said Gus to the Frenchman in the road. "I need your help. Um. Requestay le aide pour moi right away. Um. Veet!"

The Frenchman smiled. It was quite a smile. He wore peasant garb, but the way he bore himself upon his steed described a different sort of person. For one, peasants sat on horses. They didn't bear themselves, and they certainly didn't do it upon steeds. You'd get hurt. The Frenchman looked like he didn't care about getting hurt.

"Hello small boy!" declared the Frenchman. "How may I be of assistance to you this morning?"

Gus balked at the thick accent. He was trying to decide if he'd seen the man's tooth sparkle when the man in question suddenly spoke again.

"You are in a great distress, no?"

Gus nodded. "No. Yes! Yes, I am. Very great distress. We follow the horse yes? I mean–" Gus shook off his adopted accent. "Come with me please. Thomas is in trouble. Booker knows where to go."

"This... noble creature is the Bookair?"

Gus nodded.

"Then, by all means. Let us rescue your Toemoss."

Booker raced, in his way, toward the ravine. Gus clung, so to speak, to the reins.

"It is a horse?" said the Frenchman as he strolled alongside them.

"Yeees," said Gus noncommittally.

"He plods along with the fierce determination."

Gus nodded.

Booker stopped.

"No, no, don't stop now Booker. Where's Toemoss–Thomas?"

Booker brayed, rolled his eyes, and sat down heavily on a large flat stone.

The Frenchman's horse whinnied. It was glorious. It was a whinny that sailed on seas of long grass, hurtled chasms, and stopped for nothing but its master's heart.

"Octo says your Toemoss is under the rock," said the Frenchman confidently.

Gus frowned. "What?"

"Under the rock," the Frenchman pointed. "Under your... Bookair."

"That's Latin," said Gus. "'*Octo*' is Latin."

"You are correct!"

"You named your horse '*Eight*.'"

"Again you are correct my small boy!"

"Why did you name your horse '*Eight?*'"

"Because," said the Frenchman frowning. "He is the eighth."

They considered each other.

"Your horse," said Gus, "Octo. Octo says that Booker says that Thomas is under the rock?"

The Frenchman nodded.

"Crushed?"

"No, no, it is probably the depression."

"He's under the rock... because he's sad?"

"No, no, I am sorry. A depression... An empty place. A place below this place."

"A cave?"

"Possibly," said the Frenchman considering the idea. "Perhaps it is a doorway."

"A doorway? To where?"

"To somewhere. To nowhere. Who can say? The nether-gloom? Purgatory? The Wastelands? It could be anywhere really where your Toemoss has gone."

Gus fidgeted. "We have to get him out of there. We have to move this rock."

"Amposeebluh," said the Frenchman sadly.

"Ampo... Impossible?" Gus translated.

"Oui." The Frenchman shrugged. "I am certain that rock weighs more than even mighty Octo." He patted his horse's haunch. Octo's muscles rippled under a glistening white hide.

Octo's face indicated agreement with his master.

Gus clenched his jaw.

"My name is Augustus Ditcher, sir. Sworn squire to Sir Thomas the Hesitant of the Table of Less Valued Knights. And if there is one thing we Ditchers can do," he raised his chin, "it's move rocks."

Unsettling sounds came to Thomas through the darkness. Slithering. Scraping. Clawing. And now scratching sounds on the wall behind his head. He froze. Sweat beaded on his forehead.

"Yesss. Much to be afraid of I think."

The voice was right behind him. Something fluttered against Thomas' neck. There was a sharp inward hiss, a brief silence, and then the owner of the voice began to choke.

"One moment, pleassse," it managed to say.

It tried to clear its throat. It wheezed. Once. Twice. It made a panicked exclamation in French that shouldn't be translated, and then a relatively small amount of chaos unfolded.

There was a loud cough near Thomas' ear, and a tiny fireball spun past Thomas' cheek and singed the hair at his temple.

Thomas' ducked.

Something hit the cavern floor like a small sack of mud. The impact dislodged another tiny fireball that shot across the floor. Philip hopped to avoid it but it burned out before it reached him. The sack twisted and spun and coughed. Each cough threw another fireball. Each fireball illuminated the scene for a moment – the writhing shape, leering shadows, panicked faces, wisps of smoke where flames had died.

Then there was silence. No one moved.

"You," the voice gasped. "You sssmell like foul thingsss from the sssea."

And then it coughed once, louder and deeper than all the other coughs. The fireball burned and spun and shot and exploded on Thomas' makeshift torch lying abandoned on the floor.

The cavern lit up.

Hunkered before them was a small knobby lizard. One eye locked on Thomas. The other darted to the torch, to Philip, to Thomas' sword.

When it spoke next, the voice was no longer from under the mountain or a time before. The voice was now the kind of voice you'd expect from a lizard no larger than a man's boot. It squeaked a little.

"Oh dear," it said.

It stood on two legs and held its front feet out in a way that said, *Everyone just calm down. We can talk about this.*

Confidence poured into the vacuum left by Thomas' evaporating fear, along with disappointment, confusion and a healthy helping of embarrassment for having been taken in, apparently. The sudden shift was disorienting and left him wary. William had told him once, in his wise and inscrutable big brother voice, "When in doubt, doubt."

Thomas lifted his sword.

"Whoa whoa whoa," said the lizard. The words tumbled over each other. "Everyone just calm down. We can talk about this."

A hollow grinding sound issued above them. Dust came down in streams. Pebbles dropped and bounced on the cavern floor. Light poured in as the stone floated up, unblocking the cave's entrance.

A head appeared. It held two hands near its mouth and yelled.

"Sir Thomas! Sir Philip! Tell me you live!"

Thomas stepped into the shaft of light. Gus was only a foot or two away.

"We're right here Gus. We're fine."

"Oh good."

Another head popped into view.

"I've brought help," said Gus.

"You brought—" started Thomas, wondering who Gus could have possibly rounded up on such short notice.

"Sir Lancelot du Lac," said the Frenchman. "At your service, mes amis."

A knight. That's who Gus could've rounded up on such short notice. Of course it was.

The lizard cowered. "Lancelot? Did he say, '*Lancelot?*'"

"Your hiss is gone," said Philip.

The lizard wrung its hands. "Part of the ambiance. Not really necessary now is it?"

"Ambiance?!" said Philip. "You were going to *eat* us a minute ago."

"Certainly not," said the lizard. It looked affronted. Its tongue flicked. "You smell terrible," it muttered.

"Pardon?"

"Please don't tell Lancelot I'm here," the lizard implored.

"Are you injured my friends?" said Lancelot. "It would grieve me deeply to learn that guests to my country had come to great harm."

"We're fine," Thomas growled. He eyeballed the lizard. "All three of us."

The lizard buried its face in its front feet.

"Three?" said Gus.

"Aye," said Thomas. "Philip, myself, and the fire-breathing dragon that ate the old lady's sister."

"Dragon?" Lancelot said and dropped into the hole.

He landed lightly on his feet and dropped to a crouch. Thomas hadn't seen or heard him do it, but the Frenchman must've drawn his sword during his leap. It glinted in the shaft of light as it followed his gaze around the chamber.

Of course it glinted. Thomas nonchalantly angled his blade into the light.

Lancelot stood slowly and sheathed his sword. "My sincere apologies for the entrance abrupt. I thought I heard you say there was a dragon."

Thomas pointed.

Lancelot laughed from his belly.

"I see. You English," he shook his head. "Always having fun. But you cannot fool Lancelot. That is a lizard."

"That *lizard*–" started Philip.

The lizard shook its head pleadingly.

"–breathes fire. And it ate the old woman's sister."

"You have no proof of that," snapped the lizard. Its eyes went wide and it clamped its hands over its mouth.

Lancelot's sword was drawn again and leveled at the lizard's heart, steady as a stalactite.

"How does he *do* that?" said Thomas. He put a hand experimentally on his sword and tried to visualize moving it as quickly as Lancelot. His mind managed to poke itself in the eye.

"I admit I have not known a lizard to speak," said Lancelot. "But certainement this is no dragon."

The lizard drew back. "I could so too be a dragon," it said. "But I'm not," it added quickly. It gave a nervous grin and tried to control its tongue.

"And I'm sure I don't know anything about anyone's sister," it said. "Girls don't come here," it explained. "And the ones that do are generally the sort that can take care of themselves and don't need rescuing by the likes of you three."

"Four," shouted Gus.

"Four," corrected the lizard amiably.

"Could you all come into the light so I can see?" said Gus.

They shifted.

"Thank you," said Gus.

"So if you'll just kindly go on your way," said the lizard. "I'd like to get back to... lizardy things."

"Basking on rocks," suggested Gus.

The lizard nodded. "Yes, like basking on rocks."

"Lurking in dark caverns," said Thomas.

The lizard nodded. It tried to recall if that was something lizards actually did.

"Breathing fire and eating maidens," said Philip.

"Absolutely not," said the lizard, thankful to be on solid conversational footing again.

"Come my friends," said Lancelot. He called to Gus, "Small boy! Send a rope if you please yes?" He turned back to Thomas and Philip, put a hand on each of their shoulders and declared, "Today is not a day for men to bother themselves with lizards."

A rope uncoiled through the hole.

"After you," said Lancelot. He held the rope steady.

"That's right," the lizard gloated. "Run from the dragon!"

"Angry little lizard," Philip muttered as they fumbled with the rope.

"That's a dragon," whispered Thomas. "It breathed fire. And *he's* going to kill it, and then he's going to take credit for it."

"It's what we do, Thomas. Rules three, six, nine, and thirteen at the very least."

Philip frowned at Thomas and climbed. Thomas followed with a frown of his own.

When they reached the top, Lancelot turned and addressed the creature. "Lancelot and his friends are not running from the dragon. We are leaving the lizard."

"Dragon," said the creature.

"*If* you are a dragon," said Lancelot, "then explain to Lancelot why did you say that you are *not* a dragon?"

"*Because* I'm a dragon!" said the creature. "That's what we do. We deceive people. And we eat damsels. And we hoard treasure. And we get vanquished by knights. But you can't expect us to do all the work."

"Did you eat the damosel these men are here to rescue?"

"Well, no."

"Can you show me your treasure hoard?"

The creature paused. "The thing is–"

"The thing is that there is no treasure hoard yes?"

"It's been a hard year," said the creature.

"Shush lizard," said Lancelot.

"Look," said the creature, "I know I haven't been entirely up front with you. But you've got quite the reputation Sir Lancelot, and if you could just vanquish me, it would mean a lot to me and my family. Look at this–"

It held its head at a striking angle.

"Imagine how I'd look on your throne room wall."

"You would look very small," said Lancelot. "And remarkably like a lizard."

"I am a *dragon*," said the creature.

"Then prove it," said Lancelot. "Prove that you are a mighty dragon. Breathe the ball of fire or the stream of acid or the lance of frost, eh?"

"Here we go," said Thomas.

There was some coughing and an embarrassed silence.

"I burned myself out on the other two," it said sadly.

"Goodbye sorrowful lizard," said Lancelot.

Thomas offered Lancelot a hand, but the Frenchman didn't require it.

"You're not going to commandeer our quest?" asked Thomas, astonished.

"I am sorry my new friend. I do not understand," Lancelot.

"The dragon, the missing sister..." said Thomas. "Where I come from – well, it's our job you see. To sort of set the stage."

"You are the... the... the stage hands?"

"We're Less Valued Knights," nodded Thomas.

Lancelot cocked his head.

"Even if this is true, that you are the lesser valued," said Lancelot, "shouldn't your betters seek to improve your reputation. For then they would be even more better would they not?"

Lancelot smiled. It involved his whole face.

Thomas looked at Philip. Philip shrugged.

"But still," said Thomas. "The quest..."

"Lancelot did not see a damosel," said Lancelot.

"No, but the dragon?"

"Lancelot did not see a dragon. And where I come from we do not take the credit, as you say, for things that did not happen. Where is the damosel? Where is her distress? Where is the mighty dragon? No. Lancelot is spectacular." He laughed from his belly again. "He does not need to boast of things that did not happen."

Well here's something new, thought Thomas. He had a strong desire to like this knight. But his claims about himself seemed too good to be true, and when in doubt…

Lancelot whistled. Octo, tethered to a makeshift pulley system, backed up and let the large stone come to rest over the hole.

Lancelot patted Octo and said, "But you *are* lucky Lancelot arrived with his horse, no? You are welcome. And now–" He leapt into the saddle. "You must dine and lodge with Lancelot tonight and tell more tales of your strange country."

"We'd be honored Sir," said Thomas, "but we're looking for someone."

"Who?"

"King Ban of Benwick."

"Oho! Then you are twice blessed my aromatic friends."

He produced an apple from a saddle bag, polished it on his sleeve and took a bite.

"King Ban is my father," he said.

~

"*I* rigged the pulley," mumbled Gus as they walked along.

"I had a notion," said Thomas.

"All *he* did was provide the heavier horse," said Gus.

"I know," said Thomas kindly.

Gus kicked a stone.

"We need to find Merlin," he said.

Thomas nodded.

"I mean *we* need to find Merlin," said Gus.

"We will," said Thomas. Maybe things were too good to be true, but they *were* good, and that was good enough for now. "We'll find him because of you, Gus. You found

Lancelot. And now we're headed exactly where we need to go to find Merlin."

Gus cheered up. "And Faux-Ambrosia was there when you needed her, wasn't she sir?"

"She was," said Thomas. He patted the hilt at his hip. The motion released a waft of odor, but the dragon was right – the aroma was of the bilge and the sea and no longer of marinated sword. Thomas reflected that for once he smelled worse than his sword.

"Hey Philip," said Thomas. "We're going to meet the King."

Philip nodded. It was indeed good news, but Thomas seemed overly cheerful about it. "Yes, Thomas. Yes, we are."

"And," said Thomas. He held his arms wide. "We stink!"

Philip blinked.

"Remember, Philip?" said Thomas. "Remember when we met Arthur?"

"I remember," said Philip. "You can put your arms down now."

"It is a funny thing about the Englishmen," said Lancelot. "They are made happy by things that should upset them, and upset by things that should bring them happiness.

"But on the other hand," he wrinkled his nose, "Lancelot finds that his new friends' observations about themselves are indeed, how do you say, on the nose."

Laughing from their bellies, they made for Benwick.

❧

"How thrilling!" said King Ban. The man was a larger, battle-scarred version of his son. A thick head of wavy dark hair framed a face with quick beady eyes, a long nose, a perfectly thin mustache, and a jaw like an anvil. He sat with unexpected poise on the edge of his seat – a massive throne draped in green and gold with huge carved paws for arms and legs and a roaring lion's head behind and above. If the throne's occupant were to rise abruptly he'd likely impale himself on polished incisors. This was not a throne for a person prone to impulse.

Ban cracked a walnut with his bare hand, popped it in his mouth and chewed, grinning. One knee was bouncing.

"Finally," said Ban. "Lancelot, did I not tell you this day would come?"

"Indeed you tell me of many things my knowing father," said Lancelot.

"Indeed," repeated Ban, chewing and grinning. "Stand my bedraggled ambassadors and tell us what our firm and constant friend Arthur, King of England, requests of King Ban of Benwick."

Thomas stood.

Ban said, "It is I no?" He chewed and grinned and watched Thomas open his mouth.

"Wait!" said Ban. He sniffed. He looked at Lancelot. "These Englishman smell worse than the last."

"Your Majesty–" started Thomas.

Ban held up one enormous, meaty hand. "Forgive me," he said. He sat back. "I am being selfish. You are worn and weary from the road." He sniffed again. "And other unmentionable places."

Ban snapped his colossal fingers. His thumb muscle bulged.

"First, the bath. Then the adventure yes?"

Thomas closed his mouth. Eager as he was to obtain information on Merlin's whereabouts, a bath sounded very nice. He looked at Philip. Philip's face declared that he was keen on a bath too.

Thomas bowed his head. "You are too kind, Your Majesty."

Ban smiled merrily. "This also I explain to Lancelot."

"Indeed you do, my well-informed father."

A lovely girl approached. "This way messieurs," she said.

Philip swallowed.

Thomas tried to contain his odor.

She escorted them out of the throne room.

ꕥ

"I'm Philip," said Philip as they walked.

"I am Patrice," said the young lady giving a small curtsey without breaking stride. "You have traveled far no?"

She smiled at Thomas. It occurred to Thomas she was trying to be gracious. "And I'm sure we smell like it," he said.

"I'm Philip," said Philip again.

The girl smiled demurely.

Philip grinned.

"We are here," said the young lady. "The sails de Ban." Her face took on an apologetic expression. "It is his majesty's small jest. Perhaps you are amused?" She pushed open two large doors.

Thomas had bathed in streams, in lakes, in barrels, and in large buckets. None of these experiences had prepared him for King Ban's Baths.

A large circular pool dominated the center of the room which was open to the sky. Palm trees grew in gilded pots around the pool, shading the man-made lagoon. Ornate shelves lined the walls and were loaded with glass jars full of what looked like pastel pebbles. A miniature dock extended into the pool. Moored to it were two floating tubs, partially filled with steaming water, modeled like war ships.

Gus, had he been present, would have chuckled at Ban's wordplay. "Le salle de bain," he would have said, and shaken his head grinning. But Gus wasn't present, and the joke was completely lost on Thomas and Philip.

"I'll take your clothes messieurs."

Philip choked.

"Our what?" he said.

"Your clothes, if you please? They shall be laundered."

Philip shot a pleading look at Thomas.

"Or…" There was a sparkle in her eye that might have been amusement. "You could leave them on the bench if you would prefer the privacy?" she said.

"Yes please," said Thomas.

"Yes please," repeated Philip wide-eyed.

She curtseyed and exited the room, closing the doors behind her.

৵

After a suitable time spent gawking in naked astonishment at the wonder that was King Ban's Baths, Thomas and Philip got down to business.

Thomas pulled a cord dangling from the mast of his bath-boat. Sails unfurled.

"How did you–" Philip's sails sprang into action. "Aha," he said.

Neither ship moved.

Thomas tried to scootch away from the dock by sloshing back and forth. It didn't work.

"Ha!" Philip pushed at the deck with a long stick. He drifted out of port.

Thomas cast about. He spotted it nestled on two hooks on the hull – a harpoon. Where the sharp end would have been on a proper version, this one sported a spongy ball.

"Yo ho ho!" he yelled and pushed at the dock.

Freed from the pier, he took more careful inventory of his vessel. There was an assembly of sponges on sticks of various sizes. Tiny green and gold pennants hung playfully from the high points. There were fist-sized barrels arrayed on a deck above the bath's water line. He peered inside the barrels. They held more of the pastel balls that filled the shelves. A row of miniature catapults lined the starboard hull.

He fiddled with one and was able to draw the armature back and down and hook it. The press of a lever caused the empty armature to snap and arc upward.

Something shifted underneath him. He reached down and drew it out. An oar.

"That was uncomfortable," he said to himself.

Something splashed and fizzed in the water nearby.

"To arms!" shouted Philip.

A pastel cannonball caught Thomas' sail, thunked off his deck and plopped into his bath. Purple bubbles foamed. Thomas sniffed. It smelled like flowers. "Jasmine?"

"Stand down matey!" yelled Philip.

"I think you're mixing your land and sea commands–"

Another cannonball hit Thomas' hull. It bounced into the open sea and exploded in bubbles.

"So that's how it is, is it?" Thomas sneered.

He selected an assortment of colors and loaded his catapults. Philip had him at a disadvantage. They were at broadsides but with the catapults only on the starboard rail, Philip could fire on Thomas, but Thomas couldn't return fire. He needed to spin his boat around. He lifted his oar.

Another cannonball landed in his bath. Pink bubbles fountained. He brushed and blew at them to make a hole, but another fountain erupted to take their place.

He gave up and pushed his oar blindly through. His ship rocked. He brought the oar down. Success! It slapped hard against Philip's ship. Thomas shifted and pushed and cheered as he spun them both. Philip's ship collided with the sea wall.

"Avast ye scurvy sea dog!" cried Philip.

"You don't even know what that means!" Thomas retorted.

Through a rainbow of pastel foam, Thomas saw Philip raise his sponge-harpoon. His gaze followed the harpoon up. On a shelf directly above Philip, jars and jars of pastel cannonballs loomed. He watched the next several events unfold in slow motion, helpless to intervene.

Philip's harpoon struck a shelf bracket and pushed it upward. Philip glanced upward, grimaced and pulled the harpoon back. The shelf settled back down. The bracket, loosened by Philip's blow, clung valiantly to the wall. But the damage was done. It faltered. It slipped. The end of the shelf dropped an inch and stopped. The other brackets held.

Philip sighed. "That was close," he said.

One of the smaller but fuller jars near the end of the shelf leaned, slid, and tinked against the outer jar. It was enough. The jar on the end slid happily off the end of the shelf, dropped through the air and splooshed into the sea. Air bubbles blorped ominously to the surface as it sunk.

Philip and Thomas held their breath. It was quiet for a moment.

And then the floral depth charge detonated. The sea convulsed. One by one the remaining jars plunged into the deep and exploded. The sea collapsed and ruptured.

"Batten the hatches?" Philip croaked.

But King Ban's fleet was no match for the perfumed tsunami. It would prove to be her final, glorious voyage.

Thomas and Philip fidgeted nervously at the table.

"We're not in chains," said Philip.

"It somehow seems worse this way," said Thomas.

"Nonsense," said Philip. "We'll be fine. Won't we?"

"We? *You* destroyed his ships."

Philip gasped. "Me?"

"You broke the shelf."

"You attacked *me*. With an oar!"

Ban and Lancelot swept into the room. They took their seats. Lancelot stared at his plate. Ban glared at Thomas and Philip. He drummed his gigantic fingers. He took a breath.

"That," he said. He shook his head. "That," he repeated. He addressed Lancelot. "That is why I love the Englishmen."

Hope bubbled up like an effervescing pastel foam and lifted Thomas' chin.

Ban grinned at them.

"I have surveyed the destruction," Ban declared. "I have witnessed the detritus of my fleet brave and noble. But what is a ship of war if it is not in danger? A farce I tell you. A pointless and boring farce."

He slammed his fist.

"Ban of Benwick is no farce. And these men this day have proved it."

Thomas laughed nervously.

"There. See?" said Philip.

"Sincerely," said Ban in a more conversational tone. "It is so very boring here. Which brings us to the point."

He snapped his sausage fingers. Servants appeared with trays of meats and cheeses, breads and fruit, sauces and gravies.

"How many kings do we face?"

Thomas blinked. "Pardon?"

Ban bit into a leg of something large and roasted.

"It was eleven last time. What is it this time? Fourteen? Seventeen?" His eyes widened. "Twenty?"

"Um," said Thomas.

"Our friend Arthur, he is at war no?"

"Well, yes," Thomas admitted. *And mostly irrelevant*, he didn't. Ban's assumptions were the life-raft that rescued them from the wholesale destruction of his fleet, and Thomas was reluctant to abandon ship.

"And," said Ban, "the enemy, it is an army of kings of course. There is no one king who alone would face Arthur or his handsome friend Ban. So therefore it must be an army of many. How many?"

"Five?" said Thomas. Five was probably not many.

Ban paused. "Five," he said.

"Five," Ban repeated. He put down his roast meat. "I do not understand. Five is less than eleven."

Thomas nodded. He was unsure of many things at the moment, but the math seemed solid.

Ban frowned. His tone was concerned. "It would be embarrassing no? To fight just five kings after eleven. Even more embarrassing I think to ask for the mighty King Ban's help against so few.

"This worries me," he said. "I am worried. King Ban is worried. Tell me, my perfumed guest, why does Arthur ask for our help against such a paltry force?"

Thomas cleared his throat. "He, er," stumbled Thomas. "He doesn't?"

Ban sat back. "With this I am relieved."

"Oh good."

"And sad. Yes, King Ban is sad and miserable. It is miserable this peace and happiness. There is no adventure in it. I do not recommend it. It is boring. So very boring..." He trailed off. He picked at his meat.

"But if you are not here to ask for King Ban's help, why then are you here at his palace?"

"Ah," said Thomas. "Merlin is missing. We understand he came to see you?"

"Oh yes," said Ban. "He had the kind words for the boy."

He gestured at Lancelot. Lancelot kept eating.

"Kind words," said Thomas.

"A prophecy?" suggested Philip.

Ban shrugged.

"What did he say?" said Thomas.

"He said..." Ban squinted at the wall. "'*This same child Lancelot shall be the man of most glory and honor in the world.*' That kind of thing."

Thomas looked at Lancelot. Lancelot shrugged.

"This sort of thing," Ban ruminated, "is not so much the prophecy as the flattery. The wizard comes here all the time. He enjoys– *enjoyed* the sails of Ban." He waved a hand. "It is no matter."

Thomas looked meaningfully at Philip. Philip grinned and gave a silent fist pump. They were on the right track, thanks to Marie.

When we get back, Marie's getting a great big kiss, thought Thomas. He thought probably too long about that.

Thomas cleared his throat. "Your Majesty, the last time Merlin was here, was he alone?"

"Ooh ho ho ho, no," said Ban. He chuckled. "He had the lady friend yes? Sparks were flying." Ban shrugged. "It happens with wizards. The sparks."

"They were fighting?"

"Fighting? No and yes. You know how it is with love," said Ban.

Thomas and Philip nodded in false affirmation.

"The loving, the fighting, the loving..." said Ban.

"He was beguiled?" asked Philip, growing worried.

"Oh certainement," said Ban.

"Against his will?" asked Thomas. After he asked, he wasn't sure he wanted to know the answer either way. If Merlin went willingly, then it meant he probably didn't want to be found. If he hadn't, then what kind of forces were they dealing with that could take Merlin against his will?

Ban shrugged. "Who can tell with love eh? But this Nimue, she seemed not untrustworthy to Ban. They complained of Arthur's sister." Ban shivered. "That one is *not* the trustworthy lady."

"Morgan?" said Thomas. "They were worried about Morgan le Fay?"

"Oui," said Ban. "Do not trust that one. Would that she had not married the fool Uriens and involved herself in my country. It will be a relief for Ban when she sails away tonight. May she never return."

Thomas and Philip exchanged a glance.

"I'm sorry, Your Majesty," said Thomas.

He stood.

"We have to go."

ঌ

Ban remained at the table. He wasn't eating.

"What's wrong father?" said Lancelot.

"I will miss them," said Ban. "The adventure, it goes with the Englishmen always. Why is this?"

Lancelot chewed and thought.

"They smelled nice," he said after a while.

Ban sighed. "It is not their usual state in my experience."

"Just an observation," said Lancelot. "One day I would like to visit this country, England."

"Perhaps you will, my remarkable boy," said Ban. "Perhaps you will."

CHAPTER XIII

THE MIDNIGHT CORVETTE

Dusk slipped by while everyone was preoccupied. Evening nodded to dusk in passing and held the door for Night. Night sauntered in like it owned the place and took a seat. It intended to stay for a while.

Thomas, Philip, Gus and Booker stalked the docks – real, full-sized docks with multi-person ships and mooring posts. These docks stretched over a channel that smelled notably different than King Ban's bygone lagoon.

At night the squires come out. More accurately, at night folks go in, except for the squires. The squires still have jobs to do: repairing battle-armor, sharpening war-blades, brushing down mighty steeds, re-stocking saddle bags, laundering undergarments, mucking stalls and stalling the inevitable – the morrow – where it all begins again.

Gus nodded at a passing squire and gave a covert hand signal. The passing squire returned it, altered slightly. Gus gave a grateful nod. There was news from England.

"Which ship is le Fay's?" said Thomas.

They stopped. The bay held barges, sloops, catboats, a clipper, two barques and even a bilander.

Philip shook his head. "I bet they have special names for all these boats."

"I bet they do," said Thomas.

Gus bit his tongue.

There were red flags, green flags, blue flags and yellow. There was a checkered pennant, a striped pennant, and a pennant with a poorly drawn animal emblazoned on it.

"No black flags," said Philip.

Thomas frowned. "Maybe she already set sail."

"I'll find out, sirs," said Gus.

Thomas nodded. "Keep the inquiries quiet."

Gus saluted and stole away, Booker in tow.

Thomas and Philip turned again to watch the ships.

"What exactly is the plan here Thomas?"

"Find the witch, find the wizard."

Philip nodded. "There's an appealing simplicity to it, I'll give you that."

He chewed his lip.

"Any thoughts on the middle part?"

"The part where we stroll onto a witch-queen's ship and accuse her of wizard-napping?"

"Wizard-napping," Philip snorted. "Merlin's done quite a lot of that himself. Wait. You can't just stroll onto Morgan's ship and accuse her of wizard-napping."

Thomas shrugged.

"Morgan. Le. Fay. It's *Morgan le Fay*. Sorceress. Queen. Witch. She's a witch-queen. Are you mad?"

"Do you have a better idea?"

Better ideas flooded Philip's mind. None of them would help them find Merlin.

They stared at the barges, the sloops, the catboats, one clipper, two barques, and the bilander, and they waited.

"I think that one there is called a dinghy," said Philip.

It wasn't.

"Takes one to know one," said Thomas.

ණ

Morgan le Fay's ship cut silently through the whitecaps. Waves lapped at the hulls of other ships in the port, but no wave ever touched the *Midnight Corvette* twice. A philosopher had once remarked to the Witch-Queen that the same was true of any ship if you think about it. He'd never been heard from again.

Morgan's ship flew her true colors: black. She always did. Her owner enjoyed disguises just as much as the next illusionist, but there was no need. No one ever saw the *Midnight Corvette* coming.

ණ

Thomas' eyes passed over the barges, the sloops, the catboats, one clipper, two barques, the corvette and the bilander.

Philip's head slowly drooped.

Thomas squinted.

"Wait," he said. "One, two, three..."

Philip yawned and stretched.

"Was that black one there before?" asked Thomas.

Philip blinked.

A squad of guards came into view. They were moving in step. Their footsteps were rhythmic but muffled. Draped in black, they moved like the shadow of a predator. Steady, smooth, focused. In the center, a fair-skinned woman in midnight robes glided effortlessly.

"Le Fay," whispered Philip.

The squad fanned out at the corvette. Two guards took position at the foot of the gangplank. Two more stopped at the top. The Queen disappeared onto the deck with the remainder.

Thomas began to sense they weren't alone. He made himself still and listened. Stall awnings flapped in the night breeze. A bat fluttered overhead and disappeared. A buoy-bell tolled its lonely rhythm on the quiet sea. Nothing unusual, in other words. And then…

And then over top of it all came the unmistakable sounds of an out-of-breath squire towing a horse with ear, nose and throat issues. The sounds grew louder and louder until the pair came to a halt behind them.

"It's that one," panted Gus. He pointed.

"Thanks, Gus," said Philip, sarcastically. "Good detective work."

"I think you're slipping," said Thomas.

"Any other timely and pertinent information you'd care to share?" Philip taunted.

Gus glanced at him and addressed Thomas, "Well, sirs, you're not going to like it."

Philip's face fell. Of course there was more timely and pertinent information. And of course Gus had it. And of course it was bad news.

Thomas, for his part, was good at imagining bad news. He preferred, when there was bad news, that the deliverer simply tell him. It spared him from his own imagined versions which were usually much better examples of what he would legitimately call bad news.

"Tell us," said Thomas.

"The battle's won," said Gus. "Arthur's defeated the five kings."

"That was fast," said Philip.

"This is bad how?" said Thomas.

"Well," said Gus. "Several knights distinguished themselves and Pellinore's son Tor has been promoted."

"Hey, good for him," said Philip.

Thomas struggled to connect the dots. "But," he said, "that's got to make Gawain angry. Arthur favoring the son of the guy that killed his father."

Gus nodded. He was still standing rigid, his knuckles white on Booker's reins.

"But that's nothing new. There's something else," said Thomas.

Gus nodded. "It's Bagdemagus."

"Bagdema..." Philip floundered.

"Gus," finished Gus.

Thomas rubbed his forehead. "Remind me?"

"Table of Errant Companions," said Gus. "Cheerful fellow. Good heart. Bit of an idealist. You'd like him."

"How's a person supposed to keep track of all these people," said Philip.

Gus reached for his pack. "I keep a catalogue, sir, if you—"

"Not necessary," said Philip quickly.

"Word in the stables is that the promotion was going to go to Bagdemagus," said Gus.

"But Pellinore intervened," Thomas guessed.

Gus nodded. "Bagdemagus was disappointed, and..."

"And?"

"And he left."

"Seems like something an errant knight would do."

"Mhmm."

A terrible thought struck Thomas. "...and, like errant knights are wont to do, he committed to a quest."

Gus nodded. "He left and he swore he wouldn't return until he'd redeemed his honor."

"This is a fun story," said Philip, "but–"

"He swore to find Merlin," said Gus.

Booker snorted. Gus realized he was being heavy on his reins and let up.

"But that's *our* quest," said Philip. It struck Philip that this was the kind of sentiment that would normally have been expressed by Thomas. It struck him that perhaps he, Philip, was getting a little too close to things. He turned to Thomas.

Thomas wasn't there.

Philip stared at the spot where Thomas had been standing. He peered behind Booker. He scanned the shuttered market stalls, the dark alley entrances, the rooftops, the dock...

Morgan le Fay's guards parted. Thomas strolled up and onto the *Midnight Corvette.*

"He's just strolled onto Morgan le Fay's ship," said Philip incredulously. "He's just–" Philip groaned with frustration and took off after him.

Booker looked at Gus. Gus looked at Booker.

"Nope. No how. No way," said Gus. "I've had enough of sailing. And ships. And sailing ships. And besides," he said, eyeing the guards, "there are places knights can go that squires and their noble war steeds can't." Gus led Booker toward the stables. "You and me, Booker," said Gus. "We're the sane ones."

৵

Gus' chattering and Booker's whinnying faded as they departed the square. After some discussion, Philip crested the gangplank and disappeared onto the corvette. The stall awnings rustled in the salty night breeze.

A shadow detached from an alleyway. A small figure pulled a dark hood close. The figure slipped gracefully along the dock. If anyone had noticed her, they might have compared her movement to the midnight queen. But an illusionist's business is helping people see what they want to see, and this is precisely what the guards saw: no one else boarded the *Midnight Corvette* that night.

৵

"The Queen will see you now," said the blackguard. He turned and entered the corvette's forecastle. Thomas delayed a moment. Philip eyed him nervously. And then Thomas followed the guard, and it was all Philip could do to keep up.

Morgan le Fay sat imperiously on an ornate wooden throne with dark upholstery. King Uriens sat beside her on an equally hefty but less ostentatious contrivance.

Everything was gilded. Aside from the close quarters, the profusion of teak, the gentle rocking and – Thomas supposed – the parrot, he might think he was in a cramped wooden palace rather than aboard a ship.

The Queen waved a long hand.

Two chairs were produced, and Thomas and Philip were sat firmly upon them.

The Queen waved her hand.

A servant boy appeared at her elbow and filled first Morgan's glass and then Uriens' tankard with a dark red liquid.

The Queen waved her hand.

A servant girl appeared with a bowl full of something. She presented the bowl to the Queen with a curtsey. The Queen selected a morsel from the bowl and motioned the girl toward the guests. Uriens seemed content with his tankard.

The Queen waved her hand.

Nothing happened.

"Speak," she said to Thomas.

"Oh," said Thomas. "Um–"

"Greetings your majesties," squawked the parrot.

Except it wasn't a parrot. Thomas had assumed the bird perched in the shadowy alcove near Morgan was a parrot, but on closer examination it definitely was not.

"G...reetings, Your Majesties," said Thomas, eyeing the pigeon.

"Squawk I bring tidings from squawk."

Thomas glared at the bird.

"Squawk I bring–"

"I bring tidings from King Arthur," said Thomas over the pigeon. He was fascinated and frustrated, but he wasn't about to go on parroting a pigeon the rest of the night. He rushed to continue. "We're here to–"

"Who," interrupted the Queen, "are you?"

"I am…" said Thomas. He looked in the bowl offered to him. It was filled with chocolate balls.

"Squawk. Straining our patience. Squawk."

"...Sir Thomas the Hesitant," said Thomas, "of the Table of Less... er, Errant Companions, Your Majesty."

"Less Errant Companions," said Morgan. "That's a new one. But it's about time."

Philip took a chocolate ball and smiled at the servant girl. He grabbed two more before she could turn away. He popped one in his mouth.

"And who is this who eats before the Queen?"

Thomas kicked the leg of Philip's chair. Philip bit down. His eyes watered and he whimpered, startled.

"This is Sir Philip the Disadvantaged of the Table of Less Valued Knights," said Thomas.

Philip blinked. As he chewed his expression slid from shock to delight to dismay. "It's grog," he said. "They've got grog in them."

"Grog?" said Morgan. "Grog?!" Her eyes flashed and her jaw muscle flexed. She seemed to peer directly into Philip's soul. "Grog is for those who frequent bilges. This is Gorean rum and midnight chocolate. Why are you here?"

"Off with their heads squawk."

Philip carefully placed his remaining chocolates on the table before him and watched the bird.

"My apologies," said Morgan glaring at the pigeon. "He wasn't always like this."

"Rude?" said Thomas.

"A pigeon," said Morgan. "He's upset." She glared at the bird. "As well he should be."

"Bad bird! Bad bird squawk," said the pigeon.

There was an awkward moment of silence.

The pigeon busied itself with a seed ball.

"Tell me," said Morgan, "for what urgent cause do the less errant and less valued members of my brother's court inflict their presences this evening upon the Queen and King of Gore?"

Thomas' face contorted.

"Gore the country," whispered Philip. "Not, you know, blood and brains and things," said Philip.

"Oh," said Thomas. "I thought we were in Gall."

"Gaul," corrected Philip. "We are."

"Right. Thank you," whispered Thomas.

"They're King and Queen here too," said Philip.

"But really?" said Thomas. "Gall and gore?" He chuckled. "I mean who would–"

"What urgent matter," repeated the Queen. Her voice bore the dangerously unamused tone mice fear in cats.

"Right," said Thomas. "We're seeking Merlin. And we have reason to believe you may have something to do with his disappearance."

The only thing that moved for the next several moments was the ship itself. Which of course meant that everything was moving. Thomas began to worry this may be his last accurate and unhelpful observation.

A wide, red smile spread across Morgan's fair face. It didn't touch her eyes. Those were as cold and calculating as a tax collector in December.

"Of course I have," she said.

Thomas was ready for this. He'd let the righteous anger build inside him in anticipation and now he opened the blast door and let her have it.

"Don't you dare deny it Your Majesty." He actually rose a little from his seat as the words piled out on top of each other.

Morgan didn't react.

Philip put a hand on his shoulder and pulled Thomas back down onto the chair.

"She's not," he said.

Thomas mentally reviewed the conversation.

"Oh," he said.

"Merlin and I," said Morgan – the corner of her lip pulled up as she articulated the wizard's name – "have had our... disagreements, but I assure you he is safe."

"Prove it," said Thomas.

Philip, both impressed with Thomas and concerned he might be sitting within the impending blast radius, let his hand drop from Thomas' shoulder.

"I'm happy to," said Morgan casually. "But I'm curious why your concern is for your court wizard and not for your King."

Thomas glanced at Philip. Philip gave a small, bewildered shrug.

"Pardon?" said Thomas.

Morgan snickered. "There certainly won't be any of *those* if we don't find my brother."

Won't be any… pardons? thought Thomas. It sounded like a threat. But he didn't need to be pardoned for anything. Did he? Thomas felt whatever control of the conversation he might have had slipping away. "Arthur is missing?" he guessed.

"That's why we," said Uriens joining the conversation with an expansive wave of his tankard, "thought you were here."

"We, um," said Thomas. "We didn't know."

Morgan's pose relaxed ever so slightly.

"Of course you didn't, dear. How could you? Are you a sorcerer? Do you have the sight?" She laughed and took a sip from her glass, her eyes never left them. "Tell them, Uriens." She bit into her midnight chocolate.

"The battle went smashingly," Uriens began. "Quite literally I might add. Smashing all around. I do prefer the hammer for just that reason. Can't convince Arthur of course. He's keen on the sword. Always has been. Can't count it against him I suppose after the bit with the stone and the lady in the lake and so on. You don't hear about many magic hammers now do you? Thor, I suppose–"

Morgan shifted abruptly. Uriens jerked. Morgan smiled. "The hunt, dear, tell them of the hunt."

"Right," said Uriens, "so there we were. Done with the battle, and Arthur wanted to celebrate so he says, 'Uriens old friend let's go hunting.' And so we do because if a king asks you to hunt, you hunt. Hang on," he said. "I'm a king."

"Yes dear, you're a king," said Morgan. "And so is Arthur."

Uriens muttered to himself. Then he shrugged and continued. "Anyway, so we went on a hunt. Arthur, myself and Accolon. Soon enough we spot a magnificent hart, and we set chase. Well we followed this hart through glen and vale, over bridge and brook until night falls, and finally the hound howls in the dark and Arthur spots the prey pinned down and exhausted. So he blows the horn meaning of course we got him."

Uriens sat back, eyes bright.

"And the mysterious ship, dear," prompted Morgan with practiced patience.

"Right!" said Uriens. He glanced in his tankard, frowned at it, and held it out to the servant.

"By this time it's too late to go back. Too dark. So we're looking for a place to camp, and we realize we don't have anything to camp with, and that's when Arthur spots the ship. Black silk sails and drapery all the way down to the water. Just moored there on the side of the river like it's been there the whole time. Which it wasn't if you ask me. All lit up with lanterns. And Arthur takes a look at it and his eyes light up and he says he's sure it's safe. That's the thing about being a king. You can say things like 'It's safe,' and then it's got to be because the King said so..."

Uriens' forehead wrinkled. "Supposed to be like that anyway."

Morgan cleared her throat.

"So we head onto the ship and there are a lot," Uriens chuckled, "I mean a *lot* of–" He glanced at Morgan. "–not entirely unseemly maidens running things."

"Twelve," said Morgan, glaring.

"Aye," said Uriens. "Twelve." His eyes sparkled.

"Well," he said, "they feed us – Arthur, Accolon and I – and help us take off our boots and it's getting late and most of us are married so we says as much and these fine young ladies conduct us to separate bed chambers there on the pretty ship. I laid down, fell asleep, and woke up right here on the *Midnight Corvette*."

He took a swig from his tankard and shook his head.

"Darnedest thing," he muttered.

"Accolon?" said Thomas. "The Black Knight? Really? Arthur went hunting with Sir Accolon?"

Morgan's eyes narrowed. "My brother went hunting with his sister's husband and her champion to celebrate their victory."

Thomas felt rebuked. The rule was simple. One was family, or one was not.

"Of course, Your Majesty," he said.

Morgan relaxed again, which wasn't saying much.

"My brother is missing," she said. "But I have divined where he might be, and now I have two of his knights before me, ready to serve no doubt?"

"How can we help?" said Thomas.

"Wherever Arthur is, he is lacking one important thing."

"What's that?"

"Excalibur," said Morgan.

Thomas sat up.

"Where is Excalibur?"

"Here of course," said Morgan. "You seem surprised. We are family," she explained. "Who better to guard the royal enchanted sword than his sister the so-called Witch-Queen? Excalibur is larger than Arthur. It represents the kingdom. Arthur is wise. He'd rather rebellious kings join the kingdom, so he does not attack them with the very symbol of that kingdom. But now," she dropped eye contact for the first time, "I believe he needs it."

"So," she said. "You can chase your court wizard. I suspect he is chasing this charlatan Nimue. Or," she held Thomas' gaze, "you can deliver Excalibur to Arthur, and when you have done, I will tell you exactly where to find Merlin."

Thomas swallowed.

Philip reached absentmindedly for a chocolate ball, realized what he was doing, and stopped.

Nodding toward Philip, Thomas asked, "Can we–" his voice cracked, "–have some time to consider things? Privately?"

Morgan smiled. "Of course," she said. "Take all the time you need." She waved a hand at the blackguard. The blackguard opened a door to a side chamber. When Thomas and Philip passed through, she said, "The *Midnight Corvette* sails in five minutes."

The door snapped shut.

&

Inside the forecastle, Morgan rolled a chocolate ball between two fingers. Her eyes tightened. "So Merlin is missing..."

She popped the ball whole in her mouth and crushed it with her molars.

"How delicious," she said.

CHAPTER XIV

A TRAP SPRUNG

Thomas and Philip found themselves in a room built like a vault. The space was smaller but less cramped than the Royal Mess they'd just left. It should be noted that no one called it the Royal Mess to the Witch-Queen's face. Not twice anyway. Currently in the vault off the mess were three things: Thomas, Philip, and Excalibur.

The sword floated inside a glass case in the center of the vault.

"Is that?" said Thomas.

"Can't be," said Philip.

A soft glow emanated from the area of the sword and illuminated their faces.

Thomas leaned in and read the inscription on the blade. "Says 'Excalibur' right on there."

Philip rubbed his chin.

"Well I'll be," he said. "Still..."

Thomas straightened up.

"Still what?"

"Could be a trap."

Thomas nodded sagely. "Like for instance, you go to grab the sword and blades come down and chop off your arm. That sort of thing?" He looked for concealed slots in the walls and ceiling.

"No, I mean this whole thing. Urien's story. Morgan's deal. Could be a trap."

They stared at the sword.

"She *is* his sister," said Thomas. "And," he gestured at Excalibur, "Arthur obviously trusts her."

Philip frowned.

"On the other hand, it's Morgan le Fay, the Witch-Queen," said Thomas.

"Who your baron conspired with in an attempt to poison... everyone," said Philip.

"Says the baron," said Thomas.

"Didn't you see them together?"

"Yes, but that's what nobility do. They get seen together."

Thomas shrugged.

"It's probably a trap." He sighed. "But what if it's true? What if Arthur is in trouble? And why would Morgan want us to take Excalibur to him if he didn't need it? Why would she trust us with it?"

"Maybe she doesn't," said Philip. "Maybe she thinks we'll fail."

The ire rose in Thomas. "I'm sick and tired of everyone betting against us, Philip." Thomas felt the room grow hot. He forced himself to breathe.

"Let's think through this," he said.

"There's the hesitant friend I know," said Philip.

"Okay," said Thomas, "worst case scenarios. One, we ignore Morgan's story, and we go after Merlin."

Philip chewed his lip. "Worst case? We never find him, because we don't know where to look. Meanwhile Arthur is murdered by whoever sent the slumber-ship. Morgan takes over, brands us traitors for failing Arthur, and takes the pigeon's advice."

"The pigeon's advice?"

"Off with their heads," said Philip.

Thomas nodded. "Right. Okay, worst case scenario number two. We go after Arthur."

"Worst case," said Philip. "It turns out Morgan is lying. It's a trap. We fall into it. Morgan takes over. We're probably to blame. Or we're dead. Or both."

Thomas grimaced. "Alright no clear victor there. Pros and cons."

"Go."

"We go for Merlin," said Thomas. "Pro: We could be heroes and finally gain some respect for the Table of Less Valued Knights."

Philip nodded.

"Cons," said Thomas. "We don't know where Merlin is. We blow our only lead. And by not going after Arthur, we could destroy the kingdom."

"And our reputation," added Philip.

"And our reputation," said Thomas.

"Kind of a wash," said Philip.

"Scenario two. We go after Arthur," said Thomas. "Pro: We could be heroes, save Merlin *and* Arthur and really put the Less Valued on the map."

Philip raised his eyebrows and grinned in consideration of the hypothetical glory.

"Cons," said Thomas, "We're getting our information from Morgan le Fay, a source with a certain dubious reputation. And by going after *both* Arthur and Merlin we could fail to help either and–"

"And actively contribute to the usurpation of the kingdom," said Philip.

"If we survive," said Thomas. He shrugged. "Bit of a wash there too," he said.

Philip scratched his arm. Thomas rubbed the back of his head.

"Thinking isn't helping," said Thomas.

"Overrated in situations like this I'm told," said Philip.

"Yeah?"

"Yep. Mum would say, 'Follow your heart.' What does your heart say?"

Thomas stared at Excalibur and tried to listen to his heart.

After a moment, Philip said, "Well?"

"Unclear," said Thomas.

"Then there's only one thing to do," said Philip.

"What's that?"

"Flip a coin."

"Philip, I'm not letting a coin flip decide the fate of humanity."

"Well," said Philip, "for one, it's not all of humanity we're talking about. Just our little corner of it here. And two, you won't be. It's just to see what the coin says. What you pay attention to, see, is how your heart reacts. If you like what the coin says, great. If you don't like it, then you know what you need to do."

Thomas considered this.

"Couldn't hurt," said Thomas.

"Can't hurt," agreed Philip.

Thomas fumbled around and produced one of the coins the port authority had given him.

"Let's say heads we go after Arthur, tails Merlin." said Philip.

Thomas turned the coin over. He turned it again.

"Heads Arthur," prompted Philip.

"Both sides are heads," said Thomas. "It's got Morgan's face on both sides."

"Oh," said Philip. "Hmm."

"Doesn't matter," said Thomas.

"No?"

Thomas knocked on the vault door.

The door opened. The blackguard ushered them into the forecastle.

"You've decided?" said Morgan.

"Yes, Your Majesty," said Thomas.

❧

It just felt right, Thomas later remembered thinking. It still felt right when the three of them, Thomas, Philip, and Morgan le Fay, stood once more in the vault before the sword.

"I can see my brother's choice in champions has improved," said Morgan. "You've made the right decision." She seemed... proud.

"You must know," she said, "that the scabbard is as important as the sword. Excalibur cuts steel, yes. And it's the symbol of office, yes. But–" She paused to make sure Thomas was paying attention.

He pulled his eyes from the sword and looked at Morgan.

"The scabbard prevents exsanguination."

Thomas nodded carefully.

"He may bleed, but it won't be his death," she clarified.

"Ah," said Thomas. "Wow."

"Because," Philip laughed with sudden insight, "if you have the scabbard, you'll keep the sword sheathed. Die by the sword, live by the sheathe, that sort of thing."

Morgan studied him. "If that's what you wish," she said.

The ship lurched.

Thomas caught his balance, then panicked. "Gus! We need my squire. And my horse."

Morgan gave a dismissive gesture. "I had them brought aboard while you were deliberating your wisest course of action."

"Oh," said Thomas. The panic dissipated, and an unsettled feeling took up residence in its stead. "Thank you." It seemed to be what he was supposed to say.

They retired to the forecastle where Morgan waved her hand, glasses were filled, and chocolates were served.

"These are very good," said Thomas. "We should take some to Gus."

Philip chose not to partake.

Thomas beckoned to the servant girl. "We'd like to take some of the chocolates to our friend," he said.

She curtsied and fetched a bowl.

"That's a different girl," said Thomas. "Isn't she?"

Philip squinted.

"Could be," he said.

The girl returned.

"Were you here earlier?" said Thomas.

The girl didn't answer.

"It's just that you look..." Thomas peered at her "...familiar."

She tilted her head so her hair obscured her face. "Your chocolates, sir," she said. She held them out to Thomas with one hand and clutched her throat meekly with the other.

Morgan rose. "We'll beat the sun to England," she said. "A cabin is prepared for you. The guard will conduct you when you're ready."

Perhaps it was the sugar. Perhaps it was something else. A warm feeling welled up in Thomas. For the first time since Fogbottom, Thomas felt as though he had his feet under him. He stood up. It reinforced the feeling.

"My Queen," he said. "We will deliver the sword to your brother." He swayed a bit. Perhaps it was the ship. "We will not fail."

Morgan smiled. "For the kingdom, my champion." She turned and glided out of the room. Uriens woke with a start and followed.

Alone in the forecastle, Thomas and Philip grinned at each other.

"That went well, I think," said Philip.

Thomas nodded. "I feel like we're finally headed in the right direction," he said.

As they followed the blackguard to their cabin Thomas remarked, "I should get Marie one of those cameo necklaces all the French girls wear."

❧

Morgan le Fay's *Midnight Corvette* cut soundlessly across the dark channel. Even with her speed and disturbing ability to travel in a straight line, it would be some time before landfall. Philip snored. Gus and Booker were bedded down elsewhere. Thomas closed his eyes, relaxed his neck and shoulders, and tried to allow the gentle rocking of the ship to do its work.

He fidgeted. He rolled to one side. He stared at the dull light beneath the cabin door. He rolled to his other side.

He was too exhausted to sleep.

Beyond bushed, straight-through tuckered-out, well-past weary, on the other side of plain done-in, there in the gloomy fog of restlessness, a notion waited. Thomas smacked right into it.

"I'm an idiot," he said.

He rolled out of the bunk and rifled through his pack. When he'd found what he was looking for he slipped out of the room, careful not to disturb Philip. He headed for the vault.

❧

Thomas reached the vault door unchallenged. There didn't seem to be a single guard on duty. He reached for the vault door and stopped just short of touching the latch.

Something wasn't right. There wasn't a single guard on duty? There was no one guarding a vault containing Arthur's most precious treasure...

He fumbled with the bundle he had extracted from his pack and unveiled Pyralis' looking glass.

"*This* will show me what I want to see."

Traps, suggested Thomas' sluggish, over-worked brain.

He frowned. "No, this will show me what I *don't* want to see. And I don't want to not see the traps. So…"

He rubbed his forehead. "A person shouldn't be expected to work out things like this in the middle of the night."

He sighed, closed his eyes to focus, and talked himself through it. "I don't want to not see traps, and the mirror will show me what I don't want, which is to not see traps. So, I won't."

Well that's rather useless, he thought. And then: "Aha. Unless what I want to see is what's really there. And what I want to see is traps. So if they're here…"

He was back in business.

"This will cut through your dastardly illusions, Morgan le Fay."

He angled the mirror at the door. The reflection was a spitting image of itself. Thomas angled the mirror at the latch. It too looked remarkably the same. He shook the mirror.

"Should've asked more questions," he said.

He shrugged, grabbed the latch, and pushed. The vault door swung open without incident.

Thomas listened for silent alarms. He wondered what a silent alarm would sound like. He scanned the immediate environment with the looking glass. The mirror-vault looked just like the real one. He stepped inside and closed the door behind him.

Excalibur floated in its glass case just as it had before. Being in the same room with it did something to a person. It felt good. Thomas had seldom been in the presence of valuable property, but when he had been, it had always made him a bit nervous. Excalibur had the opposite effect. He felt safe.

It made perfect sense for Excalibur to make a person feel like that. It also made perfect sense, Thomas suspected, for a well-crafted magic trap to make a person feel like that.

"Alright," he said. "Moment of truth."

He angled the looking glass and peered into it.

The mirror-sword floated and shined and glowed in the mirror-case just like the real one. But there was something else. He squinted. Tiny red filaments, almost invisible, wrapped the hilt and stretched toward–

Something moved on the other side of the vault door. Footsteps padded softly, the latch jiggled. Thomas panicked and pressed himself as flat as he could against the wall beside the door.

The door swung open slowly and concealed him. The footsteps paused. Thomas tried not to breathe. He focused all his attention on the other side of the open door. A soft rustling of clothing meant the wearer was moving carefully.

Thomas slowly stretched his arm and angled the mirror.

There was a small figure hunched at the sword. The figure turned its head.

It was the old lady that led them to the dragon. Lizard. Dragon. Whatever it was, that was the old woman.

"You!" said Thomas and stepped out from behind the door.

The woman froze with her back toward Thomas.

"What are you doing here?" said Thomas.

She turned.

"Um, cleaning?" said the servant girl from the forecastle.

Thomas gasped and took a step back.

That was definitely the servant girl. That was her cameo. She noticed Thomas notice the necklace, and she clutched it.

Thomas looked around. Could the girl have come in too? Could the old lady be hiding somewhere? She couldn't have been that fast.

The mirror glinted and caught Thomas' eye.

"It can't be," he said. He aimed the mirror. In the reflection, where the servant girl should be, there was the old lady.

The girl frowned at the mirror. "What is that?" she snapped. Then she caught herself and tried again in a tone as casual as a cat asking a bird about its feathers. "I mean—" She cleared her throat. "That's a lovely looking glass you have there. May I see it?"

"Who are you? What are you doing here?" said Thomas.

All pretense evaporated. The girl's face contorted with fierce determination. "I know who you are Sir Thomas the Hesitant," she said. She snapped her wrist and a thin baton appeared in her hand. She raised it over the glass case. "I will not allow you to complete your mission."

She brought the baton down. The glass shattered. A thousand tiny glass splinters cascaded onto the vault floor.

"There was a handle–" said Thomas.

"You should have stayed in the cave."

She reached for the sword.

"Wait!" said Thomas.

She grasped the hilt. There was a flash, a whimper, and then the girl fell straight through the floor.

There was a resonant sploosh beneath him and a soft scraping of teak against teak as a trap door slid perfectly back into place.

The sword floated and glowed and generally went about its business unperturbed.

Thomas stared at the space where the girl had been. He pursed his lips. He pondered the sword. He scratched the back of his head. He glanced around at all the broken glass.

"Well," he said. "This won't be easy to explain."

CHAPTER XV

THE ADVENTURE ORDAINED

"None of this surprises me," said the Queen.

Summoned by the fracas in the vault – or perhaps by the blaring of silent magical alarms beyond Thomas' ken – the blackguard had arrived and escorted Thomas to the ship's deck. There he had awaited the dawn. The sun had risen and revealed the coast, and still he waited. Now, as the *Midnight Corvette* stole into port, Morgan le Fay had swept onto the deck. She looked fresh and regal and none the worse for having spent the night at sea. Thomas' weary body did its best to keep his frazzled mind upright. Or perhaps it was the other way 'round. He was too exhausted to sort it out.

"It doesn't?" he managed.

"My brother has been king-napped. My own champion is missing. Why do you think I set traps?"

Thomas nodded blearily. He wished he was also napped. No. He wished he was napping. Not king-napping, just napping. Knight-napping. Though any time of day would do. Now, for example.

"What kind of seeress would I be if some skelpie-limmer could slip aboard, bluff her way past my blackguard, and prance away with a magic sword entrusted to my keeping?"

Thomas closed his eyes against the bright morning light. Something she said wasn't right.

"There were no guards," he said.

"In any case," the Queen ignored him, "you've proven yourself a worthy protector of the sword."

Thomas felt as though he should feel relieved that she wasn't angry with him. He was too tired to muster the emotion. Instead he nodded and allowed himself a nice long blink to rest his eyes.

He'd open them in just a moment.

The Queen was talking at him again. With great effort, he focused.

"You will take the sword and travel west. Beyond the Summer Country you will find the castle of the false knight, Damas."

"Dumb..." said Thomas. "Pardon?"

"Damas," whispered Gus behind him. "Rhymes with Thomas."

"Oh," said Thomas wobbling gently. "You've heard of him?"

"No sir," said Gus.

"Oh," said Thomas.

"But the Witch-Queen just said his name," said Gus.

"Right," said Thomas. "Did I miss anything else? I was just resting my eyes for a moment." He closed his eyes to demonstrate.

Philip put a hand on Thomas' back to steady him.

Morgan continued, "Damas and his brother Ontzlake hold my brother, your King. You will find Arthur. You will deliver the sword. You will not fail."

She nodded to a blackguard who stepped forward and presented the sword to Thomas.

Thomas swayed and reached for it. Remembering the invisible trap, he stopped and pulled his hand back.

Morgan laughed. "No more traps. No more tricks," she said. "The sword-bearer is safe to bear the sword." She waved her hand mysteriously.

Thomas frowned and reached to grasp the hilt.

"No–" said Morgan. "Don't touch that part."

Thomas reached with both hands and, eyeing Morgan, accepted the sheathed blade from the blackguard. When nothing exploded and he hadn't turned into something abysmal and the deck remained solid beneath him, he exhaled.

Morgan inhaled through her teeth. "Nope. Don't hold it that way. Look, just strap it to your horse and–" She did a double-take at Booker.

She squinted at his head.

"What an odd horse," she said.

She eyed Booker for a moment longer. Booker shifted his feet nervously. Then he adjusted his posture and lifted his head in a very horse-like manner.

Thomas had the distinct impression that Booker was trying very hard to appear as horse-ish as he possibly could. Protective anger burst into flame in Thomas' chest. He opened his mouth to defend his horse, but a thought that had been rising through Thomas' groggy mind like a bubble through a jar of molasses finally broke the surface. He said instead, "Why aren't *you* doing this?"

Morgan turned her attention back to Thomas. "Doing what?"

"Arthur gave Excalibur to you to protect. Why aren't you taking it to..."

"Damas's," said Gus.

"The false castle," said Thomas. He glanced at the ship's forecastle. "The faux-castle haha." Gus alone was amused, but he was too frightened to show it. "It's funny because you've got one too." He did his best to imitate a sailor, "A *fo-ksel.* That's how they say it." He grinned and pointed at the forecastle. Philip was shaking his head inconspicuously at him. No one else seemed to be in the mood for clever wordplay. *Fine*, he thought, and retraced the steps of the conversation. *Aha.*

Thomas straightened up and let the humor drain from of his face. "Why aren't *you* taking Excalibur to the false knight's castle?" he demanded.

He immediately regretted asking the question.

ฺ

There were stories about people questioning witch-queens. They were harrowing tales uniquely suited to their purposes which were (1) to discourage the average person from going around questioning witch-queens and (2) to highlight the bravery of those heroes and heroines who placed themselves in mortal peril when they did so. There were not, on the other hand, any stories about people questioning Morgan le Fay. There *was* a story about an attempt to tell such a story. It went like this…

Storyteller: And then the poor sap questioned the Witch-Queen!

Audience: Gasp. No, he didn't.

Storyteller: It's true.

Audience: Was he mad?!

Storyteller: By definition, I should say.

Audience: What happened to him after that?

Storyteller: If you really want to know what happened to him after that…

Audience: Yes?

Storyteller: You'll have to ask the Witch-Queen.

Thomas, it should be noted, was questioning Morgan le Fay not because he was feeling particularly brave or heroic, but because he was exhausted and puzzled and not at all aware that he was becoming a character in a story that hadn't yet been told.

ൻ

Morgan's gaze pierced Thomas. A moment ago he'd struggled to keep his eyes open. Now he found himself unable to blink. He was afraid to move, and afraid that if he tried he would discover that he couldn't.

"I would have sent Accolon," Morgan said slowly. "But you'll recall my champion has also been abducted."

The edges of Thomas' vision began to darken. He became aware he wasn't breathing. Morgan's eyes narrowed and…

She sighed and looked away.

Thomas blinked. He was surprised to find that he could. He allowed himself to breathe. That too was remarkably successful.

"And," said Morgan, "one of us can travel unencumbered by the obligations of royalty, and that person isn't me. Anyone with the truculent pugnacity to go after Excalibur will be going after Morgan le Fay, not some..." She waved a hand. "...Less Errant Knight."

The recent fright and subsequent rush of oxygen brought Thomas a welcome clarity of mind. He ignored her insult and focused on the implication – she was banking on his *lack* of reputation.

But, Thomas recalled, the thief in the night had known his name.

"Is the old lady behind all this?" Thomas blurted.

"What old lady?" said Morgan.

"The old lady... or... the girl I guess. In the vault."

Morgan was eyeing him again. Thomas braced himself.

"The girl that sprung the trap," he said.

Morgan cackled haughtily. "I'm sure she's nothing but a putterer. No doubt a minion of this interloper, Nimue, that has beguiled my brother's court wizard."

There was a clatter and commotion as sailors secured the corvette to the dock and deployed her gangplank.

"Let the sea worry about the girl. You deliver the sword." Her eyes sparkled. She seemed almost giddy. "It's only fitting that Arthur receive this sword from the hand of his own loyal champion."

She turned to depart.

"You're going after Nimue then?" asked Thomas.

"*I* go to Camelot to aid my brother's wife while she governs the kingdom in his absence. *You*," said Morgan, "should hurry."

She disembarked and allowed Uriens to help her into a waiting carriage. Thomas watched the carriage depart surrounded by mounted blackguard.

His head felt heavy. His shoulders felt heavy. His arms felt heavy. His hands– There was something in his hands. He looked down.

"Uther's boot, I've got Excalibur," he said.

"Let's just put that right here, sir," said Gus. He helped Thomas strap the sword to Booker. Booker seemed unhappy about it, but the old horse's protests were more pitiable than productive, and the sword was secured in short order.

Everything was squared away. Thomas teetered vacantly. Gus broke the silence.

"Are you certain about this, sir?"

Thomas snapped alert. "Never been better," he said.

"Sir?"

"Of course I'm tired. Thank you for asking. But it's no excuse."

"Excuse for... Are you alright sir?"

"Never been better," said Thomas. He frowned. "Déjà vu," he mumbled. He shook himself and blinked in the sun. "I'm absolutely alright. We've got a mission. Finally. A purpose."

He put a foot on Booker's stirrup. He tried to step up, but his boot slipped and slapped the deck. Gus braced him and helped him aboard Booker. Thomas sat tall on his derelict steed atop the royal ship. The morning sun glinted on the Channel.

"Have you slept, sir?" said Gus. "Perhaps we should tie a rope..."

"Nonsense, I'll be fine," said Thomas waving him away. "Boys–"

Philip frowned.

"Men," said Thomas, "we know where we're going, we know where we are, and we know where we've been. We've got a magic sword, a king to rescue, and a kingdom to save."

Gus grinned. "The adventure ordained," he said.

"S'right," said Thomas. "To the Summer Country! To Arthur! To glory!"

Booker carried him down the gangplank. Gravity carried him the rest of the way to the dock. He was asleep when he hit the platform with a heavy thump and a muffled tinkle of shattering glass.

Gus and Philip grimaced at each other. Thomas snored contentedly.

In silence, they lifted the slumbering knight errant back onto Booker and headed west.

❧

Elisante stoked the campfire.

After the initial shock of being dumped into the Channel, she'd swum for miles buoyed by rage. The adrenaline rush had made her want to fly through the water, but she reasoned survival would be a test of endurance rather than speed. She resolved three things in her heart while she swam. One, stay afloat. Two, keep a steady pace to avoid muscle cramps. Three, destroy Sir Thomas the Hesitant who obviously had no qualms whatsoever with conspiring to destroy imperfect but just kings and kingdoms, making backroom deals to become a real knight, and dumping heroines in the middle of the blasted sea to drown. At night! In the cold.

She had eventually dragged herself ashore, seething, and made camp in short order. There had been a lot of vigorous snapping of branches and overly assertive arranging of rocks and logs. A dry bush stood no chance; it became kindling. A nearby sapling would never see the forest canopy, not in a hundred years. A fish which had had the misfortune to make Elisante's abrupt acquaintance now dangled over the fire, impaled on a makeshift skewer.

The sun slowly rose over a scene where everything was either steaming – the dew-laden grass, the fish, Elisante's clothes – or steaming mad.

Elisante shivered as her soggy clothes dried. She refused to disrobe and hang them. She didn't know where she was exactly. She huddled closer to the flames. She muttered angry nonsense.

After a while, she slept. After another while, she woke. Her clothes were damp and stiff. She foresaw chafing in her near future. She didn't care. She revived her flagging campfire and sat and stared and brooded.

Doubts crept in with the morning fog. The forces forming against Camelot were powerful. She had raw talent, that much had been proven, but what did she hope to accomplish pitting herself against these people? And to what end? Her thoughts turned to her parents. Maybe she shouldn't have left. Her hand moved absentmindedly to the cameo.

The forest, for the most part, went about its business. Woodland creatures foraged. Nocturnal predators slumbered. Ancient oak trees drew nourishment from the earth and lifted it to the sun.

An acorn landed with a thump beside Elisante. She glared at it. She picked it up. She spotted another and collected that one too. Near the line where the forest carpet gave way to beach she found what she was looking for – a stone similar in size and shape to her acorns.

She placed the two acorns and the stone on a stump near the fire, and then she sat down and stared.

ෙ

The breakfast fish hung dry and shriveled and forgotten over smoking sticks that had been a campfire. A few hundred feet away, Elisante hid in a thicket and watched the deer path. Three objects were nestled there – two acorns and a stone.

A person learned in tree husbandry or basic forestry might have wondered about acorns lying on a deer path in early summer. Falling acorns are generally an autumn experience. These were not the thoughts running through Elisante's head. They were however the thoughts of the squirrel that had just rounded the bend.

It drew up short. Elisante held her breath.

The squirrel crept closer and sniffed. It listened. It shot a wary look down the path. It eyed the trees quizzically.

After a moment it shrugged, stuffed its cheeks, and loped back the way it had come.

"Yes," hissed Elisante.

The squirrel startled and spat out the stone.

Elisante clamped a hand over her mouth. Her other hand moved to her cameo, but she stopped it. This had to work without direct manipulation. That was the whole point.

The squirrel sniffed.

Elisante stopped breathing.

Keeping its eyes on the path, the squirrel reached down slowly and picked up the stone. And then it disappeared into the foliage with its treasures.

"Yes," said Elisante.

The illusion had stuck. It was a small success, literally, but it was a success. She stood and brushed herself off.

"Fooling vermin is one thing," she said, thinking out loud. "Fooling humans is another." Knights, she supposed, were somewhere in between.

She followed the deer path until it crossed a hunting track. She followed the hunting track to a crosscut. She followed the crosscut to a road. The road led to civilization, and from there it was easy to pick up her quarry's trail: Two unlikely knights, a portly squire and a feeble runny-nosed horse all trying to behave inconspicuously are just the sort of travelers people tend to notice.

~

There was a rustling in the tree branches overlooking Elisante's abandoned campsite. There may have also been some giggling. But trees don't giggle. So there probably wasn't.

CHAPTER XVI

THE PRINCE OF THE SUMMER COUNTRY

On their second day of travel, Thomas, Philip, Gus and Booker reached Solsbury Hill in Somerset. The bucolic vista was worthy of a fairy tale. A stone bridge arched over the River Avon. Tall green and golden grasses swayed in soft breezes. Songbirds whistled and darted between blooming willows. Heavy bees laden with pollen bobbled from one happy wildflower to the next. Above it all, puffy white clouds floated lazily in a canary blue sky.

If human experience stopped there, things would have been a great deal more tolerable. But it doesn't. Willow, grass, and nettle pollen waged war on sinuses and tear ducts. Horse flies harassed, biting flesh and burrowing in hair. The sun on their faces felt like they were standing too close to the fire. And the humidity had reached a percentage one normally only encounters under water. The Summer Country in the summer was a wonderful place to look at but a bothersome place to be.

In short, the weather was heavy. It inspired slouching and labored breathing which is how the party was occupying itself now atop the hill. The country was spread out below them with all of its moisture-engorged flora, meandering fat bees, and annoyingly cheerful songbirds.

"What's that?" said Thomas. Philip squinted. Gus stepped up beside him.

"It's a tent," stated Philip.

Gus gasped. "It's a pavilion," he declared.

A colorful tent had been erected in the field below them. A shield in matching colors hung on a pennant-post next to it. A man in shining armor sat on a stump outside the tent. He seemed to be whittling.

"It's a knight errant!" Gus exclaimed.

"I'm a knight errant," snapped Thomas. "You don't see me putting up tents in the way and sitting around whittling."

"He'll want to joust," said Gus. "It's what knights errant do, you know, between times."

"Between times of what?" shot Thomas.

"Questing," said Gus. "We could try it sometime, sir."

"We *are* questing."

"I mean jousting, sir."

"Let's go around," said Thomas.

But the knight had spotted them. He stood and waved enthusiastically at them. "Ho there!" he called.

"Pretend you can't hear him," said Thomas.

Thomas aimed for a ridge obscured by high brush.

"It's no use sir. He's coming to meet us."

Thomas risked a glance. The knight had mounted and was riding up the hill toward them. He was yelling in a happy, delighted way and spurring his horse, who seemed rather less happy than the man atop him and not in the least bit delighted.

"Confound it," said Thomas. "We're questing. We don't have time to stop and chat with random knights lounging in pavilions." Those were the words he said, but his thoughts were consumed by memories of his one and only previous joust. The knight currently trotting up the hill was probably not in possession of Pyralis' Gauntlet of Smashing Success, but Thomas had no other reason to expect a second jousting attempt to turn out substantially better than the first.

"You'll want to talk to this one," said Gus. "Those are Bagdemagus' colors."

The pavilion knight was upon them.

"Hello, knights!" said Bagdemagus grinning. "Fight me on horseback or admit yourselves recreant and hand over your... steed," he concluded after some consideration and a shrug. "And your squire," he added.

"Wait. What?" said Gus.

"And your armor," said Bagdemagus.

He surveyed their armor.

"Forget the armor," he said.

He was growing less delighted as he inventoried their belongings. "What kind of knights are you?" he was about to say. He didn't say it, because he spotted a parcel strapped to Booker. The parcel itself wasn't much to look at, but the expressions on the curious individuals in front of him when he noticed the parcel were.

"You can keep the squire. I'll just take the horse," he said. "And everything it's carrying."

"This is robbery," said Thomas.

"Highway banditry!" said Philip.

"You are just a thug," said Gus. "Sir."

Bagdemagus, already sitting high on his horse, drew himself up.

"I'm a knight errant. Aren't you?"

He was looking at Thomas.

"Ha!" said Philip. "No we are not. We are Less Valued. Now we'll just be off."

"Strange," said Bagdemagus. "Less Valued, you say?"

Thomas frowned.

"My apologies. You struck me from afar," he said eyeing Thomas, "as something more."

Thomas clenched his jaw. His fist tightened on Booker's reins. His leather glove creaked and crackled.

"Oh no," said Philip.

"Sir?" said Gus.

Bagdemagus waved a hand toward the field beyond indicating, seemingly, that they were free to pass. "...if you are not what you seem," he said.

Bagdemagus and Thomas locked eyes. A fuzzy plump bee bumbled between them. Neither man blinked.

Thomas squinted.

Bagdemagus squinted.

"I am," said Thomas.

Bagdemagus grinned. "It would appear that you are."

Philip groaned.

⁂

There was a breathless moment between concussions. In that moment – after Bagdemagus' lance struck Thomas' shield but before Thomas struck the ground – Thomas had time to ponder the efficacy of the shield in general. It occurred to him that it might be better to try to deflect a blow than absorb it. He determined to try this alternate usage if an opportunity should again present itself.

Ah, he thought, as the ground approached. The ground was much larger than a lance. Deflection, he noted, became increasingly challenging to implement as the size of the approaching object increased.

He had a one-word epiphany. *Roll.* And then he smacked flat into the ground, and everything went black.

⁂

It was dark. A fire crackled. Muffled voices drifted to Thomas through the ringing in his ears. He was lying on something painful.

It was his back.

He opened his eyes and pushed himself up onto his elbows.

Bagdemagus, Philip and Gus were chewing. The delicious smell of something roasting caught Thomas' attention. His stomach growled.

"He's awake!" said Gus.

"Aha!" said Bagdemagus. He pulled Thomas up and handed him a greasy leg of something. Thomas ate and drank a mug of cool water and ate some more.

When he could finally focus, his heart sank. He looked for Booker. He casually noted the lay of the campsite. A stump here could be used as an obstacle. The clod of earth there could twist a careless ankle. The black shadow cast by the tent could make an enemy hesitate. If he kept his back to the fire, it would be easier for him to see his opponent and harder for his opponent to see him. His opponent could make use of all these things too. It didn't matter. Surprise was the thing–

Thomas pulled a burning log from the fire and yelled, "Philip, Gus, run! And you–" he said, waving his fiery club at Bagdemagus. "I can't let you have Booker. And I can't let you have what he's carrying. We have to save King Arthur and find Merlin. I cannot fail. I will not!"

Nobody moved.

Thomas waved the club, trying to model the behavior he desired.

Still nobody moved.

"He knows, sir," said Gus.

Bagdemagus nodded.

"And he's made us a deal."

"Oh," said Thomas. He lowered the log. "What sort of deal?"

Bagdemagus, chewing again, pushed a rock toward Thomas with his foot.

When Thomas had stowed his makeshift weapon back in the campfire and taken a seat, Bagdemagus spoke.

"For bravery displayed in mounted combat–"

Thomas wondered if he meant the joust.

"And for love of Arthur," Bagdemagus continued, "and our shared fellowship, I will leave you your horse, your gear, your squire, and your personages."

"Our... Thank you," said Thomas.

"And," said Bagdemagus smiling magnanimously, "You may ask any questions you desire. I will answer you thrice."

Thomas frowned.

Gus grinned and bounced his knee. "This is great!" he said.

Philip shrugged and chewed.

"Um," said Thomas. "Where–"

Bagdemagus stood and threw his arms wide. "You have come to the Summer Country, my friends." He sighed and surveyed the darkness so contentedly that Thomas looked to see what he was seeing.

Moonlight gave a colorless glow to the fields and hills. The edges of the forest held a deeper dark behind them. It was the kind of scene that could have done with some fireflies drifting just above the long grass, but this part of the world didn't know fireflies. There were bats flittering here and there. And an owl.

"It will be mine one day," said Bagdemagus. "And I will be the King of the Summer Country."

A shooting star arced above them.

"Okay," said Thomas.

Bagdemagus sat back down.

Thomas waited a moment and then tried again. "But where is–"

"Beneath a rock," said Bagdemagus. "In Cornwall."

Thomas blinked. "Who?"

"Merlin of course. You wanted to know about my quest."

"*Your* quest?"

"But I can say no more. He made me swear on the Four that I wouldn't reveal his location, and he cannot be saved."

"We'll see about that," grumbled Thomas. "Does anyone else know?"

Thomas was having dark thoughts of errant knights disappearing. They did it all the time. As far as he could tell, an errant knight appearing was the suspicious thing.

"But I will tell you this," said Bagdemagus. "Merlin's rock can only be lifted by the one who put it in place. And now you have your three answers."

"But I haven't asked my questions yet," Thomas protested.

"I have given three answers."

"But they were *your* questions."

Bagdemagus smiled and crossed his arms. He seemed quite pleased with himself. "I have played this game once or twice before," he said.

They stared at the fire.

"Hold on," said Thomas. "You're an Errant Companion."

Bagdemagus nodded.

"Of Arthur's court."

He nodded again.

"So you're duty-bound to help us find the false knight Damas."

Bagdemagus frowned. "You're thinking like a Less Valued Knight," he said.

Thomas nodded. "It's what I am," said Thomas.

"Is it?" Bagdemagus let the question hang. When Thomas didn't reply, he shrugged and said simply, "I, of course, am not."

"What's that supposed to mean?" said Philip.

"If *I* rescue Arthur," said Bagdemagus, "Arthur will have been rescued."

The fire crackled. If anyone had been looking at Gus, they would have seen his face slowly decompress.

"Oh," he said.

"Oh? Oh what?" said Philip. "What 'Oh?'"

"If *he* rescues Arthur," Gus repeated, "Arthur will be rescued."

"That's what he just said. And I think we can all agree on that. Can we all agree on that?" asked Philip, nonplussed.

"But if *we* help Arthur..." said Gus.

Bagdemagus gave an approving nod.

"Arthur will escape," Gus finished.

"He's got it," said Bagdemagus. He winked at Gus. Gus beamed.

"Rescue. Escape. The whole point is getting Arthur safe," Philip stammered. "Isn't it?"

Thomas jabbed at the campfire with a charred stick. Ashes smoldered and scattered.

"Isn't it?" repeated Philip.

"The one time I actually ask for help…" mumbled Thomas.

"You're really not going to help us?" asked Philip.

Bagdemagus smiled and nodded. "Because I care," he said.

In the distance, a river burbled. A fox rustled in the brush. Tree branches creaked in the night breeze.

"Anyone up for some riddles?" said Bagdemagus.

"No," said Thomas.

"Nine Men's Morris?"

"No," said Thomas.

"Charades?"

"I'm going to bed," said Thomas.

ߐ

Elisante browsed the swords in a barrel on the edge of the smithy. Small towns were the hardest places to maintain an illusion. In a large city or in the middle of nowhere, expectations were broad. In a small town, everyone expected to know everyone. And everything. And they generally did.

Perspiration beaded on her forehead. Her jaw muscle flexed.

The heat of the forge didn't bother her. The smell of cooking iron was bracing but not unpleasant. But the noise – pounding hammers, pumping bellows, hissing steam – it was disrupting her concentration. She gripped her cameo. It centered her. Reminded her of her sister. Bolstered her resolve.

She selected a sword, drew it from the barrel, and altered her voice to something someone might expect from a gruff supply officer on leave.

"How much?" she said.

After some brutish banter, the smith was happy to put the sword on the soldier's commander's tab and throw in the scabbard too... with the understanding that the smith's good name, superior workmanship, and congenial support of the local boys would be mentioned where these things are talked about. Pubs mostly.

Sword in hand, Elisante procured a private room at the town's only tavern, shut the door, and got to work. Her craft was improving rapidly, but here now was the true test. She tried to recall the details of the impostor-sword – the jewels in the pommel, the length and girth of the grip, the direction of the leather wrapping, the design of the cross-guard and its etched filigree, the roaring lion rain-guard.

Details were important, but less-so than she once imagined. A material forgery of Excalibur would need to look and feel like the real thing. It would require precise measurements, the vision and the touch of a master weapon-smith, exposure to weather, the wear and tear of battle, and evidence of regular maintenance.

But Elisante's illusion, like le Fay's fake-calibur, needed not to look like Excalibur, but rather what people expected of Excalibur. Expectations could be as demanding as reality, or more so, but there was wiggle-room with expectations. It helped that she knew a little about the main person she needed to convince – the turncoat, the traitor, the Judas: Sir Thomas.

They were all the same, knights. Delusions of grandeur, when frustrated, lead to an oversensitivity to being overlooked. Thomas would feel slighted, neglected, undervalued. He'd have a well-nurtured ego. He'd expect symbols of power to be... to be...

She made the sword more ostentatious, longer, wider, heavier. She made it gleam. She encrusted the scabbard with jewels, gave the leather an oily sheen, and worked in the smell of earth, horse and musk. She imbued it with authority. She bathed it in privilege. She stamped it with validation.

When she finally withdrew her attention from the task, the room's only candle had burned to the nib and snuffed itself. The street outside the tavern was empty and still. The room below was silent. Someone snored quietly behind a shared wall.

She shuttered the window and climbed into bed. She tried to sleep, but her mind wouldn't rest. Doubts overtook her. She was too late. She wouldn't be able to make the switch in time. She'd be suspected. She'd be spotted. She'd be found out.

She gripped her cameo. She remembered. She focused.

How was she supposed to move inconspicuously now, with a sword like this?

If she posed as a mercenary or soldier – as a man with a sword – it would only be a matter of time before she'd be called upon to use it. She wasn't prepared for that.

A huntress? It was Nimue's favorite guise. But it wasn't Elisante's style. A princess? Princesses didn't carry swords. Not even ornamental ones. Ridiculous, but true. She could pose as a princess anyway and carry the sword, but she would stand out.

A prince?

Princes carried swords. If a prince used a sword it was because he wanted to, not because he was necessarily expected to. In fact, one might expect a prince to not be particularly useful with a sword. Princes drew attention, but sometimes the best place to hide was right out in front.

A prince would work.

She dreamt that night of two princesses. One searching, the other lost. She awoke in a cold sweat, ate a cold breakfast, commandeered a princely horse, and rode out of town.

She had one chance left to stop the false Sir Thomas, foil le Fay's plot, make Nimue proud, and prove she was worth something to someone. To anyone. To herself.

She rode faster.

CHAPTER XVII

THIMBLERIG

The hot, wet sun clawed its way over the horizon and pushed itself into the sky. Thomas extracted himself from damp bedding and surveyed the campsite grumpily. He realized what he was looking at was Gus. He realized what Gus was doing was cooking.

"Fish from the river," Gus said. "Beans from his supplies." Gus nodded at Bagdemagus' tent. It was snoring.

Thomas took the plate. His mood threatened to improve. He suppressed it.

"How long have you been awake?"

Gus shrugged. "My pa says, 'If you teach a man to fish you'll feed him for life, but it can take a lifetime to teach some people how to fish, and the whole point of fishin' is to get away from some people, and anyway you better learn to fish Gus."

"He sounds like a wise man," said Thomas. He found himself staring at Bagdemagus' tent.

"It's a questing beast," said Gus.

Thomas looked closer. Sure enough the front was done up to look like a monster's face. The pennant, had there been a breeze at all, might have wagged like a tail. Instead it drooped sadly.

Gus laughed. "And he snores. Just like the beast's belly, see?"

Thomas chewed.

He nudged Philip with a boot.

"Wake up," said Thomas. "There's fish. And beans. And we've been assailed by a questing beast in the night. And we've got a road ahead of us."

"Pa says, 'When you embark on a journey of a thousand miles, begin with a step in another man's shoes. Saves wear and tear on yer own.' Ha ha."

Gus chuckled to himself, sighed, and started cleaning the cooking gear. A short while later, Booker was laden with commandeered supplies, and Thomas, Philip and Gus were putting distance between themselves and the questing beast with the sleeping Summer Prince in its belly.

ꟹ

Thomas was walking fast. Philip matched his pace with effort. Gus was jogging, pulling Booker, stopping to breathe, and generally having an awful time of it.

"Sir," he panted.

"We'll find a town or a village or a hamlet or something. A crossroads even."

"Sir," Gus managed again. He was wheezing now.

"A hermit maybe. Or a hunter. We'll find someone, and if they can't help us they'll point us to someone who can and–"

In a strategic moment between a puff and a heave, Gus blurted, "Sir!"

"–and if they don't know this recreant Damas surely they'll know someone who does. I mean how recreant can you be if no one knows about you or where your evil fortress and foul prison are?"

They came to a crossroads.

Thomas halted in the middle, hands on his hips. He looked left. He looked right.

"Some kind of signage would be appreciated," he mumbled.

Gus caught up. He bent double, with one hand on his chest and the other hanging on Thomas' sleeve.

"Sir," he said.

"How are you holding up Gus? Long way to go."

"It's–" said Gus. He leaned on his knees. Under his sweat-drenched bangs, he squinted northwest. He pointed. "It's. That way."

"Opinion noted," said Thomas. "But one thing you'll learn, young squire, is that looks can be deceiving. That way might *look* like the road to a ne'er-do-well's lair, and the other like a road to…" Thomas peered down the other fork. It looked exactly like Gus' fork. Neither fork looked like the road to a ne'er-do-well's lair.

"Maybe they look more sinister at night," suggested Philip.

"It's that way sir," repeated Gus. There had been too much color in his face and then not enough, but now a more normal Gus-color was seeping back in. He straightened up experimentally, and when he didn't fall over he said, "He told me."

"Who told you?"

"Bagdemagus, sir. I beat him last night at charades. He told me how to get to Damas'."

"Did he now?" said Thomas, relieved, disappointed, and annoyed. "What else did our illustrious friend, our most splendidly resplendent snoutband, our vainglorious, self-possessed smellfungus..."

He realized he was being loud and the surroundings had gone quiet – a bad combination in an unknown land.

"What else did he say?"

"Well," said Gus. "He said that after he found he couldn't free Merlin, he had stayed at Damas' brother Ontzlake's place. And a night or two ago, guess who showed up?"

"Who?"

"Yeah, who?" asked Philip.

"Accolon," said Gus.

"The Black Knight?" blurted Philip

"Morgan's champion," said Thomas thoughtfully.

Gus nodded.

Thomas chewed his cheek and pondered. "Arthur gets king-napped by a false knight, and Morgan's champion shows up at the king-napper's brother's."

"Sir Bagdemagus says that Ontzlake is a good fellow who would be even better if he could get out from under his brother. I asked him why he left Ontzlake's company, and Sir Bagdemagus said, 'Two reasons.'"

Thomas waited.

"Which were…?" prodded Philip.

"One," said Gus. "He said Accolon showed up and was riling Ontzlake. Ontzlake told Accolon that something was going on at Damas', and the last Sir Bagdemagus saw, Accolon was headed to Damas' with a fierce countenance and a fiercer sword."

"So Bagdemagus just left Accolon to it?" said Philip incredulously. "A black knight. Headed for Arthur. I don't trust that guy," he declared.

"I do," said Gus. "I mean Sir Bagdemagus is Morgan's nephew and all, but–"

"He's what?!" said Thomas horrified.

"That tears it," said Philip.

Thomas was of a mind with Philip on the matter, but from the moment he'd met him, Gus had demonstrated an ability to sniff out the truth and a nose for who and who not to trust. He'd taken to Thomas himself after all, hadn't he? But the matter at hand certainly had all the signs of deception, collusion, and… untrustworthiness.

"Why, Gus? Why trust Bagdemagus who wouldn't help us? He could have, but he refused. His claim that he's concerned about the honor Arthur will forfeit if he's 'rescued' rather than 'escapes' – that he's helping us by *not* helping – it's awfully convenient for Bagdemagus, isn't it? What kind of knight abandons a person who is clearly in distress just so he can continue his own quest uninterrupted? Why on Earth would you trust him?"

Philip nodded in agreement. "And some of us are clearly in distress here," he said.

"I meant Arthur," Thomas growled.

Gus raised his chin bravely. "He seems honest, sir. And I have a nose for these things if I don't say so myself. And the relationship to Morgan is just by marriage. I should have said he's Uriens' nephew. And because of the second reason he gave for leaving Ontzlake's."

"The guy is full of reasons," said Philip.

"Sir Bagedmagus has a dream, sir," Gus continued. "And despite being passed over after his heroic actions in the Uplands, he's putting his dream on hold because he knows that his quest could save the kingdom."

"There won't be any kingdom to save if we don't save the King first," said Thomas.

"That's right," said Philip.

Gus didn't reply.

Thomas sighed. "What quest is Bagdemagus on that could *also* save the kingdom?"

"The Sangreal," said Gus. "The Holy Grail. He aims to find it, sir."

"Bagdemagus is going to find the Holy Grail. Alone," said Thomas doubtfully.

"He found Merlin," he said.

Thomas glared. Gus didn't look away.

"He says he feels called, sir. He's certain that he's the one who can obtain the Grail," said Gus. "And if that's true, then it doesn't really matter what you or I think of him right now. Parson says, 'The Good Lord doesn't call the equipped; He equips the called.'" Gus shrugged. "A quest like that changes a person."

Philip scanned the party's equipment doubtfully. He opened his mouth, but Thomas saw it coming and preempted him.

"Okay, fine," Thomas begrudged. "That's an important quest."

Thomas stared down the path not recommended.

"What's this dream Bagdemagus is putting on hold?" he asked.

"He wants to be King of the Summer Country," said Gus. Gus' expression softened as he took in their surroundings. "And who can blame him, sir?"

Thomas took note of the horse flies. And the mosquitoes. And the humidity. But Gus' innocent admiration was endearing. And so was the Summer Country seen through Gus' eyes.

"No one, I suppose," Thomas conceded. Then, "Fine," he said. "I hope Sir Bagdemagus becomes the man he wants to be. The rest of us have a King to rescue."

Thomas headed down the right path. That is to say, the right-hand path toward Damas'. Some paths are happy to take a person straight to where they want to go even if they're headed in a wrong direction, so to speak.

Philip, Gus and Booker followed.

They stood at the tree-line, partially obscured, and observed the comings and goings at Damas' fortress. It was mostly comings. There was a queue to get in. The guards would call a person from the queue, question him, search his belongings, wave him forward, and call the next.

"How do we get in?" said Philip.

"We ask," said Thomas.

"Pardon?" said Philip.

But Thomas was already on the move.

"What happened to '*the Hesitant*?'" said Gus, collecting Booker.

"A quest changes a person," said Philip, throwing Gus' words back at him.

It struck Gus then that one of the many changes a person might experience in the execution of a quest might be a change from living to not living. He would've said as much, but there was no one to say it to.

"Come on Booker," he said, and hurried after Thomas the no-longer-hesitant and Philip the presumably-still-unlucky.

ණ

There are times and places where prisoners are provided room, board, entertainment programs, exercise regimens, and educational opportunities funded by a kingdom's more upstanding citizenry. This wasn't one of those times. Prisoners in Thomas' time depended on the benevolence of friends, family and strangers, or they perished. They were given a room. The state-funded benevolences ceased there. This doesn't mean they weren't given any options. They could, for example, die by execution, starvation, hypothermia, disease, etcetera. Those were just the beginning. The varieties of neglect were rather expansive.

"We have warm clothes for one of your prisoners," said Thomas to the guard. He pulled part of a cloak out of a satchel and showed it to the guard.

Covered in a sheen of sweat, the guard peered at him and said, "It's June."

"It won't be forever," said Thomas.

There was a commotion at the back of the line. Thomas got a glimpse of someone on horseback and a covered carriage. This was followed by a whiff of the most delightful aroma Thomas had encountered since Camelot – fresh-baked bread.

"Bread for your beloveds!" cried the person on the horse. It was a prince by the look of things.

The queue broke and made for the carriage. Thomas was jostled and spun by the rush. The prince was obscured by the crowd. Thomas heard Booker whinny. A strong hand gripped his shoulder.

It was the guard.

"Right. Fine," said the guard. "In you go. But the horse stays out here." And then he was past Thomas and heading for the ruckus. "Order!" he yelled.

Thomas found Gus, and together they retrieved Booker and tried to calm him down.

"Quickly, Gus. I need the sword."

"The sword, sir. Right," said Gus. "The sword with Morgan's magic traps on? That sword? Because I just want to be certain that's the sword you mean before I, you know, reach out and take hold of it. With my own hand, as it were." He laughed nervously. "In truth I'd rather like my hand to *remain* as it were, if you catch my meaning sir."

Thomas hesitated. Then he grunted and fumbled at the straps securing the sword to Booker. Most had come free already. Thomas reached for the sword, braced himself for a lightning strike or the ground to fall away, and took hold of it.

He opened his eyes. As far as he could tell he had not been combusted or deflated or turned into a pigeon.

Philip appeared. He was stuffing the end of a half-loaf of fresh bread in his mouth. He spotted Thomas holding the sword. His eyes went wide.

"Yes?" said Thomas.

"Morr olding vuh ford," Philip sprayed. Crumbs fell. He swallowed and said, "You're holding the sword!"

"And?"

"And," said Philip. He shrugged.

"Good, come on," said Thomas to Philip. "We've got to find Arthur. Gus, stay here with Booker."

Thomas turned. There in the crowd, watching him, was the prince. There was something familiar about him, but there was no time to dawdle. He had to get the sword inside while the guards were distracted. Thomas and Philip entered Damas' fortress, found a likely passage, and headed downward into the dark.

ঌ

There was a guard at the entrance to the cells. Of course there was a guard at the entrance to the cells. Thomas kicked himself. The guard dismissed the person ahead of them, made some scratches on a parchment and motioned Thomas forward.

"What do we do?" whispered Philip.

"We avoid looking conspicuous," whispered Thomas. "For example, by not whispering loudly at each other."

"Prisoner," said the guard in the bored and cryptic tone of those blessed people everywhere who have been burdened with the task of herding other people through processes.

"Um?" said Thomas. He tried to casually hide the sword behind his back.

The guard rolled his eyes up from the parchment. "Yer here to see...?"

"Oh," said Thomas. "Arthur."

The guard's face was heavy and expressionless. Every bit of energy in this man was going toward not expending energy.

"Arthur, um, Pendragon?" said Thomas.

The guard made a scratch on his parchment. "Arthur um Pendragon. Benevolences," he said.

"Um," said Thomas. "A blanket?"

"One blanket," said the guard, scratching. "Medium," he said to himself without bothering to look at the blanket. He made another tick.

"Anything else?"

"Um," said Thomas.

"Foodstuffs, footwear, creams, salves, abatements, potions, brews, concoctions, containers large, containers small, pillboxes, jewelry, contrivances, contraband..." He looked up and took note of Thomas being inconspicuous.

On the flawless visage of sublime non-expression that was the guard's face, two eyebrows lowered ever so slightly.

"What's that?"

"What's what?" said Thomas.

The guard rolled his eyes dramatically and sighed. "Behind your back. What's behind your back?"

"Um," said Thomas. He brought it around and showed the guard. "Walking stick?"

The guard made more scratches. "One sword, long. One scabbard, fancy." He looked up. "He's gonna need it," he said. "Next!"

❧

"Well that was lucky," said Thomas. "The guard letting us in with the sword."

"Mm-hmm," said Philip skeptically. "I know a thing or two about luck, see. So let me ask you: Which is worse? The prison where the prisoners aren't allowed weapons, or the prison where the guards aren't worried about prisoners getting weapons?"

In reply, Thomas hastened his search for Arthur.

They made their way along the prison corridor, peering into cells through small barred windows. Thomas had expected at least a few vacant cells and more than a few vacant expressions, but every cell was occupied and these prisoners seemed, alarmingly, content.

"Move along then."

"It's not a zoo, lad."

"Can I help you?"

Several of the cells were outfitted with armaments and desks, coats of arms and thick rugs. Thomas began to suspect that the most decorated prisoners had been here quite a while.

"Here!" said Philip.

Arthur's cell was bare. Damp stone walls, chains hanging from hooks, a spider web in the corner, a pot Thomas determined not to think too carefully about, and a single fragile wooden chair accounted for the entirety of the cell's contents apart from Arthur who, frankly, looked quite well.

"I'm starving!" said Arthur. "Who are you?"

"It's me, Your Majesty," said Thomas. "Sir Thomas the Hesitant and Sir Philip the Disadvantaged."

"Outstanding," said Arthur. "Just who I had hoped to see."

"Really?"

"Do you have any bread? I smell bread."

Thomas looked at Philip. Philip shook his head.

"No sir, but–"

"Who did you say you were?"

"Sir Thomas the–"

"Where's the girl that was here? Fetch her. I'm sure she'd bring us some bread."

"I didn't see a–"

Arthur sat on his fragile chair, hands on his knees, back straight. He began to whistle.

Thomas backed away from the door.

"What's wrong with him?" said Philip.

Thomas frowned. "Some kind of enchantment?" Whether it was going to be a rescue or an escape, Thomas hadn't prepared himself for a King who wasn't aware that he needed either. Thomas peered back through the window.

"Oh, hello!" said Arthur. "It's lovely to see your face again, dove. Did the lads tell you to bring some bread?"

"Your Majesty, it's me Sir Thomas again. I mean *still.* It's still me."

Arthur stood and moved toward the door. "Just pass it through the slot there."

"I have a blanket for you sir," said Thomas gently and clearly, feeling suddenly like he was talking to his grandmother. Scratch that. Grandma Farmer would've put up with none of this. He unfolded the blanket and fed it through the slot.

Arthur pulled it into his cell and draped it over his shoulders. "Can't eat it," he said. "But that's alright. It does get chilly here." Arthur was sweating.

"And your sword, sire. Excalibur."

Arthur's eyes, already slightly mad, grew wider.

"I knew she'd come through," Arthur said. "Family before dishonor. Pass it through."

The jewel-encrusted scabbard stuck in the slot. Thomas turned it and tried again. It was no use.

"It won't fit sir."

"Push harder," said Arthur.

"Try it without the scabbard," said Philip.

Thomas drew the sword.

It didn't look anything like Excalibur.

It was thin and dull and flimsy. The pommel was plain, the hilt was devoid of any ornamentation whatsoever, and the rain-guard looked not at all like a lion.

"That's Excalibur?" said Philip.

"No," said Thomas.

Thomas found himself filled with the dreadful sort of comfort that comes when the horrible thing you've been expecting finally comes to pass. To come this far, and somehow fail in the final step…

"There's something inscribed here," he said.

He turned the sword to try to catch the light.

"*Somnia non salvebis*," read Thomas. "Nonsense," he translated. "You will *not* be fine."

Thomas' mind raced. Did Bagdemagus switch the swords? Unlikely. Gus had stayed up with him and was up again before Bagdemagus awoke. Did Morgan swap the sword? To what end? If she didn't want the sword delivered she could have just not had the sword delivered. And the inscription seemed directed at Thomas, not Arthur...

"The prince," said Thomas, realization dawning.

"Who?" said Philip.

"The bread-prince. Outside. All the commotion. And when I went to get the sword all the straps were already undone. He switched the sword in the commotion. I should have known."

"How could you have known?"

"Because he was wearing the necklace."

"What necklace?"

"The same necklace the thief on Morgan's ship wore. The same necklace the old lady at the port wore. The prince is not a he. He's a she. Come on!"

Thomas bolted up the corridor. Philip followed.

Arthur pressed his face against the bars.

"So… no bread?" he said.

CHAPTER XVIII

CAUGHT LOAFING

Thomas and Philip burst into the courtyard blinking painfully at the sun. There was a remarkable lack of commotion. The queue had reformed beyond the gate. Guards milled about in the absent-minded manner of those whose jobs consist largely of the task of being on site. The Prince of Loaves was nowhere to be seen.

On the edge of things, Gus fed apples to Booker one by one from a bucket of unknown source. Thomas and Philip sidled over to him.

"How did it go, sirs?" Gus inquired cheerfully.

"Where did the apples come from?" asked Philip.

Booker whinnied happily. Gus chewed on a crust of bread and swallowed. "From the guards. 'In recompense for honorable service rendered,' they said. They were quite appreciative. I think they've overdone it though. I mean all I said was, 'There she goes!' and pointed." He pointed demonstratively, grinned and chewed.

Dumbfounded by the situation, delighted with his squire, a little put out for once again being upstaged, and feeling a need for absolute clarity, Thomas asked, "You mean the prince?"

Gus guffawed. "T'weren't no prince, sirs. Prin*cess* maybe. If you catch my meaning."

"Meaning, it was a girl..." said Philip.

"That's right. The whole time," said Gus. He winked.

Despite his simmering annoyance with Gus' ongoing effortless do-goodery, Philip was primarily thankful they didn't need to give chase and was coming up to speed – or more accurately, slowing down – quicker than Thomas. "They arrested her?" he asked.

Gus nodded. "Inciting commotion, negligent disorder, and careless loafing."

"But... 'loafing?'" said Philip. "I don't think that means what they think it means."

Gus shrugged. "My Pa liked to say, 'Gus, always remember, there are law-makers and law-abiders. One of 'em is never th'other and th'other ain't often th'latter and at the moment yer neither so put it back right now or so help me when we get home."

"When we get home, what?" asked Philip.

"That part varied," said Gus.

"But Gus," said Thomas, choosing to focus on delight and clarity, "how did you see through her illusion?"

"Illusion?" Gus stopped chewing. "Huh," he said. He stared at the ground thoughtfully. "Didn't reckon her for a sorceress." He cheered up and shrugged again. "Illusions work on imagination. I'm afraid I don't have a lot of that, sir."

"Uh huh," said Philip not convinced.

"Well," said Thomas. "Good work. The thing is, she's got Excalibur."

Gus' mouth dropped.

"Where is she now?" said Thomas.

"Well sir, she'd be incarcerated down below with the rest of the prisoners I suppose. Only..."

"Only?"

"Only I imagine they'd have confiscated the sword, sir."

"You imagine," said Philip.

Gus blinked. "Figure of speech, sir."

"Right. Come on then, both of you."

Gus fidgeted. "Might be better if I stayed here with Booker again yeah?"

"Oh, right," said Thomas. "Look, it's underground, and I won't lie, it's a little cramped, but focus on the mission, right? Arthur's down there. You'll be fine."

"It's not that sir," said Gus. "Well, it *wasn't* that…"

"What is it then?"

"Well... it's just... she might recognize me."

"And?"

"And she's a sorceress, sir. An illusionist. She does things to your brain."

"I thought you were immune to her charms," said Philip doubtfully.

"I didn't say I haven't got any imagination at all sir. I mean, I can imagine her..." He trailed off.

Gus shook himself. "The thing is, before, I didn't know she was a sorceress. Now I know. It's easier to be brave when you don't know you're doing it, sir."

"Gus, I believe you have more bravery in your left thumb than the false knight who built this place and the sorceress inside it combined. Plus, I don't think she's very good at sorceress…ing. And *we've* got a secret weapon. Bring the looking glass." He turned and headed for the dungeons.

Philip and Gus exchanged a glance.

"Sir," said Gus.

But not knowing he was terribly mistaken on at least two matters, Thomas strode forward unhesitantly. It's easier to be brave when you don't know you're doing it.

Gus hung the apple bucket for Booker, carefully extracted the bundle of broken mirror from Booker's cargo, and headed toward the dark doorway to the under-places.

He stood for a moment and thought about bolting. He hadn't taken a single step inside, but he could already feel the crushing weight of the ceiling and the walls closing in on him. Beneath the perpetual sheen of perspiration that envelops a person enduring the humidity of the sort he was enduring, Gus began to sweat.

Someone might ask, "What does a person who lacks imagination fear?"

"Unimaginable horrors," Gus would reply. "The worst kind."

In any case, what Gus lacked in imagination he made up for by cataloguing stories. Sorceresses were bad enough. And what could happen to a person in a tight place really got his mind reeling. Now here was a sorceress *and* a tight place, and here was Gus holding their best hope, shattered.

"I don't think she's very good," Thomas had said.

Here's hoping, thought Gus. He gripped the bag, took a deep breath, and stepped into the black.

They would all soon discover that, despite her recent failure to craft a fake-calibur to meet her own high standards, Elisante was becoming a better illusionist than any of them could imagine.

❧

There had been a change of guards.

"You shall not pass," said the new guard. "Next!"

"But–" said Thomas.

"Look," said the guard. "It says here that you've been in once already, you visited your charge, and you delivered..." He read from the log. "One blanket, medium. One sword, long. One scabbard, fancy." He squinted at the sword Thomas was still holding and frowned in approval.

"Don't see many like that anymore," he said.

"That's right!" said Thomas. "You don't. And you certainly don't see two in one day. This is that sword."

"Which. Has. Been," said the guard holding up the log book. "Delivered." He stabbed at the log with a meaty finger in the general area of some marks allegedly indicating as much.

"Next!" he said.

The old woman behind them tried to shove forward. Gus stepped aside obligingly and caught her eye. He panicked.

Gus yelled, "It's the girl it's the girl it's the girl!"

The guard's head snapped to the old woman, to Gus, to the old woman again, and back to Gus.

He relaxed. "Augustus! From the courtyard. Good job son, but not this time. The impostor-prince is safely interred in cell sixteen."

Gus eyed the old woman.

"Sorry ma'am," said the guard, apologizing for Gus.

The old woman smacked Gus in the shoulder with her bag.

Gus breathed. "Sorry ma'am. Sorry sirs. It couldn't be her." He laughed. "That's who we're trying to see–"

"Gus!" hissed Philip.

Thomas sagged.

"Oh," said Gus. "I probably shouldn't have said."

"Hang on," said the guard, double-checking his list. "Why didn't you say so?" he said.

"Pardon?" said Thomas, perking up.

"One visit per day *per prisoner*," said the guard. "I'll just put you down for one sword, long. One scabbard–"

"Actually," said Thomas. "Did she already have a sword, fancy?"

The guard scanned the log. "No... no sword, fancy nor otherwise. Says belongings: One robe, petite. One walking stick, gnarled. One necklace, odd."

"Quite," said Thomas.

"How's that?" said the guard.

"Do you always let prisoners in with all their belongings?"

"Well," the guard glanced at the old woman glaring behind Thomas. "We're not about to relieve a lady of her walking stick, gnarled. We have some propriety here."

"And the odd piece of jewelry?" Thomas asked.

"Nor the jewelry, odd," said the guard. "We're not barbarians. Look, do you want to see her or not? There's a queue."

"We do," said Thomas.

Philip nodded.

Gus shook his head, unheeded.

The old woman behind them glared.

The guard waved them beyond. He grinned paternally at Gus as they passed.

The old woman stepped up.

"Prisoner?" said the guard.

"The Prince of Loaves," she croaked.

"Sorry, ma'am, no can do. One visitation per prisoner per day."

It was lucky for the guard that he too didn't have much of an imagination. A lack of imagination had been a requirement of the post, and this guard had almost been passed over on account of being over-qualified.

The old woman glared. A more imaginative man would have found himself fleeing a thousand horrible specters or paralyzed before some chimerical phantasm or agreeably and unknowingly ushering one of the three best sorceresses in the world to a visit with her misfortunate apprentice.

The guard returned the glare with the impenetrable smile of the simple workman with plenty of hours left in his shift.

"Fine," said the old woman. "But I'll be back."

"Next!" said the guard.

ᔕ

"Ready?" said Thomas.

The trio stood at the door to cell sixteen. Thomas began to unwrap the looking glass.

"Sir..." said Gus.

"It's alright, Gus. She's no match for Pyralis' mirror. It cut right through her deceptions, and Morgan's too, in the vault on Morgan's ship. When I say go, slide the shutter back. Be ready for anything."

"Thomas–" said Philip.

"Go!"

Gus didn't move.

"It's about the mirror," said Philip.

"There's no time," Thomas said and shoved the shutter open.

Soft light spilled over them through the portal. Dust motes sparkled and turned in slow motion. Thomas' hands drifted down to his sides. Two knights and a squire gazed into the glimmer and slowly lowered their jaws.

There in the chamber – for it could hardly be called a cell – seated on a plush cushion adorning an ornate silver throne was no false prince. The person seated there looked to be the kindest, gentlest, most beautiful princess they'd ever seen, perhaps that had ever lived. If they were seated next to each other, this Lady's presence would have made the exquisite Guinevere frown, put things down too hard, and excuse herself early.

"Sir Thomas," she said. Her gaze lingered. "Sir Philip." She blinked long, dark eyelashes. "Augustus Esquire." She smiled. It made a tinkling sound. All tension melted away.

"Please forgive me. I would invite you in, but..." She laughed. Thomas thought it was the sound of the Summer Country and suddenly understood why it had enchanted Bagdemagus so.

"I'm afraid my hospitality has been constrained," she said.

Philip nodded.

Thomas' head felt swimmy. There was something in his hand. What was it?

Even Gus was fooled. Perhaps it was her increasing prowess. Perhaps, gripped by abstract fear in this small concrete space, Gus' mind was steered just as easily as the others.

"It's alright ma'am," he said.

"But it seems you have brought me something, haven't you, Sir Thomas?"

"Yes, I..." said Thomas.

"You can just stick it through that slot, dear," said the Lady.

"Stick it through the slot," Thomas mumbled. "Stick..." Stick. Walking stick. Something about a walking stick. The Lady held a staff, but nothing he'd call a walking stick.

"Um," said Thomas.

"Yes?" said the Lady, still smiling encouragingly.

"We're here for something," said Thomas.

She chuckled kindly. "No doubt you are, else you wouldn't be here, would you? I'm sure it's to deliver your benevolence, yes? Through that slot, dear."

Thomas frowned. He looked at the bundle in his hand. He rested his other hand on the hilt of his sword.

The stick. The staff. Something about a sword...

"We're here for Excalibur," he blurted.

The Lady's laughter was like a warm bath after a hard day. It made Thomas want to soak in it.

"Why Excalibur is there on your own hip, Sir Thomas." Her face grew playfully serious, like a mother conspiring with her child to play a trick on the father. "I think you'd better deliver it to the King as soon as we're done here, don't you?"

Thomas nodded. Why hadn't he already? He felt silly, scolded, and loved. And unsettled. His brow furrowed.

"I'll tell you what," said the Lady. "I have it in my power to grant my own benevolences. If you give me yours, I'll give you mine. One each. Anything you wish."

Her eyes sparkled. "What would you ask?"

"A horse," blurted Philip. Thomas looked at him. "Thomas has a horse. I'd like a horse. And better armor. And a shield with a crest on."

The Lady laughed. "Easy things."

Philip beamed.

"And you, young man?"

Gus blushed.

"Don't be shy. What would you ask?"

Gus prodded the floor with his toe.

"I can't give it if you don't ask," the Lady prodded.

Gus cleared his throat. He glanced at Thomas. He was beet red. "A kiss m'Lady?"

Her laughter was lovely and lush. "It will be yours, Augustus. One kiss."

A kiss? thought Thomas. A horse made sense. And he'd had no idea Philip had coveted his shield. Being in a position to be coveted was new. Thomas' mind drifted to Camelot's Table Hall. Being coveted was one thing. Being respected was another. Respect. That was the thing. A kiss? What was that? He had to admit the kiss Marie had given him... And suddenly there was Marie in his mind.

She smiled.

The Lady's smile had been beguiling. But Marie's smile… The Lady's smile wanted to draw him in. Marie's smile drew him out. With the Lady, he could lose himself. With Marie, he could be himself.

"Marie," said Thomas.

"Who is Marie?" said the Lady. "Tell me, and I shall give you her heart."

"You–" said Thomas. His head hurt. The light faded.

He let the cloth fall from the looking glass.

"You're not Marie," said Thomas.

He lifted the mirror, aimed it at the Lady, and peered right through the empty frame.

There in the cell – for it could hardly be called a chamber – seated on a creaky wooden stool, was a thin girl whose most obvious features included knobby elbows, straight dark hair, angular chin, sharp nose, flashing eyes, and a glowing blue cameo hanging on a thin chain around her neck. If they were seated next to each other, this girl's presence would have prompted Guinevere to summon the Queen's Watch to escort her from the premises forthwith.

She held neither staff nor stick, but a sword. Yet of all that was revealed through Pyralis' frame, the most surprising was the girl's expression. She stared at Thomas, eyes wide, face fixed in an expression of, if Thomas had to put a name to it, shame. Or fear. Or both.

Her mouth snapped closed. She fumbled with her cameo. Her brow furrowed, and her chin screwed up. She blinked rapidly.

She was going to cry, Thomas realized.

"Sister?" she said. Her voice was barely a whisper.

Philip glanced through the frame, did a double-take, and rubbed his temples.

Gus, still grinning and flush, stood on his tiptoes to peer through the frame. He gasped. He dropped and peered around the frame, then popped back up to look again.

He scratched his head.

"Sister, I–" Tears spilled down her cheeks. "How?" She folded both hands over her mouth and wept.

Philip frowned. "What's going on?"

Thomas shook his head.

"It's the frame," said Gus. "The magic wasn't in the glass, it's in the frame."

Thomas froze, afraid if the frame moved the magic might contort or wobble or slosh out and fizzle. "Okay," he breathed. "Now what?"

"It's still working," said Gus excited. "You're still seeing what you don't want to see, but so is she. It's turned her own power against her. I mean I suppose this would have happened with the glass still in it, but you would have had to get her to look at you in it while she was... illusioning."

Thomas, teeth clenched, said, "Clear as mud. Now what?"

"Ha!" said Gus in his own world. "How one perceives things all comes down to one's frame of reference. And now you've both been disillusioned. One literally, the other figuratively." Gus shook his head and sighed. "Brilliant! Pyralis' disillusioned frame of reference."

"Gus!"

"Yes sir?"

"Now what?"

Gus glanced at Elisante. The apprentice sorceress sat silent, face in her hands, shoulders quivering.

"I'd go with it, sir. You've got her right where you want her."

"Um," said Philip. "She seems really upset."

"Good," Thomas replied.

He returned his attention to the girl.

"Sister," said Thomas.

Elisante held a sleeve to her eyes. A soft voice said, "I'm sorry."

"As well you should be," said Thomas, glancing at Gus. Gus gave an encouraging nod. Philip grunted an objection.

"I'm so sorry," said Elisante. "I've been trying to make it right," she sobbed. "Trying so hard."

"There's only one way to make it right," said Thomas.

Elisante wiped at her eyes and caught her breath. "How? Anything Melly. I'll do anything."

Thomas mouthed, *Melly?* Gus shrugged.

"Thomas, stop," Philip said forcefully.

Thomas ignored him. "Give us the sword," he said.

Elisante's brows knit. She seemed to notice the sword in her hand for the first time.

"But Melly," she said. "Do you know what this is?"

"Yes, sister. Give us the sword and all will be forgiven."

Gus gave Thomas a thumbs up.

Philip fumed.

"Melly," said Elisante. "This sword could change everything. I can't..." Tears began again.

"Give us the sword," said Thomas gently. "And I will forgive you."

Elisante wept.

"Okay, Melly," she said. Still crying she made her way to the cell door and slid the sword carefully through the slot.

"Thank you sister," said Thomas.

"Melly?" said Elisante.

"Yes?" said Thomas.

Her voice was a whisper. "I love you."

CHAPTER XIX

MISSION ACCOMPLISHED

Arthur sat on his throne. It was smaller than he remembered, but memories were a funny thing. He'd seen enough of life – a great deal of it involving wizards and sorceresses and beguiling trinkets and martial weapons being handed to you by mysterious but attractive arms sticking out of lakes – to know that for a fact.

Three recent events ranked high on the list of wobbly memories. One: he'd been hunting with Uriens and Accolon, and he'd been having a wonderful time. Two: it had gotten dark and he'd boarded a ship operated by some very nice young ladies who'd offered him a hot meal and a warm bed. Three: he hadn't eaten anything since.

He drummed his fingers on his leg. Surely the maiden would be back with some bread?

There was an excited scuffle outside the throne room doors. A slot was pushed open. When had the slot been put there? Had he ordered that? He must have. And he must have had a good reason, else why would he have ordered it? Perhaps it was for the delivery of bread.

A loaf was shoved through the slot. It was a very long loaf. It made a metallic scraping sound as it slid its way into the room. It balanced for a moment, cantilevered by the end that was still stuck in the slot. There was a muffled exhortation, a grunt, and a lot of clanging as the loaf dropped onto the floor.

A shutter snapped open higher on the door and the maiden's face appeared.

"Something's happened to the bread, lass," said Arthur. He looked doubtfully at the object on the floor. "It seems to have become a sword."

"Excalibur!" said the maiden.

"Ah," said Arthur. He didn't move. "For slicing loaves?" he questioned. "Seems a bit ill-*bred*."

"Ha!" he exclaimed, and slapped his knee.

There was a moment of silence behind the door, then: "No, Your Majesty. I'm sorry. There's no bread. But you can use Excalibur to escape!"

Arthur chewed on the idea that the maiden had returned with no bread. He stared at the sword on the floor. He was beginning to feel nonplussed.

He rose slowly, endeavoring to impress the recalcitrant non-bread-bearer with his kingly grace. He weaved his way to the sword. He didn't intend to weave. He got dizzy when he was this hungry. He carefully bent, picked up the sword, and rose again without falling over. It was a cheerful moment in a string of disappointing affairs.

The sword looked like Excalibur. It felt like Excalibur. The hilt was cold, the blade hummed, and the weapon balanced like Excalibur.

"And the scabbard?"

"Oh," said the maiden. The face disappeared. The scabbard was shoved with as much care as a shove could be undertaken through the slot.

Arthur retrieved it.

It seemed to him that every time he examined Excalibur's scabbard it grew more bejeweled. But memories were wobbly, and so was he. He balanced, slid Excalibur into its sheathe and, when the face reappeared said, "Now tell me, why would I need to escape my own throne room?"

ꕥ

"He's bonkers, sir," said Gus. "I've read about it."

Thomas looked at him. "Is there anything you haven't read about?"

Gus considered this. "As a matter of fact–" he began.

"Belay that. What have you read about people who've gone bonkers."

"You've got to go with it."

"Go with it," Thomas repeated doubtfully.

Gus nodded. "If you snap them out of it too quickly, well, it'd be like throwing a bucket of cold water on a sleepwalker."

"What happens if you throw a bucket of cold water on a sleepwalker?"

Gus frowned. "I suppose they'd... well, they'd wake up too fast, wouldn't they? You want to affirm, but don't encourage. And try to get them back to bed without hurting themselves. Or you."

Thomas kept his eyes on Gus as he slowly turned his head back to Arthur.

"Alright, Your Majesty. The thing is–"

"Confound it," blurted Philip. It had been a long day. A long several days, as a matter of fact. And if you asked him, which no one had, there had been a few too many illusions going on and difficult moral choices to be made. And he was fairly certain those moral choices hadn't all been made so well by the people making them. But now they were here with the sword, and it was time to just get things over with. Having recently been a recipient of the cold-bucket-of-water therapy, Philip could attest to its effectiveness. He pushed Thomas aside and pressed his face to the bars.

"Your Majesty! It's Sir Philip and Sir Thomas… and Thomas' squire, whom you haven't met, and you are *not* in your blasted throne room. You've been imprisoned by a man named Damas. You and a whole slew of other knights. And a sorceress." He glared at Thomas. "And we've brought you Excalibur so you can fight your way out of here!"

Gus cleared his throat.

"What!" said Philip, seething.

"There's more to it, sir, according to Bagdemagus."

Philip's nostrils flared.

Thomas didn't really want to know, but he couldn't stop himself from asking. "What don't we know, Gus?"

"The false knight, Damas, has laid claim to a portion of his brother Ontzlake's estates. Ontzlake has challenged Damas to trial by combat. Damas has agreed, but seeks a champion to fight in his stead–"

"Let me guess…" said Philip.

"Damas is reportedly not a very good fighter," confirmed Gus.

Philip snorted. "A knight who's not a very good fighter."

Thomas raised an eyebrow.

Philip clamped his mouth shut.

Gus proceeded.

"Every knight who passes through Damas' land is given a choice. The arena or the dungeon."

"How long has this been going on?" said Thomas.

"Quite some time, sir. I believe there are some twenty other knights imprisoned here."

"And no one has agreed to fight for Damas in all that time?"

"Not one, sir."

"Correction," said Arthur.

Philip, positioned at the window, turned his head to see King Arthur standing, feet spread, chin raised, eyes afire.

"Your Majesty?" said Philip.

"You are wrong on two counts. First: the claim has been made that this," Arthur waved his hand expansively, "is not my throne room."

Philip examined the cell. It was definitely not a throne room.

"Tell me," said Arthur. "Is this not my kingdom?"

Philip glanced at Gus. *Is this some kind of riddle?* said the glance.

Gus shrugged in reply and shook his head.

"Pardon, Your Majesty?" asked Philip.

"Am I the King?" Arthur queried.

There was only one right way answer to this one. Philip replied confidently, "Yes."

"And what do you call the seat a king sits upon?"

"A throne, Your Majesty."

"And what do you call the room where the King sits upon the seat we shall henceforth refer to as his throne?"

"A throne room, Your Majesty."

"And where is a king's throne room typically located?"

"In... his castle?"

Arthur paused.

"In his *kingdom*!" Philip declared, relieved to be able to tell the King, bonkers or not, what he wanted to hear.

"Precisely," said Arthur. "These are Damas' and/or Ontzlake's lands – to be determined – but it's *my* kingdom. I will honor the brothers' choice of trial by combat, but I will not abide the imprisonment of my subjects to wit. Which brings us to the second erroneous claim to have reached my ears through the window of my throne room door." Arthur's deep voice reverberated in the cell. "Not one champion has agreed to fight Ontzlake, *until now*. I, King Arthur, will fight on Damas' behalf on the condition that upon the conclusion of the trial, Damas must release *all* of his prisoners. Now," said Arthur, "have the maiden return to the window, please."

Philip eased away from the window.

"I think he means you," said Philip.

"That tears it," said Thomas. "I'm growing a beard."

The boundary stone on the road leading east from Damas' toward Camelot had a boring but important job. It separated things on one side from things on the other. It also warmed lizards, supported a thriving moss colony on its north-facing side, and served as a hard thing for birds to crack snails upon.

But as is often the case, things that are essential to the proper function of a place are easily overlooked. It was possible, and indeed it often transpired, for a person to cross the boundary with a single step and remain unaware that, whereas previously they could have been described as having being in one place, they were now surely elsewhere.

It's easy to overlook a rock. It's not as easy to overlook a person. It is possible, but you have to be determined. If, for example, you were convinced you were in the right and your disagreeable friend was nothing but a mossy, lizard-baking snail-cracker, you might miss the critical point he was trying to make and stroll, metaphorically, right across a boundary line.

The bird atop the rock paused, snail in beak, head cocked. It took flight. The flapping startled a fat lizard baking on the rock. The lizard scurried under the moss. The boundary stone, for its part, tried to look busy. This is easier than might be expected, for one almost never observes a rock not doing what it's supposed to be doing.

Two of the four approaching the boundary stone on the road out of Damas' lands were jubilant, having successfully recovered a very important sword from an apprentice sorceress in a false knight's dungeon and having also successfully delivered the very same sword to a very important person who, admittedly, was still interred in the very same prison. It wasn't *the* quest, but it was *a* quest complete. And it put them one step closer to finding their beloved court wizard, assuming the Witch-Queen lived up to her end of the bargain. Thomas was choosing not to think too hard about that last part.

"Well done, sir," Gus was saying, and "Bravo," and "Huzzah," and a great many other things of the sort.

"Thank you, Gus," Thomas repeated tirelessly. He was enjoying the moment and the praise.

'Jubilant' was not an accurate word for the other two. Booker looked like a horse that had probably eaten too many apples recently. Philip marched along, tight-lipped and tongue-bitten.

A fellow can only take so much. Eventually he has to say something like, "When you two are done patting yourselves on the back, we should discuss what we're going to do about Arthur."

And so that is what he eventually said.

"What do you mean?" asked Thomas.

"What do I mean? What do I mean?! Arthur's going to get himself killed!"

"Nonsense," said Thomas. "He'll be fine."

Gus grinned. "Good one, sir."

"Besides," said Thomas. "You heard Bagdemagus. The worst thing we could do would be to rescue him. We delivered the sword. The best thing for us now is to report back to Camelot and let the higher-ups know the score. Plus Morgan will likely be there and we can get on with finding Merlin."

Philip stopped in the middle of the road. "You can't know that. You can't know he'll be okay. And you can't just leave him there despite what Bagdemagus says. Bagdemagus only makes sense to Bagdemagus.

"And all the other knights and royals who think like him," admitted Philip. "But we're not like him. Arthur's not thinking straight. You saw him. Sure he has the sword, but he's not right in the head."

"You still want to question the King, despite the tongue-lashing he gave you?"

"Speaking of that, how is it that *I* wound up taking the heat with Arthur?"

"Is that what you're upset about?" said Thomas. "I seem to recall someone shoving me aside and pushing his own face in the window and then... and then throwing cold water on the sleepwalking King!"

"Aha! You agree. He isn't right in the head."

"Wasn't," said Thomas. "You woke him up. And now he's determined to fight Ontzlake!"

"Don't try to pin that on me," said Philip. "The King makes his own decisions."

"The King who you say isn't right in the head?"

They stared at each other until Philip broke eye contact and continued down the road clenching his jaw and flaring his nostrils. Thomas, Gus and Booker followed.

In short order, they reached the boundary stone. They were all too preoccupied to take notice.

"We can't just leave Arthur to his fate in there," said Philip.

"As painful as it feels, it's what we must do if we're to follow orders, sir," said Gus. There was compassion in his voice.

"What orders?" Philip scoffed.

"King Arthur's charge to Sir Thomas on his temporary appointment to the Table of Errant Companions." Gus recited, "'*Godspeed Thomas. Let not even the King himself deter you from finding our friend.*'"

Gus explained, "He meant Merlin. Merlin is 'our friend'."

"I know who Merlin is," Philip growled.

"Thank you Gus," said Thomas, feeling vindicated.

Gus said, "Well, I think it was amazing, sir. The whole thing. Tracking down the Witch-Queen, confronting her on her own ship, wresting Excalibur from the very grip of a foul sorceress deep in the false knight's own dungeon. That's legend-making stuff right there, sir. There'll be a song–"

"You two are worse than Gawain," muttered Philip.

"Pardon?" said Thomas.

"You heard me. You're worse than Gawain. At least he's repented."

"What are you talking about?"

"The way you treated the lady," said Philip. He was stopped now, on the near side of the stone.

"That was no lady," chuckled Gus. "She was a foul sorceress from the pit of–"

"She's just a girl," said Philip. "A sad, tormented girl. And Thomas found her wound and used it to get what he wanted."

Thomas frowned. "I did what needed to be done."

"For who?" said Philip.

"Whom," corrected Gus. They ignored him.

"For the kingdom," said Thomas. His voice was ice cold and calm.

"For yourself," said Philip, burning with nothing like the fire of a thousand suns, but hot nevertheless. Very hot.

"You could learn a thing or two heeding your own girlfriend," said Philip.

"Back off," said Thomas.

"She advised the Queen on Gawain's oath, didn't she?"

"What... to eat more fruit?" Thomas snickered.

Gus recited, "'*Forever as he lives and so on fight for quarrels etcetera and to swear upon the Four that he will never stand against ladies or gentlewomen excepting the case where Sir Gawain of Orkney fights for a lady and/or gentlewoman and his adversary fights for another.*'"

Thomas glared at him.

"Sorry sir."

Philip beamed angrily. "There. Worse than Gawain."

"There are worse people to be worse than," said Thomas. "And fewer better to be better than."

"There are better people to be better than," challenged Philip.

They glared at each other.

It's tempting to say that the world went still in that moment. It didn't, of course. Booker swished his tail. Gus shifted uncomfortably. And nature stops for almost no man, but it's safe to say that three things in close proximity were doing their best to appear immovable: Thomas, Philip, and the boundary stone. All three were doing a good job of it.

Philip, finally, deflated a little.

"Look," he said. "It's not right. Something's not right."

His face became gentle.

"You're not right," he said.

It was Thomas' turn for jaw-clenching and nostril-flaring.

"Maybe you should go rescue your damsel in distress then."

Philip sighed. "Maybe I will," he said.

"Fine," said Thomas glaring.

"Okay," said Philip sadly.

"C'mon Gus," said Thomas. "We have a wizard to rescue."

"To help," corrected Gus.

"Whatever," said Thomas.

Thomas crossed the boundary, and didn't look back.

Philip watched his friend head down the road he'd chosen, then turned around and took his own.

CHAPTER XX

A FORTUNATE CASE OF BAD LUCK

Philip's feet led him back toward Damas'. He was in the right. He knew it. But as he walked he began to think that he hadn't thought things through very well. He wouldn't be able to visit the girl today – one visit per prisoner per day and all that. And what was he going to say when he did? He told himself he had time to figure that out. The more pressing concerns were where to stay, what to eat, how to pay for it, and how could Thomas be such a blithering idiot?

He wandered. He muttered. He muttered and wandered. He passed the prison entrance. "It's practically criminal the way he treated her. He knows I'm right." He circumnavigated a fountain more than once before he realized he was walking in circles. He detoured into the town proper.

"Soggy-minded wishy-washy addle-brained..." He passed a barracks, quickening his pace and descending into a mutter when he sensed he was drawing attention. "Rule Two. Know your limitations. Probably something in the

Code about not being a flea-bitten lout. There should be. Even Gawain..."

His nose turned his head without alerting his conscious mind. But his feet were paying attention and obliged. He walked right past the midnight-armored war steed tied to a hitching post without a second glance and found himself in a dimly lit, smoky tavern where his stomach informed him he was famished. If he had noticed the steed, he would probably have surmised that it belonged to the dark hooded figure in the shadowed corner with the black gauntlets wrapped around a large tankard. He would have been correct.

But Philip was peeved and hot and more than a little hungry and he'd forgotten Rule XIV, "Always be aware of your surroundings, as you can be sure your surroundings will be aware of you. Except when they're not. See Rule IX."

Rule IX, of course, read, "It's not about you. It's never about you. Except, of course, when it would be better for your superiors that whatever it is be not about them." A Less Valued Knight had asked Tuttle for clarification on this point once. Should they expect in the various execution of their duties to be closely watched or carefully ignored? Tuttle had replied, "That is correct."

Philip pressed his way to the bar. It felt rude, but this was the right way to go about things given the context. The sort of clientele that patronize a tavern outside a false knight's fortress expect a shove if they get between a man and his appetites. They'll either take it in stride if they're preoccupied, or make an issue of it if they're bored. Fortunately for Philip, these were the preoccupied sort.

"Says he can't fight," said a grizzled patron with a patch on one eye. He snorted.

"Sandwich," said Philip. He almost added, "please," until he remembered his manners. He was slowly becoming aware of his environment now that he was in close enough proximity to be breathed upon by it. He sensed that breaches of etiquette would not be lightly excused.

"Who?" said another grizzled patron with a beard tucked into his belt. "Ontzlake? Never knew him to back out of a fair fight."

"Three pence," said the bartender to Philip.

Philip counted his money and slapped three coins on the counter.

"Who said anythin' about a fair fight?" said the one-eyed patron. He cackled.

The bearded patron shrugged. "Why's he say he can't fight?"

The bartender slapped a bowl of stew on the counter.

"I asked– I said a sandwich," Philip said.

"Yep," said the bartender. "Ye did. See any sandwiches?" He took the coins.

"Hot stew," said Philip. "In June?"

"Yer in luck," said the bartender. "That there stew's only lukewarm."

"Oh good," said Philip. "Spoon?"

"Three pence," said the bartender.

"Never mind," said Philip. He pulled a stool up and sat down.

"Says he's wounded," said One-eye.

Long-beard snorted. "Who hasn't fought wounded. If ye ain't wounded ye ain't fightin'. S'the whole point. Wounded. Pah. I had my arm nearly cut off once 'n I still fought."

Another patron piped in, "I had my leg cut off once, I still fought." Philip risked a glance and counted the man's legs. There were two.

"What kinda wound?" said Long-beard.

"Through both thighs," said One-eye. Long-beard sucked a breath in through his teeth. "With a spear," added One-eye.

Long-beard whistled with sympathetic pain. "Ouch," he said.

Philip gave his bowl an experimental jiggle. The stuff in it didn't move.

The patrons occupied themselves with their tankards.

"I knew a fella had both thighs run through with a spear once and still fought," said Long-beard.

"I knew a fella took an arrow in a sensitive place. Kept fightin'," said One-eye. He chuckled. "His adventurin' days were over though."

"I knew a fella broke three lances, two swords, four shields, and a horse. Was cut up so bad, people watchin' started faintin'. Fought twelve hours straight and kept fightin'. They couldn't stop that fella. *He's* probably *still* fightin'."

"Yer spinnin' yarns, Geezer," said Long-beard.

"Ain't spinnin' nuthin. True story."

"What's his name then?"

A black gauntleted hand slammed an empty tankard upside-down next to Philip. The stew bowl jumped. Philip froze.

"His name was Accolon," said a voice like a boulder coming loose on a narrow pass. "And he fights for Ontzlake now."

Philip stared at the gauntlet. He swallowed. The last encounter with Accolon had left most of Arthur's court sore and humbled. Of course, they suspected he'd had Pyralis' enchanted gauntlet. The Gauntlet of Smashing Success... Philip squinted. This one looked normal enough. Besides the exceptional blackness of it. He tried to get a look at the owner's other hand.

The man turned and headed for the door. Philip craned his neck. The man reached for the door. The gauntlets were a matching pair. Philip sighed. It wasn't Pyralis'. Then the man was out the door and gone.

"Don't know what happened to that fella's manners," said Long-beard after a bit.

"I knew a fella had manners once," said Geezer.

"Yeah? What happened?" said Long-beard.

"Had 'em chopped off," said Geezer.

"I bet he still kept fightin'" said One-eye.

Everyone har-harred.

Philip pulled his stew closer. After a while he braved a finger-full. It was edible if you could get past its congealed nature. The trick was to stop thinking of it as stew. It went down quick after that. Philip pushed the bowl away.

"How much for a room?" he asked the bartender.

The bartender shook his head. "Full."

"Stable?" Philip had never slept in a stable. He imagined Thomas had though, and if Thomas could do it so could he.

"Round back," said the bartender. "Five pence."

Philip scoffed. "Five pence. Why would I put up with the... aroma, and the itchy bedding, and, and the whole idea of it? Why would I pay five pence for that when I can sleep under the stars for free?"

The bartender shrugged. "Rain," he said.

"It's not raining."

"Might."

Philip stared.

"Bandits," said the bartender.

"What kind of bandit is going to attack the patron of a false knight's legitimate place of business. Sounds like a career-ender to me."

"Wild animals," said the bartender.

"I'll take my chances," said Philip.

"Suit yerself," said the bartender.

☙

The warm night required no fire, but Philip built one anyway in case of wild animals. He kicked a log and watched the sparks float up. He listened to birds announce the night. In the darkness beyond the circle of light, he imagined the landscape was fairly pleasant. Lush grass, burbling brooks, wildflowers. If he watched long enough, he'd probably see a shooting star. It reminded him of another night, a lifetime ago, spent outside of Camelot.

There was one notable difference. Thomas had been there. They'd had their whole future ahead of them. He kicked another log, and tried not to imagine Thomas and Gus and Booker wherever they might be.

Something small hit him on the head. He flailed at it. It happened again. There was a splash on his arm. And then several on the ground and more hissing in the fire.

Five minutes and ten pence later – twice the original rate "'cause it's rainin' now in'nit?" – Philip made his way through the torrent to the itchy comfort, distinctive aroma, and uneasy company of warm domestics under a leaky stable roof.

A lesser man might have dwelt upon his unfortunate circumstances and let misery and melancholy overtake him. But Philip had larger concerns, like how to get back into the false knight's dungeon; and what to say to an incarcerated sorceress in whose torment he'd been arguably complicit; and more to the point, what said sorceress might say or do to him.

Sir Philip the Exceptionally Disadvantaged had a hard time falling asleep that night.

≪

Having been unlucky – the modern term for 'disadvantaged' – for as long as he could remember, Philip had developed a coping philosophy and an immunity to panic in a particular kind of situation. He had a name for the situation and more names for the events that preceded it: A *trigger* resulted in any number of *middlings* which ultimately resolved themselves in *the finish*. As he'd explained to Marie once at the Fine Pickle, each of these events may seem, at the time, fortunate or unfortunate, but it was best to withhold judgment and not to panic. It was only in hindsight that you would be able to say whether the sequence as a whole was fortunate or not. The only thing you could reliably say while the events were happening was that they were happening.

This is why, twenty-four hours after Philip had finally fallen asleep in the stable, he didn't panic when he found himself perched on a cracking branch overlooking Damas' Folly, directly above a sorceress and her apprentice as they exchanged tense words in hushed voices. He did however feel a certain sense of urgency.

Philip was listening as hard as he could. All of his attention was being directed through his ears, so when the branch cracked it sounded to him like a gunshot might sound to a person who knows what a gun is and who just heard one go off right next to his head.

His attention shifted quickly to his grip on the failing limb. He held his breath. He tried to come up with a believable explanation for why he'd apparently been hiding in a tree above two aggravated sorceresses. He was fairly certain the true series of events wouldn't be believed. He imagined, if he told the truth, it would go something like this…

"Why were you perched in the tree overlooking our secret rendezvous, petulant fool of a boy?"

"I was trying to collect a vial of cottonwood dew, ma'am."

The sorceress would look around taking note of all the cottonwoods and ask, "Why *this* cottonwood?"

He'd recite the instructions he'd been given, "It has to be the dew of a cottonwood that shadows a false knight's folly."

"Fine," they'd say, because they are sorceresses and they'd probably know better than he why it had to be the dew of a cottonwood that shadowed a false knight's folly. "But why *now*?" they'd want to know.

"Because it took me all day to get the other components," he'd say.

"And what did you need these other components for?" they'd ask if they hadn't decided already to just turn him to dust, or into a newt, or trap him inside a rock.

The stress of it all would make him blurt the rest in one breath. "To heal a baby goat for a little girl because when I'd finally fallen asleep it was in a cart someone parked in the stable and when I woke up I was miles from Damas' and I needed to get back fast so I asked the first person I saw, who happened to be the little girl, did she know where I could borrow a horse? And she said, 'Please help my sick baby goat,' and even though I needed to get to the prison to warn Arthur that it won't be Ontzlake he's fighting – it'll be the Black Knight himself, Accolon – I had just chided Thomas for mistreating ladies, hadn't I? So wouldn't that have been hypocritical if I'd ignored the little girl when she clearly needed my help?"

Then he'd have to inhale. "And she promised she would ask her father to lend me their horse if I helped her. So I said, 'Of course I'll help you! I'm a knight aren't I?' And she told me the instructions for the things her grandmother had sent *her* to find, and then off I went."

All of that would probably get him laughed at and possibly pitied but perhaps not turned into something dreadful. Until they realized how long he'd been there and suddenly turned deadly serious again and asked, "And what did you overhear, pray tell, while you were perched in the cottonwood collecting its dew?"

And because they were sorceresses there'd be no way around telling them. He'd gulp and he'd say, "You're Nimue." If they allowed him to continue after that he'd say, "And your name is Elisante. Which sounds French." This would be neither here nor there, and their blank expressions would indicate as such. "And you, Elisante, were trying to stop Thomas from delivering to King Arthur a fake-calibur—"

"*Fay*calibur," she'd correct.

"–a cursed impostor-sword bewitched by Morgan le Fay to resemble Excalibur."

"You overheard all of that?" they'd ask.

"I filled in some gaps by means of deduction," he'd say tapping his temple with a finger because he'd forget to whom he was speaking.

"Clever boy," they'd say because this was still all happening in Philip's imagination.

"And," he'd continue boldly, "while Elisante... Your apprentice?"

The older one would nod.

"While Elisante stays here looking for opportunities to aid Arthur, you, Nimue, are headed to Camelot to try to stop–"

"*Influence*," Nimue would correct.

"Right, because…" Philip would say, trying to recall Nimue's scolding of Elisante which he'd eavesdropped upon through no fault of his own, "'If it is a man's time, it is his time. Illusion can manipulate but it cannot compel. A boat can traverse the river, but it cannot stop the river."

"You learn quickly. You would make a better apprentice than many," Nimue would say with a withering glance at Elisante.

"And *you're* off to *influence*," he'd stress the word to impress Nimue, "some other aspect of the Witch-Queen's villainous plot."

"I'm impressed," Nimue would say. Elisante would fume. Philip would look smug. "You heard some; you deduced much. You don't know everything, but–" She'd grow suddenly serious. "You know too much."

His expression would change to terror. He'd open his mouth to say, "No! Wait!" But the words would never come, and the last thing he would see would be Elisante looking self-satisfied.

...And that is why the true explanation wasn't going to work at all. The branch cracked a second time.

And then it cracked some more.

It was just one long cracking sound now, and down he went.

He crashed through the latticework roof of the folly and landed hard on the floor in a cascade of debris. The impact knocked his breath away. When he recovered, he pushed himself up and opened his mouth to see what it would say.

He was alone.

"Oh," he said. "I didn't even get a chance to ask her about her sister."

And then he said something that of all people Sir Philip the Exceptionally Unlucky knew better than to say. "That was lucky," he said. Then he dusted himself off and patted himself down.

The cottonwood dew was safe, but the vial of weeping willow tears had popped open and dampened his shirt. He wrung what he could back into the vial. When he was done, he tilted the vial in the moonlight and examined the contents. There wasn't much there, but there was some. Maybe it would be enough to heal the little girl's baby goat. It was powerful stuff after all. Direct contact with weeping willow tears was not advised.

Philip's hands were wet with it. The tears went to work. Philip began to cry. Softly, at first.

He felt around for the other component – the pining cones. They were crushed. Small, quiet voices cried, "We miss our friends. We miss our family. We want to go hoooome."

"Yep," said Philip. "Exceptionally lucky." He ran for the farmstead.

It turned out there was enough of the cones and tears left to heal both the baby goat *and* the horse which, it turned out, was sick too. But there wasn't enough dew for the horse.

The horse *looked* better.

"But," asked Philip, "what does the dew do?"

"It counteracts the side effect," said the little girl.

"I'm sorry," sobbed Philip. "I can't stop crying." He tried to get hold of himself. "The side effect?"

"Nothing serious," she said. She patted his arm. "He'll just have a touch of the vapors."

This would turn out to be an understatement.

The little girl thanked Philip with a kiss on his cheek. It made him feel heroic, which just made him cry harder.

Now Philip had a choice to make: Ride to Arthur to warn him about Accolon and, possibly, try to make some sort of amends with the apprentice sorceress on Thomas' behalf. Or ride to Camelot to warn Thomas he was walking right into the Witch-Queen's trap, leaving Arthur in the hands of Elisante who was, apparently, not supposed to involve herself directly.

She certainly hasn't been doing a very good job of that, he thought.

All Philip had wanted was to stay in Camelot and keep the peace which, frankly, did a standup job of keeping itself as long as people didn't go around involving themselves in plots to kidnap wizards and overthrow kings.

Philip wiped his eyes on his sleeve. It didn't help.

Arthur had a better chance of coming out of this alive. He was *Arthur* after all – he was equipped far better than Thomas to handle his opponent. At least until you factored in the cursed sword…

To lose the King would be unthinkable, he thought.

He tried not to think about it.

Who, on the other hand, would miss a Less Valued Knight?

Philip closed his eyes and sighed.

"I would," he answered.

Weeping from direct contact with the willow tears, still hearing the forlorn voices of the pining cones lingering in his mind's ear, and breaking mighty wind fore *and* aft, Philip sped on the flatulent horse toward Camelot and Thomas. If there had been any passersby being passed by in that warm summer night, they would've heard the timeless phrase uttered by all the truest hearts when the bond of friendship is tested: "If he's not dead, I'm going to kill him."

CHAPTER XXI

MEANWHILE IN CAMELOT

Gus warmed the bench outside the office of Sir Tuttle the Authorized. The door was thick and squared perfectly with the frame, preventing him from making out what Thomas and Tuttle were saying to each other on the other side despite Gus' best efforts. A sign on the door read, "*Better to remain silent and be a fool than to speak and be one too.*"

Gus knew the real quote. It was taking everything in him not to unpack a dagger and start carving corrections. He tried not to look at it.

There was a sudden exclamation behind the door and then laughter from one party – not Thomas and not kind. Furniture, probably a chair, scraped heavily against a wooden floor, and then the door burst open and slammed shut. There stood Thomas, face tight, shoulders stiff, fists balled. He glared at Gus.

Gus stood up. "How did it go?"

"He didn't believe me! He laughed at the idea that *Queen* Morgan le Fay would trust a Less Valued Knight with Excalibur. He thinks I'm making the whole thing up!

He, and everyone apparently, are under the assumption that Arthur and Accolon are still out on an extended hunting holiday."

"Did you tell him that's when the king-napping happened – on the hunting trip?"

"Aye. He said Uriens is here in Camelot with Morgan and, 'Isn't that an odd place to be for someone who's allegedly been king-napped?' and 'They haven't said anything about it, and wouldn't they have if it were true?' and 'Oh, by the way, where's the court wizard you swore to find?' And then he said if I don't stop grasping at straws and get back out there and find Merlin 'since I so nobly staked the reputation of the whole Order on it' the next straw I grasped would be the last."

"I see," said Gus.

Thomas sat down heavily.

"What now, sir?"

Thomas stood back up. "Morgan is here like she said she would be. We delivered Excalibur. It's her turn to deliver Merlin. Let's go."

Thomas took a step and stopped. "Where do you think she'd be?"

"In the Queen's suites, sir, would be my guess."

"Right. Follow me."

❧

The bright and airy halls of Queen Guinevere contracted and grew cool as Thomas and Gus entered the guest wing where the King's half-sister held her shadow court.

Gus began to shiver. "Why have we always got to meet sorceresses in cold and cramped and clammy places? Why can't it be in sunny meadows or bright forest glades or cheery taverns?"

"Would that help?"

"Yes. Maybe," said Gus. He shook his head. "No."

"She just sets things up this way to intimidate us."

"It's working."

Two blackguards guarded a black door at the end of a long hall. The only light came from a few dark candles slumped and drowning in their own tallow. Thomas approached fearlessly. He hoped for Gus' sake that that was what he looked like. He tried not to think about how he really felt.

He opened his mouth, and the words came out too loud for the space, "Sir T–"

The blackguards withdrew their crossed halberds sharply, and one of them pushed the door open with a gauntleted arm.

"Ah," said an oily voice from inside the chamber. "Our hero has returned. Tell me, Sir Thomas the Hesitant, were we successful? Or shall I have the stocks prepared?" She laughed.

Gus whimpered. Thomas braced him with a firm hand on his shoulder.

"There is nothing to fear, Augustus Ditcher, we are agents of the King."

Thomas strode into the chamber.

Morgan was perched on a throne identical to the throne on her corvette with one noticeable difference – this one wasn't attached to a room that bobbed relentlessly. Thomas' stomach was doing unpleasant things anyway.

Thomas gave a courtesy bow. "The sword is delivered. Now–"

Morgan waved a hand. "Of course it is. Chocolate?"

A hooded servant girl appeared at Thomas' side offering a bowl of midnight delicacies. There was something familiar about her bearing. Her face was hidden by the hood and obscured further by her hair. A glint of candlelight reflected from something at her neck. A chain–

Thomas hit the bottom of the bowl sending it and the candies flying. He yanked back the girl's hood with one hand and grabbed the chain and pulled with the other. The girl gasped. The chain broke and came free in Thomas' hand.

"Aha!" he said.

The girl looked surprised, terrified, and completely unfamiliar. Thomas opened his hand and looked at the pendant.

It wasn't the cameo.

"Um," he said.

The bowl wobbled noisily on the floor in quickening circles until it finally came to rest.

"You may release my servant now," said Morgan, amused.

Thomas grimaced apologetically at the girl. He let go of her hood, and after a confused moment hot with embarrassment, he handed her the necklace.

"Sorry," he said.

She reached for the necklace, paused to glance at Morgan, then snatched it.

Paralyzed by his mistake, Thomas watched her and another servant scramble to collect the bowl and scattered morsels.

Morgan said something.

"I was sure she..." mumbled Thomas. He stared at his empty hand.

Gus elbowed him.

Thomas looked up. Morgan seemed to be expecting a response.

"I'm sorry," said Thomas, "I–"

Morgan's face was placid. Gus shivered.

"In the future, Sir Thomas, a polite 'no thank you' should suffice."

Thomas nodded. His panicking mind clung to the words, "In the future." Having a future was good. One that involved more of Morgan le Fay? Not as much, but details could be worked out later.

"Now," said the Queen. "If that is all?"

Thomas glanced around at the remaining staff. That one had his hand resting oddly on his hip. A concealed dagger? That one's lips were moving. That one wouldn't look anyone in the eye. That one looked him in the eye too long. He couldn't decide if the room was too hot or too cold.

What had she asked?

"Why am I here?" he said to himself. His head was swimmy. The last time he'd felt like this had been in the false knight's dungeon with the sorceress. The other sorceress.

Morgan was weaving some spell to distract him and make him forget why he was there. The realization made Thomas certain he was right where he wanted to be. The recognition brought calm. The calm brought clear thinking, and the clear thinking made him angry.

"No, that is not all." He glared at the Queen. "I'm here to hold you to your side of the bargain, Witch-Queen."

Gus blinked, moved to take a step back, thought better of it, and decided motionless was the better way to go.

Morgan raised her exquisite eyebrows.

Thomas strained his peripheral vision. As far as he could tell, he seemed to still be human-shaped. His still-human gut told him to not show all his cards.

"So where is he?" he said.

"Where is whom?" said Morgan.

"Where is *who*?" corrected Gus.

"Shh," said Thomas.

"Ah, the squire," said Morgan.

"You know who," said Thomas.

"You know whom," corrected Gus.

Thomas turned to Gus. "Are you certain?" he said. He lowered his voice. "For example I'd say, 'You know who I'm talking about!' I wouldn't say, 'You know *whom* I'm talking about.'"

"But you would say, 'You know whom it is I seek.' You'd be speaking of him, which is whom, not he which would be who."

"Whom," corrected Thomas.

"No–" said Gus. "Oh, I see what you did there. Ha!"

They laughed the convivial laugh of the easily amused. As the laugh wound down, Thomas remembered where he was.

Morgan stared.

"Right," said Thomas. He cleared his throat. "Merlin! Where is Merlin? You said if I delivered the sword you'd tell me where you're keeping Merlin."

Morgan relaxed. "Oh that," she said.

"Yes, *that.* What other 'that' is there?" *This is infuriating*, thought Thomas. *She's toying with me. Oh…*

Thomas had an older brother. One of the first things you learn from older brothers is how to *not* be entertaining when you're being toyed with. Being boring is the survival instinct of the younger brother.

He forced himself to be dull.

"Where is Merlin?" he asked trying to sound like this was a tedious detail and not something he cared too terribly about. It was the same tone he'd used to some success with William in phrases like, "Where is the shovel?" and "Where is my shoe?" and, when he was supposed to be watching her, "Where is our sister?"

"Oh very well," said Morgan. "I'll have my son Owain take you to him in the morning. You can release your beloved court wizard and play the hero."

There was a sparkle in her eye.

"And when my brother returns having overcome yet another extraordinary adventure, I'll be certain to let everyone know whom it was who came to his aid."

Gus frowned and mouthed a couple of who's and whom's.

"Not so fast," said Thomas.

Morgan raised an eyebrow. It meant he'd ceased being boring. Thomas dialed it back.

"We know Merlin is trapped under a rock only *you* can move."

"Is he?" said Morgan. It seemed to be a genuine question.

"We have it on good authority."

Morgan blinked. "And whose authority would that be?"

Thomas saw no harm in revealing his source. "Sir Bagdemagus," he said. "Of the Summer Country," he added, feeling generous.

Morgan chuckled. "Of the Summer Country? My nephew? Spilling family secrets, I see."

Every artist has a favorite palette. Morgan's palette contained fifty shades of lies. She pursed her lips, steepled her long fingers and considered her canvas. Finally she said, "Yes. Yes, you've caught me. But it's not quite as my nephew told you. Any of my kin can remove the..." She waved a hand carelessly. "...the rock. Owain can do it."

"Not so fast," said Thomas, again. He made a mental note that if he was going to keep doing this sort of thing in the future, he was going to need some more stock phrases. He'd also forgotten about being boring. It always happened.

Morgan raised another eyebrow.

"Bagdemagus is your kin. Why couldn't he move it?"

"Good one, sir!" said Gus.

Morgan glared at Gus. "Blood," she said after a moment.

Gus' face drained. He swallowed.

Morgan turned her withering gaze back to Thomas.

"Yes, that's it. The enchantment requires blood-kin. Bagdemagus is from Uriens' family, but Owain is my blood. Any more questions?"

Thomas thought hard.

"Good," said Morgan. She stood. "It would behoove you, Sir Thomas the Hesitant, to learn who you can trust and who you cannot."

"Whom you can trust," blurted Gus. "Confound it," he said and braced himself to be turned into something less Gus-like.

ൿ

Neither Thomas nor Gus spoke until they were beyond the Witch-Queen's borrowed domain.

"I don't trust her, sir."

"Nor I, Gus."

"And I don't trust her son, neither."

"Owain," said Thomas thinking.

"Do you trust him?"

"Marie does."

Gus fidgeted.

Thomas gave him what he hoped was a confident, reassuring look.

"I'll go ask Marie's counsel. We'll go from there."

"Um," said Gus.

"What is it?"

"It's just – perhaps tomorrow would be better, sir? To visit your Lady Marie. It's late is all. And if you go right now she's going to want to know where you've been."

Thomas didn't follow.

"Well, I've been on the road, haven't I?"

"Right you are, sir. And you've the aroma to prove it."

"Oh," said Thomas. "Right. Tomorrow might be better."

"I'll inform Madame Rhapsody you'll be calling."

"You're a good man Augustus Ditcher."

"Thank you, sir."

ൿ

Several hours, a pair of meals, and a barrel of elbow grease later, Thomas stood outside Guinevere's chambers smelling freshly laundered.

He stood straight, sucked in his gut and said, "Brace yourself, Gus," but he was primarily saying this to bolster himself.

"For what?"

"For whom," corrected Thomas. He widened his eyes and mouthed the name, "Madame Rhapsody."

A pair of hands came from behind Thomas then and gently covered his eyes.

Thomas stiffened. He had thought he was already stiff. If the hands had belonged to Madame Rhapsody he would already be being berated. But these hands weren't those hands. If these hands belonged to the person he suspected, then it was perfectly alright to be growing tingly around them. If the hands belonged to someone else, he was going to be in big trouble for involuntary reactions he had no control over but for which he'd almost certainly be mercilessly judged.

There was a silent, breathy giggle near his neck. It sent goose bumps careening every which where. He grabbed the hands and pulled them away just in time to keep his nervous system from short circuiting.

"Marie! What are you do...ing... here...?"

Thomas was used to seeing her dressed for court – which was stunning – or dressed for casual evenings – also stunning – but he wasn't prepared for the sight he beheld now.

She smiled and lifted her chin the way she did. Her eyes sparkled. "I'm ready to go!" she said.

She was dressed for travel.

"Ready to..." Thomas gave Gus a quizzical look. Gus laughed nervously. "You look..." He shook his head and smiled. "You look stunning."

"Thank you," she said.

"You told her... What did you tell her, Gus? A-ha ha."

Gus coughed. "She had some questions sir. Good ones I might add. One led to another, and I couldn't not answer the lady sir. Told her the whole story, didn't I? Might have taken some liberty with the orders, sir."

"Marie I–"

She slipped her hand into his.

"Walk and talk," she said and pulled him down the hall.

ᯓ

"Where are we meeting Owain?" said Marie, still pulling Thomas. "The livery?"

"Yes, but–"

"This way," she said and tugged him down a side hall. "Short cut."

Gus struggled to keep up.

"I need to make sure..." said Thomas huffing. "...we're on the same...page here."

Marie stopped. "Of course we are! Why? What page are you on?"

"What page am I...?" said Thomas.

In the presence of Marie, Thomas often found himself confused and not really minding it. There had been a reason he was seeking Marie out though. He was certain of it.

"Gus," he said. "Catch me up."

Gus reached them and trotted to a stop, panting. "Trying to, sir," he said.

"I mean, what do we know?" He tilted his head toward Marie.

Marie crossed her arms impatiently.

Gus gave her a cautious glance and began, "Morgan le Fay promised to reveal Merlin's whereabouts if and when Thomas delivered to Arthur the sword Excalibur which had been placed in Morgan's safekeeping by Arthur for unknown reasons which I frankly find ill-advised but that's how the story goes. Thomas delivered the sword and

Morgan has dispatched her son Owain to escort us to Merlin's location. Knowing through Bagdemagus that only the person who placed it can move the stone under which Merlin presently abides, and being assured by Morgan–" Gus coughed meaningfully, "–that indeed she *and/or* her blood-kin can remove it, we seem bound to accept Owain's assistance in the successful resolution of Thomas' quest to achieve the liberation of Merlin, the preservation of the kingdom, and a modest increase in the amount of dignity that is generally afforded the Less Valued."

Marie crossed her arms and tapped her foot.

"This is what Gus told you?"

"Mm-hmm," she said.

"And you're okay with this?"

"Of course." *Can we go now*, said her posture.

"You're okay with Owain, the son of a witch, leading me – us – leading us to who knows where on the advisement of said witch?"

"Uther's boot," said Marie. "Owain is not the man his mother is."

Thomas snickered.

"You know what I mean. He's Arthur's nephew! He's a member of Arthur's court. What is your problem with him?"

"Well, for one, he's a real son of a witch."

Gus snorted.

"A witch who seems to have upheld her end of your bargain."

"Are you sure you're not just eager to go on an adventure?"

Marie's eyes flashed dangerously.

"Get out of those stuffy court..." Thomas was out of his element. "...clothes for once."

Her lips thinned. She glared at him.

"Do something worth talking about instead of talking about things worth talking about?"

She sighed. "Okay, maybe. But that doesn't mean I'm not right. Look, being one of Guinevere's ladies, you get a sense of which knights are knights because they're knightly, and which knights are knights because they're not."

Thomas let that sink in. "Which am I?" he said.

"You're the sort that wonders which kind he is," she said.

"Aaand, which sort is that?" he said.

She frowned. "Come on," she said. "We have a wizard to dislodge."

Thomas grinned and let himself be pulled along. "No really, which sort am I?"

"Apparently the sort that won't *stop* asking the question, even if it's for his own good."

Gus resolved in his heart that if one day he could be a knight, he'd be the sort that was a knight because he was one and not because he wasn't. He hurried after them.

৵

Philip was blubbering. Owain was trying, awkwardly, to comfort him. A horse nearby was breaking wind rather impressively.

Thomas, Marie and Gus skidded onto the scene.

"Don't touch me," said Philip waving off Owain.

Owain held up his hands, took a step back, and noticed the new arrivals.

"Ah, Thomas. Good. This is your friend, yes?"

"Y...es," said Thomas. Was this Philip? It seemed to be, though Thomas had never seen him like this. Was Philip his friend? "Yes," Thomas said again with more commitment. "What did you do to him?"

Philip shook his head. "It's not. It's not. It's." He took a shaky breath and turned a hopeless face on them. "It's the tears," he said and sobbed some more.

Marie moved to comfort him. This Philip accepted.

"There, there," said Marie. "Have a seat."

"Marie," said Owain, bowing. "Mum didn't say anything about you coming along."

"Well I am," she said glaring. She turned her attention back to Philip. "Use your words dear."

Philip held his head up, blinking, and fumbled in a pocket. He pulled out a broken vial.

"Okay," said Marie. "Someone broke your vial?"

Philip shook his head. "*I* broke my vial."

"It's alright. You broke your vial. There are more vials. Guinevere has lots of vials. I'm sure she–"

Philip shook his head.

"There was something in the vial wasn't there? Something important?"

Philip bit his lip and nodded.

"What was in the vial, Philip?"

"Tears," said Philip. "Tears." He moaned. "Will. Will." He couldn't get it out.

"Oh," said Marie. "Oh, my."

"What is it?" said Thomas.

Gus said, "Weeping willow tears by the looks of it, sir."

Philip pointed at Gus and nodded. Then he gave a frustrated grunt, stood up, and came at Thomas. "You!" he bellowed.

Thomas threw his hands up. "Wait wait wait. I didn't have anything to do with this."

Philip shook his head. He wiped at his eyes with a sleeve. "Not this," said Philip. He threw the vial aside. "Well, yes this. Indirectly." Whatever influence the tears had held, they were now bowing to Philip's fury. "Would you like the bad news? Or the *bad* news?" he said.

Thomas, faced with his sobbing, frustrated, and now gloating friend gave the only answer he could.

"Um," he said. "The bad news?"

"Accolon is at Damas', and it's Accolon that Arthur's going to have to fight, not Ontzlake."

The expression on Philip's face read, *What do you think of that?*

"That–" said Thomas. "That is bad news." In fact, it was far more unsettling than Thomas cared to admit. *At least Arthur's got Excalibur*, he thought.

Philip's face relaxed. "But Accolon doesn't have the gauntlet. I checked." He seemed especially pleased with himself on this count.

"The gauntlet?" said Owain.

"The Gauntlet of Smashing Success," Thomas clarified.

Owain frowned and nodded.

"Surprised you don't know about it," said Thomas, suspecting that Owain in fact knew plenty about it.

"I–" started Owain.

"What's the *bad* news?" interrupted Marie, taking hold of the conversation by its ears.

Philip turned a full-force I-told-you-so glare on Thomas. "Thomas," he said, "delivered a cursed sword to Arthur."

"Wait, what?" said Thomas. He laughed.

Gus snorted unbelievingly.

"Philip," said Marie, back in her consoling voice.

Philip shook her off. "It's true."

"What? No," said Thomas. "I delivered Excalibur to Arthur."

"Fake-calibur is more like it," said Philip. "Or Faycalibur if you like. Either way."

"Impossible," Thomas scoffed. "Who told you this?"

"The sorceress." Philip folded his arms. "Esses," he added realizing the plural was more impressive.

"You went back into the dungeon and talked to her?" said Gus. He eased backward and glanced around the livery in case any sorceresses were lurking in the shadows.

"That's right," Philip nodded. "That's what I did."

The smug expression fell. He shook his head and shrugged. "Okay, no. What are you crazy? They're sorceresses."

"But she told you this?" said Thomas.

"I, um," Philip stammered. "I overheard it while..." he pointed at the discarded vial. "I was on a quest and happened to be in the wrong place at the right time. It's kind of my thing."

"What *exactly* did she say?" Horror was welling in Thomas. If Philip was right...

"Elisante – that's the girl you tortured – told her mistress Nimue, of all people, that she failed to stop the false knight Sir Thomas the We-All-Wish-He-Was-A-Great-Deal-More-Hesitant from delivering le Fay's impostor-sword to Arthur."

Thomas went numb. He felt like he was watching himself from the outside.

"You," said Marie, puzzled, "tortured a girl?"

Thomas looked at Marie. "No," he said. He looked away. "It wasn't like that. I–" What had he done?

Thomas slumped. At the time, the ends seemed to justify the means. He hadn't felt *wonderful* about it, but great knights did what needed to be done to complete the quest, didn't they?

He had his doubts about that. And now that the end was false, it was plain to him that his means had been false too, regardless of the end.

Maybe he was false. A false knight. Sir Thomas the False...

Now, hang on, he thought.

He hadn't *intended* to deliver a cursed sword to Arthur. He hadn't *intended* for Arthur to go trying to fight Black Knights with it. And he *certainly* hadn't intended to hurt the girl to get the sword in the first place.

No, he thought. That last bit had been intentional.

He felt sick.

"That's my mother for you," said Owain.

"Were you a part of this?" said Marie.

"What? Me? No," said Owain. "Not exactly."

Thomas hugged his stomach. The light was too bright. The world was growing flat like a backdrop in a play. He was aware of Marie, somewhere distant, accosting Owain.

"Allow me to rephrase," she said. "What was your part in this?"

"Just the usual," said Owain. "Take you out – well, not *you* – take *them* out. Get them lost. Threaten them. Tell them not to come back. Permanent assignment to the Table of Errant Companions, so to speak."

"You were going to turn us into empty seats?" said Philip aghast. "Are all of those seats – are they all men you've threatened?"

Owain did some mental accounting. "Not all of them, no. Look," he said, "it's my mother, right? She and Arthur go way back. And it's not all her fault I might add. He started it."

"Enough," said Marie. "Owain, you need to go find out the rest of your mother's plot and put a stop to it."

"Fair enough," said Owain. "She does tend to take things a bit too far if you ask me."

"Too far?" said Philip. "A bit?"

Marie spun and jabbed a finger in Philip's chest, hard.

"And you," said Marie. "Yes, you were right. Satisfied? Now you're going to help undo the harm you helped do."

"Yes ma'am," said Philip.

Gus snickered.

Marie glared at him with a glare that threatened unimaginable horrors.

Gus clammed up.

And stay that way, said Marie's follow-up glare.

She softened then and turned to Thomas.

"Thomas," she began, "you'd better go explain to Tuttle–"

"No," he said.

Thomas stood holding Booker's reins.

"I'm going to find Elisante," he said. "I'm going to help Arthur."

He climbed aboard. Booker tried to look supportive.

"I'm going to set things right," he said. "Hyaah," he added. Booker ambled out of the stable.

Philip and Gus moved to stand by Marie. Owain stood close, but apart. For a long moment, they watched Thomas go.

Gus was the first to speak.

"He's the sort of knight," he said, "who's a knight because he is one. Isn't he?"

Marie nodded. "I suspect so," she said. "But this is where we find out, isn't it?"

Owain took his leave. Marie mounted a horse and pulled Gus up behind her. "Coming?" she said to Philip.

"Yes ma'am," he said. He chose a fresh horse and saddled up.

"Tears still troubling you?" said Marie.

Philip shook his head. "Something in my eye is all. I'll be fine."

It took Booker a little while to find his pace – not because he had so many to choose from, but because the one he did have kept getting misplaced. But find it, he did.

Thomas sat true and fixed his eyes ahead. His friends followed behind, keeping careful company on the road their friend had chosen.

CHAPTER XXII

THE WINDS OF CHANGE

They rode through the day. When the sun set they kept riding. When the moon rose they kept riding. When the others' horses began to flag they pressed on. Booker plodded along indefatigable. Compared to the other horses he was slower, stiffer, and moved like an animal with not enough elbows. He had the inertia of the aged – any change to position or pace required nontrivial mental and physical commitments. Both moving and stopping had long ago begun to require conscious, willful effort. In other words, once Booker got warmed up it was better to keep going than to stop and rest and try to start again.

The sun rose and they kept going. By the time the sun topped the trees they'd passed the boundary stone and Damas' fortress was within sight.

Trumpets blared. Thomas, tilting half-asleep on Booker's saddle, jolted alert.

"Hyaah!" he said, panicked.

Booker obliged by not slowing down. Thomas hopped down and ran ahead.

The field was ringed with banners, people, and colorful crepe ribbons. Two fighters clashed in the middle. Thomas stood on his toes and craned his neck to see.

The fighters were fresh. They both sported unornamented breastplates, closed helmets, and unmarked shields. It was impossible to tell who they were. Thomas squinted at the swords. Neither appeared to be Faycalibur.

Thomas breathed a sigh of relief. He scanned the sides of the field looking for Arthur, but he didn't see any waiting combatants.

Philip and Marie caught up to him. Gus trailed behind leading the horses.

"Is he on the field?" said Philip.

"No," said Thomas. "I don't think they've brought him out yet."

"Where's this sorceress-girl?" said Marie.

Thomas scanned the crowd again. "I don't know." He shrugged, worried. "She might not even be here."

"Nimue told her to stay here," said Philip. "She's got to be here."

"Well what does she look like?" asked Marie.

Philip chuckled. Then he whistled. He opened his mouth to describe her, and resorted to hand motions instead.

"What are you talking about?" said Thomas. He glared at Philip in frustration.

"What?" said Philip.

"She's small," said Thomas. "She's a thin little waif of a girl. Harmless looking. Only she's not."

"I rather thought she looked like my mum," said Gus.

"Okay..." said Marie. "So I'm looking for a buxom, middle-aged, waif. Let me guess, she's a brunette with long, curly, straight blond hair cut short and braided."

Gus frowned trying to recall.

Thomas said, "Can't say I recall the hair. She's fond of hoods."

Philip stared at nothing and smiled.

"It would seem," said Gus, "she appears however you want her to appear."

"And to you she appeared as your mum?" said Philip.

Gus nodded. "I miss me mum sometimes."

"What do we look for then?"

Thomas shook his head.

"You could use the frame, sir."

"No," said Thomas. "The frame did something to her. Or to me. No frame."

They watched the crowd in silence. The fighters on the field clashed and rebounded and clashed again. The crowd seemed mostly disinterested.

"They're waiting for the main event," said Philip.

"Alright," said Thomas. "We split up. She's gone as a prince, an old woman, a sneak-thief, and a beautiful lady–"

"How beautiful?" said Marie.

"Not very," said Thomas wisely. "But very," he added for the sake of correctness. "Her illusions work by piggy-backing on what you want to see. So, look for anything *not* out of the ordinary. Pay special attention to things that don't catch your eye. If she's hiding, she's hiding in plain sight."

Thomas, Philip and Marie moved off in different directions.

Gus stood and clutched the horses' reins. He swallowed.

In a small voice, to no one because he was alone again, he said, "What do we do if we find her, sir?"

Booker whinnied and nudged his shoulder with a well-meaning but unsettling nostril.

"Nonsense we'll be fine, eh boy?" said Gus nervously.

Booker whinnied again.

"Atta boy," said Gus and patted Booker. Gus was happy to discover that calming the horse also calmed himself. He clenched his jaw, screwed up his resolve, and scanned the crowd for the mysterious sorceress with terrible powers to contort the mind. He wanted to not find her which meant that he fully expected to be the one to find her which meant that, since he would see what he wanted to see, he was certain to come across her. He whimpered.

Booker, having failed to communicate accurately with the boy, scanned the crowd for apples.

ⴰ

Thomas shouldered his way through the crowd. It was hopeless. Too many people, too little time. He was very aware of the occasional press of the mirror's frame, stowed as it was in its satchel, tight against his person.

Too many faces. What would she be today? A princess? He looked high, to the stands. A peasant? He looked low, to the grounds. A combatant? He looked to the field and watched the fighters.

He didn't know what prize was promised these two, but whatever it was it seemed to be failing to produce the desired inclination toward violence. Or perhaps they'd reached an agreement to stop short of maiming each other and split whatever prize they had coming to them.

Someone bumped him and moved past. He re-focused, scanning the crowd again. A farmer? A mercenary? A waif?

A waif. The girl who bumped him turned. She looked him square in the eye and reached for a chain around her neck. She pulled the necklace free from her clothing and laid it against her chest. She dropped her hand.

The cameo. There was a challenge in her gaze.

Illusions work best when the illusionist shows the beguiled what he wants to see. Today, Thomas wanted to see the real Elisante. Elisante seemed more than willing to oblige.

She turned and wove her way through the crowd. Thomas followed.

ⴰ

He'd lost her. He started pressing more assertively. Several heys and watch-its later, Thomas broke through the outer edge of the throng. He was on a bluff bordered by the crowd on one side and cliffs that fell to the sea on the other. A lone tower perched on the edge of the plain overlooking the surf. The tower door was swinging closed. Thomas hurried to it, swung it open, and stepped into the dark chamber.

The door swung shut behind him. He blinked to adjust his eyes. The room was clean, quiet and empty. Opposite the door, stairs led up into the tower's high reaches and down into darkness – presumably to the beach.

He listened carefully. Sounds of the crowd behind and the sea below came muffled and distant. He searched for the fall of a foot against stone, the rustle of clothes. Nothing.

And then, *click*. He followed the sound to a door hidden in an alcove between the stairs. The click must have been the latch. He touched the handle hesitantly.

Steeling himself, Thomas twisted the latch, pushed the door, and stepped out onto a salt-crusted balcony balanced high over briny depths. The wind whistled and whipped at him. The door was flung shut in the windstorm. Elisante stood facing him, her back to the vast expanse of sea and sky. Her robe flapped and her hair whipped wildly.

Thomas put a hand on his sword. Tears streaked across his cheeks as the gale tore at his eyes.

Elisante yelled something inaudible over the wind.

Thomas shook his head.

She took a breath and yelled again.

Thomas took a step toward her.

Elisante raised a hand. *Stop*.

Thomas stopped.

Elisante was yelling again.

"WHAT?" shouted Thomas.

Elisante yelled. She had both arms thrust downward at her sides either in frustration or simply to keep her clothes from carrying her away like a kite.

"I CAN'T HEAR YOU," Thomas shouted.

Elisante yelled something back. Thomas was pretty certain it had been, "WHAT?" He took his hand off his sword. In an effort to look non-threatening he relaxed his arms and shoulders. He was afraid if he relaxed anything else he'd be blown off the tower.

"LET'S GO INSIDE," Thomas yelled.

"WHAT?" yelled Elisante.

"INSIDE!" Thomas yelled and waved her toward him. He turned and pulled at the door. It was no use against the wind. He braced a foot against the tower wall and tried again. It came free for a moment but was slammed shut again, and then Elisante was there pulling with him.

They forced the door open. Elisante ducked inside, and Thomas flung himself through the door. He rolled into the dark chamber. The door snapped shut behind him.

Silence.

Thomas fumbled for some matches, struck one and lit a candle. He looked up. There in the dim light, fierce eyes glared out at him from behind a head of hair that had been thoroughly traumatized.

"Hwah!" said Thomas and dropped the candle.

The light went out. Nobody moved.

Thomas started laughing.

"Are you kidding me?" said Elisante.

He couldn't help himself. He couldn't stop laughing.

"I'm– I'm sorry," he said. "It's just–"

The silence was deafening. Elisante was not amused.

Thomas got hold of himself, fumbled for the candle and re-lit it.

"Crikey," he said. She was just how he remembered.

She watched him unblinking.

"Seriously," said Thomas. "If you could see..." It was no use. There was no humor behind those eyes.

"Why out there anyway?" said Thomas, feeling ashamed for laughing and feeling miffed for feeling ashamed.

Elisante folded her arms and looked away. "I thought it would be more dramatic."

"I can see that," said Thomas. He honestly could.

"Is this why you came back?" Elisante snapped. "To mock me?"

"No," said Thomas, feeling that he deserved this.

"You delivered the sword to Arthur. You accomplished your mission."

"No." Thomas shook his head. That stung.

"Did you come back to watch Arthur die? What reward did she promise you? You know she'll just double-cross you. If she hasn't already. Why are you here? Haven't you done enough?"

Thomas shook his head. Explaining everything was going to be more complicated than he'd thought.

"Answer me false knight!" she said.

Thomas had had plenty of time to think on the way. He'd envisioned this conversation over and over, and he'd decided three things. One: yes, he'd been awful. Elisante was suffering deep pain over something, and he'd used that to take advantage of her. But, two: he wasn't going to shoulder *all* the blame for current circumstances regarding Arthur. And three: he was no false knight.

"False?" Thomas sputtered. "'False,' says the professional illusionist. Or is it the old port-lady in distress? Or the sneaky sneak-thief? Or maybe," Thomas gave a little bow, "the Prince of Loaves?"

Elisante blinked and shook her head. "The Prince of pardon me?" she said.

"That's what we're calling you. And you know who's false? Flimflammers. That's who. You're not innocent in all of this. *You're* a flimflammer. Just like Morgan."

Elisante gasped.

"Okay, sorry, that was harsh," said Thomas. "But the point stands."

Elisante shouted in exasperation. "My only failing was failing to stop you, you... smellfungus!"

"Klazomaniac," Thomas shot back.

Elisante shrieked in frustration. "Drate-poke!"

"Driggle-draggle!"

"Fopdoodle!"

"Muck-spout!"

"How dare you," Elisante growled.

They caught their breath and stared at each other.

Thomas sat down and pinched the bridge of his nose. "This isn't how I imagined this would go."

"And how is that?" Elisante snapped.

Thomas took a deep breath. "Why didn't you just tell me?" he asked.

"Tell you what?"

"Tell me the sword was an impostor," said Thomas.

Elisante chortled. "Right," she said.

When Thomas said nothing, she frowned at him.

"You're trying to tell me you didn't know," said Elisante.

"I didn't know," said Thomas.

"Right," she said sarcastically. She turned her head and watched him. "Then why did you try to stop me?" she said.

"I thought you were trying to steal Excalibur!" said Thomas.

"You honestly thought you were carrying Excalibur?" she scoffed. She froze. "Oh, heaven help us – you honestly thought you were carrying Excalibur."

Her face went pale. She sat down carefully.

"You honestly thought you were carrying Excalibur?" she repeated.

Thomas frowned and nodded.

She rolled her eyes. "Why on Earth would Morgan trust someone like you with a sword like that?"

Thomas shrugged. "Why would Arthur trust Morgan with it?" He spoke slowly, forming the thought as the words came out of his mouth. "I have found, when dealing with people at this level, that things aren't always as they seem. Sometimes that lesson keeps me safe. Sometimes it gets me in trouble. Knowing who to trust isn't always a straightforward enterprise.

"I mean," he said. "Do you always get that one right?"

She glared at him. "No," she admitted looking away. "I suppose not."

Thomas clenched his jaw, took a deep breath, and said it. "Elisante," he said. "I'm sorry."

She squinted at him distrustfully. "For what?" she said in the tone of a person who wasn't sure she wanted to know.

"For what happened in the prison yesterday."

"Nothing happened," she said looking away again. "You beat me. You got what you wanted."

Thomas shook his head. "But the way I did it... I could see I was hurting you."

"So what?" she snapped. "You think I haven't been hurt?"

Thomas frowned. "I think you have. And I'm sorry."

Elisante was still and quiet.

"What did you see through the frame anyway?" said Thomas. "What happened to your sister?"

She stood up. "That's none of your business." But she didn't leave.

"You're right," said Thomas. "Elisante, I'm sorry. Will you forgive me?"

She didn't answer.

"I'd like– I need your help. Arthur needs our help."

She turned and held her hand out. "Let me see it," she said.

"See what?" said Thomas.

"The frame. Give me the frame."

"Um," said Thomas.

"I think you're only repentant now because you need something. You're here because Arthur is in trouble, not because you were awful. I may forgive you. But it's going to cost you. The frame," she said and motioned with her hand again.

Thomas produced the frame. He held it firmly with both hands. If he gave it up, he'd be at a serious disadvantage. How would he know if he was just seeing what he wanted to see? He supposed he'd have to do what he'd done without the frame: trust the insight of those he trusted.

He handed it over. Elisante pulled. Thomas let go. He immediately felt better. It really had been a disillusioning frame of reference.

"Close your eyes," said Elisante.

"What?"

"Close," she said again. "Your eyes."

Thomas obeyed.

Elisante lifted the frame and looked through it at Thomas. The frame worked its magic. She saw what she was reluctant to see.

She sighed and lowered the frame.

"I can open my eyes?"

"Yes," she said.

"You saw something you didn't want to see," he said.

She nodded.

"What?"

"In truth? I saw a knight. Nothing more. Nothing less."

"That's good right? You'll help?"

Elisante sighed begrudgingly. "Fine. Yes. What do you propose?"

In all the times Thomas had envisioned the conversation, he'd never gotten this far. "Um, I guess I was hoping *you'd* have an idea. Can't you just…?" He waved his hands in a vaguely magical sort of way.

Elisante chose to ignore the ridiculousness before her. "It doesn't work that way. I can't just change events. I can 'influence' things." She seemed perturbed. "And only indirectly. And we only have Arthur's own desires to work with."

"Well," said Thomas, thinking out loud. "What does Arthur want?"

She chuckled. "I can think of one thing for sure."

"Bread?" Thomas laughed.

Elisante gave him a quizzical look, like a cat trying to figure out what, in fact, it had caught between its paws.

"You are not like other knights, Sir Thomas the Hesitant," she said.

Thomas sighed. There was a sad acceptance in it. "I know. But one day, I hope to be."

She laughed and shook her head. "Do me a favor?"

"Anything," he said, without hesitation.

"Don't hope too hard."

Thomas gave her a puzzled smile. "What am I missing? What's the one thing Arthur wants for sure?"

Elisante laughed again. She was still having trouble believing that the boy before her was for real. There wasn't an ounce of mischievousness in his eyes, let alone deceit, and she considered herself something of an expert on the matter. Up to now she wouldn't have thought twice about destroying Thomas, or at least wrecking his day. But now an inexplicable desire was rising within her to protect him.

"Oh Thomas, you great ninnyhammer, What Arthur wants…" Did she really have to spell this out? "What Arthur wants is…" She couldn't believe she was having to spell this out. "What Arthur wants," she finally said, "is to win."

CHAPTER XXIII

A TEST OF TRUE CALIBUR

The field was cleared. A hush fell over the crowd. In a pavilion erected for the occasion, Arthur knelt. An old priest placed a crust of unleavened bread on Arthur's tongue.

"*Corpus Christi,*" said the priest. "The body of Christ."

"Amen," said Arthur.

"May almighty God bless you." The priest made the sign of the cross. "*Pater, et Filius, et Spiritus Sanctus.*"

"Amen," Arthur said again and stood.

Damas handed him a helmet. "You have a dozen knights and damsels to attend you. You have been outfitted with my best armor. My shield is yours."

"And my sword yours," said Arthur. "I will defeat your brother's champion or die."

Damas looked pleased. "The former would be preferable."

"And you," said Arthur firmly, "will release your prisoners. Every man."

"You have my word," said Damas.

Arthur turned, pulled on the helmet and allowed the attendants to secure it.

"Should you live," said Damas under his breath.

A squire entered the tent and bowed.

"Speak," said Damas.

"Sir Ontzlake inquires if you and your champion are ready, m'Lord."

Damas pushed the tent flap aside and addressed Arthur. "What say you, champion?"

There was a muffled response from inside the helmet.

"Pardon?" said Damas.

Arthur raised his visor. "Ready," he said, and dropped the visor again.

Damas nodded, and they walked out of the dark sanctuary and into the hot and humid sunlit morning.

There was another muffled pronouncement from inside the helmet.

"Say again?" said Damas.

Louder now. "I said, 'It's hot, isn't it?'"

"I'm sure you've had worse."

"Aye," said Arthur.

Damas let Arthur walk ahead and motioned to a servant. "Have the cool beer brought from the cellar to my box. And women with fans." He glanced at the climbing sun. "And shades."

"And extra barrels of water," Damas said, "for the champion." It sounded almost like an afterthought.

Mumble mumble, said Arthur inside the helmet.

Damas' men helped Arthur mount his horse. He set his shield and raised his lance. He turned his horse dramatically and trotted in a tight circle at the end of the lists. The crowd booed. They didn't know who was *in* the armor, but they knew to whom the armor belonged.

A knight in black sat steady on his war steed at the other end of the field. The steed pawed the ground once and snorted.

Arthur pointed his horse down the lists and assessed his opponent – his armor, his horse, the way he sat. An experienced knight can judge another by the way he sits his horse.

There was a muffled exclamation from Arthur's helmet that was probably something stronger than, "Oh drat." It was too late for clarity though, the trumpets sounded.

The Black Knight goaded his horse and lowered his lance. Arthur did the same. They met mid-field. Each lance hit the others' shield square. There was a great cracking sound, and both men went down in a tumult of dust, splinters, and whinnying masses of muscle, hoof and tooth.

The knights rolled to their feet and drew their swords.

Thomas and Elisante pushed their way to the front of the crowd. Thomas spotted Marie and Philip on the other side of the field. Philip was gripping the rail, knuckles white. Marie was twisting her sleeve. Thomas caught her eye. She looked worried.

"What do we do?" she mouthed.

"We're too late!" Thomas said to Elisante, panicked.

Elisante shook her head and nodded to a figure making her way up the stands. The lady turned and sat. Elisante and Nimue exchanged glances, and something unspoken passed between them.

Elisante gritted her teeth. "No we're not," she said.

There was a heavy clash from the field. Arthur pushed the Black Knight with his shield and swung. His sword landed once, twice, three times, but the blows glanced off of his opponent's armor. The Black Knight let Arthur beat at him until Arthur held his sword up and examined it. Then the knight yelled and charged.

He was a sight to behold – fast and nimble despite his size and armor. Arthur deflected half his strokes with shield and sword, but those that landed bit his armor and soon Arthur was bleeding from half a dozen wounds.

The Black Knight pressed Arthur back against the stiles. There was an exclamation of muffled frustration from within Arthur's helmet. He used the stile to lever himself, pushed the knight back and went at him hard.

The Black Knight again allowed blow after blow to bounce, slide, or slip off of him. Arthur turned and aimed a blow at the lists in frustration. The sword bit the wood and stuck.

A muffled taunt came from the Black Knight's helmet.

"WHAT?" shouted Arthur yanking uselessly at his stuck sword.

"DEFEND THEE WELL NOW MISCREANT!"

"Who talks like that?" mumbled Arthur. He braced a foot on the wood and pulled at the sword. Blood flowed freely from his wounds and soaked the grass.

"I thought that was his thing," said Elisante frustrated, "pulling swords out of stuck places."

The Black Knight charged.

Marie bit her lip and held her breath. Philip shut his eyes tight.

Arthur's foot slipped beneath him, but the sword came free just as they clashed and Arthur scored a direct blow to his opponent's helmet.

The Black Knight went down.

Arthur prodded him with his boot. He looked at his sword. He shrugged, turned to the crowd, lifted his visor and–

"Watch out!" yelled Thomas.

The Black Knight rose up behind Arthur and brought the hilt of his sword down hard on Arthur's helmet. Arthur stumbled and grabbed the lists to keep himself from falling.

When he'd regained his balance, he snapped his visor shut, faced the knight and bellowed. His opponent bellowed back. They charged each other hacking and slashing.

Arthur's sword ever failed. The Black Knight's never faltered.

"So much blood," said someone near Thomas.

"I can't watch," said another.

"This is the stuff!" said a third.

"I can't believe he's still standing."

"That's a true knight there."

"Ayup full of knighthood."

"Look how knightly he endures the pain," said someone.

"Who is it you think?"

"S'pose it could be Gawain," said someone.

"Nah G'wain wears a kilt. I seen him."

"And he's left-handed."

"He ain't left-handed."

"Could be."

"S'not"

"You don't know."

"S'not left-handed. Left-handed's cheatin'."

"How d'ya figure left-handed's cheatin?"

"My pappy built stairs for Uther. Ye make em go clockwise down the tower so's the defenders can swing and the attackers can't, see? But left-handers can still swing. That's cheatin'."

The commenters were quiet for a moment.

The Black Knight was beating Arthur back. Arthur continued to bleed.

"Don't think that's cheatin.'"

"Well what is it then?"

"It just is, is all. It's an advantage – I'll give ya that. But ye can't fault a man born for stormin' castles for stormin' a castle. Ye take the adventure God gives ye."

The other man nodded. "S'long as ye got blood in ye."

"S'right."

"Which won't be much longer fer this fella here."

A trumpet sounded.

The Black Knight turned and faced the stands. Arthur bent double for a moment, then braced one hand on a thigh, leaned on his sword with the other and pushed himself upright. He was breathing hard and his head tilted around an alarming arc as he focused on Damas and Ontzlake who were talking to a lady.

"Nimue," said Elisante.

"What's she doing?" said Thomas.

"Trying to stop the fight I'd guess."

"Will it work?"

Elisante shrugged. "I don't know, but now is our chance." She pointed to a handful of maidens taking to the field with water, rags, and–

"Snacks?" said Thomas. "You're going to do something to their food! Brilliant."

Elisante led Thomas to a nearby tent. "I'm not going to do something to their food," she said, peeved. "I'm going to do something to you. Well, to Arthur. And the crowd. I can get you to him."

"Then what?"

Elisante glared at him. "I suggest you think of something fast. Here," she said. She pulled a robe onto him and then handed him a bowl of fruit.

"Now get out there young lady and attend your champion."

She smacked him on the bottom, pushed him out of the tent toward the field, gripped her cameo, and concentrated.

Thomas stumbled onto the field. "You've got to be kidding me," he mumbled to himself. The crowd was distracted by Damas and Ontzlake and their impending decision. Thomas tried to make himself small and hurried over to Arthur.

Arthur swung his head around and brought his wobbly attention to bear on the damsel before him. A large grin spread across his face. "It's you!" he said. He gripped

Thomas' shoulder. "Morgan's girl from the prison. You brought me my sword."

Arthur leaned in and said quietly. "You should know, you're my favorite." He winked. "Oh, apples!" he said. He aimed his hand at one and reached for it. The motion altered his balance and he tilted alarmingly.

Thomas caught him and supported him.

"We have to stop meeting like this," said Arthur. "I am married, you know. I wonder if Guinevere is here. She really should be here. I think this might be my last fight. That other fellow is rather good."

He bit into his apple.

"Your Majesty..." Thomas wanted to explain everything, but there wasn't time. "You've got the wrong sword. I gave you the wrong sword. That's not Excalibur."

"I knew it!" said Arthur delightedly. He held up the blade. "Excalibur slices right through steel, no problem. And the scabbard. No one bleeds like this if they've got Excalibur's scabbard. Merlin says it's because if the sword is in the scabbard, you're not fighting. But he's wrong. Yep. Magic scabbard."

"Your Majesty," said Thomas. "I'm sorry."

"For what?"

"For giving you this sword. Morgan said it was Excalibur–"

Arthur brightened. "If this sword is from my sister, I'm sure it's fine."

Thomas was horrified. "Um, no sire that's the thing. This sword is cursed. You can't keep fighting with it."

"Not to worry. I've fought with cursed swords before."

"You have?"

Arthur nodded. "Lots of times."

"Name one," said Thomas.

Arthur frowned.

"Our champions have fought bravely!" shouted Damas.

Thomas said, "Sire, you have to forfeit the fight."

"What!?" Arthur looked like that was the most ridiculous thing he'd heard all day.

Damas shouted, "And a request has been made to conclude the contest."

"You must agree to end the fight, Your Majesty" said Thomas.

Arthur patted Thomas reassuringly. "Of course I won't," he said.

Damas shouted, "We all agree, none has beheld knights so knightly as these two knights, nor nary seen a knight fight so well with so much blood spilt. But–"

"You must!" said Thomas.

"I cannot," said Arthur. "I have sworn. And besides, now I have something else to fight for."

"Sire?"

"The damsel who brought me these apples," he said. He bit again and chewed, grinning.

"Sire," said Thomas.

Damas shouted, "But my brother and I agree, the contest is not over. The fight continues!"

"But Your Majesty, your sword is useless," Thomas stammered, aghast.

Arthur seemed to give this due consideration. He stared at the sword. "A young knight taught me once that 'useless' says more about the wielder than the wielded. Remarkable lad."

"Sire–" said Thomas. But Arthur was meandering his way back toward the Black Knight, and Thomas was being pulled off the field.

"He's had a traumatic brain injury!" Thomas yelled. "You have to stop the fight."

"I had a traumatic brain injury once," said a one-eyed onlooker.

"Yeah?" said his long-bearded friend.

"Ayup. And you know what I did?"

"Kept fightin'?"

One-eye shrugged. "Danged if I remember. I was havin' a traumatic brain injury, wasn't I?"

ණ

The Black Knight drew his sword. Arthur succeeded in lifting his temporarily before dropping to a knee and leaning on it instead. The flattened grass around them was mud-slick with a disturbing dark red tint. Thomas marveled that the man was still alive.

Arthur said something too muffled to hear at distance.

The knight laughed. "'Tis no time for me to suffer thee to rest!" he cried. He charged.

Arthur pushed himself to his feet and braced himself unsteadily.

His opponent thundered forward, levelled his shield, raised his sword.

Arthur waited.

Ten yards. Five yards. Three yards and closing.

Arthur swung Faycalibur high and stepped in to bring his shield up against the Black Knight's sword arm, blocking the knight's blow.

Arthur brought Faycalibur down square and heavy on the Black Knight's helmet. The strike resounded across the field. The knight's momentum carried him forward, but his legs buckled beneath him and his falling body cut a swath in the blood-soaked earth as he slid to a halt, face-down.

Arthur stumbled backwards a few steps but caught himself.

The Black Knight pulled his arms underneath him and pushed himself up.

"Oh, come on," said Arthur in disbelief. He stepped forward and raised Faycalibur again.

"Your sword!" yelled Thomas.

Arthur glanced at the blade.

There was no blade.

Faycalibur had broken at the cross-guard. The blade gleamed in the bloody grass.

The Black Knight stood, pulling grass and clumps of mud out of his visor.

"Betrayer," said Arthur to the blade. Then, "Blast," as the knight came at him swinging.

Arthur blocked a stroke with his shield. And then another. And another. Despite the press and the slick field, somehow Arthur held his ground.

"You are overcome," said the knight. "You will not endure."

"Seems like I endure," countered Arthur.

The Black Knight's sword came down on Arthur's shield, splintering the wood.

"The blood you see is yours," said the knight. "You will not survive this day. Yield to me as recreant."

"I'd rather die a hundred deaths," said Arthur.

"One shall suffice, I should think," said the Black Knight.

"Though I lack weapon," declared Arthur, "I shall not lack glory. If you kill me weaponless, it will be *your* shame."

"There is no shame in killing a dead man," the Black Knight countered. He brought his sword down and connected. Arthur stumbled backward into the lists.

"New plan," Arthur said and pushed himself forward. He was off-balance and falling, but it was all he had left. He shifted his weight into Faycalibur's blade-forsaken pommel and smashed it into the Black Knight's faceguard.

The force of the blow reeled his opponent three strides back, but he kept his feet. Arthur was laid flat on the earth before him. The knight kicked Arthur's shield away and stepped on his gauntleted hand until Arthur let go of Faycalibur's pommel.

"Yield," said the Black Knight.

Mumble, said Arthur, face down.

"Say again?" said the knight.

"NO!" said Arthur.

"So be it," said the knight. He raised his sword.

Later, Thomas would swear the Black Knight's sword had blazed with the light of a thousand suns. Gus would insist that it was the sword in the stone that could do that, and it was thirty suns not a thousand, and anyway this was not that sword – this was the other sword.

"No!" shouted Thomas. "Do something!" he yelled at Elisante.

Elisante gripped her cameo and strained. Nothing happened.

A figure stepped between them. Long smooth hands touched their shoulders.

"Let the Black Knight see for whom Arthur fights," said Nimue.

Thomas was too fraught to be frightened of the sorceress on his arm. "Damas?!" asked Thomas. "What good will that do?"

Nimue shook her head.

"The imprisoned knights?"

"I doubt a Black Knight will care about them," said Nimue.

"Then who?" asked Thomas, bewildered.

"The fair maiden," answered Nimue. "Perhaps she should call out to him."

"Who should do what now?" Thomas asked.

Nimue's face was still and calm, but there was a glimmer of something mischievous in her eye.

"You should do it now. There is little time," she said.

"But—" protested Thomas.

"Now," said Nimue.

Thomas took a breath.

The Black Knight shifted his weight, preparing to bring his sword down.

"ARTHUR!" yelled Thomas.

The knight's head snapped in Thomas' direction, then back at his target, then back at Thomas. He seemed startled. He dropped his weapon and staggered back from the prostrate King. The sword landed on the ground next to Arthur.

"You clearly make a *stunning* fair maiden," said Elisante. She giggled at her joke.

"Well done," said Nimue. "Now the Black Knight sees what Arthur sees, but more to the point, he knows it is Arthur who sees it."

Arthur's hand moved toward the fallen sword. His fingers wrapped around the hilt.

"Excalibur," he said. "Much damage you have done me, old friend." Arthur's eyes moved up to the scabbard at the Black Knight's hip.

"And you..." he said.

Arthur rose and cut the scabbard from his opponent with a flick. "Now you bleed."

The Black Knight turned.

"Oh knight," said Arthur, "I would reward you as you have rewarded me, and I have the advantage." He turned Excalibur's blade to catch the sun. "But I will choose the better." Arthur planted Excalibur in the turf and launched himself at the knight. They crashed to the ground. Arthur knelt above the Black Knight, pulled off his helm and started punching him.

In time, Arthur leaned back. "Now comes... your death," Arthur panted unconvincingly. He raised an unsteady gauntleted fist.

"Then slay me well," said the knight, "for you are the best and most worthy knight in all the land." He turned his head and spit tooth and blood. "But I vowed to fight this battle to my utmost, and I will never yield, by body nor mouth. Not even for you... my King."

Arthur wobbled and tried to focus on the face he'd made a recent mess of.

"Do I know you? I know you. Don't I?"

"It is I, Accolon of Gaul. And of the Court of King Arthur."

Arthur's arm dropped, followed by his jaw.

"Accolon?"

Accolon coughed. Arthur's revenge had had a striking effect on Accolon's face. He was bleeding from disturbing locations. There were lumps in places where there ought not and not where there ought. Arthur's revenge had been impactful.

"But," said Arthur dismayed, "how came you by this sword?"

"How came you by yours?" said Accolon.

Arthur clenched his fist and his jaw and looked toward the dark forest in the distance, because that's the kind of place one's eyes are drawn to when one considers–

"Le Fay," he said. "My own sister delivered Excalibur to you?"

"Aye," said Accolon. "And naught but woe has it brought me, for it shall be my death."

"You're not dead yet. Tell me everything."

And so, lying there in the bloody field with Arthur kneeling over him, Accolon confessed Morgan's foul scheme. How she presumed upon Accolon's love for her to ensorcell him and obtain from him a vow that he would slay King Arthur with Arthur's own sword. And how she would slay her husband, King Uriens, and together they would rule both kingdoms forever.

Arthur sat back on his heels when Accolon had finished.

"But you and I... We hunted together. Battled together. Sang songs together. And she... she's my sister!"

"Half-sister," corrected Accolon.

"And you were like a brother," said Arthur.

"Eh," said Accolon, not completely disagreeing.

"You swore to kill me?"

"Aye. But I didn't want to. And I didn't know it was you just now when we were fighting. I swear."

"You're a traitor!"

"Not *technically*," said Accolon. He coughed a little blood. "I didn't know I was traitoring, did I? You were disguised, weren't you? You're in Damas' armor. I thought you were just some mercenary to test Excalibur upon."

"You stole my sword!"

Accolon shook his head. "I was safekeeping it. For Morgan." He coughed again. "Who was safekeeping it for you."

"But you were *using* it!"

"It's a nice sword."

"You were using it *on me*."

Accolon nodded. "True. But I stopped as soon as that fair maiden cried out your name."

Accolon pointed. They both looked, but there was no fair maiden there now. Just Thomas.

"Listen," said Accolon. "On my honor, I would not have agreed to this contest if I had known Damas' champion was you."

"Nor would I, had I known you were you."

"But," continued Arthur, "you *did* vow to kill me, by your own admission." He bit his cheek. "It's a tricky one," he said pensively. "But I can tell you one thing. I'm right sore peeved at Morgan. She and I are going to have it out when I see her again, and there shall be some shouting. Oh, how there shall be shouting. There won't be anyone in all the land who doesn't hear it I suspect."

Arthur stood, turned to address the crowd, put his hands on his hips, took a deep breath, and passed out from the exertion.

&

After the people had revived Arthur and begged mercy for enjoying the spectacle of his near-death, they sat him on a chair on the dais formerly occupied by Damas and waited for him to speak. When he'd been sufficiently propped up and was able to focus properly, Arthur opened his mouth and said:

"I am in great need of rest."

And then, addressing the crowd but looking at Thomas, he said, "Here may ye see what adventures befall oft time of errant knights."

Thomas swallowed. Now that Arthur seemed to recognize him, he rather wished he didn't.

Arthur smiled sorrowfully and turned his attention back to the crowd.

"There are some points to which we must presently attend," said Arthur.

Thomas was relieved to have Arthur's gaze pointed elsewhere.

"First," said Arthur. "Sir Damas."

Thomas' heart stopped for a moment when he heard instead, "Sir Thomas," and didn't start again until Damas was shoved forward.

"You are an orgulous man full of villainy. I award all of your holdings to your brother Ontzlake."

Ontzlake whooped. He was met with cruel stares from those whom felt the situation called for gravitas. He cleared his throat and settled down.

"Damas, you shall serve Ontzlake, who shall provide you with a fresh palfrey each year upon which you shall ride."

Someone in the crowd snickered. "It's a damsel's pony, haha." The person was elbowed – probably by a damsel – and his snickers were cut short.

"Furthermore," said Arthur, "you shall release your twenty prisoners forthwith."

"For whom?" said someone.

"Right away," explained another.

"Fine, fine," said Damas. "But the palfreys won't be necessary my Lord. I have my charger."

"You shall remit your charger to Ontzlake."

"What?!" said Damas. "Sir, it's cruel and unusual."

"Not unlike your own self," said Arthur.

Damas clamped his mouth shut, but his eyes were fierce.

"If anyone comes to my court and complains about you, I shall have your head."

Damas looked away, ashen. He was rather attached to his head, and he preferred to keep it that way.

"Second," said Arthur. "Ontzlake, you shall report to my court and be knighted."

Ontzlake laughed in disbelief. "Thank you, Your Majesty. I am most thankful that I was wounded in both thighs recently–"

"Look at him standing there. He looks healthy enough," said Philip under his breath.

Marie agreed. "His thighs look fine to me," she said.

Thomas shot her a look.

"What?" said Marie.

"–and thereby prevented from raising a sword against you Your Majesty, by God's grace."

"By his own cowardice, more like," said Philip.

Thomas shrugged. "Where does *your* disadvantage come from Philip?"

"Fair enough," said Philip. "But I don't use it as an excuse to hide behind."

"Fair enough," said Thomas.

"I wish it *had* been you I'd fought," said Arthur. "Then it wouldn't have been my own sword I faced, delivered by treason, and false-ordained for my own death."

Ontzlake replied, "It is unforgivable, my Lord, that any man or woman should find it in their hearts to work treason against the King."

"I shall reward them shortly," said Arthur. "Now," he said and stood slowly. "Where am I and how far am I from Camelot?"

He wobbled a little and grasped the chair-back.

"Two days journey, my Lord."

Arthur considered this. "Is there somewhere closer where I might have a lie down? Perhaps with doctors present?"

CHAPTER XXIV

THE WITCH-QUEEN'S FLIGHT

Four days later Accolon was dead. Arthur was on the mend, but travel wasn't advised. He summoned a handful of knights to the forest convent where he convalesced and ordered them to ride ahead to Camelot. They were to accompany the transport of a gift he'd arranged for his sister. They were to guard it with their lives and deliver it to be presented in St. Stephen's Cathedral in Camelot without delay.

Thomas, Marie, Philip and Gus joined the escort party. Thomas insisted Marie ride Booker. Marie declined. And so they trod along, Booker in tow, passing once again the boundary stone which, without having moved an inch, now demarcated not Damas' lands but Ontzlake's. This is why it's important to keep one's eyes open. When it comes to rocks and other changeless things, it's too easy to see what one wants to see.

This rock, as it turns out, was indeed a rock. Fixed as it was, it only caught a portion of the party's conversations as they passed.

"But why a gift?" said Gus. "That makes no sense."

Thomas stared at the sheet-covered object in the cart as it bumbled along the highway. Despite the desire for haste Arthur had seemed to imply, the party moved like a funeral procession.

"Morgan tried to have him killed. And she's up to who knows what else in his absence. What could Arthur possibly be sending her?"

Not knowing was driving him mad. Gus was one of those fellows who could demonstrate remarkable faith in a plan as long as he was privy to all the details and was convinced they made sense.

He stomped along. He'd run out of complaints for the moment.

"Gus," said Thomas. "Come over here beside me."

Gus obeyed.

They marched along, close to the cart.

"Take a whiff," said Thomas.

Gus obliged. He immediately regretted it.

"Oy! What is that?!"

"That, I believe, is Accolon."

"That's terrible!" said Gus. "We're transporting Accolon's corpse? Do you have any idea how gross that is? Won't it spoil the gift?"

Thomas could see the answer present itself to Gus' mind on the heels of the question. His face went pale.

"Oh," he said. He was uncharacteristically subdued for the remainder of their morbid road trip. Even Philip allowed Gus some space. They all gave the cart some space. More and more space, in fact, as time and heat did its work on that sticky, humid road through the shadow-dappled Summer Country.

Arthur had only implied haste because he had only needed to imply it. Some tasks speed themselves, coming ready-made with all the motivational impetus required to bring about a swift and energetic conclusion.

They made it to St. Stephen's in a day and a half.

ൿ

The news and the aroma of their arrival had preceded them. The Cathedral's courtyard was overflowing with lookers-on. The vestibule was crowded. The sanctuary was packed. They had come out to witness events with their own eyes. If things went poorly, they reasoned, they would want to know specifically what they should deny having seen.

Everyone was there. Except Arthur, of course. And Guinevere, who'd gone to see him. And Guinevere's staff. And Arthur's doctors. And Morgan le Fay.

"She left," said the priest.

"She left?" said Thomas, not believing it.

"Quite hurriedly," noted the priest.

"She can't have," said Thomas.

"I'm afraid she has," said the priest.

"C'mon men," said Thomas. "And ladies," he added when he caught Marie's eye. "Lady," he corrected. The correction didn't affect her expression.

"Where are we going?" said Gus.

"I would have thought you would've caught on by now, Gus," said Philip. "Where would be the worst place you could think of to go right now?"

"Damas' dungeon," he replied confidently.

Philip's face fell flat.

"Le Fay's ship?" Gus guessed.

"Closer," said Philip, annoyed.

Gus thought for a moment and then grimaced. "Le Fay's suites?" he said, in the voice of a person who doesn't want to give anyone any ideas.

Philip touched his nose.

"Le Fay's suites," confirmed Thomas.

Thomas about-faced and marched out of the cathedral. Philip, Gus, and Marie followed.

"Wait!" said the priest. "You can't just leave that here."

But they did.

Several hundred people suddenly had several hundred excuses as to why they couldn't stay and help with the body.

❧

Marie led the way into Guinevere's halls. The bright and airy chambers and breezeways were just as bright and airy with Guinevere gone. As they moved into the guest wing, the halls notably failed to contract and cool as they had previously. Things were just as bright and airy here too. And just as empty.

Thomas stood in the room where he'd confronted the Witch-Queen, clenching and unclenching a fist.

"It's really a nice place when it hasn't got a mad sorceress creeping about in it, isn't it?" said Gus cheerfully.

"Let's go," said Thomas. "She can't have gotten far."

Marie put a hand on his shoulder.

"Marie, we have to–"

Her look stopped him. She was staring at a shadowy corner of the room. Something stirred.

"You're too late," said a voice.

A figure stepped into the light.

"She's gone."

"Owain," hissed Thomas. Hissing a name with no sibilants is a tricky thing to pull off, but Thomas had had lots of practice hissing the name "William."

"I stopped her," said Owain.

"Where is she?"

Owain ignored the question. He seemed stunned.

"She tried to kill my father."

"Uriens?" said Marie. "Is he okay?"

Owain nodded.

"Are... *you* okay?" she said.

Owain clenched his jaw.

"Where is she?" repeated Thomas, focusing on the mission. He could sense he was in danger of gaining some understanding of this vacillating stampcrab. And understanding would bring compassion, and compassion would bring complications, and there wasn't any time for complications. Not now. Probably not ever. Scratch that. He kicked himself mentally, and as self-imposed penance, promised to give Owain a chance. Later. Some day.

Owain shook his head. "You won't catch her," he said. "She headed west. To Arthur."

In the stable, Booker rolled his eyes and pretended to be a hay bale.

༄

The nun had Elisante by the ear. "Out! Out, urchin!" she yelled, dragging her toward the door.

"Ow ow ow ow ow," said Elisante. "Ow."

When their feet hit the gravel outside the abbey, the nun finally let go.

"I need to see Arthur," said Eli, rubbing her ear. She was miffed. She had tried to pass as a Sister, but she'd been spotted by the first real Sister she'd happened across. This woman had seen right through her illusion, but, *urchin?* Perhaps the nun was seeing what she wanted to see after all.

"We'll handle all the seeing that needs done, young lady."

Elisante bristled, but she kept her mouth shut.

"Good," said the nun. She collected herself, but there was a tremor in her hands and a stiffness of motion that signaled weakness to Elisante.

"Besides, one visitor tonight already is one too many." The nun turned to re-enter the abbey.

"Wait," said Elisante, trying to sound concerned and finding an easy time of it. "What visitor?"

The nun straightened and looked down her nose. "His sister, if you must know. Now be gone."

There was strength in the nun's voice, but in her eyes was something else.

She's frightened, thought Elisante. *But not of me.*

"His sister..." Arthur had more than one sister, so the nun's admission was potentially ambiguous. One could hope anyway.

"Elaine?" asked Elisante.

The nun shook her head and threw a furtive glance at a high window.

"Morgause?"

Another terse shake. "You best be off now, lass. This is no place for a young lady at this hour."

The heavy door slammed shut, and Elisante was alone in the night. She stared at the window in the wall above.

"Since when is an abbey filled with nuns not a safe place for a lady?" But she knew the answer to that question already.

She moved into the shadows and started looking for handholds.

⁂

Morgan le Fay knelt by King Arthur's sleeping body. She held Excalibur's scabbard in one hand, but obtaining the sword itself wasn't going to be as easy.

The naked blade slept with the King.

His arms were crossed over the sword and his hands wrapped both hilt and cross-guard. Morgan would have to pull it free by the sharp bits if she wanted it. And want it she did.

"Hugging a blade in your sleep," le Fay quietly scolded him. "It's not safe. Not safe at all. You always were an–"

There was a heavy thump near the window, a sharp intake of breath, and a crash as Elisante landed awkwardly on the edge of a table and then brought it down with her – it and everything on it.

Le Fay let go of the blade and whirled. Arthur started and was up, Excalibur in hand, blinking and miraculously not slicing himself in half.

"Unhand–" said Elisante.

But a black cape flapped and le Fay was gone.

Elisante dashed to the window.

A dark figure darted into the trees below.

Arthur was still trying to come to terms with being awake.

Elisante cast about the room. It was a quick inventory. King, check. Excalibur, check. Scabbard.

Gone.

Ducking Excalibur, Elisante bolted for the door.

ዏ

Servants carefully occupied the space that was close enough to Arthur to demonstrate their loyalty and concern for their King and far enough to demonstrate their estimation of the length of his arm plus Excalibur.

"Wake up, Your Majesty. You've had a start."

"I am awake!" bellowed Arthur. "And I will have a go as well as a start!"

"Fully awake is what we're aiming for, Your Majesty."

"I am fully awake. And fully wroth."

Arthur noticed the furtive glances and looked to see what he was holding.

"Ah," he said, relieved. "Excalibur. She won't abscond with you again, will she?"

"Who, sir?"

"Fetch Ontzlake. Saddle my horse. Rouse the hounds. I chased her hart to her foul ships once. Now we chase the woman herself. It's her ships again if I know her."

"*Who*, sir?"

"My sister. Morgan le Fay. She has the scabbard. My sword will not be sheathed until it finds her."

ര

"Couldn't he have another scabbard made?" said one servant to another.

"Well now that's not the point, is it?" said the other.

"He complained, 'Me sword shall not be sheath-ed' didn't he? Why not just have another scabbard made if what he wants to do is sheathe it? I know a good leatherman…"

The second servant shook his head. "The missin' one is crusted with jewels. And it's magic."

The first servant considered this.

"What kinda magic?"

"Stops bleeding."

"Well," the first servant laughed, "that's on account of if ye've got the sword sheathed, ye ain't usin' it to cut people, and so they ain't aimin' to cut *you* neither."

The second servant eyed the first servant suspiciously.

"It's a *magic* scabbard. Not some kind of *morality* scabbard. Who ever heard of a morality scabbard? Besides, how it works doesn't really impact present circumstances one way or the other, does it?"

"How's that?"

"It's missn', and the King wants it back."

"WHY IS NO ONE MOVING?" bellowed Arthur.

Suddenly everyone was moving.

ര

Elisante raced through the forest. She'd lose her quarry, but then a flutter of cape would give her away and the chase would resume. Le Fay was an unparalleled sorceress, but she was on the run. Her concentration was split.

It crossed Elisante's mind to wonder why an unparalleled sorceress was running from someone who clearly had parallels. She fully expected le Fay to turn at any moment and end things. And what would Eli do anyway if she managed to catch her? But Eli's concentration was split as well, and she wasn't able to dwell on these questions. She kept running.

Le Fay broke from the trees and came to a stop on the shore of a dark lake.

Elisante skidded to a stop and ducked back into the tree line. Both sorceresses took a moment to catch their breath. Le Fay straightened, but remained facing the lake. She moved a hand and whispered something. Elisante squinted and looked for the trap.

Beneath the creaking tree branch, the creak of leather. In the whistle of the breeze, a hiss of steel. There were soldiers all along the tree line. Elisante found a shadow and wrapped herself in it. It would keep out the light, like a child's blanket keeps out the night.

The dark water roiled. Menacing shapes broke the surface. They approached swiftly but stopped when le Fay stretched out her hand.

"So!" she said, turning to face the trees where Elisante crouched. "You want to be a Lady of the Lake?" She held Excalibur's scabbard aloft. Covered in precious stones and ornamented with gold and silver, it glittered in the moonlight.

"Go fetch!" yelled le Fay. She turned and hurled the scabbard into the lake. The waters roiled. The dark shapes swarmed and clawed the sinking scabbard.

&

Arthur and Ontzlake rode fast. Horse hooves pounded. Armor clinked. Barding creaked. The warm summer night streamed past. There, ahead...

The horses came to a noisy halt at the crossroads. An old man on foot shielded his face from the shower of dirt and gravel.

"I say there," said Arthur. "What manner of man haunts a crossroad in the middle the night?"

The old man coughed. “A, um, a cowherd?”

“What would a cowherd be doing, here, now?”

The old man thought quickly. “Looking for cows?”

Ontzlake frowned. Arthur shrugged.

“While you were looking for cows, did you happen to notice a witch-queen go by?”

The old man nodded. “Yes. Yes, I did actually.”

Arthur and Ontzlake gave each other looks of pleasant surprise.

“Which way?”

“Pardon?”

“I said,” said Arthur, louder, “Which way did she go?”

“Same way as her forty knights,” said the old man, confident he’d answered the question correctly.

“And,” said Arthur patiently, “which way did *they* go.”

“Did he say ‘forty’?” asked Ontzlake.

“Same way as the little sorceress.”

“I see,” said Arthur.

The old man looked bemused. “Strange night for a cowherd what’s lost his cows. Only way it could get stranger is if King Arthur himself showed up asking which way everyone went. Hehehe.”

Arthur laughed. “If he did, which way would you tell him everyone went?”

“Oh, haha. Why, that way,” the old man pointed.

“Gramercy, cowherd.” Arthur nodded his head politely and spurred his horse.

“I’d be careful!” yelled the cowherd. “The Witch-Queen’s lost her *marbles*, if you ask me. Heart as cold as *stone*!”

The cowherd, alone at the crossroads, grumbled. “Don’t know why I bother. He never clues in. Dumb as a *rock*, that one.” He giggled then at some private joke and disappeared.

ૡ

The waters had calmed, but Elisante could still see the shapes beneath the surface. Le Fay and her men had ridden off, leaving her alone to approach the shore.

She stared at the spot where the scabbard had sunk. After a while, her hand moved to her cameo. She stood like that for quite some time.

The night air stilled. The water lapped gently. Elisante broke the chain, dropped the cameo on the sand, and walked into the lake.

☙

Dawn broke. Arthur and Ontzlake cantered into a valley adorned with dozens of marbled stone pillars. Arthur slowed his horse and stopped at the fringe of the scene.

"'Lost her marbles,'" said Arthur.

"Your Majesty?" said Ontzlake stopping beside him.

"'Heart as cold as stone,'" said Arthur eyeing the arrangement warily.

"The mad cowherd's words," said Ontzlake.

"Not a cowherd," said Arthur. "An old friend." He shrugged. "But mad? Maybe." Then as if speaking to a crowd Arthur said, "My good Ontzlake, I am afraid we have lost the trail of my sister, Queen Morgan le Fay."

"But Your Majesty, I'm sure she's this way–"

"She's escaped us again!" Arthur glared at Ontzlake meaningfully.

"Surely just a bit further, Your Majesty. The sea is near—"

"But when I find her," yelled Arthur, "she can be sure the whole of Christendom will hear of the reward I bestow her for her treason." Arthur jerked his head meaningfully at the stones.

"Ride now," he said to Ontzlake, "and don't look back."

Ontzlake shrugged, turned his horse and obeyed.

When the sounds of their passing faded, forty marble stones turned back into knights and one into Morgan le Fay, the Witch-Queen.

"Shall we run them down?" inquired one.

Le Fay shook her head. "Without the scabbard. Arthur will bleed. But he won't keep himself from violence. He'll do our work for us. I and my mother and my sisters – we will be avenged."

She stared after Arthur.

"Orders?" said the captain, when he'd worked up the nerve.

"Home," she said. "To Gore."

CHAPTER XXV

THE JUDGMENT SEAT

The heat broke that June day when Arthur and Guinevere returned to Camelot. They were greeted with fanfare and rode straight through the city followed by a mass of adoring onlookers. Arthur assisted Guinevere from her horse, dropped to one knee, kissed her hand, then took her arm and marched inside to the throne. Courtiers lined the court, knights assembled in the nave, and Nimue, notably, stationed herself where everyone was accustomed to seeing Merlin.

There was a tense moment when the priest addressed Arthur and inquired about certain logistics regarding the King's wishes as they pertained to Accolon's remains.

"Speak plainly, sirrah," said Arthur.

"I suppose the most pressing question, Your Majesty, is 'Where would you like us to put it?'"

"Where would you like to put it?" said Arthur.

The priest wisely stopped the words before they left his mouth. But the exchange broached the subject of Arthur's adventure, which he was eager to recount.

At its core, Arthur's tale was a straightforward one. He had hunted, been imprisoned, and then unknowingly fought Accolon, mortally wounded him, and obtained the freedom of himself and twenty other prisoners. But the morning wore on, and Thomas grew increasingly impressed – not the word he would have used – with Arthur's ability to fill it.

❧

"Wouldn't Arthur have known it was Accolon by his black armor?" inquired a colorful, long-bearded courtier during Arthur's recount.

"The whole point of black armor", replied a stuffy gentleman wearing too much make-up and an eye patch, "is so that no one knows who you are. You could be anyone. You could be a famous knight. You could be a nobody. You could be your mother."

"Well," scoffed the colorful man, "I couldn't be my own mother, could I?"

The stuffy gentleman rolled his eyes. "The point is: the Black Knight could be anyone. He could be Arthur."

"He couldn't have been Arthur. Arthur was on the other end of the field wearing Damas' armor."

"My *point* is that the *whole* point is that no one knows *who* the Black Knight *is*."

"Seems like something a person could figure out if he put his mind to it."

"You think so, do you? Alright then, how?"

"By the process of elimination," the colorful man replied confidently.

"The process of elimination?" the stuffy gentleman sneered.

"Yes," the colorful man asserted, "I do believe the Black Knight's identity could have been determined via the process of elimination."

"Very well," replied the stuffy gentleman. "Imagine there is a Black Knight there, by the potted fern. He is looking askance at you. He draws his sword. Quick! Who is he?"

"Well, we know he's not my mother."

"He's charging."

"And we know he's not Arthur."

"He's bellowing ferocious curses. He raises his sword!"

"Beyond those two we'll have to make certain assumpt–"

"Too late! There's a blade in your stomach. You've been killed by the Black Knight."

"Oh," said the colorful man. "That was frightening."

"Indeed."

"Can we play again?"

☙

The sun was high but the hall still cool when Arthur finally finished telling his adventure. Thomas was sweating nevertheless. He'd been listening with dread to hear how Arthur would handle his part in the story.

But now as the tale came to an end, it seemed Arthur had chosen to simply gloss over Thomas' treasonous blunder. Thomas allowed himself to unclench.

The crowd however was demonstrably put out over Morgan le Fay's sordid scheme.

"The falsehood!" shouted a knight.

Arthur nodded.

"The sheer villainy!"

Arthur concurred.

"Burn her!" yelled someone.

"A bit much perhaps," mumbled Arthur.

"Feed her liver to the–"

Arthur silenced them with a hand. "She is a kind sister," he said.

"That's right!" a blusterous but not particularly careful listener bellowed. "Wait, what?" he added.

The crowd eyed their King warily.

"...And as I live," said Arthur changing course, "I shall be so avenged upon her that all of Christendom will hear tell of it!"

The crowd cheered.

Arthur relaxed. He had recounted the tale well. So well, it had become larger than him now. It wasn't about Arthur and his sister any longer. It was about the kingdom, and justice, and bringing both to bear on the Witch-Queen who'd conspired against all of that. All of *them.*

This could be a problem, said Arthur's fading smile.

"What about the others?"

"The who?" said Arthur.

"The conspirators!"

"I didn't say anything about conspirators."

"There are *always* conspirators, Your Majesty."

"The falsehood!" yelled someone.

"The sheer villainy!"

"Burn them!"

Thomas was sweating again. The hall seemed inordinately crowded. Where had all the air gone?

Arthur waved a hand again and silenced them. "Alas, there are some details of the plot," he said, "to which we must now attend."

Thomas was certain he was going to pass out. The crowd pressed. He pulled at the neck of his tunic and focused on breathing.

A hand pressed into his. Marie. She took his hand in both of hers and squeezed. "Trust him," she said. Then she glanced past Thomas and frowned. Thomas turned to see where she was looking.

The crowd stilled. A damsel made her way to the forefront. She carried a mantle so set with precious stones it was nearly too stiff to bend. She curtsied and presented it to Arthur.

"You may speak," said Arthur, intrigued.

"Your Majesty, I come from your sister, Morgan le Fay."

The crowd gasped.

"Burn her!" shouted someone.

Arthur shushed him.

"She offers this mantle as a gift and wishes you to know she desires to make amends in whatever way pleases you." The girl bowed her head and raised the mantle.

"That's a pretty nice cloak," said Arthur quietly. He brightened. "Once family, always family."

From where Thomas stood, he had a clear view of the damsel's profile. Her hair hid her face, but her slight build, the way she carried herself, and at her throat...

Thomas drew a sharp breath.

"I accept," said Arthur.

Thomas shot a look at Nimue. Nimue noticed. Thomas pointed at this throat and mouthed the word, "Cameo."

Nimue squinted at the girl, then quickly leaned over and whispered in Arthur's ear.

Arthur listened, his face falling. Then addressing the girl he said, "I accept. But first, before I or any of my knights adorn *ourselves* with my sister's gracious gift, you will."

"What?" said the girl, flustered. "Your Majesty, I... I'm not worthy of such an honor." She smiled nervously and took a step back.

Two knights moved in and took her gently but firmly by the arms.

"It is too precious a thing for someone such as me," she said eying the mantle. A courtier took the mantle and moved behind her.

"Your Majesty, I..." The girl was growing frantic.

"Eli!" Thomas yelled. He took a step forward. Marie pulled him back.

The courtier placed the mantle on the damsel.

There was an extended puff, like a soufflé deflating, and where the damsel had been, there was now a small pile of ash and a necklace.

The hall was quiet.

Arthur was the first to speak. "She is always trying to kill me," he said. "Frankly, it's exhausting."

ණ

"As I was saying," said Arthur, "there are some details of Morgan's plot to which we must now attend."

Everyone's eyes were on the pile of ash.

There was a general shuffling of feet. Someone coughed. Someone cleared his throat.

Thomas was finding it difficult to breathe. Nimue's face was frustratingly unperturbed.

"Perhaps we should reconvene," said Arthur, "in the Table Hall." He motioned with his hand, and a round woman came forward with a broom and a pan.

Thomas pushed his way against the exiting crowd and scooped up the necklace before the woman could sweep it away. He gripped the chain tight and stared at the pendant – it was definitely hers.

This can't be, was all his addled mind was able to articulate.

Then Marie's hand was on his arm again. She drew him out of the room and down the hall.

ණ

"Where were we?" said Arthur, now settled into his siege at the Table Round.

Tuttle read from the minutes, "'And now,' sayd thee Kynge, 'there are some fewe details of the Battle of Fyve Armies and afterward, the foul schemes birthyd of the diabolical Witch-Queen, the Kynge's sister halfe by marriage, Morgan the Fae, to which now we muste attendeth.'"

Arthur frowned.

"Yes," he said experimentally. He was suddenly quite conscious of his vowels.

Tuttle began writing.

Arthur waited.

Tuttle caught up.

"The Battle of the Five…" said Arthur.

Tuttle started scratching stylus on scroll again and didn't show any sign of letting up.

Arthur sighed. "I am pleased to recall the events that preceded the events that are less pleasing to recall."

Tuttle smiled in his scroll. Both men were well aware of the value of a good editor.

"Sir Tor," said Arthur. "For meritorious combat against unremitting foes in defense of King and Country, I appoint you to the Knights of the Watch. Rise and take your seat."

Pellinore beamed. "That's my boy," he said. Tor, grinning, saluted Arthur and took the seat next to his father at the Watch Table. Across the table Gawain, red-faced, glared. Owain pushed a bowl of fruit toward him.

"King Uriens," said Arthur.

Someone elbowed Uriens who was snoring. He started and looked confused.

"For your part in the plot against the throne–"

Tuttle was writing furiously.

Nimue whispered something in Arthur's ear.

Arthur nodded.

"–in which it seems you were an unwitting and presumably unwilling party to your wife's plans of regicide–"

Uriens' brow furrowed.

"–since she was going to kill you too–"

"I daresay," gasped Uriens, "rheeally?"

"You are forgiven."

"I should expect so." The courtier who had elbowed Uriens elbowed him again. He cleared his throat and stood, bowing. "The magnanimity of Your Majesty is unparalleled. We shall endeavor to continue to serve the King by, for example, not being assassinated by our wife."

"Very good," said Arthur.

Uriens sat.

"Sir Thomas the Hesitant."

Thomas stood. Now that the moment had come, he felt largely, thankfully, numb. He let the cameo's rough edges dig into his palm.

Nimue leaned toward Arthur, but Arthur stopped her.

He gestured toward Nimue. "There is no Merlin here," he said. "In his place I have invited Nimue, the Lady of the Lake." He paused. "*A* Lady of the Lake?" he said doubtfully. "*The?*"

Nimue shrugged and nodded ambiguously.

"Right," said Arthur. "Nimue will serve in Merlin's stead. Which brings us back to the point. There is no Merlin here."

Arthur pursed his lips.

Thomas kept eye contact, and waited for the hammer. Or the axe. He started to wonder which he'd prefer. Then Arthur spoke again.

"For failure to complete a self-appointed quest. For failing the Court and the Kingdom. For his part in the events that unfolded in the Summer Country..."

Thomas swallowed.

"Sir Thomas the Hesitant will remit his ordination to the Table of Errant Companions. He shall serve at the pleasure of the King, under his appointed Table Captain, Sir Tuttle the Authorized. And he shall accept the King's forgiveness."

"I told you," whispered Marie, grinning.

"I don't understand," said Thomas. He replayed the words in his mind, but still couldn't make sense of them.

"Sir Owain," said Arthur.

Philip and Marie pulled Thomas off his feet and back onto his chair.

Owain stood. But before anyone else could speak, Pellinore cleared his throat and stood.

"If it pleases the Court," said Pellinore.

"King Pellinore, for your and your son's recent service in the Battle of the Five you have earned, at the very least, the right to speak," said Arthur.

"Thank you, Your Majesty." Pellinore cast a glance at Gawain who was still fuming. There were several apple cores and corpses of pears strewn on the table in front of him.

"Your Majesty has shown remarkable grace and mercy this day. But," he said, "what is love without justice? It is a weak and hollow thing, accomplishing nothing. If the King cannot bring just resolution against threats to the very fabric of our civilization, what does it matter that he is kind? It is true that this man," he pointed at Owain, "stopped an attack on his own father by his mother. But who wouldn't? What he did next is the matter."

"And what was that?" said Arthur.

"He let her go."

"Is this true?" said Arthur to Owain.

"Yes, Your Majesty."

"You caught a sorceress attempting to kill your father, and you let her leave?"

"Yes, Your Majesty," said Owain. "The sorceress was my mother. And, well, she promised not to do it again."

"I see," said Arthur.

Pellinore grinned smugly and sat.

"What about me?" said Arthur.

"Pardon?" said Owain.

"She promised not to try to kill Uriens again. What about me?"

"You, not so much," said Owain.

Arthur's nostrils flared.

"For your part in the plot against the throne–" said Arthur.

Gawain closed his eyes.

Owain raised his chin.

Thomas realized he wasn't breathing again. Sure, he had wished Owain harm. But that was before there was a real possibility of it. And before Owain had gone and complicated things by being demonstrably human.

"Tuttle," said Arthur.

"Yes, Your Majesty.

"What's the punishment for co-conspiring in villainous plots against myself, freeing known criminals, aiding and abetting, etcetera?"

Tuttle shuffled through some papers and produced what he was looking for. He skimmed the parchment. "Various passages... context determining... the stripping of rank and privilege... exile and/or banishment forthwith... on threat of punishment comma capital." He concluded.

"Perhaps for the King's own nephew, mercy is in order," said Pellinore in an oily voice.

Seeing Pellinore's ploy for what it was, Kay leaned over to Arthur and said, "Your Majesty, if you forgive Owain, the people will trust it isn't simply because he's your nephew. You have forgiven others here today as well."

"On the other hand," said Pellinore, "Sir Owain *did* help the Witch-Queen escape justice. If he now escapes justice himself, where does the guilt fall? On the one who helps him escape?"

It was a bold and dastardly move, and Pellinore knew it. Though his face was smooth, there were tiny beads of sweat on his forehead.

Arthur held up a hand.

"Sir Owain," he said. He sighed. "For your part in your mother's plot against the throne, I hereby strip you of your Order. You shall quit your seat at the Watch Table and leave these lands. If you return, you will be tried. And that will likely not end well."

Gawain's chair shot back. The bowl of fruit was upended and Galatine flashed. Gawain's sword came down, split the fruit bowl as it tumbled, and sank into the Watch Table's table.

"If ye exile mah cousin, ye exile *his* cousin tae. An' that," bellowed Gawain, "wid be *me*."

He turned to leave, but Galatine was stuck. He put a boot on the table's edge and yanked. Most of the Ladies eyes went skyward as Gawain's kilt stretched.

The sword came free, and Gawain pointed her at Pellinore. Pellinore stared down the length of Galatine.

"Ye murderred mah faither," said Gawain. "An' noo ye've exiled mah cousin. Ye shall catch up wi' Galatine again, King Pellinore." He turned to Arthur. "The Orkney's have dane hee haw but served Arthur, mah ain uncle, wi' loyalty an'... fealty an'... an' loyalty... an' this is howfur fowk repays fowk?"

Gawain and Arthur stared each other down. Neither man blinked.

"Sir Gawain," said Arthur. "You will put away your sword, or it will be put away for you."

"Is that richt? An' who's aff tae dae that ah wonder? Ye?" He scoffed. He turned to Pellinore. "Ye?"

"Leave it be, cousin," said Owain.

"Na a wullnae 'Lea it be,'" said Gawain.

When no one moved Gawain laughed. He sheathed his sword. "Ah cuid tak' ony o' ye," he said, "an' maist o' ye th'gither!"

"Bit fur noo," he said, "we'll just tak' this fruit. C'moan, Owain. We'll fin' oot howfur thae fellas carry oan wi'oot *us*, an' howfur *we* carry oan whin we dinnae hae tae carry *thaim!*"

He pressed the two halves of the broken bowl together under one arm and collected some of the loose fruit. It didn't work well, but he was determined. No one stopped him.

Owain waited patiently then exited the chamber following Gawain.

"An' if ony o' ye lassies wantae jyne us," Gawain yelled from the hall, "Ye'r mair than welcome tae!"

CHAPTER XXVI

THE CRYSTAL CAVE

The Hall of Tables was empty. Which is to say, it was full of the things you'd expect an empty hall to be full of. Furniture, for example. And for the people who remained – Thomas, Marie, Philip, and Gus – the ghosts of recent events.

Gus could no longer contain himself. "That was amazing!"

Philip shook his head in disbelief. "Didn't think I'd ever see anyone *banished*."

"I should be banished too," said Thomas.

Marie put a hand on his arm. "No, you shouldn't," she said.

"All Owain did was let his mum go," said Thomas. "It's not like he failed a promise, sunk the reputation of his Order, delivered a cursed sword to his King..."

Thomas punched his own leg. It was a trick to keep from crying – an attempt to turn pain to anger. It worked for a moment. But the edges of Elisante's cameo bit at his palm.

"The King pardoned you, sir," said Gus. "You are innocent."

Thomas turned on him. "You were along for the whole ride. You saw it all Gus!" He waved an exasperated hand at the empty Watch Table. "The better fellowship has been broken over much lesser crimes. So tell me how, Gus. How can I be innocent given... given everything?"

"Because the King says you're innocent," said Gus.

Thomas clenched his jaw, fighting tears.

"It can't be that simple."

"It is."

"It's not right. It's not fair."

"He forgave King Uriens," said Philip.

Thomas waved a hand dismissively. "He was barely involved. And he was nearly killed himself."

"He forgave Sir Gawain when he withheld mercy to the surrendered knight whose lady threw herself beneath Gawain's sword and–" Gus lolled his head and made a chopping motion at his neck.

"–and she was killed," interrupted Marie.

"Right," said Gus sheepishly. "Sorry, m'Lady. I get carried away."

Thomas rubbed his face. "After an inquest and a trial and an oath and a sentence! And that was all for an *accident*. And it was *Gawain*."

"Accident or not, withholding mercy is a big deal," argued Philip. "For others or for yourself."

Thomas shook his head. "It's not the same."

Gus looked at the Watch Table then back at Thomas. "King Arthur forgave King Pellinore when he ignored the damsel's plea at the well for the sake of his own quest only to pass by again later and find her eaten by lions."

Philip nodded.

"When did *this* happen?" asked Thomas.

"After the wedding," said Philip. "Remember the deer that crashed the reception? And Arthur sent Pellinore and Gawain to track down the offending parties?"

"Of course. But I don't remember this bit about Pellinore."

"You were a little preoccupied with events at home at the time, sir," said Gus.

"Oh," said Thomas.

"We all have our own roads to walk," said Philip, "Owain has his. You have yours. Be thankful our roads converge for a time. I am."

Marie put a hand on Thomas' shoulder. "You sailed to the continent and back, were tricked by a witch-queen who has a reputation for that sort of thing, nevertheless located your imprisoned King, got him what everyone believed to be his sword, and when you learned the truth you reached out in humility to a perceived enemy for help, all in order to save your beloved King and, arguably, the kingdom."

"That sounds like a hero to me," said Gus.

Thomas looked at Marie. Her smile had a way of touching her eyes. He wanted to join her there, wherever she was. He looked down, opened his hand, turned the cameo over and back again, shook his head.

The faintest of noises behind them caused them all to turn.

Nimue stood between them and the Round Table.

"I need a word with Sir Thomas Farmer," she said.

No one moved.

Thomas stood. "It's alright," he said to the others.

They rose, doubtful.

Nimue remained silent and motionless.

"It's okay," Thomas said again.

Thomas' friends filed out of the hall. Marie was last. She watched Thomas and let her hand linger on the door as it closed.

⸙

Thomas turned to Nimue and held out his hand, palm up. The necklace's chain dangled.

Nimue examined the cameo. "It's hers," she confirmed.

Thomas swallowed, hand still held out, offering it to Nimue.

"But it wasn't her," she said.

Thomas blinked.

"How–" he started, but his breath caught. He tried again. "How do you know?"

"I've known young Elisante for a long time. There is only one reason that girl would part with her sister's necklace."

"Her sister's..." said Thomas. "Oh."

"Thomas," said Nimue.

"Yes?" said Thomas. He felt far away.

"Would you like to complete your quest?"

"My... quest?"

"To find the missing court wizard."

Thomas swallowed. "Yes, I would, but–"

But that's how all of this started, and now Owain was banished and Gawain was gone with him and Eli…

"I can take you to him," said Nimue. "You will fulfill your promise; You will find Merlin."

His promise. He could fulfill his promise…

There had to be a but. Everyone with an older brother knows there's always a but of one sort or another.

"But…?" asked Thomas.

"But you won't be able to tell anyone where he is."

"Why?" said Thomas. "Because I'll be cursed?"

Nimue laughed. Thomas was struck then by her beauty. He didn't want her to stop laughing, and when she did stop he wanted to make her laugh again.

Nimue shook her head. "I suppose that will be for you to decide. Do you want to complete your quest?"

"Yes," said Thomas.

"Close your eyes," she said.

Thomas did as he was told.

"I would think a blindfold would be better suited for travel. And I should tell Tuttle I'm going probably. And

Marie. I wouldn't want her to worry. Philip too, though he'd deny ever being worried but you know he worries even about worrying sometimes. Oh, and should Gus come? I know he'd want to–"

"Open your eyes."

"Oh," said Thomas.

~

Still holding Elisante's necklace, Thomas' hand fell slowly to his side.

"Is this," said Thomas, "an enchantment?"

Nimue watched his eyes. "What is an enchantment? There is a veil, Thomas. Language that suffices on one side stumbles on the other. Come."

There wasn't far to go. They followed a path illuminated by glowing mushrooms who had found that the dark places really brought out their true colors. They entered a chamber ringed with stalagmites slick from obeying the primordial charge to catch the world's tears.

In the center was a crystal. At the crystal, an old man leaned on a white staff.

Merlin turned. He smiled. At least, his eyes smiled. Merlin had enough beard and eyebrow that one had to make guesses at what his face was doing by what his eyes seemed to say.

His eyes seemed to be saying something warm.

"Ah, the noble knight," said Merlin. "Here to rescue me from my prison."

"Are you imprisoned?" said Thomas.

Merlin shook his head. His eyes were mischievous.

Thomas looked for exits. "Are we under the rock?"

"Under. Behind." Merlin shrugged. "On the other side."

"You're able to come and go from this place?"

"After a long life and a great deal of experimentation I have found," said Merlin, "that I prefer to remain only in places which I am able to leave."

"Does Morgan know you can come and go?"

"Le Fay? What does that dabbler have to do with anything?"

"I thought," said Thomas. "It's just that– You told Bagdemagus only she could move the rock that covers this place."

"Did he now? Is that what he said?"

Merlin chuckled at Thomas' puzzled expression, but the laugh died quickly. He sighed. "Bagdemagus conveys the words but not the message, I'm afraid." Then the mischievous twinkle returned, "I told him the only person who can move the rock is the person who placed it."

Thomas smiled. "And that," he said, "would be you?"

"Besides," said Merlin, "what's the point of moving the rock? Who needs to move the rock? The whole point of the rock is not to be moved. Ask the rock! It will tell you the same thing. Seems to me there are a whole lot of people going around misunderstanding rocks. And if you can't even understand a rock..."

Nimue cleared her throat.

Merlin shook off his irritation.

"That's neither here nor there," he said. Then he laughed. "Not unlike this place! Haha."

Thomas and Nimue stared.

"Because it's neither–" Merlin started.

"Yes," said Nimue.

"Look," said Thomas. "Merlin."

Merlin raised his eyebrows expectantly. They were tremendous eyebrows. You could almost feel a breeze.

"It's time to come back. The kingdom needs you." He glanced at Nimue. "No offense."

Merlin shook his head. "It seems to me the kingdom has managed just fine without me."

"Has it? The King was nearly killed–"

"Nearly," Merlin agreed.

"Your apprentice's apprentice is missing–"

Merlin waved a hand. "Sorceresses are never quite where you expect them to be. Especially the young ones." He cast a glance at Nimue.

Nimue frowned.

"Gawain's gone rogue–" continued Thomas.

"Ah, yes, well, that..." said Merlin. "There's a long row to hoe with that one. Better get used to him."

Merlin searched Thomas' eyes for a moment, then drew himself up and took a deep breath. "Thomas," he said, "we wizards spend our whole lives trying to make people see things. It's easy to make people see what they want to see. It's harder to keep them seeing it when we're not around. But you did something most people go their whole lives without doing. You got *yourself* to see what you *didn't* want to see. And you know what you did?

Thomas shook his head.

Merlin leaned in and whispered, "You kept fightin'."

He grinned with his eyes, then he drew himself up again and declared, "Thomas, the kingdom no longer needs me."

Thomas opened his mouth to protest.

Merlin shushed him.

"But it does need," he said, "you."

Thomas was fairly certain this was the most ridiculous thing he'd ever heard.

"I watched it all." Merlin waved at the crystal. "The kingdom needs its King. And it needs guidance, yes. The King needs capable knights, wise councilors, providence." Merlin looked Thomas in the eye. "And it needs you. And your... friends. And," he flailed at Nimue, "the young one…"

"Elisante," said Nimue.

"Eli, yes. Eli."

Thomas frowned. The greatest wizard who ever lived, declaring that Camelot needed not him, but Sir Thomas the Hesitant of the Table of Less Valued Knights. It was a deep honor. It was profoundly humbling. And it was completely absurd.

"Just come back," said Thomas irritably.

"No."

"Please?"

"No."

Thomas glared at Nimue.

Nimue shrugged.

So there was Merlin – endearing, implacable, pleased as punch with himself, and as exasperating as a sword of world-changing power stuck in a rock.

Ayup, thought Thomas. *Found him.*

"I knew you were alive," said Thomas, sullen.

Merlin nodded. "But I won't be. Not forever."

"Right," said Thomas. "The candles."

"Pardon?"

"The candles. On the monument under St. Stephen's. We found the inscription."

Merlin squinted. "Remind me," he said.

"Sum ardeam..." Thomas tried to remember. "Si sum vivam. If they're burning, you're alive. Loosely."

Merlin pursed his lips. "That's quite literal."

Thomas hesitated. "Gus said–"

"Augustus Ditcher is quite fond of the literal."

"Yes," admitted Thomas. "Yes, he is."

"Sum ardeam si sum vivam," said Merlin. He looked at Nimue. "I would one day love, if I would someday live." There was a silent exchange between Merlin and Nimue. Nimue looked at her feet.

Merlin turned his gaze back to Thomas.

"That's more... the spirit of the text."

"I see," said Thomas.

"Do you?"

ಬ

Thomas and Nimue left Merlin to his occupations and returned to the small antechamber off the main cave.

"Before we go," said Thomas.

"Yes?" said Nimue.

Thomas fidgeted. "You said Elisante – Eli – You said there was only one reason Eli would part with her necklace?"

Nimue nodded.

"Can I ask?"

Nimue nodded.

"The only reason Elisante would part with her sister's necklace," said Nimue, "is that she doesn't need it anymore."

Thomas considered this. After a moment he smiled, closed his eyes, and opened them again.

EPILOGUE

After leaving Thomas to his fate with the Lady of the Lake, Marie had disappeared into the palatial recesses into which the ladies of the palace recessed, and all Philip wanted to do was sleep. But Gus had begged him to help unsaddle Booker. Philip didn't buy it for a minute. Gus had a height problem which would make saddling a horse difficult. But Booker had a height problem too.

"It's not so much his height as his shape what presents problems sir," Gus had said.

Philip gave him trouble for it, but he also knew Gus just needed some companionship. Philip did too frankly. Just not as much.

So Philip was merciful. And Gus was grateful. But when the opportunity presented itself to disentangle himself, Philip took it.

"Ah," said Philip. "Here's a thing I don't envy you having to muck about with."

"What's that sir?" asked Gus cheerfully enough from the other side of Booker.

He made his way around the safer end – which was a judgment call with a horse like Booker – and stopped in his tracks when he saw what Philip was holding. His face went pale.

"The looking glass," he said.

"The frame, more precisely," said Philip. "I can't imagine Pyralis will be very enthused about its present condition."

Gus opened his mouth and shut it a few times. Finally, in a small voice he said, "Would you return it sir?"

"Me?" Philip feigned being rather put out. "I should think it's a job for the squire of the knight to whom it was lent, I should."

"It's just..." said Gus.

"What?" said Philip. "I'm sure he won't be too angry. Might just turn you into a duck. Or a badger. And probably just for a bit."

Gus looked like he was going to be ill.

"Tell you what," said Philip. "I'll return this, if you squire my gear as well as Thomas'. For a mon–"

Gus was already nodding.

"–a year," said Philip.

Gus kept nodding.

Philip almost felt guilty, but there was something he'd been dying to try from the beginning.

"Excellent," said Philip. "I'll just be off then. To the evil wizard's."

Gus swallowed. "Former," he said.

Philip blinked and looked up from the frame. "Mmm?" he said. "Right. Former. Yes."

A pair of ladies were making their way past the livery.

Philip brought the frame up and aimed it, grinning.

"Let's see what–"

Booker's head appeared in the frame, blocking Philip's view.

"Booker!" Philip was going to say. But all of Philip's cerebral resources were suddenly diverted to help process what he was seeing.

There was something pointedly affixed to Booker's forehead.

"Is that a..." said Philip. "Are you a..."

There was a terrible crunching noise, and Philip was left holding two pieces of frame – one in each hand.

Booker chewed. And then he sniffed. His eyes began to water. Then he sniffed again with vigor.

And then he sneezed. It was quite impressive.

The next person to speak was Gus. He said, "I'll go fetch a washcloth, sir."

And so he did.

It would turn out to be quite an adventure.

ABOUT THE AUTHOR

Liam Perrin has been roughly geosynchronous for more than a few decades and likely will remain so. Most recently, he orbits the center of Earth from a position outside of Phoenix, Arizona where he tries to avoid collisions with his wife, one daughter, a miniature Australian shepherd, a Russian tortoise, and a 70-pound Sheprador who will love you to death. Seriously, she doesn't know when to stop. Unlike the author who figures he should stop right about… here.

Find out more about the Less Valued Knights series at LiamPerrin.com

Made in the USA
Lexington, KY
02 February 2019